MW01686664

Phase Two

A Novel

by

C. Scott Littleton

The Invisible College Press, LLC
Arlington VA

Publisher's Note:
This is a work of fiction. Names, characters, places, and incidents are either the product of the author's imagination or are used fictitiously, and any resemblance to actual human beings living or dead, events, organizations, or locales is entirely coincidental.
ISBN: 1-931468-09-5

Special thanks to Robynn Clairday for help and encouragement.
Second Printing, 2003.

The Invisible College Press
P.O. Box 209
Woodbridge VA 22194-0209
http://www.invispress.com

Please send questions and comments to:
editor@invispress.com

For Daisy Anna Troccoli,
The cutest granddaughter in this or any other universe!

Acknowledgments

It would be impossible here for me even to begin to acknowledge all of the people who, in one way or another, have had an impact on this book. However, a few of them deserve special mention. First and foremost, I'd like to express the warmest possible thanks and appreciation to my truly remarkable literary agent, Denice Fractious, of Literary Properties Agency of Pasadena, CA, who believed in Phase Two from the outset, and whose boundless enthusiasm, sage advice, and dogged determination were instrumental in bringing this project to a successful conclusion. Others who were kind enough to read and comment on all or portions of the manuscript at various points in its evolution include Molly Blecha, Wolfgang von Chmielewski, Rosanne Cutropia-Cummins, Richard M. Dolan, Don Ecker, Benedict Freedman, Bethe Hagens, Horace L. Hotchkiss, Mike Kawitzky, Leslie Littleton-Rodriguez, Cynthia Littleton, Eugenia Macer-Story, Linda A. Malcor, Jim Mallory, Jocelyn Markey, Mike McAleenan, Sandra Miesel, Chuck O'Brien, Udo Strutynski, Leslie A. Thompson, Tom Troccoli, and Paul Walker.

Finally, and from the bottom of my heart, I want to thank my wife, Mary Ann Littleton, not only for her unwavering support and astute suggestions, but also for putting up with all those aliens and UFOs for so many long and sometimes extremely difficult years. Indeed, the magnitude of my gratitude here can never be overestimated!

C.S.L

I think we're property. I should say we belong to something: That once upon a time, this earth was No-Man's land, that other worlds explored and colonized here, and fought among themselves for possession, but that now it's owned by something: That something owns this earth—all others warned off [by] voyagers who have shown every intent to evade and avoid . . .

—Charles Fort

Any sufficiently advanced technology is indistinguishable from magic.

—Sir Arthur C. Clarke

CHAPTER ONE

She must have been on the same train. Probably in the same jam-packed car. But the chilly, outdoor platform was teeming with early morning Tokyo commuters, all of whom were hunched against the raw, late November wind, and it wasn't until he reached the bottom of the broad staircase leading to the bowels of Shinjuku Station and was engulfed by a welcome blast of warm air that Culley Wisdom noticed a young woman in the crowd staring at him intently.

At first, Culley paid her scant attention. After nearly a decade of living in Japan he'd been stared at by more than his fair share of giggly young females who were disconcerted by the presence of a male *gaijin*, a round-eyed western foreigner—in Culley's case, a tallish, sandy-haired American in his mid-forties, with a ruddy face, hazel eyes, and a flat stomach, thanks to the hours he spent each day on his feet negotiating Tokyo's marvelous but exhausting public transportation system.

However, he soon realized that the woman wasn't giggling, and that there was something oddly familiar about her face.

Especially her eyes.

Something that took him back at least ten years.

As soon as she saw him glance in her direction, the woman turned her head away and quickly disappeared into the river of people flowing toward the main exit. However, when he finally reached one of the automated gates he spotted her again, not all that far ahead of him, and this time he decided to take a closer look.

She was extremely short, even by Japanese standards, and her chin was perhaps a shade more pointed than most East Asian chins. But otherwise, her overall appearance wasn't all that out of place: jet black, shoulder-length hair, a tiny nose, dark eyes surrounded by the epicanthic folds one would expect to find in this part of the world, a trim figure, and skin so pale that it looked as if she'd never spent a day in the sun. The same could be said of her clothes, which consisted of a pair of expensive Calvin Klein jeans, a simple white blouse, no jewelry that he could see, brown suede boots, and a black leather jacket. The rational part of Culley's mind told him there was no way on Earth—or anywhere else, for that matter—that this person could be anything other than what she seemed: an attractive young Japanese woman on her way to a college class or, more likely, an upscale job, perhaps in one of the new high-rises that had sprouted like steel-and-concrete mushrooms in Nishi-Shinjuku.

But deep down, almost unconsciously, he'd already begun to suspect that she was not at all what she seemed. There was something uncanny about those otherwise unremarkable eyes; they seemed to mask another set of eyes he would never forget, not if he lived to be a hundred and twenty.

Don't be ridiculous! He told himself. How could she possibly be here, in Shinjuku Station, of all places, masquerading as a Japanese career girl?

Nevertheless, Culley's feet seemed to have a will of their own, and despite the fact that he was already late and would probably be docked an hour's pay by his tight-fisted boss, he followed the young woman through the maze of corridors lined with boutiques, electronics outlets, camera stores, coffee shops, snack bars, kiosks, and restaurants that stretched for at least half a mile in all directions beneath the station and adjacent portions of the Shinjuku district. It was almost as if she were leading him somewhere.

Just before she ducked into a tiny coffee shop

sandwiched between a shuttered sushi bar and a Chinese noodle shop she turned to face him, and they finally made full eye contact. For the barest fraction of a second, the young woman's ordinary-looking Japanese eyes became her eyes: huge, wrap-around orbs, filled with love that bored into the depths of his psyche. At the same time, he saw their corners lift ever so slightly, just as her eyes had done.

He was sure that what he'd just "seen" was a mental image, and that no one else would have noticed any change whatsoever in her physiognomy. But if she was really here and had somehow transmitted the image, in the same way she'd once spoken in his mind . . . the implications were literally staggering!

His heart pounding like an out-of-control jackhammer, Culley momentarily lost his bearings and bumped head-on into an extremely tall, hatchet-faced Japanese gentleman wearing a black suit and tie who was heading in the opposite direction. Muttering a perfunctory "*Gomenasai*," he hurried on his way, awash with the memory of his initial encounter with the exquisite alien creature who called herself Qaazi Qaan-gaa.

* * *

He'd been on his way home after a grueling day surveying some heavily vandalized archaeological sites on a bare piece of land Graham College owned in the eastern Mojave Desert. Although he had no special interest in the Native Americans that had lived in this part of Southern California a thousand years ago, the Dean had "requested" his professional services. And, if you were an untenured professor of anthropology at a place like Graham, a small liberal arts college with a campus in one of L.A.'s smoggiest San Gabriel Valley suburbs, you took the Dean's "requests" seriously. Extremely seriously.

The temperature at noon that July day had been at least 120 degrees in the shade, and, even at seven-thirty in the evening, with all the windows rolled down, the interior of his twelve-year-old, un-air-conditioned VW van had still been hellish. To make matters worse, his impulsively chosen shortcut had turned out to be little more than a rutted desert track. And then, shortly after rounding a blind curve, the early twilight sky began to glow, bathing the sere desert landscape in an odd white light. It seemed to be coming from somewhere directly above him.

He pulled over to the shoulder, leaned his head out the window, and looked up.

Hovering about five hundred feet overhead was a large, disk-shaped object, its underside suffused by the brightest artificial light Culley had ever seen. He later estimated the disk's diameter at approximately a hundred feet, although at the time he was so dumbfounded that he forgot to grab the camera lying next to him on the seat, let alone make dispassionate observations

After a few seconds, the strange craft silently descended, fluttering like a luminous, oval leaf caught in a phantom wind. It came to "rest" about fifty feet above the road a few yards in front of him, whereupon the radio went silent, the headlights winked out, and the idling engine coughed, sputtered, and died.

Culley sat there transfixed, unable to move a muscle.

Even now, a decade later, both the abject terror and intense curiosity that engulfed him in alternate waves were still vivid. He wanted to run and, at the same time, he desperately wanted to know what the object was and where it came from.

While he pondered his next move, a peculiar, disembodied voice began to echo in his head: *It's all right, Dr. Wisdom. We won't harm you. We are your friends*. The terror was still there, but it was soon overlaid by a sense of well-being, as if all of this was really happening to somebody else.

A few minutes after Culley "heard" the calming voice, three extremely short creatures with disproportionately large, bulbous heads, huge wrap-around eyes, and wearing pale blue, luminous body suits glided out of the hovering craft.

They were surrounded by a beam of bright blue light that shimmered as if it contained thousands of minuscule diamonds.

As soon as the creatures reached the ground, the beam disappeared, and they glided noiselessly toward his van. It somehow seemed perfectly natural that their feet never actually touched the ground. One of them aimed a small object at him, and he found himself opening the door.

Supported by the tiny trio, Culley floated in the direction of the waiting disk. With great effort, he glanced down at one of the hands that clutched his arm and noticed that it had but four, pencil-thin fingers, one of which was significantly shorter than the others. What made these alien fingers even more bizarre was their total lack of anything that remotely suggested fingernails.

When he and his captors reached a point directly beneath the UFO the blue beam reappeared. Still unable to move a muscle, he felt himself rise into the air. He sensed that two of the bulbous-headed creatures were floating immediately below him while the other one hovered just above his head, although the intensity of the beam blocked most of his vision. In a few seconds, Culley felt himself pass through the thin outer surface of the alien craft and into a brightly lighted, white-walled chamber that looked like an operating room. Its most obvious feature was an oddly-contoured table that seemed to grow from the floor like a flat-topped mushroom. He could also see an array of unfamiliar devices attached to the walls and suspended from the low, luminous ceiling.

As he took in his new surroundings, Culley did his best to convince himself that he was totally out of his mind-crazy with the God-awful desert heat, perhaps—or that he was having an extraordinarily bad dream. Yes, that was it! He'd pulled off the road and gone to sleep. . . .

After complying with their "suggestion" that he shed his clothes, the creatures floated him onto the table. Then, after several more similarly clad creatures entered the pie-shaped chamber, they subjected the distraught anthropologist to the strangest physical examination he'd ever experienced. Culley was poked, prodded, and invaded in almost every imaginable way, plus a few that seemed patently impossible. Most of their instruments-including a free-floating device not unlike the CBS logo that scanned every inch of his body, and several tubes that could be inserted into a variety of bodily orifices with little or no pain-were unlike any he had ever seen or imagined.

There was an ineffable, almost magical quality to the whole scene, which seemed to confirm science fiction author Arthur C. Clarke's famous "law": Any sufficiently advanced technology is indistinguishable from magic. Culley found himself repeating it over and over again in his mind as they continued to poke and prod and scan.

The medical procedure was supervised by a taller, more robust alien whose eyes and sharply pointed chin closely resembled those of the little bulbous-headed beings who'd escorted him into the ship, but was otherwise far more humanoid in appearance. Culley's assessment was reinforced by the fact that he-unlike the short creatures, this one definitely seemed to have a gender-had ten extremely slender fingers that ended in what appeared to be fingernails.

The "Supervisor" refused to answer any questions and simply did his job. Nor did his tiny assistants have anything to say as they went about their duties, their movements jerky and robot-like in contrast to the more fluid-and human-like-motions of their taller companion. All the while, the same impersonal "voice" he'd heard in the van kept repeating *It's all right, you're safe here and it won't hurt much, just a tiny pin prick* as they deftly inserted yet another set of needles into his abdomen and testicles.

Most of this, of course, did not come back into his consciousness until long after the experience, not until Culley had submitted himself to an extensive program of hypno-regression directed by Dr. Harold Stern, an eminent Beverly Hills psychiatrist and one of the leading authorities in the field. And even now there were a few memories that remained fuzzy and incomplete, no matter how hard he tried to bring them into focus. It was as if "they" still didn't want him to penetrate certain areas of his experience.

But the principal event of the evening, which he finally recalled in full one morning in Dr. Stern's office, happened shortly after the physical examination. He'd noticed that they paid a great deal of attention to his genitals, which surprised him. Why were they so concerned with that part of his anatomy?

He was about to find out.

In a few minutes or perhaps even an hour—by now Culley had lost most of his time sense—one of his captors floated him off the examination table and into another chamber. This room was similar in size and general appearance to the first one. However, its most prominent item was what appeared to be a large, round bed, which, like the "operating table" in the previous room, was anchored to the floor and occupied most of the space. He was floated onto the bed, and "told" to relax. Once again, he felt extremely heavy and unable to move his body.

It was at this point, initially, that recollection had become difficult. Culley remembered, word for word, his dialogue with Dr. Stern while under hypnosis; he'd listened to the tape God knows how many times, trying to pull it all together:

Dr. Stern: "Okay, Culley, what's happening now?"

Culley: "I'm being floated onto the couch, or bed, or whatever it is. I'm trying to sit up, but I can't. They're leaving, now. I'm scared shitless. What's going to happen next? I don't want to talk about it."

Dr. Stern: "Relax, Culley; it's not really happening this time. Just let yourself relive the experience. If it gets too painful, we can stop any time."

Culley: "The gas! They're filling the room with a green gas or a mist, I can't really tell which."

Dr. Stern: "Are you alone now?"

Culley: "Yes. But the gas or whatever—it seems to be absorbing that funny odor, sort of like baking soda in a refrigerator, if you know what I mean, is filling the room and I can't see anything! Oh, I'm so scared!"

Dr. Stern: "Hang in there, Culley! What's happening now?"

Culley: "Okay, Doc. Now the gas is dissipating rapidly. I don't know where it's going, but it's just about gone. The musty smell's back, but not as strong. It's also getting a little warmer. I still feel heavy, but I can move my arms and legs pretty well. Oh, oh! Somebody's coming in. I can't see too well—here's still some mist. But it looks like—no, I don't believe this!"

Dr. Stern: "What don't you believe?"

Culley: "It's a woman! One of 'them.' The same big eyes and pointed chin. But she's beautiful in an exotic kind of way. Yes, very beautiful and very sexy, even though her pubic hair's blood red."

Dr. Stern: "How do you know that, Culley?"

Culley: "Because she's stark naked! What's she going to do? Oh, no! I don't believe this is happening. She's getting onto the bed with me. She's . . . she's touching me. Thank God she's got normal hands! And . . ."

Dr. Stern: "Where is she touching you?"

Culley: "My penis. It's getting hard!"

Dr, Stern: "Take it easy, Culley. Do you remember anything else about the woman?"

Culley: "Yes. She's telling me that her name is Qaazi Qaan-gaa, that she loves me, and that we're about to conceive a son. And the corners of those remarkable eyes! They sometimes flutter upward, especially when she makes love. I know something else, too."

Dr. Stern: "What's that?"

Culley: "I'm deeply in love with her, too, more in love than I've ever been or ever will be. Maybe it's all a trick. Maybe my mind's playing weird games, but I desperately want to see Qaazi again. Someday, somewhere. . ."

But Qaazi and her diminutive companions remained elusive.

Initially, he'd been a true believer, eager to share his fully-recalled sexual encounter with a beautiful extraterrestrial with anyone who would listen. Indeed, he was convinced that it was his sacred duty as a social scientist to proclaim that UFOs and aliens really did exist, and the human race as a whole would soon be forced to come to grips with this awesome fact. The end result was a moderately successful UFO book entitled *Encounter in the Desert,* which he wrote in collaboration with Dr. Stern.

As it turned out, although he made a fair amount of money from it, at least initially, the book cost him both his marriage and whatever chance he might have had of receiving tenure at Graham or any other stateside institution, for that matter. No respectable college or university wanted a UFO freak on its faculty. And so, after failing to land a teaching job of any sort in the States, he joined the ranks of failed academics, burnt-out graduate students, and kids just out of college looking for an adventure who fed the seemingly insatiable Japanese appetite for English conversation classes.

Teaching the nuances of American English pronunciation to ten stone-faced Japanese businessmen jammed cheek-by-jowl into a tiny cubicle they had the nerve to call a "classroom" was emphatically not what Culley had expected to be doing a decade after earning his doctorate in anthropology. But the job wasn't very taxing, at least mentally, and he'd had a lot of time to think. The upshot was that, after eight years of mulling over what had happened to him that evening, he was no longer sure of anything.

For a brief period after *Encounter in the Desert* hit the bookstores, Culley had been fairly active in the affairs of several of the more responsible UFO research groups, among them the Mutual UFO Network (MUFON) and the Center for UFO Studies (CUFOS). He was, after all something of a celebrity in those circles. He also regularly contributed to a variety of Internet lists devoted to UFOlogical subjects. But the kooky, New-Age nonsense he kept encountering, even among ostensibly "serious" UFO researchers, caused him to question the validity of his memories, including the ones dredged up by Dr. Stern.

The two pieces of possible physical evidence, a small red mark on his neck and a bad nosebleed, had disappeared long before he'd sought professional help. In fact, the more he thought about it, the more it seemed that his ex-wife Lorna, the Graham Tenure and Promotion Committee, most of his colleagues, and the polite, close-cropped Government types—he never found out exactly which agency (or agencies) they worked for—who'd pestered him for a while after the book appeared had been right all along, and he had hallucinated the whole damned thing!

After he moved to Tokyo, he did his best to slide beneath the UFO community's radar, as well as that of the Government and whatever the aliens—if indeed they weren't figments of his imagination—might be using to keep track of folks they abducted.

* * *

Until this morning . . .

Pushing aside the *noren*, Culley threaded his way through the crowded coffee shop to the small table where the person who had triggered these memories sat, menu in hand, looking for all the world like an ordinary Japanese customer. As he approached, she put down the menu and smiled up at him with that love-filled half-smile he remembered so well. And then the corners of her eyes once again lifted ever so slightly.

He stood there staring at her, open mouthed.

Unless his mind was playing massive tricks on him, this beautiful, fashionably dressed young Asian woman had to be Qaazi Qaan-gaa. There was no other rational explanation. "Someday" was today, and "somewhere" was here, in a crowded Shinjuku Station coffee shop. Although he'd often fantasized about what he might do or say if this moment ever came, his throat suddenly went bone dry, and he found himself unable to utter a single word.

Dearest Culley, a well-remembered voice whispered deep within his psyche, *please sit down. I am indeed who you think I am. And yes, I did "suggest" that you take that particular train and that you follow me here. I apologize for being so manipulative, but it was the only way I could be sure that we would meet.*

Incapable of either a mental or a verbal response, he simply took a deep breath, exhaled, and slowly lowered himself into the chair across from her.

The waitress came over, pad and pencil in hand.

"Do you want something to eat?" Qaazi asked pleasantly in unaccented but hyper-correct American English. "Or perhaps a cup of coffee? I have begun to cultivate a taste for that beverage, although I still cannot metabolize more than a few sips at a time."

Culley nodded dumbly. The last thing on his mind at the moment was food, but he badly needed something to relieve the dryness in his throat.

In overly-polite but otherwise equally flawless Japanese, she ordered two coffees. Then she reached across the small table and touched Culley's hand. "For your information," she said, switching back to his mother tongue, "I am fluent in twelve Earth languages, including Mandarin, Cantonese, Korean, Vietnamese, Thai, French, Spanish, German, Russian, and Arabic, as well as Japanese and your variety of English. I am able to communicate fairly well in several others, but those are the languages that have been imprinted on my brain."

She paused, obviously waiting for a response.

"Qa-Qaazi?" he finally managed to stammer, "You—you really do exist? I'm not hallucinating?"

"Please believe me. You are not hallucinating. I am Qaazi Qaan-gaa, the same 'exquisite creature' you once made love to, and I too have often fantasized about this moment." She studied him for a moment. "Our son looks much like you."

Culley's eyes widened. They really had conceived a son. But where was he? Was he here in Tokyo?

"No, dear Culley, he is not here," she replied, answering his unspoken question. "They have not—haven't—English contractions are so difficult!—let me have much contact with him. That has always been the way of the Clan in these matters."

By the time the coffee arrived, Culley had regained some of his composure. He slipped out of his topcoat, then managed to smile at the waitress and take a couple of sips from his cup. Qaazi followed suit. After a couple of more swallows he asked: "Does our son have a name?"

"Yes, two names. One, Jaazaanii, was given him by the Clan. But I have also named him Adam, in honor of the mythical figure many of your people consider to be the first human being." She projected an image of Adam in Culley's mind; he had his mother's eyes and tiny nose, but otherwise his features had a more "human" cast to them. He was dressed as Qaazi had been when he'd first met her, that is, in a tight-fitting, luminous body suit. Culley's highly emotional reaction to the image pleased her, and she told him so telepathically.

"I—I really don't know what to say. He's a beautiful boy!"

"Yes, he reflects the best of both of our genomes. I am so glad you like him! If all goes well, you will meet him very soon."

Culley's mind projected intense eagerness to become acquainted with his son. Aloud he asked, "What does the other name you mentioned mean?"

Qaazi started to reply but then stiffened. The slant of her eyes shot upward. "We are being observed," she whispered, "by an Agent of the others. "

"A-a what?" Culley stammered.

"A SESO Native Agent, a Man in Black. He is seated alone at a table near the door. But please do not look at him."

"I don't understand. What's SESO and what's a—"

Qaazi silenced him with a firm but gentle telepathic command. Her thin lips formed themselves into a frown. "There is no time for me to explain. We must leave here immediately."

Thoroughly confused, Culley gulped the rest of his coffee and rose swiftly to his feet.

"One more thing," she said, giving him a small kiss on the cheek. "Please, until I have reprogrammed your implant, you must make your mind as blank as possible, at least when it comes to thinking about me or Adam. It is very important! And do not be surprised by what happens when we leave this place."

Following her instructions as best he could, he waited while Qaazi took care of the bill. Then, hand in hand, they left the coffee shop and merged with the crowd in the underground corridor.

As they walked in silence toward one of the exits that led to the street level, Culley noticed a tall, dark-suited Japanese man about ten feet behind them. His thin, hollow-eyed face looked familiar. Yes, of course! It was that odd-looking guy he'd bumped into shortly after he'd spotted Qaazi.

He followed them into the temporarily empty passageway. A moment later, Qaazi whirled around, reached into her purse, withdrew a device that looked vaguely like a TV remote control without any visible buttons, and aimed it at him.

The Man in Black immediately crumpled to the floor.

He is not seriously hurt, her mind whispered, in what Culley later realized was less than a tenth of the time it would have taken her to convey the same information verbally, *and will eventually regain consciousness, so we must hurry. Please remember, your mind must remain thought-free! It is vitally necessary. My own people may also be monitoring us.*

Doing his best to suppress his thoughts about Qaazi and what he'd just seen her do—a well-nigh impossible task—

Culley quickly followed her up a flight of steps, barely avoiding a young couple heading in the opposite direction, and onto the congested sidewalk. He noticed that their feet barely touched the pavement, and that he hardly felt the icy, late November wind that knifed across the station plaza, causing others to muffle up. He also saw that she still held what he'd begun to think of as her "magic wand." In any case, by the time a crowd had gathered around the unconscious figure at the base of the exit staircase, she'd already flagged down a taxi.

"I promise to explain as much as I can as soon as it is safe to do so," Qaazi said as the automatic door opened and they settled into the back seat. "But for now, I must ensure that your mind stays blank for a while. Please forgive me."

She aimed the "magic wand" discretely at his midsection.

Almost immediately, Culley felt himself drifting off and was unable to make out the address she gave the driver. His eyes closed, and he sank back against the seat, barely able to move. Turning his head weakly to one side, he realized that they had turned onto Meiji-dori and were headed in the general direction of Harajuku, the trendiest and most youth-oriented section of the city.

That's an appropriate place for an alien to live! I wonder if she's ever been shopping on Takeshita-dori or watched the kids dance in Yoyogi Park on a Sunday afternoon?

He also realized dimly that he'd left his topcoat back in the coffee shop and wondered if he'd ever see it again. *Hope it's not too chilly where we're going. . .*

But before these thoughts could fully crystallize, a thick black fog swirled across his consciousness, and within less than a second all but the most autonomic of Culley's mental functions had come to a full and complete stop.

CHAPTER TWO

Dr. Wilma Gibbs, distinguished Caltech professor, Nobel laureate in physics, and current director of a government agency so secret that even the President of the United States had no idea it existed, shifted her considerable bulk to a more comfortable position and stared intently at the printout. The tiny veins in her broad, coal-black forehead stood out as she did her best to make sense out of it.

He couldn't possibly be dead; that much Wilma knew for certain. The carrier beam broadcast by Professor Cullen Wisdom's alien implant still registered, along with his heartbeat and several other vital signs.

But what the hell had happened to the man's locator signal?

"You're absolutely certain the monitors are all working perfectly?" Wilma barked. "The locator signals never completely disappear, even when they're abducted!"

She lifted her massive head and fixed her eyes on Tom Johnson, her young assistant, who sat across the cluttered oak desk from her nervously fingering a sheaf of documents covered with mathematical symbols.

"We've run five separate diagnostics, Dr. Gibbs, and they all indicate that everything's operating perfectly," Tom replied after a moment's hesitation, scratching his neatly trimmed blond beard and averting his eyes so as to avoid the older physicist's withering stare. It was a habit he'd developed in graduate school while writing his doctoral dissertation under her direction.

"Any ideas?"

"Well, maybe . . ."

"Maybe what?"

"Could Wisdom have had another encounter with his alien girlfriend? The one he wrote about in his book. There's a faint indication that he left the station with a female companion. Maybe she switched him off so she can have him all to herself. . . ."

The gray-haired African-American physicist grinned that toothy grin that had so endeared her to the world press when she went to Stockholm to accept her Nobel Prize. "Well, I suppose that is a possibility," she chuckled. "Lord, knows, anything's possible when we're dealin' with these folks. Their technology's 'bout as far ahead of ours as it's possible to get. Otherwise, we could home in on the carrier beam and get a fix on him."

Tom nodded as she handed him the printout. He stared at it intently for the better part of a minute, pursing his lips and absently pulling at his left earlobe.

"Dr. Gibbs," he said finally, looking up at her through thick, wire-rimmed glasses, "I wonder if it's finally time to bring the President into the loop. I mean, maybe they're about to begin Phase Two. Wisdom would be an obvious choice for it. After all, he is—or was—an anthropologist and could serve as a mediator between our two cultures. Cultures are still cultures, no matter how complex they may be technologically. Right?"

The older scientist frowned. Her star pupil, who, she was convinced, would someday earn his own trip to Stockholm, was often right about things like this. It was this gut-level ability to come up with the solution to a problem before all the data were in that had endeared him to her in the first place. Her mind worked the same way. But somebody had to play Devil's Advocate.

"There's also the possibility that it's simply an operational failure," she replied evenly. "You just said that cultures are cultures, and you know damned well that no culture, even theirs, can possibly be perfect. So far, we've only been able to tap into a handful of their implants. How do we know that such glitches don't happen all the time?"

"We don't, Dr. Gibbs. But something tells me this was deliberate. I can't explain why."

Wilma smiled at him again and stuffed the printout into her voluminous handbag.

On the surface, she and Tom couldn't have been more different.

Thomas Fielding Johnson, Jr., had grown up in Marin Country, the only son of a wealthy San Francisco stockbroker, and had attended Stanford almost as a birthright, while Wilma Gibbs was the over-achieving granddaughter of an illiterate, East Texas share-cropper, himself the grandson of slaves, and had attended Spellman on a full scholarship.

Nevertheless, they'd both been seduced by the arcane world of theoretical physics, and both had received doctorates from Caltech, she more than a generation earlier, of course, back when black faces, male as well as female, had been scarcer than hen's teeth on the famed Southern California campus. Later on, she'd been invited to join the Caltech faculty, and, by the time Tom surfaced in one of her seminars, shortly after she was awarded a Nobel Prize for her work on super-string theory, Professor Wilma Gibbs was a world-renowned theoretical physicist. However, she immediately recognized a kindred spirit, one who was every bit as bright as she was. (Indeed, she sometimes suspected that he was even brighter!) And so, when Wilma was tapped to be the director of MJ-12, as the agency was still called by insiders, despite several official name changes in the course of the past fifty-odd years, she could think of no one she'd rather have as her chief assistant than her former student and protégé, Dr. Thomas Fielding Johnson, Jr.

As soon as his initial shock and disbelief wore off, Tom had jumped at the chance to be part of something he'd heretofore dismissed as science fiction. Now, after two years of working with him in the supercharged, super-secret atmosphere of MJ-12, she had no reason whatsoever to regret her decision. The boy had performed brilliantly. Her only complaint was that he still couldn't bring himself to get over being a graduate student and call her "Wilma," even in private!

"Okay, Tom," she said as her mind drifted back to the present, "Let's brief our colleagues. Most of 'em are out in Nevada at the Groom Lake test site and shouldn't be hard to get a hold of. But I'm not quite ready to go to the White House, not until we make better sense out of this."

The Director reached into her bag again and withdrew a small, irregularly shaped metallic object, one side of which was covered with tiny, multi-colored bumps. She pushed it across the desk.

Tom picked up the device, turned it over a few times, and then handed it back to his boss.

"Yes, I guess we need to take the thing apart one more time," he said, reading her thoughts. "Wisdom's locator signal has *got* to be in there somewhere."

Wilma nodded slowly.

They'd both spent more hours than they cared to count in the lab tinkering with what she'd come to think of as the "gizmo." It had been salvaged earlier that year by an MJ-12 team from a disk that had crashed in a remote region of northern Montana less than thirty seconds before the craft vaporized. Late one evening, as they passed the object back and forth, Tom had accidentally discovered that if he tapped one of the bumps a few times a human subject's image would appear on one of the lab monitors. It was hit or miss at first, but as time went on they were able consistently to access the data broadcast by a small number of implanted abductees. Cullen Wisdom was one of first they'd been able to identify. They couldn't actually read the squiggles that accompanied his and the other images they'd accessed, but they somehow "knew" what they meant. Wilma's best guess was that the object was a receiver tuned to a particular batch of alien subjects, perhaps those "serviced" by the crashed disk.

In any case, although they'd taken the device apart hundreds of times, it steadfastly refused to yield any further information. Oh, they could disassemble it, all right, but its components were impervious to x-rays, MRIs, and PET scans, as well as to high-speed drills, lasers, saws, acids, heat, and everything else they could think of using to penetrate its secrets.

Nevertheless, one more attempt certainly wouldn't hurt.

Wilma returned the alien device to her bag, gave it a firm pat, and then heaved herself out of her chair. Tom was already at the office door, holding it open for her.

"Yes indeed, my well-brought-up young friend, we've got more work to do. That gizmo's gonna tell us where Wisdom is if I have to zap it with an atom bomb!" she said, as they walked toward the elevator. It was almost evening, but the rolling Virginia countryside was still faintly visible though the tinted glass that formed the corridor's exterior wall.

As they stood waiting for the car, Wilma suddenly smiled the kind of smile mothers smile when their favorite offspring says something exceptionally clever. It reinforced Tom's very private assessment that his mentor was, in a great many respects, the most beautiful women he'd ever seen; her unlined ebony face glowed with a unique inner radiance that set her apart from all other women of his acquaintance, including those who were less than half her age and size.

"You know, Tom," she said softly, "the more I think about it, the more I think you may be onto somethin' important here."

"You mean you now think we should go to the President, after all, Dr. Gibbs?"

"No," she sighed, shaking her head; someday he *had* to loosen up! "I meant the part about poor Dr. Wisdom being an ideal candidate for a Phase Two operation. Yeah, he'd be just the sort of person I'd pick if I were in their shoes, or whatever they call those things they stick their little feet into! Which means we've gotta find out what's happened to him. Meanwhile, I want you to alert our people in Tokyo."

"I've already called them. The section chief said they'd launch a quiet investigation immediately. Hope you don't mind my jumping the gun on this. . . ."

The elevator door opened, and he stood aside to let her enter. After the car began to descend, she turned to face him and flashed one of her famous grins. "If you hadn't called 'em, I'd have thought you were slipping. Let's hope the poor guy's still in Japan somewhere."

"Or at least on this planet," Tom added softly as the car reached the lobby.

* * *

Junior Native Affairs Specialist Qaazi Qaan-gaa glanced nervously at the comatose Native who slumped beside her on the seat. It was not Culley's current physical condition that worried her; his breathing was regular, and he would regain consciousness soon enough with no permanent after-effects. Rather, it was the possibility that he had already given them away. Even though his mind seemed to be empty of all but the most autonomic sensations, he might still be broadcasting compromising thoughts on a wavelength she couldn't pick up. She had to get him to her dwelling as fast as possible so she could reprogram his implant.

The rush hour traffic on Meiji-dori ground to a momentary halt, and she briefly considered levitating the taxi ever so slightly so as to make better time. But then she noticed that the driver carried an implant and realized that such an action would probably cause him to panic, which could, in turn, trigger a scan by a robot Monitors, should one be overhead. The corners of her eyes began to flutter upward. *Why did I not have the good sense to bring the instruments with me? Then I could have—*

Qaazi's anxious thought-stream was interrupted by the unmistakable wail of a solitary coyote. Startled, she cautiously probed the immediate vicinity to see if she could pinpoint the source of the sound, but to no avail. To the best of her knowledge, there were no such beasts anywhere in Japan, let alone in downtown Tokyo, and the taxi driver gave no indication, physically or mentally, that he had heard anything unusual. Qaazi remembered hearing a similar wail that evening in the California desert just before the flyer ascended, although neither Jaahaap, the Command-Pilot, nor her kinsman (and co-conspirator) Waangaa, the Technician, seemed to notice it.

She was, of course, capable of picking up simple mental images from a variety of non-human terrestrial creatures. But these cases were different. Whatever it was that had just spoken to her was no ordinary coyote, any more than the one in the desert had been. Both of them conveyed essentially the same message: *Do not worry; all will be well. You and Dr. Wisdom have an important task to accomplish. All will be well.*

As the strange ululation died away, a wave of reassurance swept over her. The years of planning and conspiring had not been in vain. The incident in the station was a chance encounter, and the Monitors had not yet been alerted.

Her eyes stopped fluttering. They were safe, at least for the moment, and, once his implant was reprogrammed, all would indeed be well.

* * *

Culley Wisdom gingerly massaged his pounding head and stared blankly at what appeared to be an ordinary ceiling. His thoughts were jumbled together like a pile of badly stacked bricks. *Let's see, now, I got off the train at Shinjuku—it was Shinjuku, wasn't it? And then Qaazi showed up and I drank a cup of coffee and—and she zapped that guy on the steps. Don't know why, but she must have had a good reason. Then we—we rode in a taxi somewhere. Oh, I forgot, I'm not supposed to think about her. Shit, my head hurts! Feels like a hangover, but I don't remember getting drunk; it's too early in the morning for that, anyway.*

Where the hell am I now?

"We are in my apartment," a vaguely familiar voice answered from somewhere off to his left. "You are lying on a bed. I am sorry it was necessary to render you unconscious, my love, but it was the only way I could keep you from thinking about me and giving them our location. You will—you'll feel much better in a few minutes. And yes, you were correct. My dwelling is located near the place where the young people shop and dance."

Culley turned his head slowly—and painfully—to the left.

The first thing he noticed was her undisguised eyes, those huge, wrap-around eyes that seemed like tear-shaped pools of liquid ebony. Then he saw that the rest of her face and head matched the memory he'd cherished for so many years: her elfin chin was sharply pointed; her mouth was but a narrow slit framed by thin, bloodless lips; her exquisite nose was minuscule, hardly more than a pair of protruding nostrils; and the thick black Japanese hair had given way to wispy tresses the color of sun-bleached straw.

So it hadn't been a dream. She was really here!

Still clad in the same jeans and white blouse she'd had on earlier, Qaazi was seated in a small armchair, her legs curled beneath her in a very human way. She'd removed her leather jacket, and the blouse accentuated the tiny but perfectly formed breasts he remembered so vividly.

"No, dear Culley, you are neither drunk nor dreaming," she continued. "And yes, I did 'zap' the man who was following us. In a few hours he will wake up feeling much worse than you do at the moment."

Qaazi grinned impishly and tapped her forehead. "May I get you a drink of water or a cup of coffee, perhaps? As I told you, I've developed quite a taste for it."

He shook his head and gazed at her for a few seconds, doing his best to get his bearings. Then, as the pain began to subside, he remembered something she'd said—or had she "thought" it at him?—just before he went under. No matter, but it did seem to be important. Something about not being monitored. Then there was that guy on the stairs—

"The Man in Black in the station is not our principal concern at the moment," Qaazi assured him. "He is still unconscious, and it will be many hours before he will be able to report to his Masters. And even then he will not know what we intend. But my own people are a very different matter." She pointed to a small dish on the bedside table.

Still dazed, Culley sat up and focused intently on the dish. After a second or two he noticed that it contained a tiny metallic cylinder, no more than a couple of millimeters long. The object was lying in a few drops of what he presumed was his own blood, as his chest was covered by a blood-spattered towel.

"That is your implant. I have just reprogrammed it so that it will not transmit any thoughts about me other than ten year-old memories. Otherwise, one of the robot Monitors would recognize an anomaly in your profile and report it to Colony Headquarters. But the device must be reinserted immediately, for its apparent 'failure' will also trigger an alarm. I apologize for making your nose bleed. It is something we cannot control, especially when the device has been in place for a long time, although reinsertion rarely causes any serious bleeding. Do you understand any of this?"

Culley nodded. An implant did make sense; it's what he would use on a chimp or a bear if he wanted to keep track of it. And to get the implant in, he'd first have to tranquilize the beast. *Is that what we really are to them, beasts?*

"Not to me!" she replied emphatically. "That is precisely the attitude I am trying to overcome!"

Culley suddenly realized that since this "conversation" began he hadn't uttered a word, and that Qaazi had done all the actual talking. "Are you really going to put it back in me?"

he asked aloud for the first time.

"Yes, as soon as possible. Please tilt your head back.

There are a great many things I need to talk to you about, including Adam. You do want to see him." It wasn't a question, even a rhetorical question, but a simple statement of fact. Yes, he did very much want to see his son, who should be about nine years-old by now, assuming their gestation period was the same as human females.

But the prospect of her inserting that thing into one of his nostrils and then pushing it up all the way up into his brain was unsettling, to put it mildly. It brought back memories of that evening in the desert, to say nothing of screen memories of the first time he'd been implanted at about age five.

I don't want you to put it back in me. Please don't!

Images of the fright he'd felt so many years ago came tumbling into his mind. He'd been playing in the woods behind their home in the dependents housing area at Fort Benning, and he'd gotten lost, just like Daddy said he would if he climbed under the fence. He was a bad boy, but not because he wanted to be. Something had tugged at him and made him go deeper and deeper into the woods.

Then he saw them. They were taller than he was, but not by all that much, and had big scary eyes that seemed to look right through him. He remembered the funny flying bird on their chests, the same device Qaazi had worn. She was one of them, she had to be! The creatures he'd forgotten about except in an occasional nightmare. Even Dr. Stern, the Beverly Hills shrink who'd supervised his hypno-regression, hadn't been able to dig them out.

No! This is ridiculous!

He loved Qaazi. She would never hurt him like they did, never cut a piece out of him or hurt his nose. There was nothing scary about her. But he remembered the pain and the feeling that Mom (she was still alive then) and Dad would punish him for going off alone. If he told them about the little people with the big eyes and the flying birds they'd really give it to him! And besides—

"Please lie back and relax. It won't take long." Qaazi's gentle but insistent voice jerked him back to the present.

"Do you really have to put it back?"

"Yes, dear Culley, it is imperative! I am so sorry that my people frightened you when you were a child. They incised your leg because they needed a tissue sample. I know you still have a tiny scar on your right calf. But please believe me, my love. It will not be like that time in the woods."

She smiled at him tenderly, and as she did so her eyes seemed to become even larger, if that was possible. He tried weakly to resist, but the long repressed memory of how he'd received the half-moon shaped scar soon receded, and he felt his head sink back into the pillow.

Attaching the tiny cylinder to the tip of what looked like a long thin wire, she carefully inserted it into Culley's left nostril. It felt as if someone was crinkling aluminum foil in his nose, and, as she'd predicted, it did hurt for about a second. But the pain went away immediately as she carefully maneuvered the probe deeper and deeper inside his head. He was glad that she'd removed it while he was unconscious.

"Please lie still!" she said, "or I will have to do another figure on you. Is that the correct idiom?"

Despite his lingering fear, Culley couldn't help chuckling, and that brought the hurt back for a fraction of a second. "The word is 'number,'" he replied, holding his head as still as he could.

Finally, she began to withdraw the probe, satisfied that the implant was in the right spot. When it was all the way out, she carefully wound it up and put it away in a small case. Then, after removing the bloody towel, she sat down next to him on the bed, bent down, and kissed the tip of his nose.

"Who was that guy you zapped back there in Shinjuku?" Culley asked as the hurt disappeared and he felt himself become aroused. Now was probably not the time nor here the place, but his body didn't get the message, and he did his best to damp down a burgeoning erection. "You called him a 'Man in Black,'" he went on, hoping she hadn't noticed. "I'd always assumed that the stories about MIBs intimidating people who saw UFOs were pure folklore, in the same category as the rumors about a super-secret committee called MJ-12 that's supposed to know all about you people. Is he really a government agent? Sometimes I get the feeling they're still watching me, though none of the guys that used to pester me ever turned up dressed like that."

Qaazi grinned. "No, dear Culley, the man in the station is not an agent of your government. And I have never heard of any Native organization called MJ-12. But the Men in Black are all too real, unfortunately. They are—they're—human beings whose misplaced loyalty is to a race of would-be despoilers from a nearby star-system that calls itself SESO. We generally refer to that race as the Others." Her expression turned grim. "They are evil, but we are at peace with them now, and we cooperate in a number of areas as far as the Colony is concerned. It is possible that his superiors could alert mine as to our whereabouts. I had to forestall that possibility, at least for the time being."

Ignoring, for the moment, the intense erotic sensations that were coursing through his body, Culley propped himself on an elbow and stared at her with concerned eyes. "Look, are you in some kind of trouble, I mean with your own people?"

She silenced him by placing one of her supple fingers across his mouth. "I will shortly answer all your questions as best I can. And yes, there will soon be ample time for what you're thinking about, too. I wish it as much as you do! But we must leave now. My ship—we call it a flyer—is hidden in the mountains west of a city called Takayama, and we must reach it before the Man in Black regains consciousness. Then we shall fly to the Antarctic Base, where our son resides, and rescue him."

Culley nodded dully and stood up, still struggling to control his erection, while Qaazi retired to the bathroom to re-disguise herself.

When she returned, he helped her carry a pair of large but ordinary-looking suitcases, the contents of which would have blown the mind of even the most sophisticated human computer scientist, down to the lobby and out to the sidewalk, where she hailed another taxi. As they settled themselves in the back seat, she kissed him again, this time on the lips. It took every ounce of his will power not to undress her on the spot.

"We have waited ten years, dear Culley. Surely we can wait a few hours longer," she whispered, her mind adding an erotic memory image that did little to help his immediate problem. Then, as she realized what she'd just triggered, she abruptly changed the subject and did her best, mentally as well as verbally, to help him think about something else.

"The first part of our trip will be rather prosaic, I am afraid," Qaazi continued matter-of-factly. "It will be by what the Japanese call the Bullet Train. Do you know it? Ah, your thoughts tell me that you have—you've—ridden it several times. It's ironic—that's the right word, I believe, is it not?—that it will take us ten times longer to reach the city of Nagoya than it will for us to reach the Antarctic Base, once we've recovered the flyer?"

Culley smiled and finally managed to put his horniness on hold. "Yes," he replied with a chuckle as the cab turned onto Omote Sando and headed in the direction of Tokyo Station, "ironic's definitely the right word! But I do have a couple of questions about this trip we're about to—"

You are wondering why we must "rescue" Adam and why it is necessary for you to accompany me, her mind replied before he could finish his sentence. I had originally intended to bring him with me, but that proved to be impossible; we have our rules, just as your people do.

"Yeah, I'll bet you do. But you haven't answered my questions. What's the big hurry? Wouldn't it be safer for us to lay low until the heat's off and then go get him?"

Qaazi shot him a quizzical look? *I do not understand, her mind replied. Why should we lower ourselves? And I do not feel warm—*

Then Culley's figure of speech suddenly made sense, and

she grinned as broadly as it was possible for her tiny mouth, even when disguised, to grin. *Please forgive me. Your metaphors are sometimes difficult to interpret. But 'lying low' at the moment would be impossible. There is a good reason for us to hurry, despite the heat.*

"A few days ago," Qaazi explained, switching back to the verbal mode, "I received a very private message from a most reliable source saying that they are about to send Adam back to our home planet to complete what you would call his primary education. Many Earth-born children his age are sent home for several years; I was too. I knew it was coming, but not so quickly. We must spirit him away as soon as possible so that the three of us can begin our life together as a family."

"But why take me along? Isn't it more dangerous? I mean for Adam as well as for us."

"Again, I had hoped it wouldn't be necessary. But the SESO Agent, the Man in Black, has seen us together, and I cannot leave you alone here. They would almost certainly find you before I could return with our son. To make matters more complicated, I expect to be recalled to Colony Headquarters for reassignment in the very near future, and that means my plan must be put into operation immediately."

Her disguised eyes misted slightly. "I am so sorry that everything hasn't worked out the way I had originally intended. Please believe me! I had no intention of putting you at risk."

Still not quite able to put it all into focus, Culley put his arm around her and held her close. "Okay, Qaazi," he said, "I forgive you. But only on the condition that you tell me what this is really all about. My head's so full of questions that if I don't get some answers soon I think it'll explode!"

Alarmed, her "Asian" eyes widened and their corners shot upward, breaking for a fraction of a second the biotension that maintained the disguise. But she soon realized that this was simply another figure of speech. Qaazi's eyes relaxed and she smiled as broadly as her tiny mouth would allow.

"Dearest Culley," she whispered, "I promise I will do my best to keep your head intact."

CHAPTER THREE

While the taxi driver-surreptitiously guided, she later confessed, by her wondrous wand-expertly negotiated the crush of cars, trucks, vans, motorcycles, bicycles, and other vehicles that perpetually clogged even the widest avenues of central Tokyo, Culley learned that his beautiful companion was an Earth-born "Colonial," a human-alien hybrid whose chromosomes contained a great many human genes.

"Without those genes, my love, we could never have conceived a child," she said softly, caressing him with her disguised but still extremely expressive eyes.

Once again, he felt himself harden. She quickly averted her eyes and began to tell him about her ancestral home.

Qaazi's alien ancestors came from several planets that orbited sun-type stars in the constellation he and his fellow humans called the Pleiades, some four hundred light-years from Earth. The most important of these planets was called Niivaanaa, which she referred to as "the home world." (Yes, she assured him, the Sanskrit word nirvana did indeed derive from an attempt by some early Indian contactees to pronounce the home planet's name.)

"Niivaanaa is the sixth of seven planets that orbit a star we call Aandaaz. I believe you call it Pleione," Qaazi added.

Culley wasn't all that familiar with the astronomical details of the stars that made up the Pleiades, but he did recall dimly from a class in Greek mythology that Pleione was the wife of Atlas and the mother of the Seven Sisters—Alcyone, Asterope, Electra, Maia, Merope, Taygeta, and Celaeno—for who the other stars in the cluster were named.

He also knew that the Pleiades loomed large indeed in world mythology, from ancient Greece to Japan and a great many Native American cultures.

Qaazi grinned, her disguised but still razor-thin lips pulling back to reveal tiny but perfect teeth. "Yes," she said, "I remember learning some of these stories when I was a student at the Academy. They gave special attention to the myth your ancestors told about the giant who held the planet on his shoulders. We found it very amusing-although it was also apt, I think, in that Aandaaz—that is, Pleione—was in fact the 'mother' of Pleiadian civilization, first on Niivaanaa about twenty-thousand Earth-years ago, and later on several planets that orbit the nearby stars you call Merope and Alcyone. Of course, it took us much longer to discover how to travel as far as your system."

As the taxi negotiated the snarl of mid-morning Tokyo traffic, he tried his best to imagine generations of Pleiadian engineers laboring to figure out how to cross four-hundred light-years in a reasonable length of time, but without the rapid-fire montage of mental images Qaazi projected, it would have been impossible. Indeed, for what seemed the thousandth time since she'd come back into his life—had it only been a couple of hours ago?—Culley simply shook his head, not in disbelief, but in wonder.

By the time they reached Tokyo Station, Culley's head was swimming and his crotch was back to normal.

Her "briefing," as she called it, continued as they made their way to the Yaesu side of the station, where the Bullet Trains departed. Before climbing the flight of stairs to the platform, he helped her deposit two large suitcases filled with exotic Pleiadian equipment, including the device she'd used to reprogram his implant, in a pair of coin lockers. He asked her why they simply didn't take them along. The bags were bulky, but not all that heavy, and their marvelous contents might prove extremely useful somewhere along the line.

"There is nothing in them that could be of any immediate

help to us if we are discovered," she replied. "When we return to this place with our son, their contents will perhaps prove valuable to us. But at the moment it is better to 'travel light'—that is the right expression, is it not? It may become necessary for us to move quickly, and these containers would slow us down. In any case, my flyer is equipped with the same implements."

He had to admit that she had a point. If in fact they were being followed by SESO or by her own people, or by the CIA, or by whomever, and they had to make a run for it, two large suitcases would indeed be a hindrance.

After they boarded Hikari 47, the sleek, blue-and-white Bullet Train that would take them to Nagoya, and were firmly ensconced in their unreserved seats (Culley was surprised to see the two vacant seats appear as if my magic, and suspected that her wand had something to do with the fact that no one else seemed interested in occupying them), Qaazi picked up where she'd left off in the taxi.

The first Pleiadian probes arrived here about thirteen thousand years-ago, just before the end of the last Ice Age. In response to his unspoken questions, she replied that yes, by that time her people had figured out how to bypass "Einstein's speed limit"—that is, the speed of light—by riding what she called "time-waves," and thus were able to cross the vast interstellar void that separated their two home worlds with relative ease.

"I do not fully understand the theory behind it, but our technicians are able to harness the enormous energy released by the phenomenon you call time, much as humans have learned how to harness the energy of the wind or of expanding gases.

"Of course, in those days, our propulsion system was still quite primitive, and it took even the fastest of our ships almost an Earth-year to get here," she confided. "Now, we can make the trip in less than three of your months."

Five hundred light-years in three months!

As he began to grasp the full magnitude of Pleiadian

technology Culley couldn't help feeling like an intelligent Australian Aboriginal who had come face-to-face with a loving and sympathetic member of Captain Cook's crew. But it soon became apparent that their respective situations were even more ironic than that analogy might suggest.

While they shared an *obento*, a box lunch containing a variety of cold Japanese delicacies, including rice, dried seaweed, and several raw sea creatures, she described the comprehensive, almost hive-like social, political, and economic unit to which she and all other Pleiadians belonged, which she referred to simply as "the Clan." The Clan seemed to have few Earthly analogues except among the most primitive hunting and gathering societies. It was as if he'd encountered a band of Australian aborigines with a technology ten thousand years ahead of Captain Cook's! The idea was staggering, especially to an anthropologist.

Still struggling to accept what he was hearing as something other than the stuff of dreams, he listened intently while Qaazi told him about how, with the help of several like-minded kinfolk, including a cousin named Waangaa and a half-sister whose name he didn't quite catch, she'd been able to keep track of his whereabouts. She also him told that after Adam had been weaned and sent to the Antarctic crèche, she'd managed to have herself transferred from the North American Service to something called the East Asian Bio-transformation Program. There, she learned how to re-arrange the shape of her eyes and the color of her skin, hair, and eyes in such a way as to approximate the human physical type closest to her own (the program was restricted to Earth-born "Colonials" with human-type hands), and to speak Japanese and several other languages of the region. The knowledge was fed directly into her brain via her implant; it was painful but far more effective than the "primitive" teaching methods still used by his people. Qaazi was currently in the final, "field" phase of her training. Her superiors had provided her with fifty million in perfectly counterfeited ¥10,000 notes plus an equally well-forged

Japanese passport in the name of "Kazuko Hoshimura" (literally, "First-Daughter Star Village"), a drivers license, and several other documents, all of which she produced for Culley's inspection. About half of the original amount of cash was left.

"You'd better not flash this wad at anybody else, Hoshimura-san," he said as she returned the money and the documents to her purse. "Japan's a pretty safe country, but I still wouldn't take any chances. Now if this were L.A. . ."

Qaazi nodded gravely. Then, with an intensity and fervor he hadn't noticed before, she spoke at length about her plans for the future and about how that she hoped to convince her superiors that Natives like himself were not inherently inferior to her kind. The chief stumbling block here seemed to be an alien from the home world named Qaazgaa, the chief of her former unit and a hidebound conservative. He also seemed to be a powerful figure in Colonial affairs, a Clan Elder with a lot of influence, especially among those who were not Earth-born like herself.

After years of careful planning, she and her co-conspirators were apparently on the verge of launching a revolution against the policies perpetuated by Qaazgaa and his fellow conservatives, especially the policy that prohibited free and open contact between their two cultures. One of her immediate goals, she added cryptically, was to put an end to something called "the Project," at least as it was currently conceived.

Culley started to ask her about it, but began to wonder how much more new information he could absorb before his neurons rebelled. He desperately needed a break.

To make matters more urgent, the pressure on his bladder after drinking several cups of *ocha*, or Japanese green tea, had become intense. He excused himself and made his way to the front of the next car and the nearest western-style rest room. As he relieved himself, he wondered whether Pleiadians were subject to similar pressures.

Yes, her mental voice intruded, *though not as frequently.*

We metabolize liquids more slowly than humans. Someday, I hope you will have the opportunity to use one of our 'cleansers.' I think you will find it an interesting experience.

I'm sure I will, his mind replied with a bemused smile as she projected an image of what seemed to be suction tubes attached to his private parts.

When he returned to his seat, he sensed some reluctance on her part to talk about the Project, so he changed the subject and asked her to tell him more about "the Others," the race she'd referred to as "SESO."

Qaazi heaved a deep sigh that registered both visibly and mentally. "The name SESO is an acronym," she explained. "It stands for the Sqktkkj Exxvngh Sjrkhk Oojbqk."

"The Sqk-? Jesus! You've gotta be kidding!"

She shot him a puzzled look, then smiled. "Yes, of course! Your reference to that religious figure—he was one of our subjects—is an expletive. My rendering of these words is only a very crude approximation. The Others themselves rarely use the full name in ordinary conversation, as it comes from a long dead language which most of them now have as much trouble pronouncing as we do! That is also ironic, is it not?"

Culley nodded his head and returned her smile; by this time he was way past being surprised by anything she might say or do.

"But the difficulty of articulating their true name is the least of the problems associated with these creatures, "Qaazi went on, her thin smile fading. "When the first SESO contingent arrived here some five thousand of your years ago, we knew nothing about them. We hadn't encountered them in our own explorations. Nevertheless, their technology was nearly equivalent to our own, and we were overjoyed to discover the presence of another highly advanced race in this region of the Galaxy."

"I'll bet that joy didn't last very long."

"No, it did not. We soon learned that they were bent on a ruthless exploitation of Earth and its indigenous inhabitants, just as some of your people have systematically exploited the less complex populations living in the southern hemisphere."

Culley shuddered slightly. The dream was beginning to turn a bit nightmarish around the edges. "I get the message. But what do these Others look like? Are they humanoids?"

Qaazi nodded and projected a mental image of a tall (by Pleiadian standards), thin, extremely ugly creature with black bulging eyes, pencil-thin arms, three-fingered, claw-like hands, and a gray, wrinkled skin that covered what might best be described as an insect's carapace. Indeed, despite its overall humanoid proportions, the image closely resembled a picture he'd once seen of a praying mantis. At the same time, it appeared more than a little reptilian. She then adjusted the image to include a jet-black robe, high collar, and monk-like hood, which were apparently the race's standard costume.

As the image of the Other faded, Qaazi switched back to the verbal mode and told him that the SESO home world was in a star system his people knew as Zeta Reticulus: "It is much closer to your system than to ours, but the environment there would be far more alien to you than that of Niivaanaa."

Culley remembered that in the process of researching his book he'd run across several references to the star Zeta Two Reticulus, which was about thirty-six light years from here. An amateur astronomer in Ohio named Marjorie Fish had identified it as the home base of the UFO that abducted Betty and Barney Hill back in the early sixties. It made sense, as the description of the aliens that abducted the Hills certainly didn't match Qaazi's!

"When the Others are fully clothed and wearing helmets instead of hoods our human subjects sometimes mistake them for taller, Niivaanaa-born members of the Clan," she went on, picking up his thoughts. "Nevertheless, even your unsophisticated ancestors were usually able to distinguish between us and the Others, who were far more likely to be perceived as demons and evil spirits. Only in what you call modern times have we and the small, genderless androids we manufacture to perform routine tasks—three of them escorted you to my ship that evening—been systematically confused with the Reticulans."

Culley grimaced, recalling the tiny, bulbous-headed creatures that had sacred him half out of his wits on two occasions in his life. Most of the UFOlogists he'd read tended to apply the catchall label "Gray" to any large-eyed E.T. A few researchers attempted to distinguish between the "Grays" and the somewhat taller "Insectoids" (or "Reptoids"), who were generally held to be far less positively disposed toward human beings than the "Grays." But the reality was clearly far more complex. Maybe his ancestors did have a better handle on all this. Gods and demons, antithetical supernatural categories, evil creatures wearing robes and black hoods—a lot of things began to fall into place.

"Did your people ever fight a war with the Others?" Culley asked, his eyes narrowing as he continued to reflect on what she'd just told him. "I've always suspected that there was some truth behind the ancient Greek myth of the war between Zeus and the Titans, or the one in the Bible about the destruction of Sodom."

"Yes," she replied grimly, "we did fight such a war. It was a terrible conflict. Both sides employed the most horrible weapons you can imagine and a great many of your ancestors perished as a result. And yes, those that survived did indeed attribute the vast devastation to a war between angry gods."

She paused while she brushed back a stray black hair that had fallen across her disguised forehead. It was a gesture he would see her make more than once, both in and out of her disguise. "In the end, the Others were forced to abandon their attempts to exploit your planet, although our victory was by no means complete, and a great many problems remain."

"What do you mean by that? Isn't the peace treaty or whatever the two of you worked out still in force?"

"Oh, yes. The peace holds, at least for the nonce"—*I've always wanted to use that word; did I use it correctly? Your mind is nodding; thank you!*—"but it is fragile, and they will do anything to make trouble for the Clan, despite the fact that we do cooperate on specific missions that relate to the Colony as a whole, which is why they are occasionally observed aboard our ships, just as we are sometimes join their crews. Indeed, in such situations they often attempt to convince the Natives—I mean humans—they encounter that we Pleiadians are the results of their genetic manipulations and that they are the true lords of the Colony. What utter and complete nonsense! No wonder your researchers are so confused! If it were not for the demands of the Project, their outrageous lies could easily be put to rest!" The intensity of her righteous indignation was reflected in a cartoon-like mental image of an exceptionally ugly, black-robed Other posturing imperiously before a frightened clutch of human abductees.

Once again, Culley's neurons were on overload, and he simply nodded his head. Hesitantly, his mind framed a question about "the Project," as it was the second time he'd heard her use the expression. But his thought-stream once again immediately bumped into the mental equivalent of a brick wall, and so he shifted his thoughts back to the role of the "Insectoids" in the overall scheme of things.

"Yes, the Others are also represented on what we call the Colonial Council," she replied to his unspoken question, "but as you can imagine there is no love lost between us. The situation is broadly analogous to the 'cold war' your people waged against the Russians for so many decades, only our 'cold war' has lasted for five thousand years and shows no signs of ending."

Qaazi ignored Culley's mental objection that the United States never actually fought a "hot" war with the former Soviet Union and stared at him intently, her pseudo-East Asian eyes reflecting the seriousness of her concern. "I assure you that I had no way of knowing that we would encounter one of their Agents so soon after our meeting!"

"It's not your fault, Qaazi. The guy was probably in Shinjuku on some other business—and maybe he didn't put it all together before you zapped him, I mean that you were about to violate your 'Prime Directive.'" Then he smiled. "By any chance are you familiar with one of our television series, actually a whole bunch of series now, called 'Star Trek'?"

Qaazi returned his grin. "My associates and I frequently found it amusing, although the creator, a person named Roddenburg—"

It's Roddenberry, Culley's mind corrected. *The late Gene Roddenberry.*

"Yes, that is the name. I was told that he carried one of our implants. I presume that we conditioned him to insert the idea of non-interference into his programs."

Qaazi thanked him mentally both for his forgiveness and his optimism and snuggled close, cradling her head in the crook of his elbow. They fell silent, and from all indications she was soon fast asleep. At least her eyes were closed, though he wondered whether she really slept in the way humans did. Culley noticed that her right hand lay inside her ample purse and appeared to be clutching something. It had to be that remarkable wand, an object that epitomized the vast gulf that separated their worlds.

Glancing to his left, Culley caught a fleeting glimpse of the sea before his vision was obscured by the blackness of a tunnel, and he realized that they'd just passed Atami. Another hour to Nagoya. There, assuming JR lived up to its reputation for punctuality, he and Qaazi would immediately board a local express for Takayama, where they planned to rent a car and drive to the spot where her ship lay hidden.

The Bullet Train emerged from the tunnel and, after a brief flash of sunlight, passed into another, much longer one. The interior lights came on, causing Qaazi's serene and apparently sleeping face to be reflected in the window glass. As he stared absently at her reflection, his thoughts returned to what she'd just told him about SESO and the Men in Black.

Could the creatures from Zeta Reticulus have had a hand in what happened to him at Graham in the aftermath of his first encounter with Qaazi, despite the fact that he was a Pleiadian subject? Maybe the Dean, a consummate asshole named Frederick A. Fyfe, was really an MIB! Come to think of it, he did favor dark suits and ties. . . .

Then there was that other asshole.

Professor Sidney Levine, a Carl Sagan wannabe if ever there was one, right down to the "bilyuns" and "bilyuns," was an extremely short, media-wise astronomer in his mid-fifties with a bushy, pepper-and-salt beard who, like his famous role model, had managed to make a second career out of debunking UFOs on local TV talk shows. When some unsuspecting caller or guest had the temerity to report seeing an anomalous light or object in the sky, Sidney would lean back in his chair, grin his supercilious "I know more about this subject than you could ever possibly learn," and tear the poor, unsuspecting wretch to shreds.

To make matters worse, at least as far as Culley was concerned, Sidney Levine's late mother had been a distinguished anthropologist, almost as famous, in her day, as Margaret Mead, and he was convinced that he knew far more about anthropology than Culley did, even though he'd only taken one course in the subject as an undergraduate, and that only after his mother threatened to cut off his spending money if he didn't. Moreover, despite his advancing years, Levine thought of himself as God's gift to womankind, especially young, nubile womankind, as well as the walking embodiment of hip, and he regularly peppered his casual speech with teenage expressions like "awesome," "chicks," "cool," and "dude." He was partial to Tommy Hilfiger shirts, Eddie Bauer pants, and Air-Jordans or whatever brand of expensive basketball shoes that happened to be "in" at the moment; indeed, Culley suspected that the man's shoe closest must rival that of Imelda Marcos!

Whenever Sidney encountered the hapless anthropologist in the Faculty Club or some other public place on campus he would ask him in a loud voice whether he'd had any more trysts with his "ET chicks" or to share the "latest news bulletin from the space dudes." Such sallies invariably brought howls of laughter from Levine's cronies, including Dean Fyfe.

Culley did his best to stand up to his colleague's taunts, but with little success, and the end came swiftly.

Early one morning-ironically, the day after *Encounter in the Desert* made the L.A.Times' bestseller list for the first and only time, Fyfe called Culley into his office to tell him that TAPCOM, the dreaded Tenure and Promotion Committee, had turned him down for tenure. The Dean was businesslike and detached and did his best to maintain an "I'm-just-doing-my-job" façade; indeed, the bastard actually went so far as to wish Culley good luck! But the unspoken message was loud and clear: There was no place at a "respectable" institution like Graham for anyone who believed in UFOs, let alone had the gall to publicly announce that he'd been seduced by a space alien! Fyfe's massive bald pate, crisscrossed by tiny blue veins that bulged and glowed bright red whenever he was angry or agitated, was as smooth and as pale as a newborn babe's bottom.

Culley only had one class that morning, and when it was over he decided to pack it in for the day, go home, and tell Lorna the bad news. Things hadn't been going well between them lately, and this turned out to be the last straw. After a horrendous, door-slamming row, she packed a suitcase and stormed out of the apartment.

She returned several weeks later, and they remained together for the better part of another year while Culley searched in vain for an academic job elsewhere. But their marriage was in deep trouble. As it turned out, when Lorna finally left for good and filed for divorce, he actually felt relieved.

If only Qaazi had come back into his life earlier.

If only—

* * *

Culley's reverie was interrupted by the four chimes that inevitably precede a Japanese public announcement. They were followed by a mellifluous female voice, the same recorded voice one hears on virtually every train in the country, saying that they were about to pull into Nagoya. By the time the announcement had been repeated in English he and Qaazi had joined the line of passengers waiting to get off, as the train would remain in the station for less than a minute and a half.

Barely exiting the car before the doors slid shut, they hurried along the crowded Shinkansen platform, looking for the exit that would lead them to the one from which the Takayama Express was due to depart in less than five minutes.

I sense the presence of a Man in Black, Qaazi mental voice suddenly whispered.

"Good Lord, where?" Culley exclaimed aloud, his momentary panic blocking any attempt at coherent telepathy. He turned his head and searched frantically for any sign of a tall man in a black suit.

"I do not know exactly where the SESO agent is," she replied softly, switching to the verbal mode. "He does not seem to be same one we encountered in Shinjuku Station; however I do sense that one of them is nearby. The mental signature is unmistakable."

But the Man in Black's "signature" soon faded, and, with a little covert help from the wand, they managed to board the Takayama train just as the doors were closing.

As they settled into their seats, Qaazi gave the train one more psychic scan and then smiled at him.

"I don't believe that your Dean Fyfe is a Man in Black," she said innocently. "Indeed, he does not appear to carry any implant. But I agree that he is an—an asshole, as you so vividly put it. The way his bald head glows when he becomes angry reminds me of Qaazgaa. From your memory images, they seem very similar in a great many ways."

"Did you—?"

Yes, her mind confessed, she'd triggered and then shared his recollections. She added that she was extremely sympathetic about what had happened to him at Graham. Professor Levine had no business treating him that way!

Less than overjoyed, Culley mentally thanked Qaazi for her sympathy but went on to assert that he really didn't appreciate her triggering his daydreams or "messing around" inside his head without his permission; it was getting to be a habit.

"Look," he grumbled aloud, "I'm still new at this telepathy business, and maybe someday I'll learn how to impose blocks like the ones you regularly set up. But please let me have a little mental privacy, okay? Is that too much to ask?"

Qaazi's face fell—to the extent that even a fully disguised Pleiadian face is capable of falling.

"No, it is not," she replied contritely. "I-I'm so sorry. I shall never again intrude on your memories without your permission. And I promise not to 'mess' with your mind in any way unless it becomes vitally necessary." She went on to explain that there might be times when, as in the taxi, she would have to take control. She hoped he would understand.

. . .

Culley accepted her apology and gave her a small kiss on the cheek, much to the consternation of an elderly passenger sitting across from them. Nevertheless, the fact that she could roam around in his psyche at will was still unsettling. And his lack of choice in the matter, despite her promise to respect his memories, was downright frightening. Something he'd learned a long time ago in a mythology class seemed to be relevant here. Yes, of course! It was the ancient Sumerian myth of Inanna, the Queen of Heaven, and her mortal lover Dummuzi. If he remembered correctly, the goddess eventually destroyed. the poor, love-besotted shepherd. But the image was fleeting, and Qaazi gave no indication, mentally or verbally, that she'd picked it up.

His mild scowl rapidly transformed itself into a tender grin. Changing the subject, he projected a cartoonish image of Dean Fyfe complete with glowing forehead. "Maybe someday you or one of your people will mess around inside his head," he chuckled. "I'd love to be there when that happens!"

"Perhaps you will be. But we have more immediate things to be concerned about at the moment." She paused and cocked her head to one side. "I still do not sense the presence of a Man in Black on this train. But we still must be careful. If the SESO Agent did spot us, he may have alerted his superiors, and they will indeed put two and two together to make four, as your mind just put it."

As the Takayama Express climbed higher into the increasingly rugged mountains, they admired the scenery and spoke mainly of inconsequential things, much like ordinary human lovers. She did mention something called "the Project" several times in passing but seemed reluctant to elaborate, so he let it drop, at least for the moment. In any case, she scrupulously refrained from uninvited forays into his psyche, and their earlier tiff was long forgotten by the time the train finally reached Takayama. When they stepped onto the platform, Qaazi scanned the immediate area carefully, but could detect no cause for alarm.

It was now well after three o'clock in the afternoon, not the best time of day to begin a long drive into the heart of the Hida range, which lay to the west of the city. Nevertheless, the faster they moved, the safer they would be. Spotting a red-and-white Nippon Rent-a-Car sign, Culley led the way across the station plaza.

Although the car rental agency was housed in a modern concrete building, its next door neighbor was a quaint, Japanese-style wooden house that currently served as a souvenir shop. Takayama was a charming old town, with narrow, lantern-bedecked streets lined with lovingly restored buildings, and, under ordinary circumstances, he would have suggested that they linger a while in this last bastion of the "old Japan." But these were far from ordinary circumstances.

Just before they entered the Nippon office Qaazi gave the area another quick sweep. There was still no evidence, visual or psychic, that they were being followed. They both began to relax.

With a little more luck, Culley told himself, he and "Ms. Hoshimura" just might pull it off!

CHAPTER FOUR

Hajime Nakamura, the Man in Black whom Qaazi had zapped in Shinjuku Station, sat in the same station coffee shop where he'd spotted Qaazi and Culley nursing a glass of heavily sugared ice tea while he waited for the signal from SESO. He had returned to see if he could find any clues as to the *gaijin*'s identity, and with a little mental prodding, the proprietor produced the topcoat the man had left behind when he and his Pleiadian companion suddenly bolted. But the coat contained no identification or traceable items, and so, after pilfering a few ten-yen coins he found in one of the pockets, he returned the garment to the elderly woman who ran the place, telling her that it wasn't his, after all.

Damn that Pleiadian bitch! Nakamura's head still throbbed from the pressure exerted by the translator wand. But the tall, sober-faced Native Agent did his best to ignore the pain and to prepare his mind for the transmission process, which would demand intense concentration. A high-security message of the sort he'd asked permission to transmit required an extremely tight beam, and that meant close proximity. The ship had to be almost directly overhead.

Nakamura had awakened in Keio University Hospital—what a primitive place it was compared to the medical facilities provided by the Masters!—and was immediately confronted by a team of puzzled doctors who wanted to run a battery of tests on him. But, with the aid of his implant (one of the Keio physicians, a respected professor, also carried a SESO device), he soon was able to convince them that he felt fine and that he would return the next day for the tests.

Moreover, except for her *gaijin* companion, no one saw the Pleiadian bitch aim the wand at him, and so he was spared the bother of dealing with the local authorities.

As soon as he'd signed the necessary forms and shown them his forged National Health Insurance card, Nakamura left the hospital and headed for the nearest coffee bar, where he immediately made mental contact with SESO Central and then, between sips of iced tea, put the finishing touches on what he hoped was a concise yet comprehensive report of what had happened to him.

In addition to registering his outrage at the female's sudden and unprovoked assault, he included some comments about the curious, almost egalitarian way in she related to the *gaijin*. The fellow was definitely not one of their wretched "Native Companions"; he would have picked that up immediately when the man almost knocked him down a few minutes before he spotted the Pleiadian. And besides, the Pleiadians generally treated the Natives who served them little better than household pets—a far cry from the straightforward way the Masters treated their black-suited Native Agents (in pre-modern times, the MIB uniform in this part of the planet had been a black kimono and hakama).

To be sure, the life of a Man in Black was often difficult. The Masters expected absolute loyalty and instant obedience and didn't take kindly to mistakes. But the rewards were many, not the least of them being a life-span more than quadruple that of ordinary Natives. Indeed, all things considered, Nakamura was pleased that his long-deceased parents had been selected to produce a SESO Native Agent. Someday, the Reticulans would triumph, and he and his fellow MIBs, in concert with the Masters, would help the human race would realize its true destiny in the stars! How he longed for—

With no more warning than the Pleiadian bitch had given him, an alarm went off in his head with a force that felt like a blow. He reeled slightly, and then, putting all other thoughts aside, he concentrated intensely on the report he'd prepared.

A booming voice echoed just behind his forehead:

This is SESO 5.13, on reconnaissance over the Sea of Japan. Transmit on my signal—and the message had better be important!

A second or so later the signal arrived in the form of a sharp buzz, and Nakamura began to transmit. In less than two more seconds the report had been received by the SESO scout, and was already being relayed to the nearest base.

When the scout's acknowledgment finally arrived—it seemed like hours, but was actually only about four seconds after he finished transmitting—it concluded with the words for "well done" in both Japanese and Reticulan.

Nakamura-san relaxed. In fact, he actually allowed himself to smile faintly. Who knows? he told himself, I might even be in line for promotion after this coup! One could never really predict how the Masters would react, especially Djrnk-sama, the female Master to whom he reported. But that scout pilot would never have added "well done" if his superiors hadn't authorized it.

The kid in Shinagawa, whose photographs of a SESO ship he'd been assigned to confiscate, could wait a few more hours. He'd earned himself a little R&R, as the North Americans put it in that strange language that was so easy to comprehend but so frustratingly difficult to speak.

After "broadcasting" an appeal on a mental frequency unique to his fellow MIBs asking for their help in locating his quarry, Nakamura put his implant on standby, which meant that all but the most important messages would be deferred. His headache now completely gone, he left the coffee shop and headed for the nearest hostess bar.

* * *

The Nippon Rent-a-Car agent accepted Qaazi's perfectly forged bank card and driver's license, both of which bore what Culley had come to think of as her Japanese *nom de terre*, with no hesitation whatsoever. However, much to his dismay, he soon discovered that his alien companion, with all her well-nigh magical capabilities, didn't have the faintest idea how to operate an automobile. It seemed that Qaazi's teachers hadn't considered the skill necessary for an East Asian assignment, and had therefore omitted it from her conditioning. (When he asked her how she'd managed to get to Tokyo in the first place, she replied that it had been a long and difficult trip, first by bus and then by train, with a great many missed connections and mistakes; this, he later discovered, was why she so readily agreed to his suggestion that they rent a car in Takayama.)

At first, Qaazi had insisted that she could easily master such a "simple technology." But Culley, who carried his regularly renewed California drivers license and an international driving permit, as well as his passport, on his person at all times, managed to convince her to let him be listed as the rented Toyota's principal driver. Amused by the irony of the situation, he promised to teach her how to operate a "Native vehicle" once they'd settled down somewhere. Indeed, the more he thought about it, the more he realized that her inability to drive a car was equivalent to his own inability to knap flints or to make and use a boomerang; both skills reflected an extremely simple technology, yet few civilized human beings could perform these "primitive" tasks without extensive training and practice.

We're all prisoners of our technologies, he told himself, and smiled broadly at her when her mental voice reluctantly murmured agreement.

Once they left the city, the road became narrow and winding.

To make matters worse, as they drove deeper into the Hida Mountains the temperature dropped and the peaks disappeared under a shroud of dark, menacing clouds. Here and there, patches of mist swirled around the Toyota, obscuring visibility and causing Culley to suspect that it might snow before they reached their destination. However, Qaazi assured him that road conditions wouldn't be a problem. She patted her purse and transmitted a mental image of the remarkable device it contained.

They had just passed through a small village perched on the edge of a deep gorge when a large truck bearing a load of firewood suddenly turned onto the main road from a side street began to climb a steep hill. Their speed slowed to a crawl as traffic piled up behind the heavily laden vehicle. Without uttering a word, verbally or psychically, Qaazi reached into her purse, withdrew the wand, and aimed it at the truck. A moment later, the driver abruptly turned off onto an unpaved lane, and they were able to resume normal speed.

"The driver carries one of our implants," she said with an impish grin. "I simply 'suggested' that he take a short cut. I hope the poor man does not become lost."

Instead of thanking her, Culley drove for a few minutes in silence, then abruptly pulled over to the side of the road and shut off the engine. He stared blankly through the windshield at a sign advertising Yokohama Tires, barely visible through the freezing fog.

Alarmed, Qaazi broke her promise not to probe his psyche and quickly learned the reason for his strange behavior. Triggered by her casual use of the wand, which symbolized the almost supernatural power differential between her people and his, the mystical experience he'd had on the train had once again grabbed hold of his psyche, only this time it was overwhelming. As he remembered the details of the Dummuzi myth, his hands clutched the wheel so tightly that his knuckles turned white. The goddess Inanna decided to visit her sister Ereshkigal, Queen of the Underworld, and took the mortal she'd coerced into being her lover with her. But somewhere along the way Dummuzi angered her, and she left him behind in the Land of the dead.

He also recalled that this myth wasn't limited to ancient Sumeria. The Babylonians knew the goddess as Ishtar, in Anatolia she was Cybele, and the Romans called the ill-fated lovers Venus and Adonis. Of course, in most versions of the story the goddess relented and "resurrected" her lover as a god, but always under her benevolent thumb.

Culley relaxed his pressure on the steering wheel and stared at Qaazi as if seeing her for the first time. Was she really a counterpart—or maybe the grand-daughter of a prototype!—of Inanna, Ishtar, and those other ancient goddesses? And was he doomed to play the role of Adonis, if not Dummuzi? His hands began to shake, and the only thing he could think of was how to get away from this place as fast as possible-alone!

Struggling to keep the corners of her eyes under control lest the bio-tension program be damaged, she quickly extended a multitude of mental tentacles and wrapped them gently but firmly around his throbbing psyche, caressing and soothing as best she could. She also apologized for breaking her promise not to intrude, but it was obvious to both of them that this was one of those occasions where that promise had to be broken.

"Dear, dear Culley!" she added verbally, "Please believe me! I truly love you and have no intention of doing what that figment of your ancestors' imagination did to her unfortunate lover. Yes, I'm sure that our presence engendered the myth that so haunts you at the moment, for I am not the first of my kind to love a Native. But I promise that I'll never harm you. I am *not* Inanna. I am not a divine being of any sort. Remember. I cannot even operate this vehicle! Is that something you would expect a goddess to admit?"

It took a moment or two for her "therapy" to take effect, but she gradually felt him relax. She hugged him close, and they sat that way for almost five minutes, neither of them speaking or thinking coherent thoughts at each other. It was as if they'd managed somehow to transcend time and space.

Yet despite the warmth of the moment, a residual resentment of her god-like power over him lingered deep within Culley's psyche, apparently at a level that Qaazi couldn't penetrate, for she gave no indication whatsoever that she was aware of it. He also began to wonder, again in this newfound corner of his mind, whether the intense love he still felt for her had somehow been programmed, either by Qaazi herself or by who knew what.

Then, as he pondered this possibility, a tiny voice—not hers—intruded into his consciousness and told him that all would be well and that he and Qaazi had an important duty to perform, a duty to both their races. Like Dummuzi, the voice added, he had no choice.

The tiny voice faded and he soon began to suspect that he'd imagined the whole thing—including the mystical experience itself. Qaazi seemed as oblivious to the voice-if there'd really been one-as she had been to his lingering feelings of resentment. Perhaps she has no choice, either, he told himself.

The "spell," if that was the right word for what had come over both of them, was finally broken by a passing police siren. Culley shook his head to clear his jumbled thoughts and apologized for behaving so badly. "I know you're not a goddess. But maybe what just happened to me is why your people are so nervous about suddenly revealing their presence. I'm a practicing atheist, and yet it seems I'm still not immune to irrational visions."

She nodded, but quickly added that she didn't think it was a huge problem. "You did get over it," she said, "and I am sure that others of your kind will, too, despite what Qaazgaa and the others believe. But now you must resume driving. The place we seek is not far from here."

* * *

That place, it turned out, was a small, supposedly abandoned *jinja*, or Shinto shrine. It was located on the edge of a picturesque village whose high-gabled, thatched farmhouses, called *Gassho zukuri*, could have formed the subject matter of an antique wood-block print. Qaazi had located the site with the help of the master computer. In years past, it had occasionally served as a sort of "safe house" for surface expeditions.

However, when, shortly before dark, they finally pulled

into the graveled parking area next to the shrine, it was obvious that the Kumo-*jinja* was anything but abandoned. On the contrary, despite the awful weather, it was festooned with paper lanterns and crowded with visitors. The local *matsuri*, or shrine festival, was in full swing.

"This location certainly seemed deserted when I landed here several Earth-months ago, but it appears that someone at Headquarters failed to scan it thoroughly enough. You see, we are as 'human' as you are in many respects; we are not gods!" Qaazi frowned as she gathered up her purse, glanced at her reflection in the rear-view mirror, and made a few passes at her disguised hair with a soft brush—a very "human" gesture, Culley told himself; definitely not the sort of thing a goddess would do.

"I suggest that we mingle with the worshipers and then, when the festival is over and they've all returned to their homes, we will uncover the flyer and leave," she went on. "It is located about a hundred meters behind that building over there, in a forest clearing covered by a thin layer of dirt. I was unable to hide it as completely as I would have liked."

"Hope it's still there and in one piece," Culley muttered. "Even in Japan, people do sometimes steal things they stumble onto."

"It is there," she responded quickly. "I can sense it."

They got out of the car, walked beneath the twin cross-beams of the *torii* gate that marked the boundary between secular and sacred space, and joined the crowd in front of the thatched, Ise-style shrine, whose simple, unpainted wooden facade blended easily with the tall hinoki trees that flanked it on either side, and which grew in thick stands on the hillside that loomed behind the low building.

The last ceremonial procession of the afternoon was just coming in. A team of traditionally clad young men and women bearing a *mikoshi*, or portable shrine, on their shoulders and shouting "*Wa shoi!*" bobbed and weaved its way through the crowd. When the bearers reached the open space in front of the *jinja*, they deposited the *mikoshi* on a pair of sawhorse-like stands, then bowed to the local priest and posed for the inevitable group photograph.

After the team dispersed, it looked for a moment as if the festivities might be over for the day, and that they could soon make their way to the flyer. But then they realized that another, more sacred ceremony was about to begin, one in which the local divinity would be "drawn down" into the persons of the *miko*, or "shrine virgins" who served the shrine. By now it was completely dark, and the majority of the onlookers had departed. Qaazi and Culley were the only outsiders among the fifty-odd warmly clad people who stayed for the evening ceremony, and thus there was no way they could remain anonymous. So they decided to join in the festivities and slip away into the night when the opportunity presented itself.

Qaazi was still worried about the Man in Black she'd immobilized in Shinjuku. He'd almost certainly alerted his black-robed SESO superiors by this time and, with their help, might be closing in on them at this very moment. But a surreptitious scan turned up no evidence of his—or any other MIB's—presence in the immediate vicinity.

The *guji*, or chief priest, was impressed by Culley's command of Japanese and his familiarity with Shintoism and readily accepted Qaazi's story that he was a visiting American scholar interested in local Shinto customs, and that she was his Japanese host. Folding chairs were provided for them in the front row of the audience, a portable kerosene heater was placed in front of them as a gesture of respect, and the ceremony got under way.

An elderly gentleman, who introduced himself as the *sekinin sodai*, or head of the local shrine association, stationed himself next to Qaazi and Culley and did his best to explain the meaning of the dances, which were performed to traditional music played issuing from an excellent CD system.

How typically Japanese, Culley's mind observed: Heian era dance music amplified by state-of-the-art electronic equipment! (He also realized that he didn't feel very cold, despite the absence of his topcoat and the fact that a few random snowflakes were now dancing in the lantern light; Qaazi had to be up to something, although this time he silently thanked her.)

After much bowing, both to each other and to the shrine's chief *kami*, who turned out to be the Sun Goddess Amaterasu Omikami, and the chant-like reading of several prayer scrolls, the three priests in attendance retired and a contingent of eight teenaged *miko* attired in simple white kimono and bright red *hakama* skirts, took center stage. Forming a line, they performed a series of very ancient dances commemorating the descent of Amaterasu's grandson Honinigi to Earth from the High Plain of Heaven so as to extend his divine grandmother's sovereignty to the mortal world and found the Imperial Family.

Then another strange thought hovered at the edge of his mind: The myth these girls were acting out seemed curiously like what he now knew about Qaazi's people. Could the prototype of Honinigi be an early emissary from Niivaanaa? Could Amaterasu, the Shining Lady in the Sky, be one of Qaazi's ancestors?

She gave him a mental nod. Yes, this myth, like the Sumerian one that has so bothered you, is most probably a skewed reflection of our presence. Your Bible is filled with such myths. So is your modern science fiction.

He smiled in his head, picked up her acknowledgment, and returned his attention to what the elderly sodai was saying.

". . . the *miko* will now ask the spirits of Honinigi and Amaterasu to enter their bodies and join us for a sacred meal. Please to watch carefully!"

The tempo of the dance increased.

The recorded music stopped, and one of the younger priests began to beat a small drum. Culley remembered reading somewhere that the ancient *miko* were true shamans, and that this tradition lingered to the present in some of the more remote parts of rural Japan. These wholesome-looking teenagers seemed to be the sorts of *miko* one might find at any Shinto shrine rich enough to support their presence: the daughters of local worthies whose service as "altar girls" brought honor to their families. But as the dance got wilder, their eyes began to glaze, their long hair swirling about their shoulders as their heads tossed back and forth, he wasn't so sure. Qaazi appeared to be thoroughly mesmerized by the performance, her heartbeat now synchronized with the accelerating drum beats.

Suddenly, one of the girls, slightly older than the rest, gave a small cry and fell to the ground, her body twitching uncontrollably.

"The *Kami-sama* have come," the old man said in a hushed voice. "I must attend to them." He and the priests formed a line facing the writhing girl and bowed deeply.

For the first time since the drumming began Qaazi sent Culley a clear mental message: *Look! Something has definitely possessed her. No, it's not one of my people or an Other, as you're now thinking. It is an elemental force connected to this location, a form of energy most of your scientists still refuse to acknowledge-although its presence was probably sensed by the people who built the shrine. The Clan is also in harmony with such forces, or "spirits," which is why the place was selected to be a safe house, once we assumed it was totally deserted. . . .*

Culley stared at the girl, whose contortions were slowly subsiding. Her fellow *miko* had long since stopped dancing, and had joined the priests in bowing to the newly arrived spirits. Finally, helped to her feet by the priest who had done the drumming, she bowed deeply to the shrine three times. At a signal from the *guji*, she and the other *miko* hoisted a large box, slung between two long poles, to their shoulders. Then, followed closely by the three priests, they led a procession that wove its way around the shrine precincts. The old priest said that they would circumambulate the jinja three times, after which the entire "congregation" would consume the sacred food and sake the box contained and, by so doing, would share in the mystical presence of Amaterasu and her grandson.

"The elemental force's essence has now passed from the girl into the offerings," Qaazi whispered.

She and Culley joined the procession but politely declined the place of honor directly behind the young women. They slotted themselves in as far back as they could and, as they passed behind the shrine for the second time, Qaazi signaled to him that on the third pass they ought to slip quietly into the shadows and make for the flyer.

They had managed to drift to the end of the line, and, when the elderly couple directly in front of them turned left to return to the well-lighted space in front of the honden, Qaazi and Culley ducked into the forest and kept going straight. Once in the deep shadows of the *hinoki* and *cryptomeria* that covered the hill behind the shrine, they were effectively hidden from view, and, as quietly as possible, they made their way toward the spot where the flyer was hidden.

The soft, spongy ground, which by now was covered with a light dusting of snow, completely muffled their footfalls, and the path was easy to follow, even in almost total darkness. Like most Japanese forests of this sort, especially those within the precincts of a Shinto shrine or Buddhist temple, it was carefully maintained, and devoid of thick underbrush. After about ten minutes, they came to a small clearing.

It didn't take Qaazi long to uncover the flyer. Using her wand, she peeled away several square yards of snow-covered dirt and exposed a section of what proved to be the top. Then, from a distance of about fifty feet, she aimed the instrument at the exposed portion, and the ship slowly rose through the false earth covering.

It was about thirty feet in diameter, and stood on three spindly looking legs. Except for its smaller size, the object that now loomed in front of him seemed almost identical to the saucer-shaped craft Culley had encountered so many years ago in the California desert. He began to shiver uncontrollably as the memory came flooding back.

Qaazi sensed his fear and once again did her best to calm him. "It was aboard such a ship that we first met," she whispered, "although as you've noticed, this one is smaller. It is a scout-class flyer. There are no elaborate laboratory or 'Project' facilities such as we had on the ship you remember. But it is propelled by the same anti-gravity, reverse electromagnetic force field as the larger ones and can easily take us anywhere we wish to go on the planet." She stared intently at the undercarriage. After a second or two, they were surrounded by the same blue beam Culley remembered so vividly.

Taking hold of Culley's hand, Qaazi gently but quickly guided him into the beam and up toward the ship.

The last time this had happened to him he'd been heavily sedated. But this time, with all his wits about him, it was an almost indescribable experience. Culley felt slightly light headed, and the feeling persisted for a few seconds after they were aboard.

"We experience a similar sensation, although it soon becomes routine," she explained matter-of-factly as he shook the cobwebs from his head.

In answer to Culley's unspoken question as to why they hadn't simply floated through the woods, she told him that her wand needed some minor adjustments after the intense scans she'd been making, and until these adjustments were made it would only work properly, at least in this mode, in the immediate vicinity of the ship. However, the tools she needed were on board, and once the necessary adjustments were made the remarkable instrument would allow them to float anywhere and penetrate the molecular structure of any known substance, Earthly or Pleiadian.

She climbed into one of the contoured seats and motioned to him to take the one next to her. "I keep telling you that our technology is far from perfect; our things sometimes need fixing, just as yours do."

With a few deft hand movements, Qaazi activated the flyer's systems. A low orange light suffused the cabin, illuminating the instrument panel that Culley had noticed earlier.

"Someday I will teach you how to operate one of these ships. But there is no time now for a lesson. Let's see if the ceremony has ended."

She passed a finger over the control panel and a portion of it immediately became a small screen showing the surrounding area. A few people still lingered, and the priests and the *miko* were carefully packing away the sacred box and other ritual paraphernalia.

By this time, the chill he remembered experiencing the first time he'd been aboard a Pleiadian ship had become evident, along with the unpleasant odor. Either the wand's cold-suppressor didn't work aboard ship or she'd turned it off.

Qaazi apologized mentally for deactivating the wand and stared intently at a small blue light, which soon winked out. "Remember, ten years ago you were naked," she added verbally with a wry grin. "But it will become warmer in a few seconds. As you've probably guessed by now, our average body temperature is several degrees lower than yours-Niivaanaa is colder than Earth-and most of us are more comfortable in lower temperatures. However, I'm an exception; too many Native genes, I imagine. So do not—don't worry about my comfort. I can easily adapt to either temperature. As for the odor, it is a by-product of the propulsion system and there is not much I can do about it, at least in a ship of this class. Now if this were a Project flyer. . . ."

She started to make another adjustment, then swung around to face him again. "By the way," she added, "you'll be happy to learn that the standard climate at our bases, including the one we're about to visit, is warmer than aboard our ships. It is a small concession to the many humans—we call them Native Companions—who live there. We could, of course, condition them to accept Niivaanaa-like conditions, but it is less traumatic simply to raise the ambient temperature a few degrees."

Culley's thoughts immediately returned to the unnatural warmth he'd felt back at the *jinja.*

Her eyes lifted slightly as she begged him to forgive her for not asking his permission first. He assured her that she could warm him up any time she chose—and in any fashion she wished. . .

"Please have patience, dear Culley. There will soon be ample time for the sort of warming you have in mind. Meanwhile, you may be interested to know that such open-air temperature adjustments can only be maintained for short periods, even with the aid of a wand. Indeed, for your sake, I'm glad that we were able to break free when we did!"

As she spoke, the air became warmer, and Culley unbuttoned his jacket. It had also warmed up slightly just before he meet Qaazi for the first time. That was after the—

No, she assured him, the green mist had nothing to do with climate control. "It ensured that neither of us would transmit any harmful bacteria or viruses during the act of procreation," Qaazi explained matter-of-factly, adding mentally that it did indeed absorb most of the "ambient odor" one experienced aboard their ships, although the gas bore no chemical relationship whatsoever to baking soda.

She was about to apologize for not having a supply of the stuff aboard her flyer when Culley suddenly interrupted her thought-stream.

"Baking soda?" he asked incredulously.

"Yes. If I remember your book correctly, that was the analogy you used in describing the substance to Dr. Stern."

Culley shook his head slowly. "I don't give a hoot about baking soda or its effect on 'ambient odors,'" he chuckled, "but I'm glad to hear that our son's conception was as antiseptic as it was pleasurable!"

CHAPTER FIVE

While they waited for the ceremony to end, Qaazi did her best to explain how the saucer-shaped craft worked. She spoke as simply as she could, but much of what she told him was still way beyond Culley's ken.

It seemed that a pair of rotating generators at the base of the disk produced something called a "gravity-free, anti-mass field," a side-effect of which was the unpleasant odor he'd noticed. These generators tapped the Earth's own electromagnetism, but in order to do so they consumed small amounts of fresh water. There was more than enough water in the "tank" for the trip to where Adam lived, but if, for some reason, they wanted to go on to the Moon or to Nuurgaa, which he knew as the planet Mars, they'd need to take on a few more liters. Exactly how the water contributed to the production of the anti-mass field, or how the field itself worked, was beyond her ken, too; she was a Native Affairs Specialist, not a trained technologist.

"In the final analysis," she added, "we both take our technologies for granted. The anti-mass field is as 'magical' to me as the inner workings of a computer are to you. So you see, dear Culley, as I keep telling you, we're really not all that different!"

As she spoke, Qaazi mentally released the bio-tension that compressed her eyes and darkened her skin and hair. It was the first time he'd actually seen her do it, and the process was startling. When it was complete, he was once again confronted by those huge, wrap-around eyes that had burned themselves so deeply into his memory. Indeed, it suddenly struck him that her pale, undisguised face, although exquisite, was almost that of a fully-formed, "adult" fetus, a contradiction if ever there was one.

Qaazi immediately picked up his thoughts. "Not really," she replied verbally as she slipped out of her jeans and blouse and into a tight-fitting, faintly iridescent blue uniform similar to the one she'd worn that night in the Mojave, "our 'child-like'—I believe the proper scientific word in English is neotonous—features are a direct consequence of our biological evolution. All highly intelligent species are relatively neotonous. Most contemporary human adults are far more child-like in appearance than their nearest primate cousins, the ones you call chimpanzees."

She paused for a moment to check the scope. The ceremony was still in progress, despite the light snowfall.

Culley glanced at his watch and saw that it was almost ten o'clock. "It shouldn't last much longer," he said, stifling a yawn. "I'm sure the farmers hereabouts get up early, like farmers everywhere. Even on snowy mornings." It had been a hell of a long day and had every prospect of getting a great deal longer before it ended. He began to wonder when—or where—he'd ever hit the sack again.

I'm sorry, dear Culley, her mind whispered. *I realize that your body is fatigued. I will do my best to help you stay awake until we have rescued our son.*

With that, she turned to face him again, and picked up the thread of their previous conversation. "Yes," she continued aloud, "we've evolved further in the direction of neotony, at least externally, than your people have, although we Earth-born Colonials are far less fetal in appearance than the rest of the Clan, thanks to the massive number of human genes we carry on our chromosomes." The corners of her mouth lifted in the barest suggestion of a smile. "As a matter of fact, some of our home-planet kinfolk consider us hybrids to be rather ugly. Especially our five-fingered hands and fingernails. "

"It's obvious that they have no taste whatsoever!" he

exclaimed, feeling physically if not mentally revived. Her grin widened, and he wondered whether it was in response to his compliment or simply a reflection of the fact that he was responding to her mental ministrations.

I'm glad you appreciate my physical appearance, her mind responded. *I'm also happy to see that you're feeling better. We shall—or is it will?—-need all of our wits about us when we arrive at the Antarctic Base. . . .*

As he watched Qaazi complete the transformation process, Culley suddenly realized that, unless his tired memory was playing massive tricks on him, her features hadn't changed a wit in ten years. That meant that—

"Your memory is correct," she once again interrupted, this time verbally. "I haven't aged more than a few days, at least by Native standards. Nor will you, my love, after I persuade them to arrest your aging process, just as they do those of the Native Companions. I would do it myself right now if I had the capability. You will not become younger than you are now, nor will you live forever. No one does. But don't worry; we will have many centuries together."

Centuries. The thought was staggering!

"Yes it is a staggering thought," Qaazi continued, fixing her huge eyes on his. "I hope you will not tire of me." Her voice was even, but he could sense the anxiety that lurked behind her words, although her mind blocks were firmly in place and no specific thoughts or images accompanied them.

For a fraction of a second, the resentment he'd felt earlier evening returned to haunt him: *Why won't she let me share whatever's bothering her?* But the feeling faded almost as fast as it had come. "I doubt very much that'll ever happen," Culley replied with a chuckle. "Especially if we continue at this pace. You'd better get me some of that anti-aging stuff fast!" He projected an image of himself bent over and hobbling with a cane.

They both laughed, and some of her anxiety seemed to give way. But the underlying tension was still there.

"No," Qaazi said after their laughter had subsided. "That

is not what I meant. Of course, I too will age, but it will probably take more than an Earth-millennium for me to become physically equivalent to the image you just projected. It's something else. Our laughing together just now brought it clearly into focus."

She hesitated for a moment, and then plunged ahead, her mind blocks now in total disarray. "I-I do not really have what you call a 'sense of humor.' None of us do. That's why I was so puzzled when you laughed about the temperature and about Adam's procreation being free of infection. We have assembled a vast amount of information about your history, your biology, and almost every conceivable aspect of your cultures. But despite all our knowledge, we have yet to fully understand this most curious phenomenon. Please, dear Culley, please help me to develop a sense of humor so we can regularly laugh together as we just did. It is very important to me!"

Culley unstrapped, leaned across, and took her in his arms. She didn't cry; undisguised Pleiadian eyes couldn't. But she would have if she'd had the ability. "You just made a pretty good beginning," he said softly. "Okay, you're on. But I'll love you even if you never get any of my jokes!"

She smiled up at him, although it was clear from the general tone of her once again heavily shielded thought-stream that she was deadly serious about this. That's part of the problem, he told himself as quietly as he knew how.

But she picked up the thought, and several minutes passed with no communication of any sort between them.

Then, still brooding over her inability to understand "Native" humor, Qaazi reached across the control panel to make an adjustment in one of the instrument lights; the color shifted from pale blue to deep purple when she passed her gloved hand over it. As she leaned toward him, Culley noticed that her uniform bore the same stylized insignia he dimly remembered seeing when she and the others had approached his van. It was indeed a feathered serpent.

"Did your people by any chance have an especially

strong impact on the Indians of central Mexico a few centuries before the Europeans arrived?" he asked, hoping that the change of subject would lighten her mood.

Qaazi gave him what was obviously meant to be a quizzical look, although her almond-shaped eyes dilated slightly rather than widening in the human fashion. "Why, yes, we did," she replied. "In fact, my own great-grandfather was in charge of a team that visited region. How did you know?"

He tapped the insignia on her chest.

"Of course! I forgot for a moment that you are an anthropologist, that you are—you're—trained in your planet's culture history and know about such matters as Quétzalcoatl, the feathered serpent god. Yes, I'm afraid we did have an impact on ancient Mexico. As you suspect, my great-grandfather was also a 'rebel,' who regularly violated the Sacred rule of Non-Interference. Perhaps it runs in the—"

The corners of her eyes suddenly shot upward. She cocked her head slightly to the left, as if she were listening to something that only she could hear. "A Man in Black is now less than a kilometer from the village," Qaazi said after a long moment. "We must leave immediately!"

She did a quick scan of the shrine precincts. The ceremony was over and most of the worshipers had departed, although the sensors told her two adult males were still in the immediate vicinity of the shrine tidying things up. No matter; they had to get away now.

"We can use the cloaking device. It should give us some cover. But I will have to get us off the ground before it will work. Here we go!"

With that, Qaazi eased the flyer into the air, and within a few seconds they were hovering above the trees behind the *jinja*.

"They have spotted us!" she exclaimed, pointing a super-long forefinger at the scope.

Culley could see the two men clearly, and after she made

another adjustment, he was able to hear their startled voices as well.

"Are wa nan des'ka?" one of them shouted, pointing up at them.

The other man, who had the stolid, work-worn face that comes from years of wading in rice paddies, simply stood there open-mouthed. "*Dame des' yo*!" he muttered after a second or so, and the two of them began running toward the parking area. Culley could empathize with the pair of terrified *nofu*, or famers, but the immediate problem was the MIB.

"Where's our 'friend'? Is he getting closer?"

"No. He seems to have stopped on the opposite side of the village. I do not know why. It is hard for us to read their thoughts, especially this far away. Ordinarily, I would send out a probe. It's a ball of light that works on the same principle as the wand. But that would only give us away. We had better cloak ourselves." The bubble was instantly surrounded by a thick grey fog, although the screens still showed a clear view of the ground beneath them.

She moved her hand over the control panel and, with no sensation of speed whatsoever the artificial fog bank gave way to clear night sky, and within less than ten seconds Culley could see below him what looked like a map of central Honshu. Both coasts were clearly visible, as were the lights of Tokyo and Osaka, which looked like glowing blobs at each horizon. They had reached the upper edge of the atmosphere.

"Jesus H. Christ!" he said. "Now I understand why you people sometimes simply seem to disappear. Did we go faster than light?"

Qaazi laughed quietly, her eyes still focused on the scope. "Is that one of your jokes? If it is, it is very funny." She continued chuckling, while Culley looked at her blankly. "No, I can assure you we're still very much in a sub-light, plasmadynamic mode," she explained. "Although it is sometimes possible for this ship to approach the speed of light for brief periods, especially when it is able to tap localized energy fields like the one that 'possessed' that young woman, it is not equipped with a time-dilating, interstellar drive, and even if it were, I'm not 'checked out'—that is the right expression, I believe—on that mode of propulsion. We do not engage the interstellar drive until we're well away from any inhabited planetary body. It is far too dangerous."

"Amazing. . . But we seem to be parked, or at least we don't seem to be moving. I thought the idea was to get to where we're going as fast as possible."

"We are safe here," Qaazi said, swiveling so as to face him. "However, there are a few things that I must do before we attempt to enter the Base together. The first is to make a few more adjustments to your implant. I've already attenuated your locator signal, which also carries your more complex thought patterns. Any intense or hyper-emotional thought automatically alerts the Monitors to take note of a subject's location and state of mind. Indeed, if I had not altered your signal, they would long since have discovered us, as we've both been thinking some rather intense-and intimate-thoughts lately!"

She smiled wickedly, then resumed her mater-of-fact tone. "Unless an alert is triggered, the Monitors do not ordinarily access this signal except when they are actively tracking a specific subject, or if there is a loss of vital signs in the carrier beam."

"You mean they're still receiving a signal from my head? I though you simply switched me off."

"No. That too would have alerted them immediately. Your carrier beam is telling them that you are alive and well, which is all they care about ordinarily. The attenuation program can, of course, be overridden, but the chances of this happening without a mental trigger are extremely remote." She concentrated for a second, then passed one of her thin fingers across a small, irregularly shaped device that protruded from the control panel. A tiny, holographic image of Culley's face appeared surrounded by a shifting pattern of colored lights that winked on and off like a tiny Christmas tree gone berserk.

"I assume those lights reflect what I'm thinking at the moment and that your guys could home in on us immediately," he said, staring at the image. "Maybe you'd better turn it off before they do!"

She nodded. "Yes, those are your current thoughts. And yes, they could easily locate us—but please don't worry, dear Culley, this information only registers on my locator. It is not being disseminated."

Qaazi once again passed a finger over the device. The lights disappeared and Culley's image began to fade.

"Even if the Monitors do happen to discover that your locator signal is missing from your implant's normal carrier beam," she went on after the image was gone, "they will assume that it is a—a glitch in the system and go on to the next task. There are too many subjects and too few Monitors. But now we need to convince the gatekeepers at the Antarctic Base that you are a Native Companion returning with me from a surface mission."

Culley winced. "Do you really have to take that thing out again?"

"Yes. It is extremely important. The portable equipment I had with me in Tokyo was not capable of making the extremely fine adjustments that are needed. Please tilt your head back as far as possible. There should be no bleeding this time, as it has been less than a day since I reinserted it."

She carefully inserted a hair-thin wire into his left nostril, her long, extremely supple fingers deftly manipulating the probe until it reached the implant, which was embedded deep within his frontal lobe. When she pulled the tiny cylinder through one of his sinus cavities he felt a couple of seconds of fairly intense pain. But almost before he realized it the implant was out, had been reprogrammed by the ship's computer, and was back in place.

"That was the first time I have performed this operation

on a totally conscious Native," she told him. "I hope it didn't hurt too much."

Culley sat up and rubbed the side of his nose gingerly. "Well, no," he grumbled. "But I hope it's the last time! It's not exactly a pleasant experience. And besides, my stomach's growling. Do you realize that we haven't eaten anything since that *obento* on the train God knows how many hours ago? As you can tell, I'm no longer tired, but I'm starving to death!"

Her eyes dilated and the corners shot up. "No, not literally," he quickly assured her. "But we were so eager to get to the flyer that we totally forgot about dinner. By any chance is there any—"

"Of course!" she exclaimed. "How thoughtless of me! My nutritional needs are not as pressing as yours, and I failed to notice your problem. Please forgive me!"

Reaching into a compartment beneath the control panel, Qaazi produced several small yellow wafers, together with what looked like a transparent cyclist's squeeze-bottle full of a dark green liquid. "These will sustain you for at least twenty-four hours. I don't think you will like the taste very much, but they are all that we have at the moment."

She was right. The wafers tasted like library paste, and the liquid wasn't much better. But they assuaged his hunger, and he began to feel better. He passed the bottle back to Qaazi, who took several sips.

"Is this your standard fare?" he asked after he polished off a second wafer.

"Yes, although at our bases there is usually a much greater variety. It is, as your mind suspects, a synthetic product. We do not habitually consume other life forms. Indeed, our androids have been bio-engineered to eat no food at all. They take nourishment directly from light and recycle their waste products. Some of your food is difficult for us to digest, despite the fact that we have what amount to three human stomachs." She smiled as he tried to picture what such an organ might look like. "But I promise to adapt as best I can to this most important aspect of your culture."

I sure hope so, his mind responded. *I'm really glad to hear that you guys at least have stomachs!* Grinning impishly, he projected an image of a juicy, charbroiled cheeseburger, surrounded by thick, golden brown French fries.

Qaazi's face turned slightly green and she projected a mental gag. Then she settled herself once again in the pilot's chair and engaged the plasmadynamic drive. Within seconds, they'd left Japan far to the north and were hurtling silently southward through the far upper reaches of the atmosphere toward their final destination at the bottom of the planet.

* * *

In the cramped living room of a small, wood-frame bungalow perched on the edge of a dried-up canal in Venice, California, Sally Linker sat facing two pieces of crystal and a sputtering candle. Her eyes were closed, and the creases in her forehead betrayed intense concentration. Suddenly, as if she'd finally managed to surmount some hidden barrier, Sally relaxed, opened her eyes, and leaned her head against the back of a worn armchair. "I am ready for questions, now," she said in a soft and slightly hesitant voice that was clearly hers yet colored by overtones and stilted inflections that were absent from her ordinary speech.

A twenty-eight year-old legal secretary and part-time graduate student in Clinical Psychology at UCLA, Sally Linker been "trance channeling" seriously for about a year and a half now, ever since she'd become a disciple of the legendary new-age guru Carlos Castillana. The current session was a demonstration for a small group of close friends and neighbors, although she did sometimes accept money for one-on-one sessions in which she attempted to discover information about her clients' past lives and to help them with a variety of personal problems. Needless to say, Sally made sure that her UCLA professors knew nothing whatsoever about these activities, as channeling was *not* a widely accepted form of psychotherapy.

Ordinarily, she channeled what she referred to as her higher or “astral” self, but this time she was certain that another entity had possessed her, an entity she had never before encountered.

Several of those present raised their hands, including Sally’s current boyfriend, Sidney Levine—the same UFO-debunking Sidney Levine who had played such a decisive role in the “Wisdom case” at Graham College several years back. As it happened, Levine, now firmly divorced for the third time, had moved to Venice, and they’d met at party in a mutual friend’s apartment. One thing had led to another and for the past year or so she and Sidney had been sharing the same bedroom on a more or less regular basis.

Sidney was infatuated with her long blond hair, her enormous, waif-like blue eyes, and especially her zaftig body, which he lusted after continuously. And the fact that she seemed equally fascinated by him did wonders for his already considerable ego, despite the difference in their ages and the fact that she was a committed New-Ager.

Stroking his beard, he condescendingly allowed the woman sitting next to him, one of Sally’s long-time clients, to ask the first question.

“Are you Sally’s higher self?” the woman asked.

“No,” the entity replied. It was the channel’s voice, although the overtones were deeper and somehow more masculine.

“Who are you, then?”

“I am what you would call an alien.”

Sidney couldn’t contain himself any longer. “Do you have a green card?” he asked, glancing around the room to make sure that the others had picked up his witticism. There were some nervous chuckles plus a few dirty looks from the true believers.

But Sally, her eyes tightly closed, paid no attention to her boyfriend’s barb, nor, it appeared, did the entity she was channeling.

“I do not understand the question,” it said through Sally’s

lips. “Could you explain what that means?”

Levine smiled smugly and shook his head. It was obvious that he considered the whole business to be totally absurd.

“Are you an extraterrestrial?” someone else asked.

“Not in the technical sense, as I was born on this planet. But my ancestors came from a star cluster you call the Pleiades.”

There was a general gasp, and even Sidney Levine’s eyes opened a bit wider.

“Do you have a name?” the first woman asked.

Sally’s head lolled forward until her chin rested on her chest. “My name is Waangaa,” the entity answered. “But now the session is over, and you must all leave immediately. I have a very private message for the channel.”

* * *

The glistening, ice-bound coast of Antarctica soon appeared on the horizon, and they rushed toward it at a speed far faster than anything Culley had experienced so far. High-speed approaches were apparently the norm; anything more tentative might be interpreted as an attempt by the Others to probe the entry way—or so she said. Then again, maybe she was simply showing off.

Qaazi reacted indignantly to this last interpretation. “I am not a ‘show-off!’” she snorted. “Some of us are, I must confess, but not me. I assure you this maneuver is necessary.”

Culley apologized for harboring such a thought, but nevertheless steeled himself for whatever might happen next. The fun and games were over, at least for the time being, and the hard part was about to begin. The big problem now, it seemed, was to make it past Clan’s security system, which had to put any security system he’d ever heard of to shame, and with no interference from the Others. *Ah, well,* he thought, *if I’m about to enter the Realm of the Goddess, I hope I can handle it without blowing this whole otherworldly operation—if that’s the right word for it.*

Reading his thoughts, Qaazi projected a degree of exasperation he hadn't noticed before, and, in a short but rapid telepathic burst, she told him to forget about goddesses. How many times did she have to tell him she wasn't one? She also did her best to convince him that all would be well and that they would shortly be a family in the true sense of the word. Then she began the steep descent.

The ocean soon enveloped the flyer, and, as they sank deeper and deeper, Culley hoped that his alien (he started to conceptualize "extraterrestrial," but then remembered that Qaazi was Earth-born) lover was correct and that their quest would be successful. He settled back in the chair and watched the submarine panorama unfold.

In a few minutes they passed through some sort of huge iris into a dimly lit, rock-cut tunnel or shaft. As the "gate" spiraled closed behind them, the water disappeared, and they floated noiselessly in the center of the dry tunnel, which seemed to angle gently downward toward what seemed to be the bowls of the earth.

Despite Qaazi's continuing attempts to disabuse him of such thoughts, he couldn't help but identify with Dummuzi descending into the Underworld in the company of the Goddess, and some of the panic that had seized him earlier began to resurface. But this time she was prepared for it, and immediately applied a soothing mental balm: *My dearest Culley, do not let that myth disturb you; this is not that underworld. It is only a base-and not the most important base, either. The only reason we are here is to rescue our son from the Crèche. Please believe me!*

The panic subsided rapidly and a strange calm came over him; it was almost as if he were a spectator watching a man called Culley Wisdom descend into the nether regions with a beautiful alien. Aloud, he said: "Thanks-for whatever you did. I think I can handle it now."

"Good!" Qaazi responded as the brightly lighted docking bay began to loom in the distance. "If you can keep your mind as blank as possible, and your heart and pulse rates down—I can help you regulate your physiology—we should have no trouble making it past Security."

He gave her a mental nod, adding: *Adam, my lad, I hope someday you'll appreciate what your old man went through to get here—wherever "here" is. . . .*

The flyer eased into the bay and came to rest next to several other disks, some of which seemed far larger than Qaazi's.

She aimed her wand at the flyer's bulkhead. A few seconds later, he found himself standing next to his beloved in the center of a circular, light-filled lobby of some sort. Just below the high, domed ceiling shimmered a large hologram depicting, in three dimensions, the same winged serpent that Qaazi wore above her left breast. While he contemplated the ethereal object suspended overhead, her voice once again echoed in his head: *It's called the* Gaandaa, *and is similar to the sorts of symbolic objects you anthropologist call totems. I will be happy to tell you more about it—to be your "informant"—after we've accomplished what we've come here to do.*

Culley's mind indicated his eagerness to learn more about her "totem," and reflected on his earlier suspicion that the Clan was essentially a high-tech analog of the Australian aborigines, including the latter's proclivity for totemic symbolism.

Remember, she intruded, *you must keep your thoughts as bland as possible!*

Sorry about that.

These mental exchanges were apparently well-shielded, but it seemed that the more mental energy he displayed, the more he would be liable for a full mind-scan. And that might prove to be a disaster.

There were three other humanoid creatures present whom Qaazi seemed to ignore. They were extremely short and looked far more "alien" than his undisguised Pleiadian companion, although they wore the same uniform as she, including the feathered *Gaandaa* insignia. These tiny beings, he realized with a slight shudder, were the androids she'd mentioned. He remembered seeing several of them in the examining chamber that evening ten years ago in the Mojave. . . . .

Picking up his thoughts, Qaazi quickly assured him that androids were docile creatures incapable of performing sophisticated tasks, including any form of coercion, without the direct mental supervision of "real" Pleiadians like herself—all of whom were at least a head taller. Nevertheless, as he took in the scene, Culley's heart began to beat faster than it did at the end of a fifty kilometer bicycle race, and he could feel his pulse pounding in his temples. But before they'd floated more than a couple of meters, he felt his bodily systems relax as Qaazi activated a circuit in his implant.

He took a deep breath, exhaled slowly, and followed her steadily toward the exit at the far side of the "lobby." It seemed to take forever, and he was sure that something would give them away, that it would all be for naught.

However, after what seemed to be a few routine questions from a bored female Security officer, who looked as if she had better things on her mind than the unscheduled arrival of a Senior Native Affairs Officer and an oddly dressed Native Companion, they passed without incident through yet another iris into what her mind whispered was the main corridor. It was brilliantly illuminated, and the walls, floor and ceiling all seemed to have been made of a smooth and apparently seamless material that emitted a steady, white light.

It is now safe for us to mind-speak more openly, she whispered softly in his head. But it would be a good idea for us to remain as silent as possible, as spoken English is rarely used between Native Companions and ourselves, especially in places like this.

Okay, got the message. Can I ask you what you and the guard back there talked about? Was she concerned about me?

Only the fact that you do not look much like one of our Companions. I told her you had just come in from the field, and were about to return there under my direction. She was also fascinated by the meaning of your name.

She's not the first, he responded ruefully. *But since we're on the subject of names, there's something I've been meaning to ask you: what does "Qaazi" mean in your language?*

It means "Precious One." We all share the surname "Qaan-gaa," of course, which means "of the Clan."

What an apt name! You're certainly precious to me!

Thank you, but we must not allow too much emotion to seep into our thoughts. There is always the possibility of leakage.

I'll do my best. Though if things get hairy, you may have to take over—just like you a few minutes ago and in the taxi.

She looked puzzled for a moment, then smiled in his head. *You and your metaphors! Yes, if a "hairy" situation arises, your Precious One will do what she must.*

They moved rapidly and effortlessly, their feet skimming along just above an orange track embedded in the luminous floor. From time to time, they passed what seemed to be entrances to side passages, and now and then they overtook or were overtaken by others as they moved steadily deeper into the complex.

After a few hundred meters, they turned into one of these smaller passages, which, Qaazi's thought-stream indicated, led to the place where the children were kept. So far, nobody had questioned their right to be there, and it was beginning to look as if Qaazi's plan might just succeed, after all. A number of "Colonials," including one whom she identified as a descendant of immigrants from a planet called Aaraa, which orbits Merope, as well as several androids, and two thoroughly human females clad in toga-like costumes who had to be "Native Companions," passed them without so much as a second glance. Indeed, the security hereabouts seemed almost too lax, as if they were being led deliberately into a trap of some sort. It had been too easy, much too easy. But Qaazi gave no indication, mental or otherwise, that they might be heading into a trap.

In a few minutes they reached a large door. Qaazi pointed her wand at it, and it slid open.

We have reached the crèche, her mind whispered so softly that he could barely "hear" her words. There is no trap; no fearsome Underworld Goddess awaits us behind that portal. Only our son and his mentor Waangaa, the kinsman I told you about on the train. They are expecting us. Please trust me!

Keenly aware of the beads of sweat that had begun to form on his forehead, he steeled himself and followed her through the door, which slid closed behind them with a faint but decisive click.

CHAPTER SIX

It took Culley a couple of seconds to get used to the dim light. Compared to the light-filled corridors along which he and Qaazi had just floated, which were suffused with an intense white glow that seemed to come from everywhere at once, the place they were now in was shrouded in gloom.

As his eyes adjusted, he realized he was in a fairly large, low-ceilinged room, roughly rectangular in shape. In the center of the room was a low, free-form table or platform on which sat several dimly-lighted computer terminals and key pads similar to the ones he'd seen on Qaazi's flyer. In front of each of these" work stations," or whatever they were, was a seat that rose from the floor like a mushroom on a stalk. Along the far wall he could see a row of doors similar to the one that had closed behind them. He also noticed that the luminescent orange "glide strip," which had made walking unnecessary, was gone. From here on, if this wasn't their final destination, they would have to use their legs, a prospect Culley welcomed, as his left knee was beginning to cramp from inaction.

I once was a student in a room like this. She accompanied her thought with a memory-image of a row of Pleiadian children, herself included, hunched over terminals simultaneously assimilating both the information that was being fed directly into their minds via their implants—each of them wore a helmet-like device composed of multi-colored wire filaments—and the data that appeared on the screens in front of them. It was not a happy image.

Where are the children? We seem to be alone. At least I

don't see anybody else around.

That is correct. They are most likely in a sleep cycle at the moment. The living quarters are behind those doors. Their minds can only stand just so much input before the pain becomes intense, and they must be allowed to rest periodically. Qaazi projected a deep mental sigh. *Life in a place like this is difficult for me to describe; you have nothing remotely equivalent to it. The children have little if any real contact with either their biological or their ceremonial parents. The only adults who impinge on them directly are the teaching techs who monitor the input. I remember—*

Suddenly she froze, and even her mental voice ceased for a few seconds. *Oh shit,* Culley thought, *my hunch was correct; they've discovered who we are and where we are and are coming to get us. The hairy situation has arrived!*

"No, no, dear Culley!" she finally whispered aloud for the first time since they'd entered the Base. "You could not be more wrong. Our 'situation,' as you call it, has grown no hair—what a curious metaphor! I have just picked up the thoughts of the kinsman who awaits us. He informs me that it is now safe for us to speak verbally as well as mentally."

Culley started to say something, but before he could utter a sound, one of the doors in the far wall slid open noiselessly, and through it stepped a uniformed male Pleiadian, a Colonial with five-fingered hands, but extremely pale skin and hardly any hair at all. The newcomer was holding a small figure by the hand.

"I am called Waangaa," the Pleiadian said immediately in fluent but extremely stilted English. "It is good to see you again, Doctor Wisdom. May I present to you your son, Jaazaanii, whom my kinswoman Qaazi has named Adam in honor of the mythical founder of your race?"

The boy was extremely short for his age, at least by human standards, and he had his mother's eyes—or a least a fair approximation of them—as well as her sharply pointed chin. But in other respects, Adam could probably pass for a

Eurasian, if the light were dim enough. His hands were five-fingered; both his hair and complexion were slightly darker than Qaazi's; and he definitely had a hint of his father's prominent nose. Culley noticed these features immediately, and was pleased that his son's human heritage was clearly visible, too.

Father? Adam's mind said hesitantly, staring up at Culley with those luminous black eyes, the corners of which rose slightly as he did so.

Without a word or coherently transmittable thought Culley picked the boy up and hugged him close. He could feel the warmth of Qaazi's mental glow as it mingled inextricably with his own and Adam's, forging an unbreakable triple bond. Then, as the immediate emotional impact of seeing his son for the first time began to wear off, Culley held Adam at arms' length and was about to say something when Waangaa's flat but urgent voice suddenly cut him short.

"I regret the necessity to interrupt your first conversation with your son," the Pleiadian intoned, "but we must leave now. Do not worry, my cousin has programmed your implant so that the four of us can send and receive shielded telepathic transmissions. But once we leave this chamber wc must not speak aloud in your language, or they will become suspicious. Qaazi and I can, of course, converse with one another and with Adam in our language, but you must remain silent until we return to the flyer that brought you here. Do you understand this? It is very important."

Culley nodded numbly, his emotions wobbling like a top that has lost its spin. Qaazi's mind quickly intruded, affirming her lover's awareness of the gravity of the situation.

"That is good," Waangaa continued. "With some difficulty, I have managed to delay Jaazaanii's departure for one Earth-month and have arranged for the three of you to fly to the part of North America where we first met. Yes, Dr. Wisdom, as you now suspect, I was the one who supervised your medical examination. But please remember, do not speak and keep your mind as blank as possible."

They exited the classroom and soon were locked into place a few centimeters above the ubiquitous orange glide strip. Once again they floated through a crowd of uniformed Pleiadians, the majority of whom were obviously the end products of millennia of cross-breeding with human beings. Like Qaazi and Waangaa, he mused. They also encountered several groups of Native Companions, who reflected the full spectrum of the human race, although the majority were tall, blond, and Nordic in appearance and were clothed in white, ankle-length robes that trailed behind them as they floated along the strip. They wore vacant, beatific smiles that caused Culley to wonder whether the white robed humans might be under the influence of a drug of some sort.

No, Qaazi's mind whispered quickly as they turned a corner and threaded their way into one of the corridors that led to the gate. *They are not drugged. They serve us willingly, although they are, of course, heavily conditioned, both physically and mentally.*

Where do they come from? Are they abductees?

In a way. In the early days of the Colony, our contacts with human beings were far more open. Your technology was so primitive then that ours could not possibly contaminate it; we were universally perceived as supernatural beings—goddesses and such. She grinned as he picked up her last thought.

Okay, okay; don't rub it in! Culley's mind protested. *But seriously, it's another example of "Clarke's Law." Remember? Any sufficiently advanced technology, et cetera.*

Yes, that's a good way of putting it. In any case, the cults that sprang up necessarily had leaders, and such individuals came to have a close association with their "gods," that is, our representatives. When my ancestors began pulling back from direct contact in the most civilized regions, about three of your millennia ago, they took some of these priests (and priestesses) with them. Such persons formed the nucleus of the Native Companions. In return for their total devotion and obedience, we gave them an almost unlimited life-span and freedom from ordinary human afflictions. Indeed, we still sometimes use Companions as our "emissaries" in dealing with humans. As I told you, you're supposed to be on such a mission, and—

Waangaa's mind suddenly intruded. *Again, I regret that I must interrupt your exchange of thoughts, but we are approaching the docking bay. From here on, Doctor Wisdom, please reduce your own* thought-stream to elemental matters, such as eating and sleeping, as even the best blocks can be penetrated by Security.

The Pleiadian's warning had barely faded from Culley's mind when three uniformed "Colonials" emerged from a side corridor and rushed past them on some urgent errand. As the trio disappeared around a curve, he received the fleeting impression that one of them had probed his mind. Neither Qaazi nor Waangaa seemed to notice. Nevertheless, he resisted the urge to report the event, as the mental activity that would take might make matters worse. Instead, he forced himself to concentrate on the glowing strip as it slid beneath them and did his best to block out all other sensations, physical as well as mental.

A few minutes later they came within sight of the Security Gate, which was much more crowded than when they arrived. Several Pleiadians waiting to exit eyed them curiously and then seemed to whisper among themselves.

Culley noticed that the corners of both Qaazi's and Waangaa's eyes lifted ever so slightly, then returned to normal as they regained control. So did those of his so far mentally silent son. As they glided slowly up to the Gate, Qaazi, Waangaa, and Adam engaged in a rapid verbal exchange in the incomprehensible Pleiadian language.

The same security guard who had passed them through earlier was still on duty—or at least she seemed to be the same one. Culley had difficulty telling full-blooded Niivaanaans (or Aaraans, for that matter) apart. In any case, he did his best not to think about her, as per Waangaa's instructions, and instead concentrated on food. At first, he attempted to visualize a plate containing those tasteless wafers Qaazi had given him. That ought to be innocuous enough. But then, without any warning whatsoever, the cheeseburger image he'd projected when he ate the wafers once again took center stage in his mind.

Oh shit! That guard's gonna gag and the game'll be over!

Qaazi must have noticed the slip, too, as he suddenly felt lethargic and heavy-headed. He was dimly aware that something had taken control of him, but at first he didn't know what or why. Then, somewhere deep inside, he realized that it was Qaazi and that his survival was at stake.

Dimly, he noticed that the guard was aiming a wand at him and peering intently at a scope. He also could see and hear Qaazi and Waangaa talking with the guard and one other figure who looked vaguely familiar.

Yes, of course! That figure over there was one of the trio of Pleiadians who'd rushed past them earlier, the one who'd probed his mind. Qaazi held Adam by the hand and, while she spoke to him and the guard, she seemed to be doing her mental best to allay their son's fears; for some reason he found himself able to understand most of what she was saying to the boy.

As this scene unfolded, Culley stood rooted to the spot. He felt curiously detached from what was happening, as if he was watching himself from a distance. It reminded him of that first time in the desert a decade ago, when Qaazi had tranquilized him with her wand. But there was one crucial difference: this time he was able-within limits-to control his faculties and to key his thoughts into his implant in a way he never thought possible. He felt little if any real fear, only resignation; *shikata ga nai*, as the Japanese say; the phase kept swimming though his mental fog. The waves of panic that had swept over him several times since Qaazi had come back into his life were conspicuous by their absence. He suspected that this was her doing, and he made a mental note to thank her for it if they got out of here intact.

Then the security guard aimed a larger, more complex looking instrument at him, and he realized that Qaazi could no longer shield him. He was on his own now. The panic began to return with a vengeance, but before it could take hold his mind went completely blank.

When awareness returned, it was dream-like. The guard was asking him about SESO in a strange language he knew he couldn't understand. Nevertheless, he found himself answering her in the same liquid syllables. Gradually, he realized that it was Pleiadian; that was why he'd been able to understand what Qaazi was saying to Adam. The guard seemed to think that he was really a SESO Native Agent who had infiltrated the crèche in order to kidnap a Pleiadian child.

What a silly idea! He told the huge-eyed female as much in unaccented, idiomatic Pleiadian, although how he'd come to master the language in such a short time was a complete mystery-unless Qaazi had somehow infused it into his brain before she lost control.

The crazy dream went on for what seemed like hours. Qaazi, Adam, and Waangaa were in it, too, together with the other Pleiadian he'd recognized. They all asked him questions in both English and Pleiadian, even Adam, who insisted his name was really Jaazaanii. He felt something insinuate itself into his head, and then Qaazi's extremely faint but insistent mental voice pleading with him to resist and to maintain the disguise she'd devised for him.

Disguise? What disguise? Yes, of course! He was supposed to be a Native Companion on some kind of external assignment.

At one point in the proceedings he was dimly aware that Qaazi's eyelids had risen sharply, and he resigned himself to whatever fate was in store for him. It was, after all, only a dream—or a dream within a dream, perhaps. Nevertheless, the questions and the probing continued unabated.

The cheeseburger image seemed somehow to be crucial. Why would a Native Companion harbor such a disgusting image? Companions weren't supposed to know about those things. But a SESO Man in Black would probably eat them with relish. He could feel the probe bore deeper and deeper into his psyche, and there seemed to be nothing he or anybody else could do to block it.

Culley's spirits-to the extent that he could come to grips with them-sagged almost beyond recovery.

Then, in desperation, he reached into the small area of his brain that was still (he hoped) shielded and hit upon a ploy: make them think that the cheeseburger image was a feeble attempt at a joke. He somehow "knew" that despite their overwhelming seriousness-a trait which Qaazi had recently confirmed-the Pleiadians sometimes laughed at the impulsive behavior of their Native Companions, much as human parents might be amused by the antics of a mischievous child. In any case, no would-be SESO infiltrator would be dumb enough to call attention to himself by trying to be funny. It was a long shot, but he couldn't come up with anything better, and the probe was beginning to penetrate the last of his mental defenses.

He laughed uproariously, both mentally and out loud. The security guard's mind, amplified by the huge machine, did what appeared to be a double take and the probe stopped moving, which was exactly what he hoped would happen. The cheeseburger image, Culley's unshielded thought-stream confessed, was simply an unthinking attempt at humor. He had recently heard about such abominable Native dishes and, thinking the image amusing, pretended to desire one. He humbly apologized for his lapse and begged forgiveness.

After a long moment, during which the guard indicated that she had indeed been mildly amused by the repulsive image, he received the impression that his questioners were satisfied with the forged mental "credentials" Qaazi had programmed into his implant. The probe disappeared, and the strange dream faded into the deepest blackness he'd ever experienced.

The next thing he remembered was reclining in a seat aboard Qaazi's flyer, fully strapped in. Qaazi was in the pilot's chair, and Adam sat beside her, his tiny fingers flying back and forth across the control panel. Water streamed over the transparent bubble that covered the cabin as they rose rapidly to the surface.

Culley shook his head several times and then leaned toward Qaazi. What the hell happened back there? His memory was still extremely fuzzy.

"It is safe to speak, now," she said quietly, flashing him a wide grin. He realized that it was the first time he'd actually heard a voice—other than in his mind—since they'd left the crèche. "I am so proud of you!" she continued. "Adam is too. With Waangaa's and our help you maintained the disguise perfectly!"

"Disguise?"

"The one I programmed into your implant when we hovered over Japan. I was afraid that they might suspect you were a SESO Native Agent and that I was a traitor."

"Yeah, I sort of remember somebody asking me about SESO—in Pleiadian. You and I were supposed to be on some kind of 'outside' mission. But how was I able to speak the language? I couldn't speak or understand a single word of it at the moment."

"The kind of emergency language conditioning we gave you wears off very quickly. Waangaa and Adam helped me maintain the illusion that you were a Native Companion. If it had failed, you might have been disintegrated on the spot or perhaps remade into a real Companion. Either way, our dream would have come to an end."

Culley's head throbbed, and he rubbed his temples gingerly. "When I saw your eyelids go up, I thought it was all over."

"It almost was. We had hardly any mental energy left. But then you decided to laugh about the plate of Native food you'd visualized. You were right, by the way; no SESO Native Agent would ever have done such a thing. It convinced the Security person to accept our story, especially after you proved to be capable of speaking Pleiadian and didn't have any knowledge about the SESO base where they house and train their Agents. If you hadn't thought of that brilliant strategy, the probe would soon have revealed the truth about us. There was nothing any of us could do to help you at that point, but you carried it off brilliantly!"

Qaazi paused while Culley's mind indicated that his memory had begun to return and that he remembered most of what had happened back at the gate. "By the way," she added, "officially, I'm taking my son along to give him flight experience while I transport you to your surface assignment, which, of course, I will monitor closely, although not in the way they expect." She laughed softly. "Such a thing is unusual, but not unheard of."

"Yeah, that's great. But what went wrong? I mean in addition to the cheeseburger business. The disguise was already in place. How did they get the idea that I might be a SESO spy? Was it that guy who probed me when we left the crèche?"

"Yes, although we didn't realize it at the time. For some reason, you didn't seem right to him, and when he probed your mind. Remember, *all* humans are still considered subjects, even Native Companions, and may be probed at will. He managed to penetrate one of the blocks I inserted and received the impression that you had no knowledge of our language. This was inconsistent with the outward indication that you were a Companion. Occasionally, SESO agents have managed to penetrate our bases disguised as Native Companions, and he assumed that you were such an intruder."

Adam, his eyes still riveted to the control panel, spoke for the first time. "It was when you accidentally visualized the-the cheeseburger that they really became suspicious. We had to act rapidly. I have recently discovered that language imprinting is always unpleasant, even under ideal circumstances. I hope we did not cause you too much pain."

Culley winced slightly. "Well, all I can say is that my head still feels like people have been walking around in it. But I know why you did it, and I'm profoundly grateful. You certainly saved my bacon! "

For a long moment, both Adam's and Qaazi's minds registered puzzlement. The mental image of sizzling pig flesh flashed back and forth between mother and son. Suddenly the boy's huge eyes sparkled, and he looked up at his new-found father. "Ah! I understand!" he exclaimed. "That is a most interesting idiom. Yes, Father, I was happy to help save your bacon. So was Mother!"

As Adam turned his attention back to the array of lights on the panel, his mother's mind nodded vigorously. *I too am glad to see that your bacon is intact, she signaled, adding an extremely private mental image that was definitely not meant for Adam's mind.*

Culley couldn't help cracking up, though he did his best to hide the source of his mirth from his son. *You're making great progress in the humor department, my love*, he replied, using the intimate mode that had already begun to become second nature to him. *I hope it won't be too long before we once again become a bacon sandwich!*

By this time, they had cleared the water and were climbing rapidly toward the stratosphere. Culley glanced at the scope but couldn't make any sense out of what saw and then swiveled his chair so as to face Qaazi. "Can you tell me where we're headed? From what Waangaa said, I gather we're not going back to Japan, at least not right away."

"No," she replied, "It would be too dangerous now. We will stay for a while at an unused 'safe-house' in the California desert. I still hope eventually to settle in Japan, as I think it would be the ideal place for our experiment. But we can discuss that later. Let us relax and enjoy ourselves for the first time as a true family!"

* * *

Wilma Gibbs cradled the phone against her thick neck as she used her mouse to locate the places Tom Johnson mentioned as a series of detailed maps of Tokyo's Shinjuku Ward flickered across her screen. She'd sent Tom to Japan, aboard an Air Force jet, to supervise operations there almost immediately after they'd left the MJ-12 facility the previous evening.

"Yes, Dr. Gibbs, the Japanese intelligence people can definitely put Wisdom in Shinjuku Station yesterday morning at approximately 8:30 a.m., Tokyo time. His roommate, another American expat named Hotchkiss, told me that he left their apartment as usual around quarter of eight and didn't seem in any way agitated or nervous. We also confirmed that his English conversation school is a ten-minute walk from the station in a district called Kabuki-cho. It's a weird area for a school, full of bars and strip clubs. But Japan is like that, it seems. Everything's jammed next to everything else.

"Anyway, I just left the place. Guess what? He never showed up yesterday! Also, the local intelligence people have found a taxi driver that has identified Wisdom's picture. Seems he was accompanied by what the driver said was a beautiful but slightly exotic-looking Japanese woman in her early twenties. What's even weirder is that the guy says that Wisdom was comatose-or passed out-for most of the trip, and seemed in a daze when they got out. The lady had to help him walk. Even in Japan, 8:30 in the morning is a bit early to be dead drunk, especially when you're on the way to work and were cold sober when you left home less than an hour earlier."

Wilma, who'd been listening intently, was silent for a second, then grinned. "Yeah, it's weird alright. This lady turns up just about the time we lost him. What do you think, Tom? Could she be—"

"I don't know, Dr. Gibbs. They've checked out the address where he took 'em. It's a large, rather expensive apartment house, the kind the Japanese call a 'mansion.'

They're currently checking to see if any of the tenants fit the lady's description." He paused briefly. "Just a minute. I'm getting a message from the local station chief. Yes! One tenant, a single woman named Hoshimura—it means 'Star Village' in Japanese—does fit the description. I guess I don't have to tell you that she's not at home, and that all of her personal belongings are missing. I'm calling from the Embassy, which is about fifteen minutes by subway from the apartment house. I'm about to head over there and see—"

"No," Wilma interrupted. "Let's let the locals trace Wisdom and Ms. Star Village. I need your help with the gizmo."

"Okay, but there are a couple of more things you ought to know. There was a close-up UFO sighting last night at a small Shinto temple—or is it shrine?—in the mountains west of the city of Takayama. Japanese Intelligence is investigating it as we speak. Seems a couple of farmers saw a disk suddenly rise from behind the main building as they were tidying up after a festival. I suspect it was partially surrounded by one of their cloaking devices, but the object was clearly visible for a couple of seconds before it shot out of sight. Are you *sure* you don't want me to go out there and check it out?"

"No, I need you here. If Wisdom and his girlfriend were aboard that saucer, they're long gone from Japan by now. If not, I'm sure our Tokyo people can handle it. But you just said you had a couple of things to tell me. What else have you turned up?"

Tom hesitated for a second. "Well, it may be totally unrelated, but shortly after Wisdom and his companion disappeared from the station a tall, thin Japanese man wearing a black suit was found lying in a coma at the foot of one the exit stairs. The Tokyo paramedics took him to Keio Hospital, a major local medical center. But as soon as he came to—it was several hours later—he left the hospital without saying much of anything. There was no way they could hold the guy. By the time they discovered that his IDs were phony, he was long gone."

"Are you thinkin' what I'm thinkin'? "

"Yes. All the outward signs—the black clothes, his physical appearance, the perfectly forged IDs—do suggest that he could be an MIB, though exactly what happened to him and whether he has any connections to either Wisdom or the Pleiadian female is still unclear. If you don't mind, I'd like to go over to the hospital and talk to the doctors who treated him before I leave. If he's what I think he is, maybe the Reticulans are involved here, too, and that could get sticky."

"Okay, Tom, check the guy out as best you can and then get on back here as soon as you can. We've gotta get back to work on the gizmo. Once we get a fix on Wisdom, the pieces will begin falling into place. Somethin' big is about to happen, I can feel it in my bones."

"I have the same gut feelings, Dr. Gibbs. I'll stop by the hospital on the way to the plane. Glad I studied some Japanese when I was at Stanford! It's been getting a workout! See you shortly!"

Wilma hung up the phone, shifted her considerable bulk to a more comfortable position, and stared intently at the momentarily blank screen, gathering her thoughts. One of the few indisputable things MJ-12 had managed to discover about Earth's alien "visitors" in the course of the last fifty-plus years was that the Pleiadians and the Reticulans were not bosom buddies.

Yes, indeed, if Tom's hunch was correct, things might become sticky, especially if the bug people learned that a Pleiadian was openly consorting with a human being.

Extremely sticky. . .

CHAPTER SEVEN

They soon left Antarctica far behind. After crossing the southern tip of Africa, where the lights of Cape Town were faintly visible far beneath them, and then the South Atlantic, they began angling northwest across South America. Early evening gave way to late afternoon and finally to morning as the flyer outraced the sun.

As he sank back and let the chair enfold him, Culley noticed, for the first time, that Qaazi had adjusted the temperature and that he felt comfortable. "Thanks for remembering to turn up the thermostat, or whatever that light controls," he muttered. "The last thing I need after what I've just been through is to wake up freezing!"

He was also relieved to learn that the flyer was not being pursued—or even under close scrutiny by the Monitors. However, to ensure that they would arrive at their destination undetected, Qaazi and Adam concentrated intently and, using a procedure that Waangaa had recently developed, disengaged the device that automatically signaled their presence to other ships in the vicinity and allowed Headquarters to track them.

"At first," she explained, "they will think we've crashed. But by the time they stop scanning those mountains down there, the ones you call the Andes, we will have arrived at our destination and my cousin is convinced there is no way they can reconstruct our path."

"I hope to hell he's right. I was wondering how you were planning to avoid being tracked by your radar, or whatever you use."

She assured him once again that the procedure was working, and that they had just vanished from every Pleiadian scope.

"How about my people?" Culley asked. "How do you guys manage to avoid being picked up by our radar? I know it's pretty crude by your standards, but doesn't it cause you at least some inconvenience?"

"Yes, it does—or rather it did. When you first invented that device, it caused us a great many problems. It not only 'picked up' our ships, but also interfered with their operation. There were a number of crashes and mid-air collisions. But we eventually discovered a way to shield our flyers against the beams. Today, except in rare instances, your scanning devices simply do not recognize us."

After performing a brief set of calculations, Qaazi announced that they would arrive at their destination in the Mojave Desert in approximately twenty-five minutes.

Culley took a deep breath, and then expelled it slowly. "I've always intended to return to the States someday," he said softly, "but I never dreamed I'd make the trip in a flying saucer . . . or end up in a place near the spot where it all began."

Qaazi looked up from the instrument panel and grinned as warmly as her undisguised lips would allow. She said nothing intelligible, either mentally or verbally. But her smile and the tender telepathic vibrations that accompanied it spoke volumes.

* * *

The remainder of the trip was relatively uneventful. On two occasions, Qaazi spotted Pleiadian flyers on the scope. She and Adam immediately began evasive maneuvers, and they managed to avoid detection. Over the Isthmus of Panama a SESO ship came within three kilometers of them, but made no attempt to communicate. Qaazi said that this was not unusual, as the two groups generally ignored one another unless they were engaged in a joint operation or there was clear evidence of a Treaty violation.

Between these encounters, she and Adam were able to explain the flyer's operation in some detail—the boy was eager to do so—and Culley even handled the controls for a few minutes. It proved to be somewhat easier than he'd expected. The hardest part was keying his implant to what she called the flyer's "receptor." Once the connection was made, he simply had to move his hands over the colored lights on the control panel. Each controlled a specific motion: up, down, forward, reverse, etc., as well as the rate of acceleration. At Qaazi's urging, and, with Adam's enthusiastic encouragement, he pushed the "throttle" up to approximately Mach 30 for a few seconds but then relinquished the controls to Adam, saying that he'd better quit while he was ahead. Still, in a pinch, Culley thought he just might be able to get the thing airborne and control it well enough to make an emergency landing.

"That is the idea, Qaazi told him. "Next time, you will lift us off! "

"Your sense of humor's really beginning to blossom! No, my Precious One of the Clan, not unless both you and Adam are totally incapacitated, and the whole SESO fleet is in hot pursuit."

The three of them laughed together and Culley began to suspect that, unless something untoward happened, they would soon become a close-knit, loving family—the kind of family he'd always wanted but, until this moment, had never really had. The prospect almost moved him to tears.

Qaazi smiled at him warmly, and then turned serious. "There is something I have been meaning to tell you, something . . . something rather embarrassing," she said hesitantly. "I've been avoiding the subject, but now, since we are thoroughly committed to the plan and have some time at our disposal, I cannot postpone it any longer, especially since you are thinking such wonderful thoughts about us. It has to do with what we call 'the Project.' I know that you've been wondering about it."

He had indeed. Culley leaned forward in his seat, eager

to hear about this piece of the puzzle, which seemed to be extremely important.

"Yes, it is very important," she responded, picking up his thoughts. "But I had better begin at the beginning, as you sometimes put it."

In the early days of the Colony, Qaazi explained, the Project was pure science, an attempt to explore the extent to which two homologous species that had evolved along closely parallel lines hundred of light-years apart could interbreed. At first, no Pleiadian could even have sexual intercourse with a human being without some major anatomical modifications. But a relatively simple procedure was eventually developed that enabled viable offspring to be conceived in approximately one out of every ten attempts. And once such offspring appeared, there was usually no further necessity for the operation, as their human genes would more often than not endow them with reproductive organs that were fully compatible with those of the Natives. At the same time, the fertility rate increased markedly.

In short, as the generations unfolded-with an average life expectancy of more than a thousand Earth-years, a Pleiadian generation averages about two hundred years-a hybrid race slowly began to take shape: one that was still thoroughly Pleiadian in culture and in overall physiology, but with a great many "human" traits in its genetic make-up. Both she and Waangaa belonged to this category, as did well over half of the Colony.

The presence of so much human DNA in the Colony's gene pool, Qaazi explained, greatly facilitated its adaptation to the Earth's environment. Among other things, they were less sensitive to Earth's lower atmospheric pressure, which at sea level is equivalent to an extremely high altitude on Niivaanaa and Aaraa.

Then, approximately two hundred Earth-years ago, a series of catastrophic stellar accidents that affected not only Aardaaz, but the nearby star systems as well, and caused Niivaanaa and the other Pleiadian home planets to lose crucial elements in their atmospheres. As a result, the populations were bombarded by a variety of lethal cosmic particles.

Before we fully realized what was happening," Qaazi said, "we became susceptible to a variety of fatal diseases which even our medical knowledge has trouble coping with." Her words were accompanied by images of Pleiadians obviously devastated by disease, their shrunken eyes a dull brown instead of the luminous black he'd found so irresistible. "It was rather like the terrible AIDS epidemic that is currently spreading so rapidly among your people."

Culley shuddered and projected a very nasty mental image of his own plus a question. . . .

"Oh, no! Please don't worry! We—even those of us with a high Native DNA count—are totally resistant to AIDS; and besides, we could easily cure it and a host of other human diseases, which is one of my complaints against those who set Colonial policy. We will—we'll talk about that later. But by far the most important effect of this bombardment was the loss of our fertility, even among those who managed to resist disease. Millions of us became sterile, and we found ourselves face-to-face with the possibility that we might soon become extinct."

She paused while Culley assimilated her mental images of an increasingly childless milieu as Adam picked up the story. "At first," he said with a rush in his childish but, at the same time, ultra-precise voice, "we were able to compensate for the loss of these atmospheric elements by synthesizing substitutes. But we soon began to run out of the necessary chemicals. The only viable alternative, aside form burrowing deep beneath the surface and living like-like moles—yes, that is the correct Native species, I believe—or covering the home planets' cities with huge and extremely expensive protective domes, was to find a set of otherwise compatible planets orbiting stars that do not produce the life-threatening particle and emigrate. But such stars are extremely rare. The nearest one to Niivaanaa is ten thousand times farther than

Earth."

The boy paused for a second, took a deep breath, and plunged on eagerly, his huge black pupils glistening. "Then, while the Elders were debating what to do next, our scientists made a major discovery: those of us with significant amounts of human DNA—Colonials like Mother, Waangaa, and me, were able to resist the effects of these particles. You receive massive doses of them daily, and they have no ill effects whatsoever on your bodily functions, including your ability to reproduce."

Culley swiveled around to face his son, awed by the lad's display of intellectual as well as mechanical precocity. This was some kid he'd fathered!

"Okay, Adam, now let me see if I can guess the rest," he interjected as Qaazi's mind beamed at his glowing reaction to their offspring's knowledge. "For the last hundred years or so, you've been systematically exploiting our DNA, in direct violation of your own policy of non-interference. That's what the Project's all about these days, isn't it? I've already made at least one contribution to it, and more will eventually be expected. Am I correct?"

"Yes, Father, you have indeed made a contribution to the Project, though whether you will make more contributions is a matter yet to be determined. But it is not as simple as you seem to think. Only about fifteen percent of all human beings are able to contribute the requisite DNA, although some communities, such as East Asians and Northern Europeans, seem to have a larger number of genetically qualified individuals. The capability is inherited. You come from a long line of 'contributors.' Both your father-my grandfather-and his father, that is, your paternal grandfather, carried Clan implants, and their DNA was also harvested. By concentrating on particular lineages, like the Wisdom family, our scientists are able to study the long-term effects of their genetic experiments, and to identify the range of potential donors."

Dumbfounded by what he'd just heard, Culley stared at

his son in disbelief. Then he smiled and shook his head slowly. "So Dad carried an implant. And Grandpa, too. That explains a few things. Dad once said he thought he saw a UFO, but it was years before I met your mother, and he never mentioned anything about meeting any aliens. We were still living in Japan at the time. I wonder if—"

"No," Qaazi interrupted, "he had no idea whatsoever that his DNA was being exploited. Neither you nor the others in your family had any choice in the matter. We simply took what we needed or performed our experiments and then did our best to prevent the persons concerned from remembering what happened to them. Remember, it was—and still is—a matter of survival. According to the tapes, the procedure worked well enough with your father and grandfather, although, as I know you remember, neither of them was very happy or content with his life. Indeed, had you not consulted Dr. Stern, you would still be having bad dreams and be in much worse shape mentally, but you would not know why. Then there is the way we obtain the DNA. . ."

She paused for a very long moment, and the corners of her eyes began their tell-tale lift. So did Adam's. "We cannot extract what we need directly from your chromosomes," she continued evenly. "It must be in combination with our own genes. Moreover, for reasons we still don't completely understand, our systems can only accept DNA from a three to four months-old, unborn fetus, and, to be effective, to give our people the protection they need, the 'Native' component of that DNA cannot be more than two or at best generations removed from a fully human 'donor.' It is therefore necessary to produce a great number of hybrid embryos."

Culley chuckled. "So you go around seducing guys like me and the rest of the Wisdoms, right? "

"As Adam just said, it is—it's not that simple. What happened to you and your father is, of course, one way we go about producing such an embryo; it is standard procedure for 'special' donor families. And, of course, in our own case, it was natural and loving. But there is, I'm sad to say, another, far more common and less pleasant way."

The angle of her eyes became acute, and she gulped slightly as she wiped away a tiny bead of sweat—or was it perhaps the Pleiadian equivalent of a tear?—that had formed on her left cheek. "It involves surreptitiously removing ova from Native women, fertilizing them with our seed mixed with that of a male human 'donor,' and then re-implanting the eggs in their uteruses," she continued evenly, doing her best to sound clinical. "When the females are about three months pregnant, they are abducted again and the embryos are removed. The fetuses are kept alive, at least for a while, in an artificial environment and the DNA we need is systematically extracted. The majority manage to survive this trauma and grow up to be members of the Clan. But many do not."

As she spoke, Qaazi transmitted a series of stark mental images, each of which was tinged with sorrow. The first was of a young, obviously human woman with frightened eyes lying on her back on a table, her legs drawn up, surrounded by a team of uniformed Pleiadians, one of whom was reaching into her vagina. It was followed by an image of a tiny, humanoid fetus with huge eyes suspended in a transparent tank of some sort. Several tubes led into the tank, which appeared to be filled with a colorless liquid that gave off what looked to be sparks. The third and final image was of a lifeless fetus, its body shriveled and hanging limp, being removed from one of the tanks.

Culley shuddered. He'd read several accounts of such "operations," one of which included a vivid description of a live fetus in a transparent, liquid-filled container. But until now, despite his own experience, this aspect of the UFO phenomenon had seemed much too far-fetched to be believed.

"Yes, dear Culley," she responded verbally, her voice quivering with emotion and moral outrage, "the terrible things we do to these unfortunate women and their unborn offspring do defy belief. They are utterly inexcusable, and bring no honor whatsoever to the Clan. If only we had the sense to lift the veil of secrecy and initiate open and direct contact! Waangaa—he's a survivor of one of those awful tanks—and I are convinced that if your people knew about our situation and about how badly we need your DNA, most of them would gladly help us. There is so much that we could give you in return."

As Culley digested what he'd just learned, a plethora of questions popped into his head all at once: Was she absolutely certain that his father had no inkling as to what was really going on? Had he ever made any contributions to this other process? Had Adam ever been in one of those tanks? And was there any danger to his species from what they did?

Qaazi put an arm around his shoulder. "Dear, dear Culley—always so many, many questions! No, I assure you that you were never 'milked'—except by me!—and that you're the first of the Wisdoms to have any conscious awareness of our presence. And yes, a small amount of DNA was extracted from our son while I was pregnant. But he was spared the tank, except for the short period when the precious DNA was removed, after which, praise be to the Winged One, he was reinserted into my womb. We rarely if ever subject naturally-conceived fetuses to that awful procedure, except during extractions. I should add that he was also spared the necessity of being 'presented,' as one of your researchers has phrased it, to a human mother for bonding, as I was available to perform this task. But the majority of infant hybrids are periodically 'presented' to their human mothers in the course of subsequent abductions. It is necessary to their physical and mental development. Of course, if parents and children, Pleiadian as well as human, were allowed to live together in families as you do, this would no longer be necessary."

She glanced lovingly at their son, then turned back to face Culley. "As to your last question, I wish I knew the answer. The amount of short-term physical damage to your race, above and beyond that sustained by the hybrid fetuses we remove, seems to be nil. Nevertheless, one of my goals is to encourage our scientists to study this matter in depth. "

His huge eyes sparkling with eagerness, Adam once again jumped headlong into the conversation. "One of the crèche Techs recently told us that our scientists are on the verge of developing a synthetic gene, which will solve the problem permanently. Have you not heard the same thing, Mother?"

Qaazi shook her head. "No, Adam, I haven't. I have been out of regular communication with our technicians for some time now. But we have all heard this before, so I'm skeptical. It may simply be-propaganda? Yes, that's the correct word, I believe."

Adam seemed disappointed. He'd been so eager to share this news with his mother, so Culley decided to change the subject. "How do the Others react to all this?" he asked. "Surely they must be aware that you're exploiting our DNA. Don't they consider that a violation of the Treaty?"

"Yes, they do, but as they have no need for your DNA, they cannot claim that we are expropriating a resource that might be shared. But the Project remains a—a bone of contention, yes?—between us, and they regularly accuse us of hypocrisy in our dealings with our subjects-that is, when they are not spreading the lie among their subjects that they bio-engineered us!"

Culley was about to ask another question when Adam, who'd been watching the scope intently, suddenly looked up and touched Qaazi's arm. "Mother," he piped, "I believe we are about to arrive at our destination!"

She glanced at the image on the scope, checked a couple of incomprehensible read-outs, and verified her son's words. "Yes, we have just crossed the shallow body of water you call the Salton Sea. That means we are but a minute or two from the Mojave Desert. It is time to contact the young human female who awaits us."

* * *

Shortly after SESO Native Agent Hajime Nakamura broadcast his appeal for help in locating the Pleiadian female and her *gaijin* companion, he received an urgent telepathic message from an MIB named Chang, who had just spotted what had to be the same pair while passing through Nagoya Station.

Chang was based in North Korea and didn't have a SESO vehicle at his disposal at the moment. Nevertheless, at Nakamura's urgent request, he put his own assignment on hold and followed them (on a later train) to Takayama and then "borrowed" an ordinary Native vehicle from a parking lot and eventually tracked the female and her companion to an obscure mountain village. That was the best he could do, as he did not recognize the female's unique mental signature, and was therefore unable to pinpoint her exact location—until he witnessed what was almost certainly a Pleiadian flyer take off from behind a small shrine a kilometer or so from his location.

It was too dangerous for the Korean MIB to remain for any length of time in possession of a "borrowed" vehicle, and besides, he had other work to do. So, after reporting what he had seen to his Japanese colleague, he abandoned the vehicle near the same bus stop Qaazi had found when she first arrived and went on his way, once again via public transportation.

Nakamura was delighted by the news and thanked Agent Chang profusely. He immediately said sayonara to the pretty bar hostess with whom he'd intended to spend the night, retrieved his jet-black, SESO-enhanced Nissan sedan from the parking garage, and headed for the Toi Expressway. After driving all night and mentally coercing several traffic officers to look the other direction and using the advanced technology supplied by his Masters to negotiate the icy mountain roads, he reached the Kumo-jinja around eight o'clock the next morning.

A small crowd had gathered in a snow-covered clearing behind the shrine to watch a team composed of an Air Self-

Defense Force colonel, some space scientists from the Ministry of Science who'd been helicoptered in from the Tsukuba science complex outside Tokyo, and several National Police Agency investigators take measurements, check for radiation traces, and do all the other silly things his unenlightened fellow Natives did when they attempted to "document" a UFO landing or take-off. There were also several UFO buffs from the UFO Kaikan in Osaka, as well as a Fuji-TV reporter and cameraman.

It didn't take the MIB long to discover that there were two primary witnesses, both of them local farmers. The two men, wearing parkas and knee-high rubber boots, stood together at the periphery of the crowd, obviously embarrassed by all the attention they'd received.

Nakamura approached the pair, bowed, and then handed them phony name-cards that identified him as a representative of the non-existent "National Scientific Investigative Agency." He knew that they had been interviewed exhaustively by the real authorities, but he counted on his formidable appearance and demeanor, to say nothing of his impressive "credentials," to impress them with his importance. Moreover, the fact that his fellow Japanese rarely questioned the veracity of what appeared on a name-card gave him an advantage in these kinds of situations not enjoyed by Western MIBs.

"You will please tell me whether you noticed the presence of an exotic-appearing young woman, seemingly a Nihonjin, in the company of a middle-aged, Japanese-speaking *gaijin*, in the period immediately before the UFO appeared," he said softly but firmly, staring at each of them in turn and adding as much mental coercion as possible (neither seemed to carry an implant of any sort).

The two men looked at each other for a second, then one of them, whose name was Kojima, nodded his head. "*Hai*, Matsumura-san and I did see a *gaijin* of the sort you describe—although they all look alike!—in the company of a striking young woman, a city dweller who said she and her companion had come here to study the matsuri. They were very polite. And the *gaijin* spoke our language very well."

"*So des' ne!*" Matsumura added gravely, "never have I heard any foreigner speak as well. The *Guji*—he is standing over there—was also very impressed with his knowledge of Shinto lore. But they disappeared shortly before the ceremony ended and did not partake in the sake. We thought they had left, although I heard the *omawari-san* say that a car, a rented car, was left in the parking area in front of the shrine. But you must know all this by now."

"By any chance did the *gaijin* tell you his name, or that of his female companion?"

"No," Kojima-san replied. "But I overhead one of the *omawari-san* say that the drivers of the rented car were named Hoshimura and *Wi-su-do-mu*, or something like that. A curious name, even for a *gaijin, des' ne*?"

Nakamura allowed himself to give them the ghost of a smile, then bowed once again and thanked the two farmers politely for their information. Then he became grim. "You must say nothing of what we have just spoken about to anyone, *wakarimas'ka*? It is extremely important."

Kojima and Matsumura assured him that they understood and would keep the conversation to themselves.

Although he was careful to maintain the solemn mask appropriate to a Man in Black as he walked away from his "informants," inwardly Nakamura-san wanted to shout for joy. He had established beyond the shadow of a doubt that the Pleiadian who'd attacked him in Tokyo and her lover, or whatever he was, had been here the previous evening. And he had learned the *gaijin's* name! "*Wi-su-do-mu*" *had* to be Professor Cullen Wisdom, an American who had written a book some years ago about a romantic episode with a beautiful "alien" female. Although the American professor was a Pleiadian subject and therefore not officially of any concern to him, Nakamura had heard that Wisdom-*sensei* was currently living in Tokyo. "Hoshimura-san" was almost certainly the name used by the Pleiadian female. That was also important, but the fact that he now knew who her lover was would be most appreciated by the Masters.

He had to report in immediately.

At first, he considered broadcasting the essentials in the same way he had earlier. But the more he thought about it, the more it occurred to him that he should request a face-to-face meeting, as he suspected his Mistress would eventually call him in anyway so as to probe his mind for all the relevant details.

In any case, if in fact a Pleiadian female was having a love affair with a Native, that is, above and beyond the immediate demands of the Project, which even the most conservative Masters and Mistresses agreed were legitimate. It would be a clear violation of the Rule of Non-Interference. And according to the Treaty, if the Pleiadians broke their own Sacred Rule, SESO was entitled to recompense in the form of a greater share of Earth's bounty.

As he guided his vehicle out of the parking area and onto the recently cleared road that fronted the shrine, he found himself actually thanking the Pleiadian bitch and her pet *gaijin* for being kind enough to assault him and thereby bringing their nefarious scheme-whatever it may be-to his attention!

Activating his implant, Nakamura sent a priority-one message to SESO Headquarters requesting a face-to-face meeting with his black-hooded Reticulan Mistress.

CHAPTER EIGHT

Scrunched down as far as it was possible to scrunch and still see over the dashboard, Sally Linker sat in her eight-year-old Subaru Legacy station wagon peering through the windshield at the bright blue, smog-free desert sky. Next to her sat Sidney Levine, who'd begged her to take him along after she explained what her new entity had told her.

At first, she'd said no, not only because Waangaa had told her to come alone, but because she was afraid that Sidney would never let her live it down if the whole thing proved to be a hoax.

"Hey," he'd protested, "you know I don't believe this shit, but what the hell? Maybe something weird will happen and I'll have to shift my mental gears. And besides, Babe, it's a long trip out there alone!"

So she gave in, and here they were, waiting for extraterrestrials. To Sidney, who was currently on sabbatical leave, it was a lark, a welcome break from the dull routine of writing a boring paper about an obscure, well-nigh invisible comet that might or might not return someday.

But Sally took her "assignment" extremely seriously. She was convinced that Waangaa was exactly who and what he said he was-somehow, she "knew" that he was a male-and that her skeptical boyfriend was about to get the shock of his life, though she did wish the aliens would hurry up. The suspense was killing her.

Thanks to a humongous pot hole, the bag of groceries they'd picked up in Barstow now lay on its side, half of its contents strewn across the back seat. She hoped that at least some of the eggs had survived. The alien entity hadn't told her exactly what to buy, only that one of the creatures he directed her to meet would probably be hungry for breakfast, of all crazy things, and she was to use her own best judgment.

"Who the fuck knows what aliens eat for breakfast? Or for lunch, for that matter. Maybe they eat each other!" Sidney had exclaimed with a condescending laugh as they wandered the supermarket aisles.

As she continued to scan the sky, small fingers of fear began to clutch at Sally's throat. Channeling an ET in the safety of her Venice living room was one thing; sitting out here in the middle of nowhere waiting for a bunch of them to appear in the flesh, as it were, was another scene altogether.

What if Sidney's wrong and we're the breakfast. . . .

Maybe she should have brought Carlos Castillana, her mentor and former lover, after all, instead of Sidney. Carlos would have been eager to come, and she'd been on the verge of inviting him several times since Waangaa had intruded into her mind the previous evening, and even now she briefly considered calling Carlos on her cell-phone to ask his advice. But Sidney had been adamant. The last thing he wanted was for her to go off into the desert with "that horny bastard Castillana," or have anything to do with him, for that matter; indeed, this was probably the real reason Sidney had insisted on coming along.

In any case, she'd left a voice-mail message for her Century City boss requesting an unpaid leave of absence, called a fellow student and asked her to tell their UCLA Psych professor that something important had come up (she was careful not to say what) and that she'd have to miss the next couple of class sessions, and locked up the house. The only real problem, aside from keeping Carlos in the dark, had been her five year-old cat, and that was solved by an elderly neighbor who promised to look after the creature while she was away on her "trip."

Her new entity, who somehow seemed familiar, even though she was sure she'd never channeled him before, had instructed her to meet the occupants of an alien craft in front of a deserted ranch house deep in the Mojave Desert and wait for further instructions. Although Waangaa's first message had been vague as to who (or what) these occupants were-she remembered him saying something about a "family"—his second message, which she received shortly before she left, had included a set of very precise and detailed directions on how to get to the landing site, as well the command to go food shopping en route.

That message had been one of the clearest psychic communications she'd ever received, in or out of trance. And so, after driving half the night to Barstow, and then, after another hour and a half doing their best to follow Waangaa's directions-shortly before dawn, a wrong turn took them to the gate of the Goldstone Deep-Space Tracking Station, which caused Sidney to quip that maybe the folks they were going to meet were homing in on its radio beams-they eventually found themselves at the end of a pair of unpaved, sand-filled ruts that had taken all of Sally's considerable driving skill plus the Subaru's four-wheel drive to negotiate.

But this had to be the right place.

The imposing escarpment, studded with oddly-shaped rock formations, which Waangaa had described in such detail, was right where it ought to be. So were the rambling, one-story, concrete block ranch house and the extra-large wooden barn that stood a couple of dozen yards to the left of the house. There were also a couple of sheds, an old-fashioned windmill, and a large corral, also empty, next to the barn. Everything looked normal enough and in fairly good repair, yet there was a sterile quality about the place that didn't quite ring true. It was as if somebody-or something-had decided to build a full-scale model, or movie-set, perhaps, of a working desert ranch, but had stopped short before adding the finishing touches.

She noticed, for example, that no one had bothered to do

any landscaping whatsoever. No shrubbery except a forlorn pair of stunted, spiky-leafed Joshua trees that had been overlooked when the ground was cleared; no flowers, either alive or dead; no kitchen garden; just bare, sandy, weed-covered ground, front and back. At the same time, the open space in front of the house was totally devoid of the rusting car parts, discarded refrigerators, children's toys, and broken farm machinery that inevitably littered front yards in this remote part of the Mojave.

Even Sidney found it unsettling, which was probably why he was uncharacteristically silent as they watched and waited.

Idly bushing back stray strands of her long blond hair, Sally shivered slightly, despite the fact that the outside temperature was already well into the eighties. She'd always supposed that these sorts of encounters happened in the wee hours of the night, not in broad daylight. Indeed, the whole business was almost too bizarre, even by her "New-Age" standards, and the more she thought about it, the more she wished she could simply pack it in and go home. But every time she seriously considered leaving, something she couldn't quite identify seemed to take hold of her and prevent it. So she took another sip of stale coffee from a thermos jug, and continued to sit there, waiting as patiently as she could under the circumstances.

As the sun climbed higher, she closed the car windows, started the engine, and turned on the air-conditioner. Waangaa's final message, which she'd received shortly after leaving Barstow, had assured her that "they" would arrive at 9:38 a.m., local time, but according to both her digital watch and the dashboard clock it was now exactly 9:36, and there was still no sign of anything extraordinary.

She was beginning to think that maybe Sidney'd been right all along and the whole thing was a figment of her overactive imagination, when a strange voice—definitely not Waangaa's—suddenly echoed in her head.

"Hello . . ." she muttered. Sally's eyes widened,

revealing a mixture of anxiety and intense anticipation.

We are almost there, the voice said in what she soon realized was a female intonation. *Are you ready to receive us?*

An odd but comforting calm settled over her.

"Yes, I'm ready," she said aloud in an even voice. "Everything's cool."

Sidney's eyes suddenly became as big as saucers, and then closed tightly as his head lolled back against the headrest.

Unlocking the car door, Sally Linker slowly stepped outside, tilted her head back, and stood motionless, staring intently at the cloudless desert sky directly above her head.

* * *

Djrnk, the deputy regional commander of SESO operations in East Asia, adjusted the scope and did her best to scan the thoughts of the Native Agent waiting below in the cold Hokkaido dawn. Her coal-black, bulging eyes, which, like those of a terrestrial insect, were multi-faceted, reflected her intense concentration as she plumbed the depths of the Agent's mind.

She could, of course, probe his mind as they spoke, but that would be much less efficient. His request to make a face-to-face report was highly unusual, and she wanted to squeeze every possible bit of information from him before he could erect any mental barriers, accidental or otherwise. This was most important, for if what Nakamura had relayed, first via the recon pilot and later directly through Headquarters, proved to be correct, it could have profound implications for SESO, to say nothing of her own career.

The Agent was waiting patiently, but his mind was churning in anticipation of meeting his Master. In a matter of seconds, Djrnk managed to extract from it the essence of what he had come to report, including the name Cullen Wisdom.

As soon as Nakamura's mental images had been transferred to the central SESO computer, together with her annotations, she signaled her pilot to begin the descent. The egg-shaped craft dropped silently, hovered a meter or so above the surface, and then, after the landing pods extended, settled slowly to the ground. The snow-covered forest glade was large enough to contain both the Agent's helicopter and the ship with room to spare. But it was far removed from any human habitation save for a small Ainu village about two kilometers to the north. Djrnk laughed to herself about what the local shamans might be making of their landing. Perhaps it would give them a new lease on life. Someday, when SESO was powerful enough to defy the Treaty, she might return and take her rightful place as a living Ainu god. But the business at hand needed to be tended to; it was time to confront Agent Nakamura.

When the hatch opened, Djrnk mentally invited the shivering Man in Black aboard her ship. He accepted eagerly, as the weather was freezing, and the SESO heating device sewn into his jacket needed repair. She noted the problem and told him her technicians would take a look at while they conferred.

By the time he reached her private quarters, the warm, dry air that circulated through the ship had removed the chill. Pulling her jet-black hood forward and drawing her robe more tightly around her, Djrnk fixed the MIB with her faceted eyes, and waved him to a seat across from her. "Nakamura-san, I am ready to receive your report," she said in heavily accented albeit grammatically perfect Japanese. "Please begin." Then she and leaned forward, projecting polite expectation. The Master knew that her visitor had some fluency in the SESO language, but felt that his Native dialect would perhaps include some nuances that might be missed if they used hers.

"I am honored to be here, Djrnk-sama," he responded in kind. Bowing deeply, he eased himself into the chair she'd indicated. "What I have learned may well be extremely important to the SESO cause, and I felt that you should hear it directly from my lips and mind." Nakamura knew that she had the power to probe the thoughts behind his words;

indeed, he was sure that she'd already done so. Nevertheless, as per her command, he immediately launched into his report. When he'd finished, he rose, bowed again, and waited politely for her response.

Djrnk leaned back in her chair and steepled her six, sucker-tipped fingers in what might have been a parody of a common human gesture where it not for the fact that Reticulans regularly did it, too. "You are correct," she said after several seconds. "I did, of course, extract the essence of your report before we landed. But I also learned much from your verbal presentation. Your mind dredged up a few details while you spoke that were not available to me in your static memory. You will be pleased to hear that your assessment was accurate; what you have learned could be extremely important to SESO. I wish you to drop your current assignments and join me in pursuing this matter; your immediate superiors will be informed."

The slit that served her as a mouth formed a rough caricature of a human smile. "You should know," the Reticulan continued, "that the Native who has bonded with the Pleiadian is an American *sensei* called Cullen Wisdom—an odd name, is it not?—who has lived for some time in this region."

Nakamura smiled back at her. "Yes, Djrnk-sama, I immediately placed the name when I learned it. Did he not write a book about his romantic experience with a Pleiadian female doing her Project duty? The Clanswoman who now calls herself 'Hoshimura' must be the one he wrote about."

"Yes, I believe you are correct in that assessment. It is indeed a major violation of the Treaty. I want you to monitor the vocal communication apparatus in the dwelling place Wisdom-*sensei* shares (or shared?) with another North American Native in case he attempts to re-establish contact. This will tell us where he and the Pleiadian female, most likely a Native Affairs Specialist called Qaazi Qaan-gaa, have hidden themselves, and perhaps their offspring as well. You can do this from the ship. I have already arranged to have Agent Chang install a device in the base of the apparatus. It will tell us not only what was said, but where the communication came from."

Djrnk extended a thin arm and clasped the Agent's elbow. "Again, you are to be commended for your diligence in this matter. Rest assured that it will be rewarded. Meanwhile, I invite to you make yourself as comfortable as possible aboard my ship." Then she shifted to the telepathic mode and indicated that it was time for him to leave.

Her rictus quickly faded, but Nakamura was ecstatic. Bowing one more time, he thanked her profusely in her native language and left the chamber.

As the door slid closed behind him, a Reticulan voice—not Djrnk's—sounded in his head telling him where he would find his quarters. But Nakamura paid scant attention to the voice, for he was so elated that he could hardly contain himself. Indeed, for the first time in his artificially extended life he actually felt giddy.

* * *

"I have locked onto her. Ms. Linker is responding to our control now. Her mental pattern is stable, and I am about to put her into a deep trance. It will be safer that way. I'm sure you now understand why. . . . Her male companion's mind is also under our control, although he bears a SESO implant, and I cannot quite—"

Qaazi's eyes rose slightly, and she zoomed in close on the inert figure who sat in the passenger seat. "That is the Sidney Levine you visualized on the train!" she exclaimed. "Here, see for yourself!"

Culley peered at the scope. "Well I'll be God damned! What's that bastard doing out here? "

She concentrated for a moment on the young woman, then smiled. "He is her boyfriend. That is why he has accompanied her. I'm sure this is not what Waangaa had in mind, but it would appear that we are stuck with him. That is the correct expression, I believe."

Culley simply nodded his head; the irony of the situation was delicious. That asshole was about to get the shock of his life; indeed, it just might send him 'round the bend!

Adam frowned. "So that is the man who hurt Father at his college. Perhaps we should—"

"No, Adam. Professor Levine's presence may in fact be helpful to us, although when he awakens he will probably have great difficulty adjusting to the fact that you and I are real."

"You can say that again!" Culley muttered under his breath as Qaazi zoomed in close on the young woman. They watched her pale blue eyes widen as she caught sight of the flyer, which was hovering at less than a thousand feet.

"Is she a total zombie yet?" Culley asked, adding a mental image that explained the reference.

"No, she does not resemble such a mythical creature. But her trance state is now complete and she will respond to my directions until I cut off the beam. As you suspect, Sally Linker-that is the young woman's name-carries one of our implants. I will have to reprogram it immediately, of course. Your former comrade will be more difficult to handle. I have switched off his mental functions, and I'm sure I can disable his implant. Reprogramming him, however, will be impossible, as I do not know the SESO codes."

As Culley stared at the images on the scope, which were now overlaid by a series of unreadable squiggles that seemed to represent the subjects' vital signs, Culley couldn't help but recall his earlier experience, which had occurred less than dozen miles from where the girl and her lover awaited them.

"Yes, my love," Qaazi whispered softly, "your image contained the same set of information. I monitored it continually as we closed in."

She tapped lightly on what she called the "locator matrix," and the spot where her flyer had touched down so many years ago appeared on the scope. He could see the bend in the road and the sere rock walls of the small canyon;

nothing had changed, and a flood of memories, both fearful and loving, washed across his mind. Then, after another quick tap, the focus shifted back to Sally Linker. *I share your memories*, her mind continued. *We have come almost full circle. But now we must descend.*

Qaazi made a couple of passes across the main control panel, and the saucer-shaped craft soon began to flutter earthward. As he gazed at the scene below him, he could make out some ordinary looking buildings, which Qaazi magnified on the main scope. Yet aside from a few rattlesnakes and scorpions, he could detect no evidence of any living creatures other than the girl and Sidney Levine. That barn hadn't held any livestock for a good long time, if ever, Culley suspected. Although he couldn't quite put his finger on it, there was something odd about that whole complex down there. It looked ordinary enough, but at the same time-

"Your thoughts match those of Miss—or is it Ms.?—Linker and her companion," Qaazi said. "They have come to the same conclusion, a correct one, I must say. For reasons I do not know the site was never fully 'decorated'—that is perhaps the best way to put it. However, unlike the 'safe house' in Japan, this one does appear to be deserted, except for our—our welcoming committee, as you mind just put it. This time, the main computer was right for a change!"

"I sure hope so," he muttered, stifling a yawn.

Qaazi laughed softly and made an adjustment in the rate of their descent, as well as in the mental program she was using to keep Culley alert.

"By the way," she went on, "my cousin finds Sally Linker as attractive as you seem to find me, and therefore feels that she will be an asset to us in more ways than one, if you follow my meaning." Her words were accompanied by a rather explicit mental image involving her cousin and the girl, who was now deep in trance.

"I get the message. Does she know?"

"No, but she will shortly. Waangaa plans to join us as

soon as he can. We may have to relocate Professor Levine before my cousin arrives."

By this time, the flyer was hovering a few feet off the ground and had begun to kick up some dust. Qaazi told Adam to extend the three landing pods, and they settled gently to earth. She shut down the drive, opened an iris, and the three of them floated over to where Sally stood, immobile as a statue. As they approached her, Culley noticed the young woman's huge, elfin eyes. Except for their pale blue pupils, now almost completely dilated, they could almost be Pleiadian—

Yes, Qaazi's mind injected, *she does carry an unusually large number of our genes; that is another reason why Waangaa selected her.*

The woman began to shiver. Qaazi aimed the wand at her head, and the spasms soon stopped. *It's all right now, Sally*, she projected, *no one will hurt you.*

Then she gestured to Culley: "Could you and Adam please help Professor Levine out of the vehicle?"

Sidney was still sitting in the passenger seat. His eyes were now wide open but staring straight ahead with hardly a blink.

Culley opened the car door, leaned across the comatose astronomer, and tugged on his left shoulder. Adam took hold of his right arm, and the two of them managed to guide Levine out of the Subaru and into a standing position next to Ms. Linker. He was breathing erratically but otherwise seemed to be in an even deeper trance than his girlfriend.

Qaazi said, "The house is locked. However, my wand, as you call it, is now fully charged and capable of transporting us through almost anything. Please line up behind me. Adam, could you see that our new friends are directly in front of you? Yes, that's right. Culley, you will bring up the rear."

Holding the instrument in front of her, Qaazi concentrated for a fraction of a second. The device began glow with an intensity he hadn't noticed before. It soon transformed itself into a ball of shimmering blue light about the size of a small grapefruit, and she led them through the closed and locked front door. (As she later explained, the beam from the transformed wand "opened a hole" in the door's physical makeup, and the molecules of their bodies literally passed between those of the wood. A similar process had occurred when they beamed aboard the ship. This process, known as "translation," was always accompanied by an intense blue light that contained what she called "transformer beads," glittering points of white light that facilitated molecular interpenetration.)

Once inside, she pointed the wand, which had now resumed its normal shape, at a light switch. A second or so later Culley heard the faint but unmistakable throb of a single-cylinder gasoline generator, and several electric light fixtures began to glow dimly, augmenting the daylight that leaked in through the cheaply curtained windows.

Still tingling slightly, but otherwise no worse for the experience, he found himself standing in the sparsely furnished albeit otherwise unremarkable living room of what appeared to be a perfectly ordinary, albeit somewhat shabby human dwelling. While he got his bearings, Qaazi floated Sidney Levine into an adjacent room, which he presumed was a bedroom. She returned almost immediately and focused her attention on Sally, who was now seated in an armchair next to one of the windows. Tilting the pliant girl's head back, she inserted the same thin wire she'd used on Culley into one of her nostrils and retrieved an implant.

"It has been inside her a long time," Qaazi said, holding the tiny object up to the light. "This may take longer than I anticipated. But do not—don't worry. Professor Levine is not, for the moment, at least, a problem, and Ms. Linker's thought patterns will not project very far in her current state. I need to get some more equipment from the flyer. And we must also get it out of sight." She glanced at her son. "Adam, could you please help me translate it into the barn? The building was designed to accommodate flyers."

The two of them left the house, this time conventionally, and returned to the disk-shaped ship, which glinted brightly in the mid-morning sun.

Despite Qaazi's best efforts, Culley was now on the verge of total exhaustion. He stretched out as best he could on a lumpy old sofa-they sure didn't waste any of their technology on the furniture!-and looked over at Sally Linker, whose head remained tilted back, ready for the second phase of the operation. Her eyes, which by this time had lost all trace of the fear they'd betrayed when the flyer landed, were glazed over, and she was breathing normally. Her long denim skirt had hitched up past her knees, revealing a small, half-moon shaped scar on her right calf.

"Welcome to Phase Two," Culley muttered, half to himself, as he idly rubbed his own calf. "They seem to like your genes, too. I wonder—"

He started to say something else, but before he could utter another syllable his hand relaxed, and he drifted off into a slumber almost as deep as the coma-like trance that still held Sally Linker and, he presumed, Sidney Levine firmly in thrall.

CHAPTER NINE

The first thing Culley noticed when he finally opened his eyes was that he was no longer on the sofa, but firmly tucked into a smallish but otherwise comfortable double bed.

The second thing was that he was hungry enough to eat a horse!

He glanced at his watch and realized with a start that unless it was totally out of whack he'd been asleep for almost twenty hours, which meant that it had been at least two days since anything substantial had passed his lips. Christ, was he famished! Even one of those bland Pleiadian wafers would taste delicious at this point!

Then he began to notice the unmistakable odor of freshly brewed coffee and frying bacon. He sat up and confirmed his earlier suspicion that he was alone. He also noticed that someone had piled his clothes neatly at the foot of the bed. As he reached for his shirt, the door opened, and Qaazi entered the room carrying a tray of what was most definitely *not* Pleiadian food.

"Good morning!" she said cheerfully. Although she'd changed back into her jeans and tee-shirt, she hadn't resumed her East Asian disguise, and the mid-morning desert sunlight streaming through the still-drawn but paper-thin curtains highlighted the near albino quality of her natural hair. Her enormous, wrap-around eyes glistened brightly.

"Hi," Culley muttered, staring hungrily at the tray. Without another word, she put the tray on his lap, kissed him lightly on the forehead, and sat at the foot of the bed while he wolfed down the bacon and eggs. In less than two minutes the plate was completely empty.

"Thanks, Qaazi! That was excellent!" He drained the last few drops of coffee, set the mug down on the tray, and pushed it to one side. "It has to be the best damn breakfast I've ever eaten! Did you by any chance have a hand in cooking it?"

Qaazi's thin lips parted in a grin.

"Yes," she replied. "It was I who prepared your breakfast. The cold storage unit—the refrigerator—was empty, but Sally brought with her some basic provisions. She showed me how to cook the chicken ova and the bacon. I wanted to put the bacon between two slices of bread"—her smile grew broader as he remembered their conversation aboard the flyer—"but our new friend informed me that you don't eat bacon sandwiches for breakfast. In any case, I'm pleased that you have enjoyed my humble culinary efforts."

Culley brought his left wrist up close to his face; his watch seemed to be working fine. "A whole fuckin' day! "he said after a moment's reflection. "Sorry to poop out on you like that. I was completely zonked by the time I hit that sofa. Did you guys have any trouble getting me in here?"

Qaazi shook her head. "Most of the heavy work was done by my' wand'"—she patted the right front pocket of her jeans—"although Sally Linker lent what I believe is called 'moral support.' We were careful not to awaken you. And please don't worry; I was the one who undressed you after Sally left the room."

She paused while Culley yawned a couple of times, rubbed his eyes, and thanked her for maintaining his modesty and for letting him sleep in.

"There was no reason to disturb you—and yes, as you suspect, I did help slightly," she confessed, once again patting her pocket. "I was well aware of how tired you had become. Please forgive me. . ."

"You're forgiven. I feel wonderful! But what about our unexpected guest? Has Levine freaked out yet? It would serve the bastard right!"

Qaazi heaved the Pleiadian equivalent of a sigh of relief. "I am—I'm—pleased to say that Professor Levine has behaved far better than I imagined he would after scanning your memories. I revived him a few hours ago. He is, of course, still in something of a daze, but he told me to tell you that he is extremely sorry for everything that he said about you at the college and wants to make amends. Indeed, he wants to join us!" She smiled and shook her head as she picked up Culley's thoughts. "No, my love, my wand is not responsible for Professor Levine's—or Sidney's, as he prefers to be called—new attitude toward you, as I can only disable, not reprogram SESO implants."

Culley grimaced. "Where is he now?"

"He and Sally—Ms. Linker— have taken Adam with them into the nearest town, the one called Barstow, to purchase more supplies. Incidentally, you'll be pleased to hear that she is adapting extremely well to her new circumstances. I have learned that, unlike Sidney, she has long been sympathetic to the possibility that beings like Adam and me exist."

"I'm not surprised. I assume it was one of the reasons why Waangaa picked her. Hope he doesn't get too upset about Levine being here, too. . . ."

She inclined her head in a mock bow, then withdrew her wand and casually pointed it at the tray. Culley watched in silent fascination as it gently lifted off the blanket and slid over to a small bedside able. He'd already seen—indeed, experienced!—what the device could do on several previous occasions, but the effect was still impressive.

Then, her thought-stream brimming with erotic images, she quickly disrobed and slid into bed next to him. *It is time for us to make our own bacon sandwich*, her mind purred.

Culley was beside himself with joy. *At last!* his mind shouted loud enough to be heard by any telepath within a fifty-mile radius. *I was beginning to think this moment would never come . . . yes, it's definitely bacon sandwich time!* he added as he nuzzled her tiny ear. *Unless—*

"Do not worry, my love. Our new friends and Adam will be gone for a while. I thought it would be good for Adam to experience Native—pardon me, *human!*—culture directly as soon as possible. Our son has learned a great deal from the holotapes, but there is no substitute for first-hand experience."

She began to fondle his penis and testicles. "I, too, am extremely 'horny,' as you're so fond of saying," she whispered softly, her supple fingers having precisely the effect she intended. "The first time we made love, I initially conceived of the act as my duty to the Clan, something I had been trained do so as to conceive a child on behalf of the Project. But I soon realized how wonderful it was, especially with you, dear Culley. Now, I would like to repeat that experience, if you have no objections."

"None whatsoever, my Precious One of the Clan!" he exulted and held her close, smothering her face and neck with ardent kisses. His ten-year fantasy was about to become as real as it is possible to get.

"God, how I love you!" he whispered softly. But a few seconds later Culley's body tensed and his massive erection began to wilt. "Are you sure Adam'll be safe?" he asked anxiously. "I'm sure they'll take good care of him. Levine may still be a monster, despite what you've just told me, but he's not that kind of monster. But it seems to me that whoever's out—or is it up?—there looking for us might spot him more easily out in the open. And besides, he does look different."

Qaazi quickly assured him that Adam was as proficient at bio-transformation as she was, and that there was nothing to worry about as far as her people were concerned, at least not for a while. "They will be looking for a specific neural pattern that apparently no longer exists," she went on to explain. "If a passing Monitor does happen to scan him, he will simply appear to be one of millions of ordinary Native 'subjects' who have been implanted. The same thing now holds for you and Sally, as well as me, I might add. And Professor Levine's SESO implant no longer broadcasts anything. So please don't worry."

His anxiety relieved, Culley kissed her passionately and began stroking her inner thighs. She responded by once again caressing his penis, this time with her tongue as well as her fingers. "How long do we have before we need to begin worrying about your people? " he asked as his organ swelled to mammoth proportions.

"At least two weeks," she replied between kisses. "You must remember that what Waangaa and I have done is unthinkable—yes, that is the right word—as far as the Clan is concerned. Eventually, of course, they will be forced to conclude that I've reprogrammed our implants. But until they do, we're safe from detection."

"You and your cousin certainly seem to have covered all the bases." Sensing her puzzlement, he told her mentally that the metaphor derived from a game called baseball and that he'd explain it later. Then his mouth sought out her small but exquisite nipples, while his fingers eagerly probed what lay beneath her blood-red pubic hair.

"Aieee!" she cried, and threw herself on top of him. He entered her immediately, and her slim hips began to undulate, drawing him in deeper and deeper. After what seemed an eternity, but was actually only a couple of minutes, Culley could hold back no longer, and he poured his love into her. As he did so, she moaned incoherently, both mentally and verbally, and her body began to shake violently. Leaning backward, she thrust her pelvis against him in a series of spasms, and squeezed until she had drawn out every drop he had to give.

Their love-making was as much mind-to-mind as it was body-to-body. Indeed, at one point in the course of what seemed to him to be an endless mutual orgasm they levitated several inches above the bed, and the effect was indescribable.

Finally, their pent-up passion fully spent, she slid off of

him and nestled her body in his arms. "That was one for the record books of at least five planets," he whispered softly.

Qaazi didn't reply verbally, but her mind concurred as she traced abstract figures on his chest with the tip of one of her tiny fingers. Then cocking her to one side, she suddenly sat up. Culley noticed that the corners of her eyes had elevated slightly.

"We shall soon cease to be alone," she exclaimed as she slipped back into her tee shirt and jeans." The time has come to put aside our naughty pleasures and pay attention to our son and our new companions. Come, dear Culley, put on your pants! We must help them bring the supplies into the house."

* * *

In the days that followed, while they waited for word from Waangaa as to their final destination, the four of them did their best to adapt to their new circumstances. Much to Qaazi's dismay, all Pleiadian items had long since been removed from the "safe house," and she had to "make do" with ordinary human technology—except, of course, for her wand and the equipment on board the flyer, most of which she didn't dare use for fear that it would reveal their presence to a passing Monitor.

The generator, housed in one of the sheds, proved to be in good working order, and the fifty-gallon drum that fed it was still filled almost to the top with gasoline, which meant that Qaazi did not have to waste precious mental energy powering the system with her wand. The well was operated both by the windmill and, when the breezes failed, by a small electric motor. The resulting water pressure, while far from heavy, was more than sufficient for their purposes.

Nevertheless, despite the ready availability of water and electricity, which meant that they could survive here indefinitely, Waangaa's continued silence added an undercurrent of uncertainty, if not anxiety, at least as far as the adults were concerned. (Adam was firmly convinced that his former mentor would arrive momentarily and transport them to Japan or some other exotic Native region, where they would live happily ever after.)

Sidney Levine proved to be highly adaptable. Once he got over his initial shock and dismay, he managed to go from consummate skeptic to true believer, reinforced, as it were, by the presence of what he'd come to call the "smokin' saucer," almost over night.

However, when he learned that Qaazi's people came from the Pleiades, he was nonplused. "They're mostly B8 stars, much hotter and brighter, as well as a hell of a lot younger that our good ol' G2 Sun. Shit, any planet that orbited Pleione at the same distance we orbit that flaming ball up there would be much to hot to support any kind of life, let along a high-tech civilization!"

Qaazi nodded gravely. "Yes, Dr. Levine—Sidney—you're quite correct. But Niivaanaa is more than ten times farther from Aandaaz—or, as you call it, Pleione—than Earth is from its primary. At that distance, our home star is about as bright as your Sun, although it appears much smaller in the sky. And the quality of its light is different. The ultraviolet radiation is far more intense, which is why we and the other creatures that inhabit Niivaanaa evolved dark, protective lenses, which, in turn, at least among our species, led to the evolution of larger pupils. Also, the fact that much of Niivaanaa is perpetually shrouded in mist reinforced the necessity for larger and more efficient eyes."

The astronomer scratched his scraggly beard, then coked his head to one side. He was still doing his best to come to terms with this challenge to everything he'd taken for granted about the absurdity of UFOs and aliens and the poor, deluded fools who took them seriously. He was now a true believer, but it was still hard for him to jettison his ingrained skepticism, which, as Culley had learned all too well, had become an integral part of both is public and private persona.

After a long moment, Sidney said, "Okay, that all makes good sense, but I'm surprised that rocky, Earth-like planets are that far away from Pleione, as well as Merope and the other Pleiadian stars Culley tells me your people have colonized. You'd think they'd be gas giants, like Jupiter and Saturn. I'm also surprised that a species as complex as yours could evolve so damned quickly! Pleione's only about a hundred million years old! The Sun's four and a half billion years old, and life's been evolving on this planet for at least half of that time."

Qaazi said, "You must realize that all solar systems are unique. In ours, the gas giants-there are three of them, all about the size of the planet you call Jupiter-orbit very close to Aandaaz. The same situation obtains in the two other Pleiadian planetary systems we've colonized. However, you are, of course correct, when you say that Aandaaz and its neighbors are much younger than your star. Our mythology"—*yes, dear Culley, we have one, too! Someday I will tell you more about it*—"suggests that our remote ancestors evolved elsewhere in the Galaxy and migrated to Niivaanaa perhaps two- or three-hundred-thousand years ago, as you reckon time, but whence they came and exactly when and why are still unknown. We do know that they soon lost the technology that allowed them to travel from one star system to another, as we only reinvented it about twenty-thousand of your years ago. Perhaps they were—what is the correct word?—yes, marooned. At least that is what some of our researchers now suspect."

Qaazi paused to brush a stray strand of pale, almost invisible hair from her undisguised face. "In any case, once they found themselves on Niivaanaa, our ancestors must have evolved the protective lenses I just mentioned rather quickly"—she pointed to one of her jet-black eyes—"although some Clan scholars suspect that we originated on a planet with a similar sun, and thus already had them when we arrived on Niivaanaa. But this is still highly conjectural."

Culley, who'd already heard most of this, said, "I gather there's no archaeological or fossil evidence for these early folks."

She shook her head. "No, none whatsoever, at least not

yet, which is why many of our researchers deny the validity of the mythological evidence."

He glanced at his former enemy and smiled. "I guess things are the same all over. As you know, we've got more than our share of skeptics who refuse to accept the evidence of you guys' presence in our mythologies. But I know one who's changed his tune lately, right?"

Sidney nodded, and then shook his head slowly, just as Culley had when Qaazi told him about Aandaaz and Niivaanaa for the first time en route to Tokyo Station. "Only twenty-thousand years ago," he muttered softly, staring at her incredulously. Then he began to laugh uproariously. "Yes indeed, it's a brand new ball game! So keep on pichin' me them curve balls, and I'll do my best to hit em'! "

Before Qaazi could finish saying "I don't understand . . ." Culley quickly explained the essence of Sidney's metaphor, whereupon she admitted that she, too, had much to learn about "curve balls" and "ball games," to say nothing of the inner core of the human psyche, which, despite her ability to read thoughts, still remained elusive.

* * *

One evening after dinner, Sidney took Culley aside and did his best to apologize for sabotaging his career at Graham. "Please understand," Levine said with uncharacteristic seriousness, "when I first saw your book I really did think you were a flake. So did that shithead Fyfe, although he didn't like you for a bunch of other reasons, too. Mainly 'cause you're *much* smarter than he is, and he knows it."

The bearded scientist put his arm around his former colleague's shoulder. "Look, Culley, I know I was an arrogant asshole. Shit, in the absence of a body of hard evidence, we skeptics were absolutely convinced that anybody who believes in UFOs and all-powerful aliens is a total whacko." He paused for a moment and looked Culley square in the eyes. "But I think the real reason that scientists like me come down so hard on guys like you is that our egos simply can't handle the possibility that we're not the most enlightened creatures in the universe, and that there are folks out there that make us look like ignoramuses. I realize that now, of course, but I hope you can understand where I and the others were comin' from. The bottom line here is that I'm really sorry about what happened at Graham. I hope you can forgive me. . . ."

As he spoke, a small tear dribbled down his cheek and disappeared into his beard.

Culley accepted Levine's profuse apology, but remained slightly standoffish. You didn't forgive the sort of shit he had pulled all that easily—or quickly.

In any case, Sidney was brimming over with questions about Pleiadian science and technology, which Qaazi patiently answered as best she could, just as she'd done for Culley. He was also extremely curious about SESO, especially after he learned that he was one if its subjects. "It's sorta like the lab rats suddenly realizing that somebody's controlling the maze," he quipped as they sat on the porch watching the stars. "And that there's not a God damned thing they can do about it! But I gather you want to change all that, at least as far as your crowd's concerned."

"Yes, Sidney," she replied, "that is what Phase Two is all about. Indeed, Waangaa and I hope that SESO will soon follow our lead after we receive permission from the Elders to begin the new experiment."

"I sure as hell hope so. But from what you and Culley have told me, they're a bunch of mean mothas! Sure wish I'd ended up in you guys' maze rather than theirs. . . ."

Now and then, Qaazi sensed the presence of other human beings in the immediate vicinity, some of them in helicopters, and Culley couldn't help wondering whether the CIA, the FBI, MJ-12, the MIBs, or whoever had somehow managed to pick up their trail. He also wondered why a place this isolated—their nearest neighbors, the mostly elderly residents of a small mobile home park, were almost ten miles away—hadn't been trashed beyond recognition by malicious teenagers, outlaw bikers and off-road enthusiasts, druggies, and other unsavory types. She assured him that they were in no immediate danger from any human beings and explained that the "Starbuck Ranch," as the property was called locally, had been protected by an invisible "psychic fence": a force field that affected the minds of would-be intruders and discouraged them from coming any closer.

Culley laughed when she mentioned the name of the place. "I doubt whether it has any connection with the famous coffee folks, as they sure wouldn't do much business hereabouts!"

"The name was probably selected in much the same way my 'Japanese' name was, with 'star' as a component, although one of our people may well have been aware of this coffee company," Qaazi said with characteristic seriousness after he explained what Starbucks was. "Someday I promise to investigate this matter on the master computer. But of more immediate importance to our current situation is that Waangaa managed to convince a passing Monitor to deactivate the 'fence' when he arranged for us to stay here. Otherwise, our new friends would have been unable to meet us. I do not possess the right equipment to reactivate the field permanently, although I have been able to bring it into temporary operation. Once we are gone for good, the field will collapse. Until then, the five of us can penetrate it at will, but it will convince all others to go on their way." (In answer to his unspoken question about the Kumo-*jinja*, she told him that such protective devices were deemed unnecessary at "safe houses" in Japan, which was one of the reasons why she still hoped to settle there eventually.)

Their "new friend" Sally proved to be a bright and cheerful, if sometimes awestruck young woman. She and Adam, who seemed to be making a remarkably rapid (and painless) adjustment to life outside the communal crèche, soon became extremely close, and he regularly accompanied her and Sidney on shopping trips and other errands. Sometimes, when they were in Barstow, they would take him to a video arcade, where his prowess proved to be awesome. His favorite games-and she savored the irony each time they played them together-were the ones that involved battles between humans and aliens.

Indeed, Adam's delight in such games caused Sally to exchange a handful of Qaazi's counterfeit yen for dollars at a local Barstow bank so she could buy Adam a cheap laptop computer and several computer games, including an updated version of "Space Invaders." Adam loved the "primitive" machine and, with a little help from Qaazi's wand, soon figured out how to reprogram Sally's cell-phone in such a way that he could use it to log onto her AOL account without leaving any traceable "digital fingerprint," although in spite of this safeguard, Qaazi ruled out his use of e-mail, as it would quickly give them away to anyone who might be monitoring the account.

Once he had the system up and running, Adam found the plethora of Internet sites devoted to UFOs highly amusing, while his mother took an opposite view: "It is so sad that so many imaginative people must grasp at straws, while the truth is all around them, waiting to be revealed. Someday, my love. . ."

Culley, who recalled his own abortive attempts to discover the "truth" about UFOs and aliens on the Internet, couldn't help but savor the irony here. "Yeah," he said wryly, "someday you and I are gonna set up the UFO site to end all UFO sites! And we'll let Adam be the webmaster!"

The blonde channel also took it upon herself to augment Adam's meager wardrobe. With his mother's wholehearted approval, she bought him several more tee-shirts, a UCLA-monogrammed sweatshirt, a leather jacket, and a pair of high-topped basketball shoes, which he asked for after noticing them on other boys his age, at one of the outlet stores on I15 a mile or so west of downtown Barstow. She also gave him a black-and-silver Oakland Raiders cap, which he loved and always wore backwards, à la the style he soon observed among most pre-teens. The clothes and other necessities were paid for with dollars she received at a local bank in exchange for some of Qaazi's seemingly inexhaustible supply of counterfeit yen.

As it turned out, Sally's station wagon wasn't the only "Native vehicle" at their disposal. The morning after their arrival Adam discovered a twelve year-old, slightly beat-up Ford Bronco in a shed next to the barn. It was registered to a "P. Starbuck," and, for a time, they suspected that they might not be alone. But a careful search turned up no evidence whatsoever that anyone had lived there recently. The Bronco seemed to be in good mechanical shape and started immediately when Culley turned the spare key he found in the glove box.

Qaazi's best guess was that a team from the Native Affairs Service, most likely accompanied by a properly attired Native Companion, visited the ranch periodically and saw to it that everything remained operational and ready for instant use, including the Bronco. This, of course, would mean that the place was still listed in the main computer, and that Waangaa had been wrong. However, the renewal month on the vehicle's license tag was October, almost a year away, and it was reasonable to assume that the next visit would be timed accordingly. Nevertheless, the sooner they left for their permanent location-somewhere in Japan, she only hoped-the better would be their chances of success. If Waangaa would make contact and let her know what was happening! (She didn't dare use the flyer's communication equipment, as that would be spotted immediately.)

After a few days, they settled into something resembling a routine. When Adam wasn't off somewhere with "Aunt Sally" and helping his mother maintain the psychic fence, he and his father explored the nearby desert, where they searched for Indian artifacts and fossils. "Uncle Sidney" sometimes accompanied them, as he'd often tagged along behind his anthropologist mother on similar explorations when he was a small child, and grubbing in the ground for projectile points was nostalgic. But for the most part, Culley and Adam went off into the desert by themselves. They had long conversations, and Culley was soon profoundly impressed with the range and depth of Adam's knowledge, not only about Earthly matters, but also about Pleiadian technology and science. Sometimes he had to pinch himself to remember that the lad was only nine years-old! As Qaazi had indicated, the boy's practical knowledge of the world, or at least of Culley's world, was almost nil. But Adam was eager to learn, and their times together in the desert were as loving and as profound, in their own way, as the ones he shared with Qaazi.

* * *

One day, while she and Adam were in Barstow, Sally decided to rent a pair of eighteen-speed mountain bikes. She was a dedicated cyclist, and was determined to teach Adam how to ride. The boy took to the sport immediately, and soon was urging Uncle Sidney and his parents to try it, too. So back to the bike shop they went, this time in the Bronco, and returned with three more bikes.

Like her son, Qaazi had never been near a bicycle. But, with the aid of her wand, plus a few lessons from Sally and Culley, who had ridden extensively while in college, she soon became an excellent rider. As for Sidney, although he sometimes sported spandex shorts, he hadn't actually been on a bike since he was ten years old, despite Sally's constant urging, and it took him a while to get the hang of it again. But after a couple of days of frequent spills he became proficient enough to accompany them on rides along the old prospectors' trails that cris-crossed the nearby desert. Sometimes they explored abandoned mines, and sometimes they simply rode to the top of the serrated butte that overlooked the ranch and gazed at the view, especially at sundown.

Early one evening, as Qaazi, Culley, Sally, and Adam-Sidney had opted out of the ride because of a sore back-sat watching the twilight afterglow bathe the snow-capped peaks of the southern Sierra Nevada in myriad shades of pink and purple, the Pleiadian outlined her plan to establish an experimental community in which her people and humans would live together as equals, each learning from the others.

"We Pleiadians know so much about your history and your cultures, far more than you yourselves know," Qaazi observed as the colors faded, "but we still don't understand what it means to be a human being, despite ten thousand years of sharing the planet with your species. That is what my 'revolution' is all about."

Culley, of course, was already familiar with the general outlines of "Phase Two," but to Sally, hearing it for the first time, it had the force of divine revelation. Like Sidney, she'd become a "convert" and was fired with the zeal of a newly-minted true-believer.

"Where do you and Culley plan to set up your community," she asked eagerly, zipping up her down jacket against the nighttime desert chill. "And will be Sidney and I be a part of it?"

"You will if you wish to be," Qaazi replied. She was still wearing a tee-shirt and seemed oblivious to the cold. "As to where we will eventually settle, Culley and I have discussed this matter on several occasions. I would prefer to establish our community in Japan, as, of all contemporary human civilizations, that of the Japanese comes closest to approximating my own. I think they would have a natural affinity for our ways, and they have a long history of borrowing from other Native cultures without losing their identity. But Culley has reservations, and he knows the culture rather well. What do you think?"

"Gosh, Qaazi, I really don't have a clue. I've never been to Japan or any place else in the Orient, but they do seem to be pretty adaptable, and their economy's awesome. I guess it's because they work harder than we do. Anyway, that Subaru down there"—she pointed to the barely visible car parked in front of the house— "runs better than any American car I've ever owned, so maybe you've got a point."

"The vehicle *is* a fine example of Native craftsmanship," Adam injected. "But I am curious as to whether a member of the Clan had something to do with its design. You may have noticed that its emblem—the more accurate English word is logo, I believe—is a stylized image of the Pleiades as seen from Earth. Am I not correct, Mother?"

"Yes," she replied, brushing a stray strand of well-nigh invisible hair from her cheek. "If I remember correctly, the word 'Subaru' means 'Pleiades' in Japanese. I'm sure we had no involvement in the vehicle's design, although the image-the logo-it bears does perhaps indicate the extent to which the Japanese are subconsciously in tune with us."

"Well, at least they didn't call it Zeta Reticuli," Culley said with a touch of sarcasm. Then he turned serious. "But Qaazi's right. I do have some serious reservations about our locating permanently in Japan. For one thing, Sally, that 'awesome' economy's not doing all that well at the moment. Things are beginning to get a little tense over there. The last time their economy got shaky, back in the thirties, the militarists took over the country and started a war. It's also too damned crowded, too cramped. We'd do better to find a spot in a less populated part of the world. Say, a place like this, or maybe somewhere in the Australian outback."

He sifted some dirt through his fingers, leaned forward, and fixed his gaze on those wondrous eyes. "But the most important reason for looking elsewhere is that the Japanese are far too group-oriented. They have a saying that 'the nail that sticks up will be hammered down.' You're too much of a rebel, too much of an individualist to be happy in a society that thinks that way, no matter how eagerly it absorbs new technologies. It would be too much like what you're trying to escape. Sure, I did fine in Tokyo as a professional *gaijin*, but I always intended to leave someday. I really wish you'd reconsider."

Qaazi said nothing, verbally or mentally. But it was clear from her demeanor that she was still strongly inclined toward settling in Japan. Culley resigned himself to what seemed to be an irrevocable decision on her part; after all, if she ever did realize her dream, the effect on humanity would be incalculable, and it really didn't make that much difference where the experiment began.

By this time, the Sierra peaks had all but disappeared from view in the gathering darkness and it was time to return to the warmth of the ranch house. Qaazi led the way on the ride back, illuminating the trail with her wand. "What a remarkable instrument! "Culley mused. "Is there anything it can't do?"

"It has its limitations," she replied as he pulled along side her, "but I must teach you how to use it, just in case. Here, you take the lead. "She passed the wand over to him as if it were a baton in a relay race. "Key your mind to it in the same way we showed you when you piloted the flyer."

Holding the small stick in front of him, he concentrated on maintaining the light. At first, it grew dimmer, but soon the trail once again became as brightly illuminated as if they all had powerful headlights.

"Large—I mean great job, Father!" Adam exulted. "But you must keep up your concentration!"

Culley laughed nervously as the trail became as clearly illuminated as if they all had headlights. "I think I'm beginning to get the hang of it," he said as he passed the wand back to Qaazi.

That means that our experiment has begun in earnest, her mind exulted. You have begun to master two of our most important devices. Someday you and the others will learn how to build them; that will be Waangaa's task.

* * *

Later that evening, while Culley and Adam repaired to the shed to tinker with the Bronco's engine, and Sidney, whose back still bothered him, slept fitfully, Qaazi and Sally sat at the kitchen table drinking coffee.

"Up there on the hill you said Sidney and I could join your group if we wanted to," Sally said hesitantly, her chin cupped in her left hand as she stared intently at her newfound alien friend. "But I get the distinct feeling that there's more to it than that. Am I right?"

Qaazi was silent for almost five seconds. "Yes," she finally said, "you are correct. There is more to your presence among us than you realize. Have you ever had any dreams about holding a tiny, odd-looking infant?"

"None that I remember. A few years ago I thought I was pregnant, but when I went to a clinic to see about getting an abortion they told me it was a false alarm, although I do have the feeling that something really strange happened to me shortly before I learned I wasn't pregnant."

Qaazi sighed and patted Sally's arm. "There are some exceptionally strong memory blocks in your implant that I cannot remove without first accessing the flyer's master computer terminal, and that would immediately betray our presence. But I can tell you that you and my cousin Waangaa, who directed you to come here and help us, once conceived a child. The fetus was removed three months later and placed in a gestation tank. To the best of our knowledge, it did not survive. I'm so sorry."

Sally blanched. "I don't understand!" she exclaimed. "They said I wasn't pregnant."

Qaazi went on to explain the Project and how a great many fetuses didn't survive the tanks. "It is not Waangaa's fault, dear Sally. He had no control over the procedure. This is one of the reasons why he insisted that you be the one to help us. He still loves you very much."

Sally's head was awhirl. So the entity she'd channeled was both a clandestine lover and the father of a child she'd only carried for three months and who was probably long since deceased. It was almost more than she could assimilate.

"I realize that all this must be extremely disconcerting," Qaazi continued. "But my cousin hopes that you will give him what I think is called a second chance."

The blonde channel wiped away a tear and brushed back a stray strand of hair that had fallen across her forehead.

"Well, I guess there's not much use crying over past history. And like you said, it wasn't his fault. But if I ever conceive another kid by your cousin—assuming I decide to, or if I have any choice in the matter—I sure hope it'll a normal pregnancy!"

Qaazi put her arms around Sally and hugged her close. "Dear, dear Sally," she whispered softly. "That is what Phase Two is all about. Waangaa and I want to end the exploitation of your race. I assure you that you do have a choice and that whatever may happen in the future in this regard will be 'normal' in every respect. But perhaps your relationship with Dr. Levine is such that. . . "

"No majorly important problems there, at least as far as I'm concerned," she replied after gulping down the last of her coffee. "I've been seeing Sid for about a year now, ever since I broke up with Carlos, but we don't have any firm commitments. He's basically a nice guy, even if he does have a wise mouth, and we've had some fun times together. But I really don't think I'm in love with him. Let's wait and see what develops when Waangaa gets here and I find out what's behind that voice in my head, okay? I mean, like, when I'm fully conscious and in control."

As she recovered from the shock and pain of learning the truth about her short-lived pregnancy, Sally once again began to experience the exhilaration she'd felt when she first realized what she'd gotten herself into, thanks to Waangaa's unceremonious intrusion into her psyche a lifetime ago, or so it now seemed. Her huge blue eyes, no longer tear-filled, glistened with anticipation. Yes, she would be delighted to give Qaazi's cousin as many chances as he wanted-or needed! For better or worse, she was about to achieve every New-Ager's fondest wish: an unsmudged window on Ultimate Reality!

CHAPTER TEN

"Tell me about Lorna, "Qaazi murmured. "I have some general impressions and images, of course, but I cannot put them all together into a coherent pattern—at least not without a deep scanner, which I wouldn't want to use on you now, even if I had one handy. But we have been together almost two weeks now, and it is time we shared this memory."

She cuddled against him, head pillowed on his chest and the tips of her toes brushing his knees. They had just made love, and were still savoring the pleasure they'd given each other as the cold grey light of dawn, faintly visible through the window opposite the bed, began to encroach on the black desert night. Not a sound could be heard anywhere. Indeed, the stillness was almost palpable, as was the presence of the local elemental "spirit," whose existence Qaazi sensed shortly after they arrived. So far, it seemed happy to have them as its "guests," just as Culley somehow knew it had welcomed the Native Americans who had worshiped on this spot a thousand years ago.

He shifted position slightly, closed his eyes, and began to project a series of mental images.

Lorna had come into his life while he was still a graduate student at UCLA, in the early eighties. She was a girlfriend of an old high school buddy's new bride, and they'd met at the wedding. He was an usher, she was a bridesmaid. One thing had led to another, and, two years later, after living together for a few months, they decided to get married. By that time, Culley was close to finishing his dissertation. After a series of part-time jobs at several local community colleges and a brief stint as a museum curator, he began teaching at Graham College just as the Reagan era was coming to an end.

"It was a hand-to-mouth existence there for a while, and we needed every penny Lorna could earn just to survive. But at least I was young enough to have missed Vietnam," he sighed. "Indeed, there were times—"

"You were lucky to have missed that terrible war," she injected. "My team flew a number of reconnaissance missions over the Vietnamese and Cambodian battlefields. The amount of senseless killing and sheer brutality displayed toward innocent noncombatants was beyond description. It reminded me of the holograms I'd seen of how humans everywhere suffered during our conflict with the Others."

Culley shuddered slightly as he recalled the images she'd projected when she first told him about her experiences monitoring Vietnam. "Despite my being an Army brat, I've always believed that wars are avoidable. That's why I got involved in the anti-war movement when I was a kid, but I'm sure you know all about that, too."

She nodded. "We monitored that aspect as well, including, of course, your own participation. I remember gathering data from several abductees who had just finished participating in a huge anti-war demonstration in the capital of your nation. It seemed to have been an-an uplifting experience."

"I can imagine. But my opposition to the war was always expressed from a position of complete safety. I was way too young to have a draft card, so there wasn't much I could do in the way of civil disobedience. But I did the best I could"

Qaazi turned to face him. "All wars are well worth opposing, including the wars my people have fought," she said quietly, her undisguised eyes fixed on his. "I thank the Winged One that we haven't been involved in a major armed conflict for several Earth millennia. Nevertheless, I've seen a great many human horrors, also from a position of safety, since I left the Academy. The worst were during what you call the Second World War. I was still a Cadet then and it was my first direct exposure to a Native conflict. Those death camps in the country called Poland were indescribable. We really should have suspended the Rule of Non-Interference and rescued those poor people; it was heart-rending in the extreme when we had to return them to the camps after they were abducted. You cannot imagine how awful those places were. How utterly awful!"

Culley had, of course, seen grainy, black-and-white photographs of the ovens and of the hollow-eyed, emaciated corpses stacked ten deep in mass graves. But the extremely vivid mental images that accompanied Qaazi's words were almost too much for him to assimilate. "I-I once talked to a woman who survived Auschwitz," he finally managed to say, "and she described much the same thing. Have you said anything about this to Sidney yet? He must have lost a lot of relatives there or in places like it. . . . "

"No, but I will if you think I ought to. I was afraid that it might be too painful for him."

"I think he'd appreciate—not sure that's the right word—the fact that it was at Auschwitz where you first began to question the rules."

Culley stared silently at the ceiling for the better part of a minute, doing his best to suppress the images Qaazi had projected. "Someday," he finally added, his eyes still fixed on the cheap light fixture that hung above the bed, "you must tell me more about the human history you've observed. The good parts as well as the bad ones."

I promise to do so, she responded, mind to mind, *and there have been some good parts, I assure you. But we were speaking about your former wife. Let us return to that subject. Why did your marriage to her fail?*

He sighed. "There were a lot of reasons. For one thing, our backgrounds couldn't have been more different. . . .

While some of Culley's Protestant ancestors had come over on the Mayflower (or at least the next boat), both of

Lorna Belaskas's parents were first-generation Lithuanian immigrants and were about as Roman Catholic as it was possible to get. To make matters worse, his immediate heritage was decidedly non-religious; indeed, from the outset his in-laws had disapproved of Culley's atheism, to say nothing of his left-liberal politics. And the fact that Lorna, who'd only had two years of junior college, felt woefully inferior in the presence of Culley's colleagues and their wives, most of whom had advanced degrees and careers to match, didn't help matters any.

Another major bone of contention was the fact that she couldn't conceive a child. They'd gone to several fertility specialists, but none of them could come up with anything other than the fact that Culley's sperm were healthy, which made Lorna feel even more inadequate.

And then came his encounter with Qaazi.

"At first," Culley explained, "like everybody else, Lorna thought I was simply hallucinating. But after I underwent hypnotic regression, and the lost hours I spent with you gradually re-emerged, she began to suspect that I'd faked the whole thing to cover a sleazy affair with a student. She never really believed that I'd been seduced by an alien. More likely by one of my 'braless female admirers,' the kind who'll do anything to get an A. At least that's what she used to say. "Qaazi smiled at the mental image that accompanied her lover's words.

When the book came out-Lorna had done her best to persuade him not to publish it until he had tenure-and he began to appear on talk-shows, it got worse. Her parents were aghast. Even her older sister, who had liked Culley, advised her to leave him.

For the first year or so, the royalty checks from Encounter in the Desert proved to be far larger than she'd anticipated. This allowed them some luxuries, including a new BMW, they couldn't otherwise have afforded on an assistant professor's salary. So she decided to stick it out a while longer. But when Culley was denied tenure and then, after more than a year of trying, was unable to land another academic position, Lorna's patience finally ran out. One day, after a vicious argument in which he said some particularly nasty things about her family, she packed her bags, walked out the door, got in the BMW, and never returned.

He hadn't seen her since—the divorce proceedings were handled by their attorneys—although he believed she was still single and living somewhere in Southern California. How jealous she would be to learn that he now had the child she couldn't give him, and that his account of his affair with a beautiful alien was utterly and incontrovertibly true!

Poor Lorna, Qaazi's mind murmured. *I feel so sorry for her. It's almost certain that she does not carry an implant; it would have been noted in your file. But from your memory images I get the distinct impression that she really did love you, at least in the beginning, and that you cared for her too.*

Yes, I suppose that's true, he responded in kind. *But I'm glad things turned out the way they did.* He accompanied his thoughts with an extremely tender mental caress.

By this time, the bedroom was awash with the early morning sunlight, which streamed in through the cheap curtains and formed luminous pools on the walls and ceiling.

Culley yawned and glanced at his watch. "Time to get up!" he muttered, reverting to the verbal mode. "Are you still game for a shopping trip to Victorville plus a driving lesson."

"Yes, my love. Sally tells me the shopping place there—I believe you call it a mall—is 'majorly cool.' She and Adam have been there several times. She says that the stores in the Victorville mall contain a better class of merchandise than the ones in Barstow. And you've been promising to teach me how to operate a Native motor vehicle ever since we left Takayama. I intend to hold you to it today!"

Qaazi sat up and kissed him softly on the cheek. Then, grinning puckishly, she inclined her head toward him in a humorous imitation of a traditional Japanese bow and placed her hands on her forehead just above her eyes. "Now you must excuse me, oh worthy sensei, for I need to repair my human disguise."

She concentrated for a moment, and her huge eyes shrank and become more "Asian" in appearance. Glancing in the mirror tacked to the back of the bedroom door, she noted the change with satisfaction, but added that she needed to do some more work on herself before she could come into close contact with other human beings without causing any "undue consternation."

"Consternation," Culley injected with a laugh. "I like that word; it's the first time I've heard you use it. Are we doing a little vocabulary building on the sly? And I must say, your sense of humor's coming along nicely these days!"

Qaazi's semi-disguised eyes glistened with delight, and she smiled one of the broadest smiles he'd had from her. "Thank you!" she exclaimed. "I'm glad you noticed. It has not been easy. And yes, I have picked up some new words and expressions 'on the sly,' as you just put it—I do like that phrase!—from listening to the crude electronic device in the living room, as well as to you and Sally, and especially Sidney, who has a very colorful way of speaking. But the others are now up and bustling—that's another good word!—in the kitchen. Why don't you go help them bustle while I finish adjusting my disguise? "

As Culley slowly got out of bed and padded toward the door, chuckling over her reference to his former enemy's vocabulary, Qaazi's mind once again made contact with his: *I also thank you for telling me about Lorna. I realize that it was painful. Although it may be hard for you to understand, I really do sympathize with her. It's not totally her fault that you were unable to reconcile your differences.*

You're probably right, his thought-stream replied. Then he paused for a second, his hand on the door latch. "Uh . . . I've told you all about Lorna and me," he added hesitantly, once again switching back to the verbal mode. "How—how about you? In the last eighty years or so you must have had your share of lovers. I mean among your own kind. . . . "

Qaazi stared at him for a long moment before responding; her thought-stream became unreadable. "I did not become a fully adult, child-bearing female until shortly before we first met," she finally said in a flat, almost emotionless voice. "We mature at the discretion of the Clan Elders. When they decide that it's time for us to do our Project duty, or to mate, our reproductive systems are activated, and we develop breasts and other secondary sexual characteristics. We also gain the ability to ovulate."

Culley leaned against the door and shot her a quizzical look. "Do you, uh, have periods like human women?"

"Periods? I don't understand. Ah, yes! The monthly discharges human females of childbearing age must cope with. Your mental image tells me that they are considered unpleasant and unsanitary. That is not the case as far as we're concerned. We Pleiadians have learned to expel our unfertilized ova at will, along with the accompanying bodily fluids. It only takes a few seconds, not a week. Someday I hope that I can teach Sally and other human women how to do this."

"I'll bet the folks who make Kotex and Tampax'll love it when that secret gets out," he chuckled while his mind described the products he'd mentioned and how they were used. "But you haven't answered my question. I mean it's been ten years since—"

"I assure you that you were the first and so far the only male, Native or Pleiadian, whom I have 'known,' as your Bible so quaintly puts it," she replied indignantly. Her thought-stream reinforced her words with a vengeance, and he knew in the depths of his soul that she was telling the absolute truth.

Culley quickly returned to where Qaazi was standing and put his arms around her. "I didn't mean to upset you," he whispered softly, kissing the tip of her tiny nose. "But it's hard to get used to the thought that I once made love to a ninety-eight year-old virgin! Seriously, though, I hope you won't regret not having had more 'experience' before I came along."

"Don't forget that you didn't just 'come along'," she said with a wry smile. Then she brightened considerably as her eyes struggled to complete their transformation into East Asian eyes. "I really must concentrate on my disguise. If you continue to distract me, we shall never get to that shopping mall in Victorville. Please go help Sally and Sidney prepare breakfast.They are planning to drive into Barstow this morning and purchase a small television receiver. Adam will go with them. He's convinced that he can access programs by attaching a wire to the flyer and using it as an antenna. Sidney agrees."

"Okay, I'm outta here. But speaking of Adam—"

Yes, her mind interrupted, *his reproductive system is of course still dormant. But Waangaa has secretly programmed Adam's implant to trigger it at the appropriate time for humans. Unless I am mistaken, that should be in about three years.*

Culley heaved a sigh of relief. "Yeah, I guess that's about right. For a moment there I was worried he wouldn't make it to puberty until he was in his nineties!"

* * *

It didn't take Qaazi long to learn the rudiments of driving a "Native vehicle." Her gear changes were a little jerky, and her short legs had difficulty reaching the pedals—a problem she compensated for by using her wand—but by the time they reached the outskirts of Barstow she could handle the Bronco pretty well.

Nevertheless, shortly before they reached I15 Culley took over, as he was not sure that his extraterrestrial lover was up to driving in freeway traffic. Forty minutes later he pulled into the vast parking lot of the Mall of Victor Valley. It was a Wednesday, and the lot was barely a third full.

"I wonder how Sally and Adam are doing," Culley said as they left the mid-day desert heat behind and entered the mall's heavily air-conditioned atrium. "I suggested that they check out a SONY, but she said Sidney prefers Panasonics. In any case, I hope they'll have enough sense to buy a cheap VCR to go with it. Then we can watch videos together."

He glanced at Qaazi's purse. "The last time I checked, we were still doin' fine in the yen department, though if we have to stay here much longer I ought to close out my Tokyo bank account. Jim Hotchkiss, my roomie—make that my former roomie!—could do it for me, as we can access each other's account."

Much to Qaazi's relief, no one paid much attention to her, as Asian faces were ubiquitous these days in Southern California, and Victorville was no exception. It was almost noon, and she suggested that they share a small pizza, a local Native dish she'd recently come to enjoy, at one of the mall cafes before hitting the shops.

After they finished—Culley ended up eating most of the pizza—they joined the throng of shoppers that drifted through the mall from store to store. Qaazi, of course, knew about places like this, and once, when she was with the North American service, they'd abducted a couple from a mall parking lot; it had been late in the evening, long after most of the shoppers and movie-goers had left. But she'd never actually seen the inside of one. The range and variety of available goods, especially clothing items, surprised her, especially in a small city like Victorville.

"What must the malls in Los Angeles be like?" she wondered aloud. He did his best to explain that shopping malls everywhere were pretty much the same; that they generally had the same specialty shops and department stores, as well as fast-food outlets and movie theaters, and that the size of the town really didn't make much difference.

They both bought several items of clothing, mostly jeans and the like. Qaazi also insisted on buying several pairs of Levis for Adam, as well as sturdy hiking boots and a couple of shirts. She worried that the sizes might not be right, but Culley reassured her, saying they could return them if they didn't fit. "What a convenient custom!" Qaazi observed as they wandered from shop to shop, their arms loaded with packages. “In our commissaries we are expected to make do with what we are given—and, of course, there is but one size and a single style.”

In a small boutique, she found herself admiring a light blue, tight-fitting, midriff-revealing tank-top with an extremely low neckline. “Exposing one’s navel seems to be extremely popular these days among your females,” she mused, fingering the top and holding it against her chest. “It is the same in Japan, although I was never brave enough to purchase such a garment. But Sally wears one now and then, so perhaps I should as well?”

Culley grinned and nodded his head. “Hey, you’re the only hundred and eight year-old on the planet that could wear a thing like that and get away with it. Why don’t you try it on?” So she did, and when she emerged from the fitting room he gave a low whistle. “Yes, you are definitely the only lady your age who can wear it! Britney Spears has nothing you, Babe!”

“She is one of the performers Adam seems to admire. All right, I shall buy it. I’d also like to wear it now and surprise Sally and Adam when we return. I imagine Sidney will like it, too.”

“He’ll be blown away!”

Qaazi looked puzzled for a second, then picked up Culley’s mental explanation and smiled sweetly. She was proud of the way she filled out the tank-top and wasn’t at all shy about letting him know it.

They stopped briefly in a computer store, where Culley stared longingly at a new, top-of-the-line IBM laptop.

“It is a quaint instrument,” Qaazi said as her fingers idly tapped several keys. Then she smiled at her human shopping companion. ”Yet Adam might like it. It seems somewhat more sophisticated than the one Sally bought for him, but it would still be impossible, under the circumstances, for him to do more than ‘surf the net,” as you call it. The monitors would spot him immediately if he were to send someone a message. Maybe someday, when we've settled down somewhere. . ." She completed her thought with an image of her son happily typing messages to unseen cyber-buddies.

"Too bad," Culley said wistfully. "I'm sure he'd become a big-time hacker in nothing flat." Qaazi looked puzzled. "Why would he want to chop up things?"

While Culley explained, they continued their tour of the mall shops. He couldn't help thinking that she was like the proverbial kid in a candy store.

Just before they reached the exit, Qaazi noticed a large, discount record store. There was an aging but still serviceable FM radio-cum-stereo tape deck—the "crude electronic device" that had helped her expand her English vocabulary—in the living room, and she suggested that it would be nice to have a variety of music to choose from, especially as their radio reception was limited to a couple of local country-western stations.

Much to Culley's surprise, there was a decent selection of classical CD's and tapes. Scanning the contents quickly, he picked out tapes of Handel's "Water Music," Mozart's "Jupiter Symphony," several works by Mendelssohn, Tchaikovsky's "Sixth Symphony," and a recent Boston Pops/John Williams recording of three works by Aaron Copeland: "Appalachian Spring," "Fanfare for the Common Man," and "Billy the Kid."

Qaazi smiled as he placed the tapes in a carry-basket. "I will enjoy listening to them with you," she said. "Indeed, I share the widely-held view among Colonials that our own music, despite its technical perfection and harmonic complexity, is nowhere near as beautiful as yours. Music is not one of our principal art forms."

Then she moved over to the rock music section, and quickly picked out a tape by an L.A. heavy metal band called "Doctor Stupid." Responding to Culley's unverbalized question, Qaazi smiled again and pointed to a clutch of teenagers loitering in nearby.

"Most of them seem to like the sounds produced by that

group of musicians," she said matter-of-factly. "The dark-haired girl over there, the one in the tight bicycle shorts, has an implant and is easy to scan. She is thinking about buying it as a gift for her boyfriend. It appears that their music is popular among your young people, and therefore Adam ought to become familiar with it. It will help him make friends. Do you not agree? "

"Well, maybe," Culley replied, "But I'm sure it'll make your music sound wonderful!"

Qaazi grinned and then became serious. "Nevertheless," she replied, "I'm extremely curious to hear their songs and to learn why they are so popular. Perhaps we can play the tape on the device in the Bronco?"

"Sure, although you're not gonna like it!"

"Remember, I am—or rather I was—a Native Affairs Specialist. There are many things about your culture I don't like, and this music will probably be added to the list. But if Adam is expected to enjoy it, I must do my best to understand its appeal. You can help me—"

She froze in mid-sentence, her head cocked to one side, and Culley was sure she'd spotted another MIB or maybe one of her own people.

"No," she assured him after a second or two, "there is no immediate threat that I'm aware of. I was receiving a message from Sally. Actually, it was from Waangaa, but, as you know, he cannot contact me directly at this point. It would be much too dangerous. But Sally is a 'channel,' and mental messages to her from members of the Clan are considered routine and will not be closely monitored. That is another reason why he selected her. When we finally—"

"This is all good to know, Qaazi," he injected, unable to control his curiosity, "but what did he tell her? Do we have a problem?"

She shook her head and switched to the mental mode. It was nothing urgent. My cousin informs us that we must remain where we are for at least another two months. It's not yet safe to return to Japan, as both SESO and the

Monitors are now actively seeking us there. But Waangaa has no reason to believe that they have any idea of our current location.

Culley heaved a sigh of relief. The prospect of remaining in the States for the foreseeable future was good news indeed, at least as far as he was concerned. "Maybe I ought to make that phone call to Japan. If we're going to stay here a while, we'll probably need some more cash. I'll also have Jim send me my personal stuff."

Spotting a public phone, Culley dialed the international operator and placed a collect call to Mr. James C. Hotchkiss in Tokyo. After a few seconds of static, his former roommate's phone began to ring. He was about to hang up, wondering what Jim was doing out at that hour of the morning (it was shortly before 6:00 a.m. the next day in Tokyo) when he finally heard a familiar voice mutter: "*Mushi-mushi, donata des'ka?* "

The Japanese operator asked him if he'd accept a call from a Mr. Cullen Wisdom in Victorville, California, U.S.A.

Stifling a yawn, Jim Hotchkiss said "*Hai*," then mumbled sleepily, "Culley? Is that you? What the fuck are you doing in Victorville, wherever the hell that is?"

"*Hai, Culley des'*. Yeah, it's me, old buddy. Sorry to get you up so early, but I need your help."

The voice on the other end of the line yawned, and then responded: "Okay, sure, but what the hell's going on? Some hard-faced guys in dark suits with scary credentials, both local and from the States, have been here several times asking about you. Level with me, Culley. Are you in any trouble? *Honto ni?* "

"Jim, you wouldn't believe what's happened to me. Not in a million years! It would take hours to explain, and even then I'm sure you'd think I was crazy—*totemo baka des' yo.* So please trust me, okay? Anyway, here's what I want you to do. . . ."

Culley asked his roommate to close out his savings account, convert the funds into an international money order, and send it to him care of General Delivery, Barstow. He also asked him to pack up some of his belongings-clothes, books, personal papers, and the like-and mail the package to the same address.

By now fully awake, Jim made one more half-hearted attempt to find out what Culley was up to. But he knew his roommate well enough to realize that he'd tell him when he was ready, and not before. So they said their goodbyes and Culley hung up.

* * *

As Jim Hotchkiss hung up and tried to go back to sleep, he failed to notice a very faint metallic click. It activated the microscopic SESO listening device Nakamura-san's colleague Mr. Chang had clandestinely installed in Hotchkiss's telephone (at the same time, the Korean MIB had disabled a primitive device installed by the Tokyo section of MJ-12). Within less than a second, a record of the conversation, plus the location from which the call had come, were relayed to an egg-shaped craft hovering high above the Kamchatka Peninsula, at the edge of space.

Less than a nanosecond later, that record, including the Barstow address Culley had given his friend, surfaced in Hajime Nakamura's implant. In less than five minutes, he and Djrnk, his SESO Mistress, were streaking toward the Mojave Desert of Southern California at slightly better than 10,000 miles an hour.

* * *

After enduring the discordant—indeed, Satanic!—sounds of "Doctor Stupid" for a few minutes via the Bronco's tape player, Qaazi readily agreed that the music was awful but still insisted that Adam ought to be aware of it, if only to facilitate his eventual acceptance by Native children his age. Culley could see her point, especially if they stayed in the States, but made her promise not to play the tape when he was within earshot.

Then he inserted the "Jupiter Symphony" tape, and,

while Mozart's inimitable melodies soothed their ears, Qaazi told him more about her distant, almost tangential relationship with her biological parents, about growing up in a crèche, and about the plethora of half-siblings, most of whom she'd never seen. In return, he shared some additional intimate details about his own early life as an Army brat and about his failed marriage, two subjects which Qaazi seemed to find endlessly fascinating.

He let her drive again after they left I15 at Barstow, and they were so deep in conversation—Culley had raised the possibility of a trip to Las Vegas, where Qaazi could use her wand to augment their dwindling supply of cash—that neither of them noticed the presence of a California Highway Patrol cruiser until it was too late. Nor had he noticed that Qaazi had allowed their speed to reach more than ninety miles an hour!

Oh, shit, Culley thought. *This is gonna take a big bite out of our finances. Now we'll really have to make that Vegas trip! Hope they don't bother to check out her license with the people in Tokyo!*

Startled, Qaazi immediately followed his mental directions and slowed to a stop on the shoulder of the deserted two-lane road. It was too late for them to trade places. *Why can't we accelerate to any speed that is safe?* her mind queried. *There are no other vehicles present. Must we pay money to the man?*

As the cruiser pulled in behind them, Culley did his best to brief her on what to say and how to act. She could, of course, zap the guy with her wand, but that might raise a lot of nasty questions, especially if, as he suspected, the officer had already radioed in the Bronco's license number. He told Qaazi to stay cool, answer the man's questions, and show him her phony Japanese license, which was perfectly valid in California.

Do not worry, my love, I shall be as cool as that oblong green vegetable you sometimes like to eat. I cannot recall its name.

It's cucumber, Culley's mind whispered as the cruiser's door finally opened and the tan-uniformed patrolman began to walk slowly toward them. *And please, just do what he says. These guys throw the book at people who give them a hard time.*

"I shall be a meek little Japanese woman," she said aloud. "But why would he want to hurl a book at me? That makes no sense whatsoever."

Never mind! I'll explain later, he replied, doing his best to remain calm as the officer's stern face loomed in the driver's side window. *Just pretend you're a Japanese cucumber!*

CHAPTER ELEVEN

"Was I a good Japanese cucumber?" she asked innocently, but with a twinkle in her disguised eyes as she glanced at the citation.

"That you were, my Precious One of the Clan. A very cool cucumber! Your Japanese accent would have fooled me! I'm surprised you didn't jump out of the car and bow to him! But I'm glad you didn't, as you just might have come out that new tank-top!"

By this time, they'd turned off the Fort Irwin Highway and onto the first of several lonely, unpaved county roads that snaked across the barren hills and dust-filled dry lakes that dominated the desert landscape northwest of Barstow. The brilliant, mid-afternoon sun was reflected in one shimmering mirage after another.

Qaazi grinned broadly and reached between the seats, intending to put the ticket in her purse, which lay on the back seat. But, as she did so, Culley, who was now back at the wheel, swerved suddenly to avoid hitting a nasty pothole, sending the purse to the floor.

It fell directly beneath the driver's seat. She attempted to retrieve it, but couldn't quite reach that far. Neither could Culley. He offered to stop, but she demurred, as the odds that she might need the wand in a hurry before they returned to the safe house seemed to be nil. So they continued on their way, and she returned her attention to her recent encounter with Native law.

"How much money will my unfortunate driving error cost us?" Qaazi asked hesitantly.

"A bundle, maybe several hundred dollars, but we can handle it. I just hope that they don't—"

* * *

A brilliant, multicolored flash of light exploded in Culley's head. There was no pain, exactly, but as the light broke up into an uncounted number of small bursts, which resembled the dying embers of a Roman candle, the pressure became almost unbearable. Then, a nanosecond later, after briefly glimpsing a tell-tale burst of shimmering blue light, a profound darkness began to envelope him, and before he had time to think rationally about what might have happened to him-or to Qaazi-everything went black.

* * *

The next thing Culley remembered was a tapping sound. It seemed to be coming from his left. He opened his aching eyes and slowly turned his head toward the driver's side window, which framed a large male face and a set of knuckles rapping persistently on the glass. As his eyes focused more clearly, he saw that the face belonged to an officer of the law.

He glanced to his right and saw that he was alone.

A wave of panic swept over him. What the hell had happened to Qaazi? And why did his head hurt ten times worse than it had when he'd come to in her apartment?

"Sir, please open the window and unlock your door. Are you all right?" the face said through the glass.

It was not the face of the CHP officer who'd cited Qaazi; he was sure of that. The man had a flashlight, and, for the first time, Culley realized that it was almost dark, which meant that he'd been out for at least three hours.

Three fucking hours!

He rolled down the window and did his best to smile at the man, who turned out to a San Bernardino County Deputy Sheriff. The deputy's car was parked a few yards behind the Bronco, and its flashing red lights were reflected in the rear-view mirror.

"May I see your driver's license and registration, please,"

the deputy asked as he sniffed Culley's breath, which bore no trace of any alcoholic beverage whatsoever.

"Sure. I'm okay, officer. I-I was just taking a nap. Didn't want to take any chances. . ."

The officer smiled back at him approvingly. However, he carefully scrutinized both Culley's license and the Bronco's registration in the beam of his flashlight.

"You live in Japan, Mr. Wisdom?" he asked, his eyes narrowing.

Culley, whose head still throbbed, but not quite as badly as it had when the guy first tapped on the window, was startled for a second, but then remembered that the license was clipped to his international driving permit, which bore his Tokyo address along with his "permanent" one, a former colleague's cabin in the San Bernardino mountain community of Crestline. As his mind cleared, he decided to ring the changes on the ploy they'd used earlier with the CHP officer. "Yeah," he finally replied, "I just got in this morning. That's why I'm so sleepy. You know, jet-lag and all that. I'm, uh, staying with the Starbucks'. They let me borrow their car."

"Okay, sit tight. I'll be right back."

The deputy took the license and registration back to the cruiser. He returned a few minutes later and handed them back to Culley. "The car's clean and so are you, my friend. No problems. Enjoy our desert—but only after you get a good night's rest! "

"Thanks, Officer, I will."

As the deputy drove off, Culley sat staring at the retreating taillights, doing his best to sort out what had happened and waiting for his headache to go away. He was convinced that Qaazi had been abducted, 'translated' through the roof of the car by the blue beam he'd glimpsed just before losing consciousness. There was no other possible explanation.

But by whom? And why didn't they take him too?

Obviously, they, whoever "they" were, had knocked him

out in the process, and had brought the Bronco safely to rest on the shoulder of the two-lane road.

Almost immediately he was struck by another extremely nasty thought: What had happened to his son? And to Sally and Sidney? Were they safe?

Shaking the remaining cobwebs from his brain, Culley tried the ignition key and heaved a big sigh of relief when the engine turned over.

Shortly thereafter he made an important discovery. Qaazi's purse still lay were it had fallen under the driver's seat. Whoever took her must have been in a hell of a big hurry!

He grabbed the purse, fished out the wand, and placed it on the seat beside him, within easy reach. That thing just might prove to be his ace in the hole if he came face-to-face with the abductors. They would not expect a Native to have such a device in his possession, let alone any conception of what it could do.

By this time, the sun had dipped below a range of barren hills that were now barely visible against the darkening western sky. He switched on his headlights.

Maybe there was still time to get to Adam and the others before whoever took Qaazi realized where they were. Indeed, maybe they were still in Barstow. If only he had a cell-phone handy! He could call Sally and see if she and Adam were all right. But Culley quickly remembered that Sally's Nokia was hooked up to his son's laptop, and that Sidney had neglected to bring his cell-phone along when he and Sally left for the desert. So it wouldn't have made any difference. There was no way to contact them. . . .

Then another, wholly contradictory thought struck him with the force of a sledge hammer: this was the first time he'd been totally alone since Qaazi had come back into his life two weeks ago. To be sure, he'd been apart from her briefly when he and Adam had explored several nearby caves looking for artifacts, and when he and Sidney had hiked up to the top of the butte to look at the stars together-

and, at the same time, settle their previous difference. But this was different. Until now, he realized, one or another of the group had always been present. What if they had somehow all taken turns controlling his mind? Indeed, what if the whole thing had been a sham from the outset?

What if Adam, Sidney, and Sally, if not Qaazi herself, at least to some degree, really were figments of an alternate reality created by what he'd begun to conceive of as the "Alien Raj," on the model of the so-called "British Raj" that had ruled India until 1947. The major difference, of course, aside from the relative scale of the two hegemonies, was that the old British Raj had been extremely visible, while its alien counterpart was deeply clandestine. Nevertheless, by this time Culley had long since earned that it was equally, if not more ubiquitous, and that its tentacles reached into almost every corner of the planet. Maybe what had happened to him was all part of some secret experiment the Alien Raj had concocted to see how he'd react to such stimuli? Maybe her sudden disappearance was simply part of the scenario.

Yes, that had to be it! She no more loved him than a psychologist loves the rats he or she runs through mazes! It was all a sham!

But why did she leave her wand behind?

He picked up the alien instrument and turned it over a few times, examining it carefully. It was real enough, and he knew from personal experience the wonders it could perform. In less than two hours he could be just across the state line in Primm, Nevada, sitting at a roulette table in Whisky Pete's Casino; no need to drive all the way into Vegas. He could make a quick fortune and then simply disappear.

Or maybe his real duty was to be a latter-day Paul Revere and alert his fellow humans to the alien presence, like some cardboard hero in a fifties flying-saucer flick.

Maybe he ought to deliver Qaazi's wand to somebody at the Pentagon, or perhaps the CIA. One of those crew-cut Government guys who used to bother him after the book came out would probably give his eye teeth to get his hands on it! If they stonewalled him, he might try contacting one of his old MUFON or CUFOS cyber-buddies; from what he'd seen on Adam's computer screen they were still very much in business.

At the very least, assuming that the Alien Raj was far too powerful to be ousted by any form of conventional rebellion, perhaps he could become a latter-day Gandhi. . . .

But why be so damned hasty? Did he *really* want to get involved in UFO politics again, despite the fact that he now knew for certain that what they spent so much time debating was real, far more real than most of them suspected, even in their wildest dreams.

He hefted the wand again, aiming it at an imaginary roulette wheel. Even if he did decide to play the hero and lead the human race in what would almost certainly be an abortive revolt against Pleiadian and SESO imperialism—against the Alien Raj—why not use the thing to feather his own nest first? Once again, the image of a spinning roulette wheel danced before his eyes. Yeah, why the hell not make a few—

Culley's thoughts were suddenly interrupted by the plaintive wail of a solitary coyote somewhere up in the nearby hills. At first, he paid little attention to the sound, which, after all, was not all that uncommon in these parts. And he continued to visualize the mountain of chips he would take to the Whisky Pete's cashier as he surreptitiously directed the little white ball to fall into preselected pockets. But the coyote's wail imperceptibly transformed itself into a human voice deep inside his head: *It is not a sham*! the voice intoned, Qaazi does love you deeply! *The others, including Adam, are in danger and need your help desperately. You must go to them immediately! You and Qaazi have important work to do. Do not waste precious time trying to become rich or a hero. Go to them now!*

As the voice continued speaking in his mind, Culley came to realize that it wasn't really a voice at all, but rather a totally convincing sequence of intense feeling states and images. It was like nothing he'd experienced in the sub-verbal communication he'd had with Qaazi, Adam, Waangaa, and the others, even when they conveyed memory images.

But that coyote, or whatever it was, was absolutely right! Qaazi was real! So was his son Adam. Both of them *did* love him as much, if not more than he loved them. And both of them needed his immediate help; so did Sally and Sidney. He had no doubts whatsoever about that now.

Cursing himself for being such a selfish bastard, Culley realized that he had to get back to the safe-house as fast as possible, and to hell with the speed limit! He hoped that cop was long gone by now. . . .

Leaving a long strip of rubber on the asphalt, he roared back onto the well-nigh deserted road and sped toward the Starbuck ranch as fast as the Bronco could take him.

* * *

Wilma Gibbs stared intently through the lens of the ultra high-powered electron microscope at a tiny fragment that had been carefully shaved from the alien device. Her eyes were blurry from almost two solid weeks of fruitless searching for a key, any key, that would permit them to unlock more of the thing's secrets. It was even more crucial now that they'd lost a second locator signal, one belonging to a young subject named Sally Linker. She'd winked out less than twenty four hours after Wisdom disappeared.

What the hell was goin' on here?

Wilma was convinced that if they could understand the gizmo's physical structure, they might be able to figure a way to tap into another of its functions. Tom Johnson sat next to her on a lab stool, preparing the slides.

"Time for a break, Dr. Gibbs," he mumbled wearily. "We've been at this steadily since six o'clock this morning. We're both too beat to see anything important at this point." They'd been working at this killing pace ever since Tom returned from Tokyo, and it was beginning to take its toll.

Wilma looked up, grimaced, and then nodded. She rubbed her eyes a couple of times, glanced at the dried-out remains of the large pepperoni pizza they'd shared, then swiveled around to face her chief assistant. "Has it really been that long? Okay, Tom, let's give our eyes a rest and kick around some ideas."

She took a deep breath, exhaled, and then paused for a moment before continuing. "These molecules just don't make sense. We know the thing's made out of a light-weight metal that doesn't exist in this solar system, let alone this planet. Even so, the structure should be obvious. But it isn't."

"Uh, maybe we're taking a wrong tack, Dr. Gibbs," Tom ventured; he was too tired to worry about offending her with his impertinence. "Maybe we ought to be looking at some of the patterns that occur when we manipulate various parts of it. That's how we found the carrier beam and with it the locator signal in the first place."

"Yes, it was. But we've poked and prodded almost every millimeter of that sucker and nothin' new has happened. The rest of our subjects are still coming in clear as a bell. I just don't understand it. It's as if all the physics I ever learned—or taught—is dead wrong. . . ."

Tom chuckled softly. "I promise I won't tell the Nobel people!"

She shot him a withering glance, and then wreathed her tired face in a broad smile. "Well, Tom Johnson, you're gettin' positively brave in your old age! I've been waiting for you to loosen up, ever since you took your first seminar from me back in Pasadena. Let's see, how long ago was that?"

"Seven years, Dr. Gibbs," he replied, regaining his usual deference, despite his fatigue.

"Look, Tom. We're colleagues, now. Have been ever since I brought you aboard MJ-12. How 'bout calling me Wilma from now on? Okay?"

Blushing slightly, Tom smiled broadly at his former

professor. "Okay . . . Wilma. I guess I have been a little stiff. It's just that you're—you're so awesome. I keep thinking that if I don't mind my manners I'll wake up and find myself teaching elementary physics at a third-rate liberal arts college somewhere rather than sitting beside the chair of MJ-12, even if I can tell anybody about it."

He stroked his beard absently. "Look, maybe there's some combination we haven't tried yet, maybe. . ." He reached over and picked up the device, turning it in one hand and stroking the burned areas gently with the other. Then he pulled his hand back about an inch from the surface and continued to move it slowly back and forth above the burned areas. At first, nothing happened. A few seconds later, however, Wilma noticed a faint glow. It faded almost as soon as it appeared, but she let out a whoop that startled the rest of the lab team.

"Boy, I do think you're onto somethin'! Here, let me try it." While Tom held the device, Wilma ran her thick but supple fingers over the device's surface, being careful not to touch it. Again, after a couple of seconds, the glow returned, only to fade almost immediately.

Tom frowned, but Wilma's eyes glistened. "Let's concentrate on that spot there." She pointed to where the glow seemed to have started. Then, by accident, her finger happened to touch the spot.

As she quickly pulled it back, one of the locator scopes tuned to Cullen Wisdom's beam came to life. It flickered for a second, and then indicated what seemed to a location in Southern California, about a hundred and fifty miles northeast of Los Angeles. The screen also displayed Wisdom's face, overlaid with several lines of the unreadable squiggles.

"Bingo!" Tom yelled as Wilma did her best to hold the image.

She was unsuccessful. In less than two seconds the screen was blank again. But they had managed to access some sort of a back-up locator system, and, unless that system was totally out of whack, it appeared that Wisdom had somehow managed to get to the Mojave Desert, not far from the spot he'd written about in his book.

Then, as Wilma handed the device back to Tom, she fingered another spot on the device. Once again it glowed softly, and a second scope came to life; this time, it was tuned to Sally Linker's signal. Although the background was extremely fuzzy, she seemed to be in fairly close proximity to Wisdom.

"Get L.A. on the horn, Tom!" Wilma shouted. "Or better yet, the Groom Lake people. They're closer. Tell 'em to check out a location in the desert northeast of Barstow as soon as I fax the coordinates. Why in blazes have both our lost chickens turned up in the Mojave? It can't be a coincidence! Linker's a trance channel, isn't she?"

"Yes, she is" Tom replied after scrolling though her dossier. "Maybe she's communicating with the aliens on Wisdom's behalf, though there's no known prior connection between the two subjects."

While Wilma and Tom were doing their best to enhance the images that had automatically been copied onto the super-computer's hard disk, a lab technician, a young woman named Helen Gardner, beckoned to them excitedly from where she sat staring at a console. "Dr. Gibbs, Look at this!" Helen exclaimed, pointing at the screen. "A California Highway Patrolman spotted Wisdom about two hours ago. It was on a county road northwest of Barstow."

"Well, I'll be damned!" Wilma said, peering over the woman's shoulder. "Was he alone? Was Ms. Linker with him?"

"No, Dr. Gibbs," the technician replied as she scrolled through the report. "He was a passenger in an older Ford Bronco driven by a young Japanese woman named Hoshimura, Kazuko Hoshimura. The officer cited her for doing ninety-three miles an hour! She showed him what appeared to be a valid Japanese license as well as a passport. The CHP man asked for the passenger's identification when he determined that the vehicle was registered to a person named 'P. Starbuck,' a local rancher, they think, although the address is a Barstow post office box. But the Bronco turned out not to be a stolen car."

By this time, the whole team was peering at the screen over Helen's shoulder. She looked up at her boss, who instructed her to send the Japanese woman's name, along with her driver's license and passport numbers, to their people in Japan.

Almost immediately, word came back from Tokyo that there was no such person as "Kazuko Hoshimura," and that the driver's license and passport numbers had never been issued.

Wilma squinted at the blank screen. "Could that Japanese lady possibly be—?"

Then she looked at Tom, whose eyes were once again fixed on the locator scopes. He was passing his fingers back and forth across the device, vainly trying to reactivate the signals.

"The countryside around there's pretty God-forsaken, isn't it?"

"Yes, it is that," he replied without looking up, although it's beautiful in its own way. I used to back-pack in that part of the desert when I was at Caltech. There are a few scattered ranches, many of them deserted. Maybe if we. . ."

"I'm way ahead of you, boy! We're gonna get to the bottom of this! Have the Groom Lake team go over that area inch by inch, if they have to. Especially any apparently deserted ranches. Get L.A. out there, too! This 'Starbuck' person, whoever or whatever he is—I don't think he makes coffee!—has to live somewhere in that area!"

Tom nodded. "I'll get on it immediately." Then he shot her a quizzical glance. "How about alerting Alexei? His team just might be able to help us, especially since we were kind enough to share our discovery with them. I wonder if any of their subjects have disappeared."

The stout African-American scientist hesitated for a

moment. "Yes, I've been wondering about that, too. Why don't you give him a call first?"

Tom nodded, then picked up the red phone that connected MJ-12 with its Russian counterpart. Five minutes later he hung up and turned to face his boss. "Alexei sends his greetings and says to tell you that all his subjects are accounted for. He says they'll keep their eyes pealed and will let us know if anything odd happens on their screens. What do we do now, Dr. Gibbs?"

Before she could answer, Helen once again motioned to her boss to come over and look at her screen. "Look at this, Dr. Gibbs! Our 'Wisdom virus' is really paying off! A few minutes ago, the San Bernardino County Sheriff's computer logged in a report from a deputy that he just discovered a driver named Cullen Wisdom asleep by the side of the road in the same Ford Bronco!"

The young technician made a couple of adjustments and continued scrolling. "Oh my God! It was on the same highway, about five miles north of where the Japanese lady got the ticket three hours ago! No mention of her at all this time. No citation was issued, but the officer ran a check on the man's license and on the registration. It's our guy, all right, Dr. Gibbs!"

Wilma shook her massive head. This new information was almost too weird to be true. What the hell was Cullen Wisdom doing asleep—and alone—on that desert highway? And where was Ms. Hoshimura, or whoever she really was?

A few minutes later Helen returned with more details, including the fact that Wisdom was carrying an international driving permit with a Tokyo address, and that the address on his California license was that of a mountain cabin that belonged to a Graham College professor, and which had been rented to a family named Smith for the past eight years.

"Well, Tom," she sighed, "I guess the time has indeed come to call a full meeting of MJ-12. The general can handle the details, though you'd better tell him to get 'em back here on the double, before Wisdom and Ms. Hoshimura, or whoever—or whatever—she is, get back together and decide to go somewhere else. And before we loose any more prime subjects!"

* * *

By the time Culley Wisdom finally turned off the county road onto the dirt track that led, after a great many twists and turns, to the safe-house, it was completely dark. When the massive butte they had so often climbed began to loom against the night sky, he turned off his headlights and cut his speed to little better than a crawl, picking his way among the potholes by the light of the full moon. Best not to alert whoever who might be waiting for him, although as he thought about it, he grimaced as he realized that anyone with the technology to pull a person through the top of a car and into a hovering space vehicle would almost certainly know he was there.

There was no sign of life as he pulled up in front of the shed that served as the Bronco's garage. The house was dark and there was a preternatural stillness about the place that caused him to shiver. He buttoned the top button of his shirt and turned up the collar.

The Subaru was still there. It was parked along side the barn that held Qaazi's flyer. The doors were closed and the lights were off.

Culley was about to exit the Bronco when he noticed a short figure emerge from the shadows and walk stiffly toward him. At first, he thought it was one of "them," but as the figure moved out into the moonlight he realized it was Sidney.

At the same time, he saw a luminous, egg-shaped object rise up from behind the butte and glide toward his position. It stopped about twenty feet away and slowly settled back to earth, coming to rest on three five-foot landing pods. The ship was totally unlike any he'd seen at the Antarctic Base, and he concluded that it must be a SESO vehicle.

Sidney stopped a few feet in front of the strange ship and stared at him, saying not a word. After slipping Qaazi's wand into his pants pocket, Culley slowly exited the vehicle and stood facing Levine.

He was about to call out to him when another figure suddenly materialized in front of the ship, a few feet from where Sidney stood. The creature, whose hooded, insect-like head, huge faceted eyes, and mottled grey skin were clearly evident in the moonlight, was soon joined by a second figure, and the two of them began to float slowly toward him. Both carried small tubular rods.

As they approached, he began to hear a voice in his head. It wasn't as clear as Qaazi's had been under similar circumstances, and the words and images were garbled. But if the Reticulans—he was sure that's who they were—used a procedure similar to the one the Pleiadians had used, he would soon be immobilized. It was now or never.

Concentrating as intensely as he could on the interface between the wand and his implant, he slipped his hand into his pocket, withdrew the device, aimed it as best he could it at the leading creature's chest, and told it to fire.

For the better part of a second, nothing happened. Then his target suddenly fell to the ground, twitched briefly, and lay still. The second creature immediately crouched down next to a scraggly yucca tree, but was obviously confused, and, by the time it was able to react, Culley had fired again.

Just before the second Other crumpled, it managed to discharge its own device. The Bronco glowed brightly for a fraction of a second and then simply disappeared. Both creatures were now lying motionless on the ground in front of the barn. He'd done his best to "tell" the wand not to kill, but it was by no means clear that the device had understood him. Slowly, cautiously, Culley walked to where the nearest Other lay, face down in the dirt.

CHAPTER TWELVE

Sidney still hadn't moved a muscle. He seemed totally oblivious to what had just happened.

Culley had just about convinced himself that the creatures he'd zapped were still alive-he could see a slight flutter their chests-when a light-filled opening suddenly appeared in the side of the SESO ship. In it stood another robed and hooded figure, its huge, faceted eyes staring at him so intently that began to feel slightly nauseous. In one three-fingered hand it held the limp body of a young child that he had no trouble whatsoever recognizing; in the other was a small tube pointed directly at the reversed Raiders cap that perched atop the child's head.

"My name is Djrnk. I am the commander of this vessel. Professor Wisdom, you will give the instrument you carry to our subject, Professor Levine, or the life of your son will cease to exist," the creature said in thickly accented, but all too understandable English.

Culley stood there open-mouthed, unable to move a muscle, as Sidney, his eyes still glazed, slowing walked up to him. "You-must-give-me-the-wand," the astronomer said haltingly, extending his hand.

Culley had no choice. Mechanically, he handed the instrument to his former enemy and watched dully as Sidney began to float toward the ship. It was like a bad dream that was happening to somebody else.

Then another figure suddenly loomed behind the female Other. It lurched forward though the portal, knocking Djrnk aside, and covered Adam with its body. "Sidney, for God's sake, zap her!" a familiar voice cried.

Levine hesitated for a fraction of a second while Djrnk began to rise, tube in hand.

"Please, Sidney, you gotta do what Sally says!" Culley screamed, his eyes bulging with fear and his mind doing its best to make contact with Levine's.

In what seemed like slow motion, Sidney turned stiffly and faced the SESO Commander. Djrnk's coercive power still held him. But something deep inside him managed to resist, and, numbly, he tried to concentrate on the creature who at that instant was aiming her device at the child.

A nanosecond later, Sidney's brain was penetrated by the combined force of Adam's and Sally's minds. His head seemed to explode in a million multicolored pieces, and the wand finally discharged.

Djrnk staggered forward and began to fall, but she managed to get off a ragged shot at the pair lying in the doorway before she reached the ground.

Sally's body glowed briefly, began to fade, and then stabilized. Adam, who lay beneath her, was less affected by the badly-aimed discharge, although it soon became evident that he'd also been severely injured.

As soon as Culley recovered his wits, he ran over to the SESO ship. Sally was still conscious, but the fading had begun again, and it was all she could do to remain solid.

For a brief moment, everything was frozen in place. "Did Sidney get her?" she asked weakly.

"Yes," Culley replied as he gently helped the two of them to the ground. "He did. And I'm going to finish her off! "

The intensity of the "explosion" in his head had knocked Sidney out, although he didn't seem to be seriously injured. Culley quickly retrieved the wand from the astronomer's limp hand and aimed it at Djrnk, who was still sprawled on the ground directly in front of the ship. The SESO Commander's black hood and high collar had fallen away, and the bright desert moonlight now fully revealed her bug-like physiognomy.

Sally was now slipping in and out of consciousness, as well as visibility, but Adam had regained his senses, at least for the moment. When he saw what his father was about to do, his eyes, which had largely reverted to their original Pleiadian form, widened and began to lift at the corners: "No, Father! Do not attempt to kill her! It will only make things worse. Please!"

Culley hesitated for a second. Then he slowly lowered the wand.

Adam smiled wanly and his eyes relaxed as a carpet of blackness once again began to enfold his mind. But he did manage to pick up his father's unspoken question. "We did not see Mother aboard their ship," he replied in a voice so weak Culley could barely hear it. "Nor did we sense per presence. But there is a—"

"Culley, look out! The bastard's aiming it at you!" Sidney yelled as he came to.

Culley whirled around in time to see a black-clad human being who was indeed aiming a SESO device at him. He immediately brought up his own wand and, without any conscious thought, discharged it in the direction of the threat.

The Man in Black quivered for a second and fired wildly, causing a section of fence to disappear. Then he fell to the floor just inside the doorway and lay still.

For a couple of seconds, Culley simply stood there holding the wand and staring dully at the body silhouetted in the opening. Then he crouched down and peered first at his son and then at Sally. She was no longer fading in and out, but had become pale as a ghost. Adam had, too.

Straightening up, Culley took a deep breath, pulled himself together, and pointed in the direction of the barn. "We gotta get out of here fast!" he exclaimed, glancing once again at Adam and Sally, who was wearing jeans and a top similar to the one Qaazi had purchased that afternoon, the sight of which made him even more anxious about his Precious One's safety. The Subaru was still apparently intact, but there was only one place where they could get the proper medical care, a place no car could reach. And, of course, he had to find out what had happened to Qaazi.

"Adam and Sally are in pretty bad shape," he continued. Then he glanced at the three tiny bodies that lay strewn around the yard and the larger one slumped in the open hatch. They all seemed to be breathing. "I don't know how long the bad guys will be out."

"Why don't you just make 'em disappear, like what they did to the Bronco?" Sidney growled. "Shit, if I'd had the power, I'd have vaporized that bug-bitch after what she did to Sally!"

Culley smiled and gave him a high-five. "Sid, you really came through in the clutch. I doubt whether I'd have been able to buck her power."

He and the astronomer began gathering up the SESO equivalents of Qaazi's wand. "Maybe I could have done better with this gizmo," Sidney muttered, half to himself, as he examined one of the tubes. Then he brightened and grinned broadly at his former colleague. "Wanna hear something funny? When that bitch was staring at me, her mind tried to convince me that Qaazi and all of her kind were their mutants that had gotten out of hand. But I couldn't buy it, ol' buddy. It just didn't make any fuckin' sense whatsoever!"

"Yeah, Qaazi told me about how they try to put this over on us. It's a bunch of bullshit!" Culley glanced over at the SESO vessel. "Okay, my friend," he said as he tucked one of the SESO wands into his jacket pocket. "Aim the damn thing at the ship and give it the biggest mental blast you can!"

Without another word, Sidney pointed the tube at the egg-shaped craft and began to concentrate.

Almost immediately, the SESO ship began to glow with an intensity equivalent to the noon-day sun. The light was so bright that they had to shield their eyes. After about five seconds the glow began to fade, and as it did the SESO vessel slowly disappeared from sight. By the time darkness returned, the only evidence that it had ever existed were the three depressions in the dirt left by the landing pods, which were clearly visible in the moonlight.

"Jesus H. Christ!" Culley muttered as soon as he recovered his composure.

Sidney uttered a low whistle. "Yeah," he said, "that was somethin' else, all right! They probably saw it as far away as Vegas. This place'll be swarming with cops and Lord knows what all before we know it. Lead on, ole' buddy!"

Culley nodded. "Okay, I'm gonna to try to use the wand to get us into the barn and onto Qaazi's ship. If it's not there, well, we'll cross that bridge if and when we get to it. The Subaru's still there, thank God!" He paused for a moment while Sidney wiped his girlfriend's deathly pale forehead with a handkerchief.

Culley picked up Adam and held him against his shoulder with his left hand. He then walked up to the barn door, which, as he suspected, was bolted from the inside. "Line up behind me. That's it, Sidney! Move in a little closer, maybe."

When they were all set, with Sidney cradling Sally's unconscious body in his arms, Culley aimed the wand at the door with his right hand and concentrated on the interface between the device and his implant. At first, nothing happened. But then he remembered Qaazi telling him that it was necessary to clear both the wand and one's implant before shifting to another mode, in this case to the translation mode. As soon as the new mode was in place, the wand immediately transformed itself into a ball of shimmering blue light, and they passed through the thick wooden door as easily as if it had been made of melted butter.

Once they were inside the barn, Culley heaved a deep sigh of relief. The flyer was still there. He commanded the wand to remove the tarpaulin cover Qaazi had found neatly folded in a corner of the barn, and, in a couple of seconds, the Pleiadian vessel was clearly visible in the moonlight that streamed in through the barn's high, clerestory windows.

Sidney set Sally down carefully on the concrete floor and stared open-mouthed at the silvery, disk-shaped object that loomed before them. He'd seen it before a couple of times, but never with the tarp off. "How do you plan to get the thing out of here?" he asked as he leaned forward and ran his hand along its smooth, outer skin.

"The same way we just got in: by translating it through the wall. That's how Qaazi got it in here the morning we arrived, while you were still a zombie. Okay, let's line up again and get aboard."

Sidney picked up Sally again, and in a few seconds they were standing in the main cabin. Culley strapped Sally and Adam in carefully as the seats recontoured themselves to fit the limp bodies. He slid into the pilot's chair and motioned Sidney to take the seat next to him. He began to concentrate. Qaazi had said that he'd remember the procedure if and when the time came.

She was right. Keying in his implant, he passed his hand across the instrument panel from left to right, as she'd instructed him, and the interior lights came up. After a second pass the outer rim started to rotate, the lights flickering from red to violet, just as he'd remembered from his previous trips in this vessel.

Then, without any effort, the codes popped into his conscious mind and he spoke them aloud. They were in the Pleiadian language, but he knew that they would program a course that would take them to a point directly above the Colony Headquarters. After one more pass with his hand, the landing pods retracted and the ship, now glowing with the same intensity as a transformed wand, began to move forward. It passed effortlessly through the wall and hovered a few feet above the ground.

A moment later, the rotation stopped, and the disk shot up into the sky. In less than fifteen seconds they were at the upper edge of the atmosphere. They felt no g-pressures whatsoever.

Sidney almost came unglued. "Motha fucka," he muttered. "We oughta be dead, shit, nothing but grease spots, after pullin' that many g's! Hey, did we get up to light speed?"

Culley grinned and shook his head. "That's what I assumed the first time, too. No, Sid, Qaazi says these babies can't go quite that fast. But she assures me they've got a lot of ships that can."

"Do you mind telling me where we're going?" he asked, his eyes glued to the viewport.

Culley made a wry face. "Well, Sidney" he said as they streaked southeastward at God only knew how many miles a second, "if I've pushed all the right mental buttons, and if nobody gets in our way—or shoots us down, or abducts us—the next stop oughta be the Bermuda Triangle."

* * *

Qaazi Qaan-gaa sat facing Jaahaap, her former Command Pilot, in the bubble-topped cockpit of a small, two-person Pleiadian flyer. They were hovering a few hundred meters above the Pacific, about three hundred miles off the coast of northern Baja California, and had both the sea and the sky to themselves. The rays of the late afternoon sun glinted like liquid fire along the disk's leading edge.

She'd had no forewarning whatsoever when, a few minutes after Culley swerved to avoid hitting a hole in the road, she suddenly felt the familiar onset of dematerialization. Only this time it was involuntary and of such force that she knew she was about to lose consciousness. Her last conscious thought was the fervent hope that the person on the other end of the beam was Jaahaap or at least another Colonial, and not Qaazgaa or, the Winged Serpent protect her, an Other.

When the blackness faded—she had no way of determining how long she'd been unconscious—she was vastly relieved to see Jaahaap's familiar face as he ran a floating sensor over her levitated body, its cyclopean "eye" blinking as it examined her from all angles.

Within a few seconds the robot had satisfied itself that no

injuries had been sustained, and she'd been automatically lowered to a seat. Shortly thereafter, she regained control over her bodily movements.

I have informed Waangaa of your current situation and he understands why it was necessary for me to abduct you. He sends his greetings, Jaahaap's mind told her, adding that the ship was on automatic, and at the slightest hint that a Native craft was approaching within visual or radar range, the cloaking device would immediately surround them with a fog bank.

"Are you really prepared to live the rest of your natural life as a Native?" he asked, switching to the verbal mode; his speech betrayed the tension his mind had effectively masked. "And is this 'revolution' that you and your cousin are about to foment—do not worry, I have no intention of betraying either of you—a sincere attempt to change our system or simply a 'romantic' gesture on your part? That is the expression the North American Natives use, I believe."

The corners of Qaazi's eyes leapt upward. How did he know? Was there a traitor in their group?

"No," he replied, "none of your co-conspirators has revealed anything to the Elders. But it is the only rational way to interpret your behavior. I must warn you that Qaazgaa already suspects what you have in mind and is quietly taking steps to counter it. As Waangaa may have told you—it is common knowledge at Colony Headquarters—he has asked me, and probably several others as well, to find you and bring you to him."

"Is that what you are planning to do?" she vocalized in return, her tension now almost unbearable.

"No. I have no intention of betraying you. I simply wanted to find you before the others did."

Qaazi's mind remained silent, and she made sure that her shields were firmly in place. She needed time to gather her wits about her, as the Natives put it.

As you well know, his mind whispered, *we were once pledged to each other, and our parents still expect us to mate someday, if only symbolically. So do mine.*

Our parents! she hissed, her thoughts crackling with emotion. *What right do they have to interfere in this matter? They barely knew us after we were sent to the Crèche. That is something else we hope to change. We have been here now for almost thirteen thousand Earth-years, and have successfully melded our biology with that of the Natives. Why is it so difficult for us to admit that we might profit by adopting an aspect of their culture?*

Jaahaap's deep black eyes locked with hers, and their minds fully coalesced. The barriers she'd erected began to fall, one by one. *I had the same childhood experience*, his thought-voice said, penetrating ever more deeply into her psyche. *We all did. You know that. It is our system, the Way of the Clan. Yes, I do think it is possible to learn from the Natives, and that is why I am not planning to turn you over to Qaazgaa. As your intended mate, even though I will not hold you to the pledge once this matter has been resolve, I have the Serpent-given right to put you under my protection. You would have the same right if the situation was reversed. Therefore, you are effectively out of Qaazgaa's grasp. He knows I have this right, but hopes that my loyalty to the Clan will supersede all other loyalties.*

What do you plan to do with me?

We shall go to Colony Headquarters. Once there, with my help-and, I suspect, also that of your ritual-father, as we have spoken about the matter-you will plead your case before the Council, clothed, I suggest, in something other than that bizarre upper garment. Perhaps, with my help, you can convince the Elders that your ideas are correct; such things have happened before. I had originally intended to bring in both you and your Native lover, but that would not have been prudent. A SESO ship was in the general vicinity, and the power surge produced by a pair of sudden, beam-assisted abductions would almost certainly have attracted their attention. So I left him behind in the vehicle, but made sure that he would remain unconscious for approximately three hours, which is also the time it has taken you to recover.

"I consider Professor Wisdom to be my husband, not simply my 'lover'!" she retorted sharply, or as sharply as was possible in Pleiadian. "He is the father of my child. And he very much approves of my costume. But I do appreciate your concern. Is he now safe?"

"Yes, at the moment I believe he is. And do not worry; I had neither the time nor the inclination to reverse the changes you have made in his implant. But the Others are also searching for the two of you, as well as your son. The boy now seems to be their prime target. I suspect that they intend to hold him as a hostage while they accuse you, and, by implication, the Clan as a whole, of breaking its own Sacred Rule. In return for his release, they will demand concessions that the Council is not prepared to grant. Qaazgaa is afraid that the end result might be a renewal of hostilities, which, of course, would be tragic for all concerned, especially the Natives.

"But we need to speak of more immediate matters. SESO began its search for you and the boy in Japan. However, as we speak, one of their ships, commanded by Djrnk herself, is now beginning to comb the local desert."

Qaazi turned so pale she almost became transparent. Could they possibly know the location of the safe-house?

Yes, it is possible, he replied as he assimilated her unshielded thoughts. *Their methods are extremely clever. Sometimes, as you well know, they—*

They both picked up the faint telepathic cry for help, as it was broadcast hurriedly on a wide frequency. Qaazi immediately recognized the mental signature: it was Sally's.

She quickly adjusted a scope and, keying her implant to it, attempted to fine-tune the faint thought pattern. Jaahaap mentally punched in a new program, and the flyer's outer shell began to spin. In less than five seconds they were streaking toward the edge of space at over eight thousand miles an hour. As they rose, she was able to pinpoint the source of the transmission, and her former commander locked onto it as best he could. So far, only the cry for help was audible, although seemed to be accompanied by an as yet unintelligible subtext.

The location appeared to be that of the safe-house!

"The sender is a Native female," Jaahaap verbalized. "Most likely a channel—I think that is what they now call them—by the feel of the transmission. Few of us are able to project that far. Your mind tells me that she is Jaazaanii's guardian."

Qaazi's eyes lifted again. "You are correct," she answered, choosing her words carefully. "Her name is Sally Linker, and she has extraordinary power to receive as well as send. Waangaa selected her for that purpose, among others. But if she and her Native lover have been abducted, then whoever has them must also have Adam. Please, oh Sacred *Gaandaa*, let them resist!"

"They will need more than the Winged One, I fear. But I am now getting a better fix on them. Your son and the female have joined together to transmit, although the carrier thought-beam is wavering. I think they have been sedated, together with another Native, one of their own subjects. Let me see if I can amplify the transmission."

As the Pilot passed his hand over the control panel, Adam's extremely faint thought pattern became apparent: *Mother . . . Father . . . Waangaa . . . any member of the Clan who may be listening. This is Jaazaanii. I—we, my companions, Sally Linker and Sidney Levine, and I—have been taken by the Others. Please help me! Please help us both!* His telepathic plea was accompanied by fuzzy memory images of their abduction.

Linking their own psi receptors, Jaahaap and Qaazi concentrated intently. Although some of the details were unclear, it appeared that the egg-shaped craft had appeared out of nowhere, catching them completely by surprise as they exited Sally's vehicle after returning from Barstow. The boy immediately realized what was happening and tried to warn Sally and Sidney, but it was too late, and the three of them were quickly drawn up and into the SESO ship. The last external image she was able to decode—it must have been a nanosecond before they were translated through the egg's outer skin—was that of a wide-eyed and obviously terrified Sidney Levine.

"Is there no way we can rescue them?" Qaazi shouted verbally as well as mentally. "Surely the Council would approve, as Adam—Jaazaanii—is of the Clan!"

Jaahaap gave the Pleiadian equivalent of a deep sigh. "It is not that simple," he responded slowly. "Assuming I could locate the SESO ship—remember what we have just seen occurred at least an hour ago—we might be able to defeat it if we engaged in an armed struggle. But in the process Jaazaanii and his companions might very well die. No, the best thing is for us to go directly to Colony Headquarters and report what has happened and do our best to prevent Waangaa from engaging in a rash act."

Qaazi slumped back in her seat, which immediately readjusted. "Is there any evidence that they also have Culley aboard the egg?" she asked after a long moment. Ironically, it had been Qaazi herself who had suppressed his locator beam.

"Let us see if we can penetrate it."

With Qaazi's help, Jaahaap fine-tuned the scanner as best he could. They were rapidly moving out of range, and they had to work fast. However, it soon became clear that there was but one other Native male aboard the ship. He seemed to be a SESO Man in Black, most likely the one she had incapacitated in Shinjuku Station and who had been dogging her trail ever since. But at this distance—Jaahaap prudently kept them just beyond the known range of SESO monitors—it was impossible to be certain.

At first, she was relieved. Culley was almost certainly not a hostage, at least aboard that ship. But then it occurred to her that it was probably only a matter of time before they or Qaazgaa's people found him, and that all that she and

Waangaa had worked for would be for naught, despite Jaahaap's kind offer to put them under his protection. And indeed, as they continued to scan, they picked up Culley's locator beam, which seemed to be heading in the direction of the SESO egg.

Dear, dear Culley, she mused. *Are you planning to rescue them? If you are, I love you for trying to do so, but it will be impossible. You do not know what they are capable of. . .*

As these dark thoughts percolated behind her mental shields, he began, for the first time, to question her motives. Maybe Jaahaap was right. Maybe she was a "romantic," a very selfish romantic. Then, out of nowhere, the same mournful wail she'd heard so long ago in the California desert and, more recently, in the Tokyo taxi sounded in her head. Only this time the coyote's "message," really more of an induced feeling-state than a true telepathic message, was different. *You are the Chosen One, it seemed to say. All will be well . . . all will be well. He has the translator and he knows how to use it. Do not fear! He will be there. Return . . . return . . .*

Qaazi was far too sophisticated to take this sort of thing seriously. "Prayers" to the Winged One were rhetorical and not meant to be taken seriously, any more than "messages" from phantom coyotes. It was most likely a mental aberration brought on by stress; she would ask her sister Jaanii to look into it when they returned to Colony Headquarters. Nevertheless, the message, mental aberration, induced feeling-state, or whatever it may have been was certainly comforting. Maybe something quasi-supernatural *had* intruded into her consciousness, something that would eventually explain why she and Culley had been so lucky, despite the current setbacks.

And then she realized that she did not have her translator, the device that Culley had come to call her "magic wand." She'd left it behind in her purse, which had been on the floor of the vehicle when Jaahaap pulled her out of it.

Yes, all might go well, after all, although she sincerely hoped that he would remember how to use the device. They would not expect a Native to have one!

It also occurred to her that her flyer was probably still where she'd left it, in the large barn. She doubted whether the Others would dare to destroy it. Perhaps, just perhaps, Culley would remember how to activate it. She thanked the Winged One profusely that she'd had the foresight to program his implant with Colony Headquarters' coordinates.

Armed with this new confidence, a confidence tempered by her awareness that her son's captors could still-indeed, most likely would-prevail, no matter how brave her Native lover was, she turned to face Jaahaap once again and implored him to return to Colony Headquarters as fast as his flyer could take them.

CHAPTER THIRTEEN

A thin crescent of light became visible in the east, marking what astronomers call the "terminator," the shifting line that marks the boundary between day and night on a planetary disk. Sidney Levine took a deep breath and then expelled it slowly. "I always had fantasies about being an astronaut," he said softly, "but this is majorly ridiculous!"

There was a fair amount of cloud cover, but they seemed to be over the Gulf of Mexico, heading straight for Florida and the sea beyond it. It was still night, although the crescent of light that rimmed the eastern horizon was rapidly getting brighter.

"Hey, Culley, do you know where that foul odor's coming from? It smells like three day-old shit laced with perfume and sulfur," Sidney exclaimed, sniffing the air. "Does it come from some sort of field? I mean from whatever powers this thing?"

"That's what I've been told," Culley responded with a grin. "It seems we're not the only ones whose technology sometimes stinks—literally, that is. If Qaazi were here she'd know how to get rid of it, but she's not and she didn't teach me that trick. So I'm afraid you'll just have to get used to it, Sidney"

He looked up from the viewer, greatly relieved that they'd managed to pass the vicinity of the North American Base, which was buried beneath the mountains of northwest New Mexico, without attracting any attention. "Qaazi says that they have a big underground base down there. In the old days they used to have 'fairylands' near major human population centers, but they've long since been abandoned. It seems we're getting too sophisticated these days for that sort of thing. She says the Others had them, too, which must have led to some tense situations."

"Yeah, like they were the evil trolls," Sidney scowled.

Culley nodded. "It would seem so, although the whole business is pretty complicated, and I'm only just beginning to make sense out of it. Remember, we've also perceived them as gods. And sometimes we—"

"Hello! It looks like we're standing still!" Sidney interrupted. "That's impossible!"

Culley had been looking over his shoulder at Adam, and he immediately followed the astronomer's gaze. They had indeed come to a dead stop, although once again there'd been no physical sensation whatsoever. He looked at his watch. Approximately twenty minutes had elapsed since they left the ranch.

The flyer hovered for about a minute, and then, without warning, began to descend rapidly toward the surface of the sea. Although they felt nothing, it was obvious that the ship was out of control.

Sweating profusely, Culley made a few vain passes with his hands across the instrument panel and did his best to project a mental SOS. "Shit! I've watched Qaazi maneuver this thing to a safe landing twice now, but she never got around to teaching me how to do it. I'd hoped that somebody down there would spot us and bring us in. . . ."

"*Mazeltov*," Sidney muttered, half to himself.

Then Adam opened his eyes and stared though a viewport at the surface as it rushed toward them. The corners of his now completely undisguised eyes immediately rose higher than Culley thought possible.

"Father, please listen to me! You must do exactly as I say," he said in the same weak but firm voice in which he had admonished him against killing Djrnk." They are trying to contact you, but Mother has programmed your implant in such a way as to preclude that kind of communication. I will interface my implant with yours and the ship's guidance system."

The boy paused for a moment and then continued speaking, his voice getting stronger with every word: "Pass your left hand over the instrument panel from left to right just above the line of purple lights. Yes! That is correct! Now, with your right hand, inscribe a half-circle on the right-hand side of the panel."

Their headlong plunge immediately slowed, and the flyer began to descend in the familiar "falling-leaf" mode as it adjusted to changes in the earth's magnetic field, just as it had during the two previous descents he'd experienced.

There was a collective sigh of relief. "I think now that I can relay the commands from Colony Headquarters," Adam went on after another brief pause. "Please, Father, you *must* key your implant to mine."

Almost immediately, Adam's voice began to echo in Culley's head, although the words were not his: *Your son has done well. He is to be complimented. However, now that you can receive us, we will assume control of the flyer and guide you the rest of the way. Do not be concerned, you and your fellow Natives will not be harmed. We have been expecting you.*

There was a short pause, during which Culley noticed several basketball-sized sliver globes dancing in the air just beyond the view-port. Even in the full light of the tropical dawn they seemed to glow with a light that reminded him of the transformed wand. Despite the gravity of the situation, he found himself recalling accounts he'd read of the mysterious "foo-fighters" that dogged both Allied and Axis pilots during the Second World War.

Then the globes positioned themselves evenly around the disk, and the entity whose words Adam had relayed entered his mind directly: *Please listen very carefully*, it intoned. *You must hold your left hand over the small blue light in the middle of the panel. Do you see it?*

Culley nodded both physically and mentally and did as

he was told. He watched the light turn from blue to orange.

All is now in order, the voice continued. Please withdraw your hand. Do not attempt to manipulate the controls again until you receive further instructions.

In less than a minute they reached the surface of the sea. There was a slight bump as they entered the water, but still no real sensation of motion as the craft sank deeper and deeper. Culley had witnessed a similar scene in the Antarctic, but Sidney others stared open-mouthed at the tropical sea life that streamed passed the viewports; the glow from the ship, augmented by that emitted by their luminous "escorts," illuminated everything for at least a hundred yards on all sides.

When they reached the bottom, the glowing balls disappeared and a huge "door" opened directly beneath them. As soon as the flyer passed through it, the opening closed, the water disappeared, and they floated down a dimly lighted shaft hewn from bedrock. At the base of this shaft a series of tunnels branched out in several directions. The flyer automatically took one of them, and for the next several minutes it moved horizontally.

As he expected, the docking bay was a high, circular chamber, also "unfinished" in that its rock walls were plainly visible. However, it seemed much smaller than the one Culley remembered at the Antarctic base, which was puzzling, especially if this was the Pleiadians' largest installation. In any case, theirs was the only ship "in port" at the moment.

As soon as the craft came to rest, a few yards from the side wall almost directly opposite the entrance to the bay, Adam's voice returned to Culley's head: *You must now pass your right hand across the length of the panel, from left to right. This will shut down the drive and attach the flyer to the Colony's life-support system.*

Culley did as he was told, and then turned to check on his son-only to find that after this last transmission he had lapsed back into unconsciousness. Sidney leaned over and stroked the boy's forehead, which seemed hot.

Meanwhile, as soon as the rotation stopped, a flexible tube snaked out from the sidewall and attached itself to the flyer's hull. After a faint click, the main hatch spiraled open.

For a moment, neither of them moved. Then Culley unstrapped himself, did the same for Adam, and, with his son cradled in his arms, exited the ship. Sidney assisted Sally, who had regained some bodily movement but was still not fully conscious and walked like an automaton.

In a few seconds they were out of the tube and floating along a dimly lighted, rock-cut tunnel which was fitted with the same luminous track, or "glide strip," that Culley remembered so vividly. Sidney had problems maintaining his balance, but still managed to keep Sally going.

There was something oddly familiar about the tunnel, above and beyond its resemblance to the entrance to the Antarctic base. It was almost as if he'd been here before. . . .

After about five minutes they reached an iris-like gate, which automatically opened as they approached it.

The chamber they now found themselves in was circular, about thirty feet in diameter, with a high, domed ceiling, and filled with a light that seemed to have no particular source. It was similar to the "lobby" at the Antarctic base, albeit much smaller. And it was totally empty.

Where was the hustle and bustle he remembered from the last time he'd been in such a place? More importantly, where was the Security post, with its keen-eyed Monitors, its scanners, and the rest of the stuff that almost done him in?

It just didn't make sense. This was, by all accounts, the largest and most important of the Pleiadian bases: Colony Headquarters. So why did they have the place all to themselves? Where was everybody?

As Culley had anticipated, a hologram depicting the Winged Serpent shimmered just under the dome. Sidney tilted his head back and gaped at the electronic image, which contained almost every possible color imaginable plus some that weren't. Culley, however, had seen such an image before, and he concentrated his attention on three irises that were set into the wall directly opposite from where they stood. Despite the absence of any overt Security apparatus, he was certain that their every move—and thought—was being carefully monitored, and that a "welcoming committee" of some sort would soon make its appearance.

He was right on both counts. After a couple of minutes, the middle door dilated and through it floated a tall, thoroughly human-looking male of indeterminate age whose finely-chiseled cheek bones, pale blond hair and sky-blue eyes seemed at first glance almost quintessentially "Nordic." However, his attire, a loose-fitting toga-like garment that rippled gracefully as he moved, could have come from one of the ancient Mediterranean civilizations.

"We're not alone anymore," Culley said quietly. Sidney tore his gaze from the shimmering "totem" and riveted it on the toga-clad figure. Indeed, he almost let Sally slip from his grasp.

"Who's the blond, Roman-looking guy?" he whispered. "I expected to see people that look like Qaazi, but he looks as human as we do. What's he doin' here?"

"He's one of their 'Native Companions.' They're human, all right, at least genetically," Culley replied, all the while keeping his eyes on the blond man who now stood less than a dozen feet away. So far, the fellow had made no attempt to communicate, although his face was wreathed in a vapid smile.

Then a most familiar mental voice began to caress a sheltered corner of Culley's mind. It was Qaazi! She was here, after all! But where? And why wasn't she here to greet him?

Dear, dear Culley! Qaazi's mind whispered. *Praise be to the Serpent that you have finally arrived. They said you were en route. I don't know how you managed to avoid capture by SESO, but you did, and I am so relieved!*

Culley's heart skipped a beat as the familiar voice echoed in his head. *Wha-what happened to you?* his mind stammered. *Who—*

It was Jaahaap, praise be to the Winged One. Do not worry, I am well, and we will soon be together.

He heaved such a sigh of relief that Sidney was startled and wondered if they were about to be attacked. Culley quickly reassured him.

But now is not the time to share our thoughts on these matters, Qaazi's mind continued. *The Companion will shortly escort you and Sidney to my temporary quarters. Please follow him, my love. Yes, I'm well aware that Adam and Sally are injured. Two medical assistants have been dispatched to care for them. Ah! I sense that they have arrived.* The iris-like door on the left dilated and two large-eyed androids, both about a meter tall, floated toward them, their stubby legs barely touching the floor. *They will take Adam and Sally to the—I think you would probably call it an "infirmary"—where my sister Jaanii awaits them.*

Yes, her mind continued after a short pause, *as you suspect we arranged for you to land at a rarely-used, secondary docking bay; that is why there is no Security. Any unauthorized ship attempting to land there would be intercepted long before entering the tunnel. And please forgive me for not meeting you in person. I wanted to, but Jaahaap insisted that it wouldn't be proper for me to be there, at least at this time. We are all under his protection at the moment. I'll explain what that means when I see you. But rest assured that your "goddess" loves you more than ever! Please tell Sidney that I welcome him too, and that he has nothing to fear. I must break off now, but we will be together again soon!*

Still dazed by all that had happened since they'd lost control of the ship, Culley acknowledged her message, adding that he loved her with all his heart and that he would give Sidney her greetings. Then he shifted his attention to the Native Companion, who, like the medical assistants, had not yet uttered a sound.

"I bid you welcome to Colony Headquarters," the blond

human finally said in extremely stilted but otherwise unaccented English. "I am instructed by my Mistress, Qaazi Qaan-gaa, to inform you that you are all under the formal protection of Jaahaap Qaan-gaa, and therefore not in any danger, nor will you be treated as abductees. May I be permitted to add that your situation is most unusual. I have never known any other Natives to be treated in such a fashion."

Although their "host" made no attempt at psi communication, Culley got the distinct impression that he was indeed having a great deal of trouble categorizing the fellow human beings he'd been sent to greet. In any case, after clearing his throat, he continued speaking in the same stiff and archaic fashion as before:

"Before we proceed any further, I should perhaps introduce myself. My name is Tertius, and I am, as Doctor Wisdom has correctly surmised, a Native Companion. I have been assigned by the Council to escort you to the place where my Mistress now resides. She too is under the protection of Jaahaap Qaan-gaa. Please give your son to the android now approaching you. Your companion is directed to release the injured girl into the custody of the other android. Once that has been accomplished, please follow me."

As Tertius finished speaking, one of the androids approached Culley and extended its arms. The boy floated out of his father's arms and levitated just above the entity's outstretched appendages. Meanwhile, the other android gently but firmly disengaged Sally from Sidney's grasp and did the same thing to her. Then they began to float toward the door through which they'd entered, one following directly behind the other.

When the creatures, who had been utterly silent throughout, disappeared, Tertius beckoned to them to follow him.

Culley started to glide forward, but was once again immobilized by fear, the same elemental, unreasoning fear that had gripped him that first evening in Tokyo when Qaazi was about to replace his re-programmed implant. For several seconds he simply stood there, rooted to the floor, staring with terror-filled eyes at the door through which the Native Companion was about to lead them.

I don't want to go through that door again, he told himself. *Please don't make me go in there!*

Sidney looked at him anxiously, waiting for him to move. "You don't look so hot," he whispered nervously, putting his hand on Culley's arm. "Is there something about this guy that ain't kosher? You know these people. Maybe we can make a break for the UFO, if it's still parked back there." The frightened astronomer glanced over his shoulder at the entrance to the tunnel.

But this time, Culley was able to overcome his fear almost immediately. Yes, he "knew" that he'd stood on this very spot when he was five years-old; he also "knew" that he was one of the last abductees to arrive via this particular bay, and he remembered the abject terror he'd felt when they'd brought him here, despite their best effort to allay it.

But that was then. This was now.

Deep inside his head he heard what sounded like the distant wail of a solitary coyote. It had to be his imagination, but the faint ululation somehow reminded him, in an almost dream-like way, that he and Qaazi had a destiny to fulfill. And that the first step toward the fulfillment of that destiny was to follow the white-robed Native Companion to where his beloved awaited him.

Culley shook his head and rubbed his eyes. "I'm okay now," he said. "The guy seems sincere, Sidney. Let's follow him."

And so, guided by Tertius, they entered Colony Headquarters.

Culley soon noticed that this part of it also looked similar to what he had seen at the other Pleiadian installation. There were the same corridors with luminous walls and ceilings and the same ubiquitous glide strip running down the center of the floor, although it was clearly a vastly bigger complex than the Antarctic Base. Indeed, the place was labyrinthine, and without Tertius they would have been hopelessly lost.

At first, they had the corridor to themselves, and Culley suspected that they must be traversing an out-of-the-way corner of the complex. Qaazi had said that they'd been directed to a "secondary" docking bay, which probably explained the absence of traffic. Eventually, however, they floated into what Tertius said was an "arterial" corridor, and Sidney encountered the first undisguised Pleiadians he'd seen other than Qaazi and Adam.

A pair of "Colonials," dressed in luminous blue uniforms, glided by in the opposite direction. Neither gave Tertius and his party more than a passing glance.

"So that's what they wear when they're on duty," he observed as he did his best to keep his footing. "I'll bet Qaazi's a knockout in her costume!"

Realizing that she'd never worn her uniform in Sidney's presence, Culley smiled broadly. "Yes, she is that!" he said proudly. "However, the ones straight from the home planet—I've only seen one or two of 'em—are much more exotic."

They soon encountered several more parties of uniformed Pleiadians of both sexes, all of them apparently Colonials, as well as more androids and a party of Native Companions. The latter were dressed in a fashion similar to their guide. Again, nobody paid the slightest bit of attention to them.

By this time, they'd turned off the main corridor and had stopped in front of what looked like a blank stretch of wall.

"We have arrived," said Tertius gravely, gesturing toward the wall.

Almost immediately a section of it began to shimmer, and within a second or two Culley's beloved Qaazi stood before them smiling as only she could smile. She was undisguised and in uniform.

"Dearest Culley! " she said, and threw herself into his arms. He picked her up and hugged her close. She kissed him passionately, so passionately, in fact, that he wished they could be alone, if only for a few minutes.

We will be soon, my beloved, Qaazi whispered in his mind, adding a mental image that all but melted him—and made him forget, for the moment at least, the stress he'd been under almost continually since he came to in the Bronco God knows how many hours ago.

Their guide was still there, looking as serious as ever, and obviously put off by this display of affection between a fellow Native and a member of the Clan. To Culley, Tertius and his kind were the ultimate "Uncle Homo Sapiens," as it were, and he vowed that if Qaazi's revolution ever did manage to get off the ground he'd do his best to convince her to put an end to this degrading institution.

Then his thoughts turned to Adam. Qaazi's mind quickly responded that, according to her sister, who was a medical-tech, both Adam and Sally were already out of danger. She added that she now thoroughly agreed with his assessment of the Native Companions.

Culley heaved another loud sigh of relief, hugged Qaazi a second time, and passed the good news to Sidney. As he did so, Tertius finally took the hint.

The pompous blond Companion bowed deeply. After a brief mental exchange with his Mistress, he floated off down the corridor in the direction they'd come, the hem of his white robe tucked up around his ankles to keep it from brushing against the glowing glide strip.

* * *

Once they passed through the wall—Culley noticed that no glowing ball of light was necessary in this environment—they found themselves in a rectangular chamber, about the size of a large bedroom in an average-sized American home, furnished with what appeared to be built-in couches along two walls. The walls and ceiling were still luminescent, although the light level here was much lower and easier on the eyes. There was a two-dimensional version of the Winged Serpent image in the middle of one wall, just above the couches.

On the opposite wall an intricate pattern of lights slowly ebbed and flowed, forming and reforming itself into an infinity of patterns. Culley's eyes were immediately drawn to it. "That is an example of one of our art forms," Qaazi said as she waved them to seats on the couch facing it. "We call it *aandii*, which means 'pattern-forming.' It keys itself to the implant of whoever lives here and reflects his or her mood. You see? As I speak it changes." She pointed to the lower right-hand section and smiled, whereupon the colors shifted from dark red and green to pink and yellow, and began to dance more rapidly. As she lowered her arm, the pattern resolved itself into a series of spirals and the colors became more muted.

She smiled at them warmly, and once again the colors of the *aandii* began vibrating faster, forming new and ever more intricate patterns. Culley found the kaleidoscopic display fascinating and had trouble keeping his eyes off of it. But finally he turned to look at Qaazi.

"I-I know I must look pretty grungy," he said apologetically, stifling a yawn and feeling the stubble that darkened his chin. "We've all had a hard day. But I'm sure you know all about it by now—"

"Yes, I do have a general idea of what happened," she replied quickly. "Please forgive me for being so insensitive. You must be very tired and in need of refreshment after your ordeal with the Others. How frightening it must have been! Praise be to the Winged Serpent that you had my wand!"

Then she turned to face Sidney. "I need to see the device you used against the Others' vessel SESO is demanding that their flyer and their Native Agent be returned—if in fact they were not disintegrated—from wherever you sent them." Both her voice and her eyes now betrayed a degree of anxiety that disturbed Culley, although he decided not to query her about it, verbally or mentally, until they were alone.

"Sent them?" Sidney asked sharply. "What do you mean

by that, Qaazi? I assumed that both the ship and the guy were vaporized."

"Not necessarily. Please give me the device."

Sidney reached into his shirt pocket, pulled out the SESO wand, handed it to Qaazi. She examined it closely, and then smiled. "It is as I suspected. You did not disintegrate their vessel! It is now parked somewhere in another universe, one of thousands we are aware of, and can eventually be retrieved, along with the Man in Black. This may prove important."

Sidney simply shook his head. He'd been doing his best to make sense out of the physics involved in both the possibility of retrieving things from other universes and the dancing lights of the *aandii*, but could make neither heads nor tails of it. "I'm still suffering from what has to be the worst case of culture shock—isn't that what you anthropologists call it?—on record."

"Sure," he went on, "some physicists, like Wheeler, Thorne, and Sarfatti have speculated that black holes open into what they call 'worm holes,' passageways that lead to other universes. But the idea that a person or even an object could actually pass through such a hole and be stranded in another universe or dimension is absolutely mind-blowing. And that thing on the wall—shit, there's no way to describe what it does, at least in terms of the physics I know."

"Someday soon, dear Sidney, you will be as familiar with the physics of an *aandii* as you are with those of a human television receiver. But now it is time for you and Culley to become refreshed in our cleansers. Later we shall share a light meal together."

Qaazi indicated the door that led to the cleansers. But Culley hung back, and when Sidney had left the room, he immediately queried her about Adam. Was there any further news? And what about Sally?

No, she told him mentally, she'd heard nothing further since he and Sidney arrived in her quarters, but Jaanii was an experienced med-tech and Adam and Sally were in excellent hands. She added that she wanted to go to the Infirmary immediately, but that Jaahaap had urged to keep as low as possible a profile until they appeared before the Council. That was why she wasn't there to greet him when he arrived.

"When my mind spoke to you in the entrance chamber," she said, shifting to the verbal mode, "I was able to pick up some of your memory of the conflict with the Others. You were all in great danger, and I am glad I did not learn of it until afterwards. Someday I must teach you how to do more 'tricks' with the wand, although you certainly did well enough on your own! And Sally certainly deserves our undying gratitude for what she did to save our son!"

Culley nodded. "She sure does! She's a remarkably brave lady! Sidney behaved well, too, as I'm sure you know. He's become a good friend indeed." He paused for a moment, and then asked her if she knew what happened to the Others they zapped, *I mean before Sidney "relocated" the ship.*

"Their people were only stunned, I am happy to say. Adam's advice was correct, by the way. Our situation would be far worse if you hadn't taken it. But oh, dear Culley, I have been so worried about both you and Adam!"

She hugged him again, and they kissed passionately. Culley's mind sent an extremely explicit image, and the *aandii* began to form erotic images.

How long will they be gone?

Not long enough, I'm afraid. . . . The Council meets shortly to consider our fate, and we must be there.

Culley winced. "Will there be any major problems? That is, in addition to getting the SESO ship and that MIB back?"

She hesitated, and the agitation he'd noticed a moment ago reappeared." Well, perhaps a few, but none that we cannot surmount. I will explain when Sidney returns."

He sensed that there was more involved here than she was willing to admit, and that beneath the confident mental image she was attempting to project lay a mountain of anxiety.

"Tertius said something about us being under Jaahaap's protection. What does that—"

I promise I will explain everything when you and Sidney return from your baths, her mind intruded. *Please trust me! The situation is 'fluid'—yes, that is perhaps the best way to put it—and there are some matters I need to check on before I can give you a full explanation. I don't want to alarm you unnecessarily.*

Needless to say, her mental tone didn't help his peace of mind, especially as the light pattern on the wall became dark and somber.

"How long before the Council meets?" he asked, changing the subject.

"About an hour from now by your reckoning. We use Niivaanaan time reckoning here. As I think I told you, the day there is slightly longer. I shall have to teach you the system someday. But you really must spend a few minutes in one of our cleansers; if I remember correctly, I told you about them that first morning at the safe-house. I guarantee you'll feel better, and I want you at your best when we confront the Council. It will also clean your clothes if you tell it to."

"Okay, the cleanser sounds like a good idea. I haven't had a bath for almost twenty-four hours. I must really stink!"

Qaazi laughed, although her huge eyes remained serious. "Did I tell you that Pleiadians have a less developed sense of smell than you do? That is why we do not mind the odor produced by the drive that propels our flyers. Yes, the cleanser includes a 'john,' as you are wont to call it, and it will even remove your embryonic beard. I'll have something for you and Sidney to nibble on when you get back. Indeed, if you had more of our genes, the cleanser would also provide nourishment, as even we hybrid Colonials are able to ingest most of what we need through our skins as well as our mouths." Before Culley's mind could even begin to react, her thought-stream informed him with uncharacteristic curtness that now was not the time to discuss this curious aspect of Pleiadian physiology.

He hesitated for a moment and then tried one more time to probe the reasons for her growing anxiety and tension, but her shields were firmly in place. It was clear that she wanted to hold off talking about what was bothering her, and he withdrew his probe as gently as he could. He knew Qaazi well enough by now to realize that she'd tell him when she was ready.

I trust you, his mind said.

Thank you, hers replied.

She led him into a small foyer, and two seconds later a female Native Companion appeared. "This is Drusilla," Qaazi said. "She and her androids will you how the units work. Has Professor Levine finished yet?"

Drusilla was blonde and blue-eyed and looked to be in her early-thirties, although Culley knew that some Companions lived very long lives. "He is almost finished, Mistress," she replied, smiling sweetly.

Qaazi smiled back at her and started to return to the main room.

Then she paused and turned to face Culley." There is one more thing. Before you go to the cleanser, would you please return my wand? It's still in your shirt pocket, I believe. I must also collect the rest of the devices you and Dr. Levine took from the Others. For the moment, the fact that you are all under Jaahaap's protection technically entitles you to carry whatever weapons you wish to carry, which is why they weren't taken from you when you arrived. But it would not help our cause if you and Sidney attempt to bring such items into the Council Chamber. They are ordinarily forbidden to Natives, and—"

"Not a problem," he replied and handed her the wand plus two SESO tubes that he fished from his pants pockets.

Qaazi stood on the tips of her toes and kissed him lightly on the cheek, much to the waiting Companion's embarrassment. "Thank you," she said with a grin. "Someday soon I hope you will have an instrument of your own. As you have discovered, they can be extremely handy, especially in a crisis! Now go and be cleansed! I leave you in Drusilla's extremely capable hands."

CHAPTER FOURTEEN

As soon as her mistress disappeared, Drusilla was joined by a pair of androids, one of whom opened one of several oval doors set into the glowing foyer wall and ushered Culley into a small cubicle. The other android silently demonstrated how to manipulate the equipment.

"I have heard it said that you can operate a flyer, and have fired a translator device at an Other," Drusilla said in the same stilted and slightly pompous language that Tertius had used, although it was obvious that she was extremely impressed by these accomplishments. Her amazement that a Native could do such things reinforced Culley's initial disgust at the servile role played by most Native Companions in the Pleiadian hierarchy. He doubted whether any of them ever got their hands on a wand or anywhere near the controls of a flyer.

"The principle here is much the same," Drusilla went on. "You must use both your hands and your implant. These lights turn on the sonic device. Just pass your hand over them. But first you must remove your clothes. My Mistress says that you want to clean them, too. Please place them in the container"—one of the androids indicated a basket-like object that jutted out from the wall—"while the device is in operation."

"What about the—"

"It is controlled by this light here." Both she and the android pointed to a purple spot on the console. "A tube will automatically appear and attach itself to whichever part you wish to void. The green light plus the proper thought pattern will activate the depilatory system, which is only for Natives, of course."

"Okay, I think I've got it."

"The androids can help you make the proper connections. Just visualize the procedure you need."

Culley grimaced slightly, remembering his first close encounter with Pleiadian androids. "Thanks," he said, "but I'll take it from here. I'll call you guys if I have any problems." Drusilla smiled again, and she and the tiny creatures left the small chamber without another word.

As soon as he was alone, Culley stripped and passed his hand over the purple spot. Immediately, several flexible tubes snaked out from the wall and attached themselves to his nether regions in such a way that all of his bodily wastes were immediately sucked out. It was an odd sensation, but not altogether an unpleasant one. In some ways, he thought, it beat the traditional Japanese *benjo* (his legs had never quite gotten used to squatting), although he doubted whether it would ever replace the good old fashioned American commode!

Then he tried activating the cleanser itself. He passed his hands over the spots Drusilla had indicated and concentrated his mind on cleaning his body. Within a few seconds the cubicle was filled with an extremely fine mist that reminded him of what they'd done to him ten years ago just before his first encounter with Qaazi. This made him shiver slightly, both mentally and physically, but the temperature automatically adjusted, and his mind was so full of so many things now that the memory of that first encounter didn't last long.

Following Drusilla's instructions, Culley placed his clothes in the "basket" and "told" the device to clean them. Then he passed the other hand over the green light and visualized the loss of his stubble.

After about thirty seconds the mist disappeared and the lights ceased to glow as brightly. He felt remarkably refreshed and invigorated. His face was smooth and felt as if it had been professionally shaved. By this time, his clothes, now spotlessly clean and wrinkle-free, had reappeared, and he quickly dressed, feeling a thousand percent better than when he'd entered the cubicle.

As he opened the door, he almost collided with Sidney, who was leaving the cubicle directly across from his.

"It's somethin' else, isn't it!" he said. "How'd you like the toilet part?" The astronomer laughed heartily. "Hey, I've seen some weird johns in my time. But that one! Hello, how high-tech can you get? Maybe we could work a deal to export them to Japan; bet they'd sell by the millions! Seriously, the whole damned system is remarkable. No wonder these folks got here more than ten thousand years before we had any idea that there might be a 'there.'"

The two of them returned to Qaazi's quarters to find that she'd set out a tray full of the bland tasting wafers Culley remembered eating—had that only been three weeks ago? It seemed as if a lifetime had passed, maybe several lifetimes.

She urged them to try the wafers as well as some small vials of the colorless liquid.

After he swallowed one of the wafers, washing it down with the contents of the vial, Sidney smiled at Qaazi and pretended to lick his lips.

"You guys are real gourmets!" he said with a grin. "You ought to open a restaurant in Beverly Hills! You'd give Wolfgang what's-his-name a real run for his money! But this stuff"—he gagged, holding up the empty vial to the light—"sure ain't Chateau Lafitte Rothschild! Qaazi, I do appreciate the food, but I gotta admit, I'd much rather be eating sushi. Do you folks ever eat that kind of thing?"

Qaazi smiled and brushed a stray strand of pale blond hair from her face. "Some of us have cultivated a taste for Native foods, but what you have just consumed is our standard fare. It is nourishing and will sustain you far longer than the raw fish dish you just mentioned." She paused for a moment and her smile faded as she mentally acknowledged Culley's silent but insistent plea for an explanation of what was really happening.

"All right, now that you've all refreshed yourselves and have assuaged your hunger with our finest cuisine"—she grinned at Sidney again and then grew serious—"there is something I must tell you. It is extremely important. As Tertius told you when he guided you here, we are all, myself included, under the formal protection of Command Pilot Jaahaap, my former superior. You will meet him shortly. Jaahaap is the one who abducted me. He is sympathetic to our cause, although I do not think that he will actually join us. You must—"

Culley leaned forward, and his slight stutter betrayed the anxiety that had once again begun to grip him. "Uh, Qaazi," he interrupted, "does this mean you're under what we might call 'house arrest' at the moment? Is that why you couldn't come to the lobby?"

"It is not quite that simple," she replied, adding a mental plea to please let her finish. "We have a very old and very sacred custom which permits a Clan member to place someone junior to him or her under that person's personal protection."

Culley noticed that she no longer made any attempt to control the upward movement of her eyes or the patterns formed by the *aandii*, which had become dark and angular.

"It means," Qaazi went on, "that the protector assumes personal responsibility for the protectee's behavior. That is, I can do or say anything that Jaahaap allows with impunity. If I violate a rule, it's his fault, not mine. The same holds for the rest of you. At my urging, he expressly allowed you to bring in the wands, and therefore, as I've already told Culley, they weren't confiscated when you arrived. Indeed, you now have all of the rights of a 'protected' Clan member. This is why Tertius was so impressed. To the best of my knowledge, it is the first time any Natives have ever been granted full protection. So I am not under 'house arrest,' as you put it, but I felt bound to honor Jaahaap's request that I greet you here instead of at the gateway."

Along with his free-floating anxiety, Culley felt a pang or two of jealousy and asked her mentally if Jaahaap's request had anything to do with the fact that she was still technically "betrothed" to him, and whether it meant he intended to interfere in their relationship.

No, dear Culley, she replied in kind, *he has no wish to interfere. So please do not be jealous. As I just indicated, Jaahaap is most sympathetic. The reason he abducted me so abruptly, without taking the time to ensure that you would not be affected, was to make sure no one else would. But there are some grave problems.*

Sidney, who hadn't been privy to this very private telepathic exchange, scratched his beard, then jumped to his feet and began to pace back and forth. "From what you just said, it sounds as if we're home free!" he exclaimed, interrupting Qaazi's train of thought. "If this pilot guy whose name I can't pronounce is willing to let you and Culley start our commune, they can't stop you as long as you don't break any of his ground rules. Right? Or did I miss something?"

Qaazi slowly shook her head, wondering whether either of them would ever let her finish explaining. "Again, it is not that simple. Protection is not absolute. It can be overridden by the Colonial Council. Of course, such a negative decision would immediately be transmitted to Supreme Elder Yaazdaagaa on Niivaanaa, who could void the Council's action—although I doubt whether she would see fit to reverse a clear majority. She will also make the final decision if the Council is-is—"

"Deadlocked?" Culley interjected.

"Yes, that is the correct word, I believe. The Council includes two SESO representatives, and they have formally requested that our protection be overridden. That's why the Council must consider the matter."

Culley gave her a long look. "Is there any possibility that they'll vote to override?"

She paused for moment and fixed her eyes on his. "Until a few minutes before you arrived at my door I would have said that we were, as Sidney so eloquently phrased it, 'home free.' But then I received word that certain Elders were ambivalent about my plans, and that they intended to support the SESO position. While you were in the cleanser, my half-sister Jaanii, the medical tech who is caring for Adam and Sally, contacted me to say that she has heard by what I believe you call the 'grapevine' that Qaazgaa has decided to speak against me."

"From what you've told me, I gather he carries a lot of clout," Culley said.

"That is a word I have not yet learned, but from the image your mind projected as you spoke, yes, he does have a great deal of 'clout,' especially among his fellow non-hybrid, Niivaanaa-born Elders."

"What will happen if our protection is overridden?"

Qaazi's anxiety was now betrayed both by the angle of her eyes and the stiffness of her speech, which had lost some of the colloquial fluency it had achieved during their sojourn at the ranch. "If Jaahaap's protection is voided," she said, choosing her words carefully, "I could be punished for violating the Colony's long standing rule against direct and open contact. Perhaps 'punished' is too strong a word, but it might mean permanent banishment to one of our less attractive outposts—perhaps to the one we have just established on a proto-planet of the star you call Vega—or I could be reassigned to one of the cattle mutilation teams and spend the rest of my life dissecting bovine reproductive systems. The worst part would be that my memory would be altered, and I would forget everything that has happened, including you and Adam."

By now the *aandii* had become almost totally black, and lightning-like streaks raced across it menacingly.

Sidney stopped pacing and turned to look at Qaazi. "What would happen to us? Would we be 'punished' too?"

Qaazi replied slowly, her eyes straining to rise even higher, "As far as you and Sally are concerned, in all probability they would erase your conscious memories of this place and return you to your homes as if nothing had happened. However, there is also the possibility that some or all of you would be forced to become Native Companions. Culley, I am afraid, would be the one to suffer this fate. There would be a long period of conditioning. When that part was over, your life spans would be extended, and it would be a pleasant enough life. But you would no longer be fully yourselves."

"Shee-it," Sidney mumbled, as he watched the thing on the wall explode with snake-like streaks of black light.

"I am sorry to put you through this," Qaazi went on. "The risk is real. But I think—no, I'm convinced!—that we can persuade them to reject Qaazgaa's argument. Jaahaap, of course, will speak on my behalf, and I hope Culley and the rest of you will, too."

"Obviously, I'll do the best I can!" Culley exclaimed as she transmitted an image of him speaking to a group of Pleiadians. Then he frowned. "But what if Jaahaap changes his mind and decides to withdraw his protection? Are you *sure* his motives are all that altruistic? I mean, it could be a way of getting you back."

"No!" she replied emphatically. "It would be impossible, even if he wanted to. Once protection is granted it cannot be withdrawn, and only the Council and the Supreme Elder can override it. That is why it is never granted lightly."

Sidney suddenly seemed to get the message, and his face brightened considerably. "So this means that if you and Culley can convince the honchos here that what you have in mind's a good idea, we really are home free."

"Again, it is more complicated than that. They could impose some restrictions, and the Others may try to add a few of their own, just to be disruptive, especially after what Sidney did to their Agent and the ship. But what you say is essentially correct. At least I hope that—"

She was interrupted by a faint chime. Qaazi immediately rose from the couch and refastened her Sam Browne belt, which she'd loosened while they were relaxing in her quarters, making sure that the Winged Serpent badge was in the proper position.

"The Council is about to convene," she said anxiously, "and we must hurry! I hope you are both prepared to be eloquent!"

Sidney smiled. "Well, Qaazi, as Culley's undoubtedly told you, I'm not too bad on my feet. God knows I've addressed my share of rallies and protest demonstrations over the years!" He gave the clenched fist, power-to-the-people salute, and attempted a high-five with Qaazi. She didn't quite know what to do, but Culley nudged her mentally and she grinned back at Sidney as their palms met in mid-air.

This lightened the mood considerably, and the *aandii* responded by once again becoming a colorful swirl.

"The path we must take to the Council Chamber will be very interesting, I think," Qaazi said. "It is different from anything you've yet seen. Follow me, please."

She led them through the iris leading to the cleansers and then through another that opened onto a narrow corridor. It led to something she called the "Central Plaza."

As they passed through the second iris and began floating above the ubiquitous glide strip, Sidney took off his gold-rimmed glasses and squinted at Culley while he polished them on his sleeve. "These things seem to be the only items those machines back there aren't programmed to clean. I guess Qaazi's people don't need specs. Shit, with those eyes, I'm not surprised!"

"They're something else, aren't they? They were the one feature I remembered most vividly after that first encounter, the one that you and Fyfe thought was a hoax and gave me such a bad time about."

Sidney winced. "Touché! I hope to hell these Council people will listen to us better than we listened to you back at Graham," he replied as he returned his glasses to his nose. "For what it's worth, I promise I'll do the best I can to help the cause, bad eyes and all!"

Culley grinned at the nearsighted astronomer, who still found it difficult to adapt to the glide strip and moved with what amounted to a series of ragged lopes. Qaazi told him it was because his implant didn't interface well with Pleiadian technology.

"Think of it as a faculty meeting," Culley said with a chuckle as he watched his former enemy struggle manfully to maintain his forward progress. "Sidney, you may not be the champ when it comes to the local means of rapid transport, but in years past I've heard you charm the pants off many a dean. I sure hope you haven't lost the knack!"

* * *

Qaazi led them through a translucent iris and into a wide, high-ceilinged corridor that was bathed in a vibrant, red-tinged light. On either side of the glide strip loomed a jumble of rectangular structures, piled atop one another like children's blocks, and pierced by "windows" and "doors" of various sizes and shapes. Crawling in and out of these openings were hundreds of tailless, lemur-like creatures with plump bodies and thin limbs culminating in stubby, four-digited "hands" and "feet." But what really set these curious beasts apart from any animal Culley and his human companions had ever imagined, let alone heard of, was the presence of a pair of stalks where their heads ought to have been. Each stalk ended in a large, bulbous eye.

"Ech!" Sidney cried. "What the hell are those things?"

As he stared in disbelief, one of the creatures leaned out of a window and fixed both of its stalks on him. Sidney abruptly stopped his forward motion, tumbled over a couple of times, and then hung there above the glide strip gaping at the creature, eyeball-to-stalk, as it were.

Qaazi laughed as she gracefully slowed to a stop and turned around to look at him.

"Do not fear them, Sidney!" she exclaimed. "They're harmless pets, a species native to Niivaanaa we call *raaghi*. This area is what you might call a zoo. We keep them here to remind us of thc home planet."

As he watched them cavort, Culley suddenly realized that the creatures had made no sound whatsoever, which certainly set them off from any monkeys or lemurs he was familiar with. He wondered aloud whether they had psi capabilities.

"Yes," Qaazi replied, "they communicate with one another telepathically, and we can communicate with them to some extent the same way. They have no speech capability, but if you concentrate, you can hear their simple thoughts chattering in your mind."

Culley did as she suggested, and soon began to receive a series of impressions, most of them friendly enough, from the *raaghi* that climbed in and out of the building incessantly. He was even able to sort out some individual images and to associate them with particular creatures. "I have a hunch that these critters don't do all that well on the surface," he said, "and that they need a special environment. How many troops, or whatever you call them, do you have here?"

"You are correct on both counts, Culley. This is the only 'troop' within five hundred light-years. And no, they do not thrive here under ordinary surface conditions. There is something in your sun's radiation that affects them negatively. Several thousand years ago we tried raising them on an island in the Pacific, but gave it up when they all died. We could probably solve the problem, but there always seem to be more immediate priorities."

Then she turned serious. "But we too have more immediate priorities. The Council will convene shortly, and we must not be late!"

As she spoke, Qaazi levitated herself above the glide strip once again and moved forward. The others followed, and in a few minutes they glided through another iris.

This time, they found themselves in a vast circular area that was suffused with by a much brighter, greenish light. It was hard for Culley and the others to estimate how large this space was, as the horizon was shrouded in a pale green mist.

But it had to be at least several miles in circumference. The chamber seemed to be roofed by a huge dome, although the exact configuration of the ceiling was difficult to ascertain, as it was obscured by cloud-like wisps.

They had entered the "Central Plaza."

A hundred yards or so in, the glide strip rose off the floor, and they soon found themselves soaring over a remarkable landscape. Beneath them they could now see a large body of what looked like water plus several areas of dense, pale yellow foliage. Strange, winged creatures, half-bird and half-fish, floated lazily in the sky far above them, while a variety of other animals, none of which looked at all familiar, darted in and out of the yellow vegetation. Other creatures, some with long, scaly tails, lay inert in small clusters along the bright orange "beach" that bordered the grey-green "sea."

Off in the distance shimmered a cluster of glass-like structures, some of them pyramidal in shape, that looked like a city, an Emerald City, Culley couldn't help thinking. As they rapidly approached it, the glide strip was intersected by other strips, and on several occasions Qaazi and her party were forced to pause while others, Native Companions as well as Pleiadians, crossed their path.

"The Plaza is a miniaturized version of a typical Niivaanaan landscape," she told them. "It is what you might call a park or a 'habitat.' The animals you see are also native to Niivaanaa. Not all of them are real, by the way; the flying things up there are actually holograms. The Council Chamber is not far now, but we must change directions here."

Qaazi led them in a ninety degree left turn onto another floating guide strip. One of pyramids that formed the "Emerald City" loomed directly beneath them. To their right, suspended in the air, were several large crystals whose many facets shimmered in the greenish light.

"They are part of the main computer," Qaazi said, gesturing toward the crystals. "The rest of it is housed in those pyramids we just passed. They are beautiful, are they not?"

"Yeah, they are," Sidney replied. "But what's that white thing over there, beyond the pyramids, or computer, or whatever it is? It looks like a giant bird." He pointed to his right.

"Ah, that is the prime symbol of the Clan. It is an image of the Winged Serpent, the *Gaandaa.* You saw a more common representation of it when you arrived. Remember the hologram? This is another way of depicting it. The image alternates between a bird and a serpent. At the moment it is in its full avian mode."

Culley, who'd been silent since they'd entered the "Plaza," was awestruck. "I remember reading a description of all this in a UFO book a while back," he finally whispered. "At the time, I thought it must be a hallucination. But wow! Niivaanaa must be a very beautiful planet!"

Qaazi turned to face him. "No, in all honesty it is not. What we have here is an idealized replica. Actually, conditions on Niivaanaa are usually misty, which is why they surrounded the park with the haze you see on the horizon. The few times I have visited the home planet everything looked gray rather than green. In a great many ways, Earth is a far more beautiful world!"

"That's hard to believe," he said, "But I'll take your word for it. Do you by any chance know the book I mentioned?"

"Yes. It was based on an account by a woman from the region you call Massachusetts who was brought here for deep conditioning; we sometimes bring our prime subjects here for that purpose. She managed to remember a great deal after being hypnotized, and the books that were written about her are among the most accurate ones any human being has yet written about us. Her abductions were supervised by Qaazgaa personally. I was not involved, but Jaahaap, whose name she misheard, by the way, participated in at least one of them."

"Didn't the woman—her name was Betty, if I remember correctly—have a profound mystical experience in front of that image? She also had one behind some huge glass doors, didn't she?"

"Yes, she did," Qaazi replied, "although the second incident actually occurred when she was much younger. We will shortly pass through those doors. But in the case you mention, the subject was already a deeply religious person, and we simply reinforced her beliefs. The *Gaandaa* image periodically self-destructs, and is replaced by a snake, which gradually transforms itself once again into a bird. Betty was by no means the first abductee to witness this transformation; it occurs several times each Earth year. Indeed, I believe there are several reflections of it in your mythologies."

Sidney burst out laughing. "Yeah, of course! The Phoenix myth! Have you guys brought a lot of Arizona people here?"

She looked puzzled, but chuckled briefly after Culley explained the joke to her. "Yes, Sidney, I'm sure we have. But seriously, the death and rebirth of the Winged Serpent is a fundamental part of our traditional belief system. It is over thirty thousand Earth-years old and is what Culley would probably call the 'primary' Clan myth."

The astronomer paused, caught his balance, and then turned serious himself. "Speaking of myths, I'm sure Culley's long since asked you this one, but are you folks still religious? I mean, do you believe in a god of some sort, or maybe a set of gods? And is one of 'em that bird? "

"That is a hard question to answer, Sidney. No, we have long since discarded the kinds of gods many humans still worship. Those beliefs disappeared long before we began to explore new worlds. We do, however, still share a number of sacred symbols, as well as some deep-seated communal rituals. As among your people, such things help us maintain our identity, and reinforce the solidarity of the Clan. And as you've guessed, most of these involve the cult of the Winged

Serpent, which Culley calls a form of totemism."

While Qaazi continued to speak at length about the nature of Pleiadian beliefs, they left the vicinity of the Great Bird and in a few minutes the glide strip began to descend gradually toward a huge building that shimmered even more brightly than the computer crystals.

"We have arrived at the Central Structure," she said as the strip finally came to an end in front of the building. Close up, it appeared to be a complex of crystalline cubes, one piled atop the other in apparent disorder, as if a post-modern, "deconstructivist" architect had designed it while high on LSD. "It contains the Council Chamber as well as the main computer display, called simply 'The One,' which we also use to condition subjects like the woman from Massachusetts."

Culley stared at the building and then turned to look Qaazi. His face paled, and he began shake. The fear he'd experienced shortly after their arrival once again bubbled to the surface as screen memories of this place flashed through his head.

I was "conditioned " here, too, wasn't I?

Dearest Culley, her mind replied. *I had hoped these memories would stay blocked. Yes, you were brought to the Central Structure when you were five years old. Remember, you were a special subject, destined for the Project. It was in that building that you received your implant. No, you didn't observe the Winged One become the Serpent, but you did commune with the One, which means that some extremely deep-seated things were fed into your mind. I do not know what they were, as that part of your record was not available to me. I was never told why. Perhaps you will discover them when we enter the Structure. But please keep in mind that this time you are here under vastly different circumstances.*

As her mind spoke to him, he could feel her tiny mental "fingers" massaging and soothing his troubled psyche, and some of the fear began to recede. But then, for the second time in less than three hours, the "voice" of the phantom coyote echoed in his head, and the indescribable feeling-state he'd experienced in the lobby took hold of him. Whatever it was, it was far more powerful than anything Qaazi could generate, even with a massive array of equipment.

Within less than a second, his conscious anxiety all but disappeared. Intellectually, it made no sense whatsoever; the prospect of becoming a Native Companion should the Council decide to override Jaahaap's protection was still appalling, but no longer fearful. Again, it was clear that he had a destiny to fulfill!

Unaware of the episode in the entrance chamber—he'd done his best to keep it from her—Qaazi signaled her astonishment at the sudden transformation in Culley's mental state. She quickly withdrew her mental "fingers," as they were now superfluous. "I had nothing to do with what just happened to you," she continued verbally. "Something else is at work here, Culley, something I do not understand. Perhaps it is The One. . . ."

Perhaps you're right, Culley's thought-stream replied. *Your Alien Raj certainly seems to work in mysterious ways, doesn't it?*

My what? her mind muttered. Then, as Qaazi picked up his mental image of pre-modern, British India, she slowly nodded. *Yes, there is indeed a parallel. It never occurred to me, even when we flew missions over that part of your planet before the war your people fought against that monster named Hitler and his terrible extermination camps, the ones I told you about. . . .*

She paused for a moment, and then smiled at him warmly. "But I am glad you are all right now," she said aloud. "Our protector has arrived."

CHAPTER FIFTEEN

Culley turned his gaze back to the crystalline building and noticed the presence of a tallish, five-fingered Colonial hybrid who had the air of an experienced field commander. Jaahaap reminded Culley of his own father, both in the way he bore himself and in the essential goodness that animated his hybrid alien features. Deep down, he suspected, the Command Pilot was as dissatisfied with his situation as his father had been.

Qaazi immediately spoke to her former commander in the liquid syllables of their native language. Culley didn't really understand what she said, although he did make out the words that meant "welcome" and "gratitude," as they were among the handful of Pleiadian words she'd taught him.

Jaahaap smiled as broadly as he could and inclined his head slightly. "I am most happy to become acquainted with Doctor Levine," he said in heavily accented English, "and to see you again, Doctor Wisdom. You may recall that we met ten years ago in the Mojave Desert."

They locked eyes, and for a second or so Culley found himself once again reliving the event that had started him on the road to this place. Jaahaap, he now realized, was the tall alien who had supervised his physical examination.

"At present," the Pilot continued, after a pause that allowed Culley to return his attention to more immediate matters, "you and your companions are, as Qaazi has explained, under my formal protection. I know that you now understand what that means, and that there are those who would override what I have done."

The Pleiadian stared briefly at the front of the building, aligning his implant with a mechanism embedded in the nested set of rectangular crystal panels. The panels soon dissolved into a million sparkling pieces, and he led them inside. As soon as they crossed into the building, a Native Companion appeared and fitted them with what looked like transparent glass *geta,* the wooden clogs widely worn in Japan.

"We must wear these inside the building," Qaazi explained. "They will allow us to move freely from level to level. You will see what I mean shortly"

As they glided through what appeared to be an endless series of multi-colored, crystalline mirrors, Qaazi explained that the slippers automatically interfaced both with something embedded in the crystals and the wearer's implant, and thus allowed complete freedom of movement, including the capability of levitation. Thus, neither glide strips nor wands were needed in this remarkable building, which apparently reflected the leading edge of Pleiadian technology. She said that the technique was still too expensive to be used extensively, but that eventually all of their corridors and living spaces would be "coated" with the substance embedded in the crystal panels and that their ordinary footwear would be fitted with a version of the device that activated the slippers.

"In time," Qaazi told them, "glide strips will become obsolete, just as your horse-drawn vehicles gave way to automobiles and other self-powered vehicles. No viable technology ever stands still!"

On all sides were shimmering kaleidoscopes of every color imaginable. Here and there, suspended among the crystals, were holograms of the Winged Serpent and a host of other images, some of them recognizably avian and reptilian, that Culley had never seen before. The overall effect was dream-like in the extreme. No wonder this place had made such a powerful impression on that lady from

Massachusetts.

"Yes," Qaazi responded verbally for all to hear, "the crystals do have an intense impact on our subjects. The building was in part designed for that purpose."

From time to time they passed other Pleiadians on errands of various sorts in the building as well as a sprinkling of Native Companions, most of whom stared blankly at their fellow humans. The presence in this place of Natives who were neither abductees nor fellow Companions seemed to be incomprehensible to them.

"You're right, Culley, these folks are weird, "Sidney muttered. "I hope to hell they don't turn us into 'em."

"I'm with you, Sid!" Culley snapped. A yet another wave of anxiety began to build, only to be dissipated by whatever—or whoever—was repressing his fear.

After several more twists and turns, both vertical as well as lateral, Qaazi suddenly stopped and cocked her head, which Culley had come to realize meant that she was receiving a telepathic message from one of her people. As she "listened," her heart-shaped faced was wreathed with e of the biggest smiles he'd ever seen. "Waangaa informs me that he and our loved ones will be here momentarily!" she announced eagerly.

A few seconds later, her cousin stepped through one of the crystal panels. He was followed immediately by Sally, still clad in her bare-midriff top and jeans, and Adam, who was now dressed in a standard Pleiadian uniform-except for his beloved black and silver Raiders cap, visor to the rear, which was still perched jauntily atop his tiny head. The effect was at once absurd and rather touching, Culley thought, as he scrutinized his son's appearance. Adam's undisguised face seemed paler than usual, but otherwise both he and the young woman who had saved his life appeared to be fully healed, at least physically. It was the boy's first visit to Colony Headquarters, and his huge Pleiadian eyes glistened with excitement.

Defying what he knew to be the Clan's deep-seated

aversion to public displays of affection, Culley picked Adam up and kissed him on the cheek, almost knocking off his cap in the process.

Although the lad's expression registered some embarrassment, his mind affirmed that the affection was reciprocal. *Yes Father*, his tiny mental voice whispered, *I do love you. Thank you for saving me from the Others! I very much want to live with you and Mother like a fully human son and I will say this to the Council! Colony Headquarters is certainly a cool place—that is the correct expression for one my age, I believe. It is part of my heritage as a member of the Clan, and I am happy to have seen it, despite all that has happened to us. But it is not my home.* He kissed his father spontaneously for the first time, melting Culley's heart as he returned his son to the floor.

Constrained by her culture and the circumstances, Qaazi was more reserved. She put arm around Adam's shoulder and kissed him lightly on the forehead. But it was clear from the way her undisguised Pleiadian eyes glistened that she was overjoyed to see that her son had fully recovered from his ordeal.

Sally, too, was wide-eyed, but unlike Adam she seemed listless and tired, and her movements were slow and deliberate, as if it took all of her concentration simply to propel herself from one crystal to another.

"Wow!" she said haltingly, shaking her head as Qaazi greeted her. "I-I never thought it would look like this. No wonder you guys call your home planet Nirvana!" A moment later she spotted Sidney, who lumbered over to her, his arms outstretched. "Hi, Sid," she said as he enfolded her. "Hey, thanks for everything. You really came through back there."

"Hi, Babe, he whispered softly. "You look great!"

"Well, I'm still a little shaky, but the med-techs have been wonderful, especially Qaazi's sister."

Sally disengaged herself from Sidney's arms without kissing him and glided over to where Culley stood. "I owe you one, too, Culley. I don't know where to begin thanking you. . . ."

"No need to," he assured her. "I'm sure you'd have done the same for me if I'd been on that ship. But are you sure you're okay?" The blonde channel had slumped against his chest and seemed to have difficulty keeping her balance.

"She will soon be all right," said Qaazi's half-sister Jaanii, who had just joined them, in the hyper-correct but stilted American English spoken by most Pleiadians. "Ms. Linker's—Sally's—injury was much more serious than my nephew's. Her implant's interface with her brain cells was massively disrupted, and it will take some time for the connections to restore themselves. She should exert neither her body nor especially her mind for several Earth-days."

Culley couldn't help noticing that Sidney was intently watching the young med-tech, who was slightly taller that her half-sister, but had essentially the same hybrid features, including the huge, luminous eyes that had so captivated him when he had first encountered Qaazi. He also saw Sally and Waangaa exchange furtive glances and wondered what sort of private mental messages they accompanied. Culley knew that Qaazi had told the channel about how Waangaa had impregnated her and that he still found her attractive. Could something be brewing here?

Qaazi sent him a very private telepathic message indicating that she, too, had noticed a budding attraction between Sally and her cousin, adding that she was concerned about the girl's energy level. *Sally has suffered a great deal and perhaps ought to be discouraged from taking an active part in the session, at least until she regains more strength. I would hate to see her remarkable psychic capabilities irreparably damaged by a prolonged mental exchange with the Council. She should also postpone any serious thoughts about a change of lovers until our status is clarified. Waangaa agrees. We'll do our best to dampen her mind, for her own good.*

She paused for a moment and glanced at Jaanii. *Yes, dear*

Culley, her mind went on, *my half-sister finds Sidney fascinating as well. She is attracted to his beard! Indeed, you and he are the first Native males she has ever encountered other than Companions or abductees whose genitals needed medical attention after their sperm was 'milked.' Ironic, is it not?*

Culley's thought-stream heartily concurred, but before he could frame a more detailed reply Jaahaap stepped forward and gently touched Qaazi on the shoulder. "It is almost time," the Pilot said in English. "We must hurry!"

As they began to glide forward again, their slippers elevated slightly above the crystalline floor, Sally's energy seemed to improve somewhat and she grinned at Qaazi and Culley. "You guys sure have one super kid! Adam really rocks! He didn't panic, and did his best to keep my spirits up, even when the bug-lady with the grey skin and that spooky Japanese guy had us so spaced out we could hardly move a muscle."

"Thank you, dear Sally," Qaazi responded. "But I know that you saved his life. Culley and I can never repay—"

"No repayment needed! There's no way I was gonna let 'em hurt Adam! Like I said, he's a super kid!"

Qaazi beamed and said something to her son in their native language. Adam seemed embarrassed, but smiled back at her as he and Sally glided along the shimmering corridor, hand in hand.

* * *

Helen Gardner, the MJ-12 technician who, earlier in the evening, had established the indisputable presence in the central Mojave Desert of both Professor Wisdom and "Hoshimura-san," the curious Japanese lady that Tokyo said didn't exist, glanced wearily at her watch. 11:46. Almost time to go home, after more hours than she cared to contemplate staring at her monitor in hope of gleaning more information about Wisdom, Hoshimura, and Ms. Sally Linker, whose newly recovered locator signal indicated that she was out there, too, although so far that lady hadn't had any run-ins with the law.

As she idly straightened a pile of print-outs—Helen was both compulsively neat and hyper-conscientious—she toggled to the screen that displayed Wisdom's and Linker's locator signals to take one last look at them before signing out-and almost fell off her stool.

Since the last time she checked it, less than ten minutes ago, Wisdom's signal had shifted over a thousand miles to the east! Indeed, it appeared to moving in that direction at upwards of 5,000 miles an hour! Then she noticed that Linker's signal was following exactly the same trajectory. Upon closer inspection, the trance channel's signal seems to be almost in tandem with Wisdom's, although it was extremely weak and sometimes disappeared altogether.

What in blazes was going on here!

Helen picked up the phone and pressed the red button that would instantly connect her to Dr. Gibbs anywhere in the world. The late supper, followed by what she expected would be a romantic interlude with her new husband, would have to wait. Her long evening was about to turn into a very long night!

In less than ten seconds Wilma's sleepy voice was on the line. "What's happening? Must be somethin' big for you to call me at this hour."

The technician assured her boss that it was bigger than big, and after she explained what was happening, all traces of sleep disappeared from the Nobel laureate's voice. "Okay, Helen, I'll be there as soon as I can. Please get a hold of Tom Johnson, too. He needs to know about this. Call me again on the cell phone if our boy stops moving. 'Bye, see you shortly. "

Helen started to dial Tom's cell phone number when she heard him talking to one of the other assistants. "Dr. Johnson! I didn't know you were still in the complex. I just called the boss. We've got an anomaly here you need to know about."

She quickly filled Tom in on the situation, and the two of

them, together with the other techs on duty, watched as the two blips paused over the eastern Caribbean and then slowly descended. While Helen called Wilma again to report the new development, Tom scratched his beard and peered intently at the screen through his thick glasses. “Bet they’re heading for Colony HQ, “he said softly, almost as if he were talking to himself. “They have to be in a disk. Were he and Linker abducted? And, if so, by whom? And why? Or maybe it’s Wisdom’s girlfriend’s disk and they’re simply out for a spin!”

Then the blips disappeared altogether. Both Helen and Tom know that the aliens had something down there that blocked transmissions, and they settled down to wait for them to resurface.

Twenty minutes later Wilma Gibbs arrived, wearing a purple sweat suit and sneakers. She took one look at the blank screen and said, ”I guess they’re still down there. Can you replay a tape of their flight for me?”

Helen clicked on a pair of icons with her mouse, and the two conjoined blips were once again superimposed over an image of the Mojave. Then they began to move rapidly across Arizona, New Mexico, and Texas and out over the Gulf of Mexico. After remaining stationary over the island of Bimini, they slowly disappeared from view, and she stopped the tape.

Wilma said, “We know where they are now. Let’s see if we can get a more accurate fix on the spot where they first come together.” Helen rolled the tape back to that point, froze the image, and did her best to zero in on the two blips.

“Here, let me see what I can do with it,” Wilma muttered as she took over the mouse. The spot was in the same general area they’d already identified, but as she clicked her way from one level of magnification to another, it began to take on more definition than ever before. Suddenly, an array of spidery dishes, the unmistakable indication of the presence of a major radio-telescope, came into view in the lower right hand corner of the screen, although the blips were still well above and to the left of it.

"Yeah!" Wilma shouted. "Just as I suspected! They've been holed up somewhere northwest of Goldstone, 'bout twenty klicks from it, I'd say. That's as close as we've come yet!" She turned to her young assistant. "Tom, get Groom Lake on the horn and tell 'em to keep that area—you can find the map coordinates—under close surveillance. I've gotta hunch they'll be back. . . . Yes, indeed, my bright young friend, we'll have a hell of a lot to talk about when the Committee convenes tomorrow morning!"

* * *

If the rest of the Central Structure was a brilliant kaleidoscope of multi-colored crystals designed in fair measure to induce mystical experiences among Native abductees, the Council Chamber itself was wholly functional. Except for its impressive dimensions, it closely resembled most of the Pleiadian rooms and corridors Culley had so far seen, both here and at the Antarctic Base. That is, the walls were faintly luminescent, and the low ceiling also emitted light of varying intensity from a variety of hidden sources.

Three ascending rows of ten semi-circular desk-like work stations filled one end of the large, irregularly oval room. All but two of the thirty stations were occupied by uniformed Pleiadians who didn't look much older than Jaahaap, although by this time he'd learned that it was almost impossible to estimate their ages at first glance. As far as he could see, there were no androids present, and Qaazi later explained that they weren't permitted to participate in any important Clan or Colony deliberations.

However, behind two of the desks in the front row sat figures whose grey, wrinkled skin and faceted eyes that stared balefully from under jet-black hoods left no doubt as to what they were. The sight of the SESO representatives made Sidney Levine shudder, and Culley wondered if they were attempting to manipulate the astronomer's implant. If so, he hoped his former colleague could put up the same resistance he had managed during the confrontation at the safe-house. Qaazi's mind quickly reassured him that the Others would be severely reprimanded by their own superiors if, while in the Council Chamber, they attempted to coerce anyone who was under a Clan member's formal protection, no matter whose implant he bore.

The only decorations in this otherwise unornamented room were a small hologram of the *Gaandaa* that floated in the air above a desk in the center of the front, and a two-dimensional geometric image that looked like a pair of "E's" back to back, which Qaazi said was a sacred SESO symbol. It was suspended directly above the two Others.

Facing the desks were several rows of low-backed chairs that rose from the floor like misshapen mushrooms. As soon as they sat down, the chairs molded themselves to their bodies, just as the flyer's chairs had.

After everyone was seated, the Chief Elder, who, as Culley had suspected, occupied the desk directly beneath the hologram, rose and addressed them in Pleiadian. Qaazi interpreted as best she could, but had difficulty putting his words into understandable English. The gist of it seemed to be that the Council had convened to consider a demand that Jaahaap's formal protection of certain Clan members and Natives be overridden. All parties present were invited to speak their piece, either verbally or telepathically, or any combination of the two. He invoked the blessing of the Winged Serpent and the SESO *Ummo*, as it was called, on all those who came before the Council.

It was clearly a ritualized, legalistic formula, and when the Chief Elder finished, Jaahaap rose and began to speak in the precise and heavily accented English they'd heard him use earlier. "Out of courtesy to my protectees, who do not yet understand our language, I request that this session be conducted in their native tongue, which I believe all of us here understand."

The Chief Elder, whose bulbous head, absence of hair, and almost invisible nose and mouth betrayed his unalloyed

Niivaanaan heritage, glanced to his right and then to his left. When it became clear that the majority of the Council did not object, he shifted to English even more precise, if less accented, than Jaahaap's.

"The challenge to our Cousin Jaahaap Qaan-gaa's right to grant protection must be considered against the background of two fundamental questions," he said, his huge, tear shaped-eyes fixed upon Qaazi and Culley. "One is whether our cousin Qaazi Qaan-gaa should be allowed to live with the Native called Cullen Wisdom, a subject, as his mate in a fashion consonant with the customs of his people, and be allowed to raise their offspring Jaazaanii Qaan-gaa, whom they call 'Adam,' in such a context. The second and much more fundamental question is whether this Native-style 'family' should become the nucleus of an experimental community in which our people and Natives would live as equals, sharing their respective cultures, including technology."

The Chief Elder paused and glanced down at something on his desk. From where Culley sat it appeared to be a small screen or scope. "In other words," he went on after raising his head and staring intently at each member of the group in turn, "Qaazi Qaan-gaa and those who would join her experiment contend that Phase One has lasted too long, and that it is time to inaugurate Phase Two. Am I correct in these assumptions?" His eyes once again bored into Qaazi's, and there appeared to be a brief mental exchange between them, which Culley could not decipher.

Qaazi slowly rose, and for a second or two she said nothing as the corners of her eyes quivered upward. Then, as Culley's heart skipped several beats, she managed to get them under control and, after glancing at the other members of the Council, she addressed the Chief Elder in the same measured and careful tone: "Yes, Chief Elder; that is the essence of my plan. I do hope to begin Phase Two, albeit on a small and experimental scale. It is why I violated Clan custom and took my son from the Antarctic crèche. In retrospect, my action may have been hasty, as it led to his abduction and subsequent injury by members of a Reticulan survey team."

She glared at the two SESO representatives, whose insect-like features remained impassive, at least to Culley, then once again locked eyes with the Chief Elder. "But despite what has happened," Qaazi continued, "I do not regret it. However briefly, my son has now experienced what few of our people have ever experienced: the sensation of being part of an immediate, nurturing family rather than simply a crèche—no matter how competently it is managed. And that is something he will never lose."

As Qaazi sank back into her chair, Culley detected a slight rustle among the Council members. Then one of the SESO representatives fixed his facets on Qaazi and began to speak. Culley was surprised at how clear and colloquial his English was; it was far better than either Jaahaap's or the Chief Elder's, to say nothing of Qaazi's, at least initially.

"Yes," the Other said, his voice betraying no emotion whatsoever. "One of our officers did detain the Clanswoman's child. But with good reason. The boy's mother and her Native lover"—he shifted his gaze to Culley—"are plotting to violate your Rule of Non-Interference. If SESO must obey this rule, then all concerned must obey it. That is what the Treaty says. Need I produce a copy?"

The Reticulan paused while all eyes in the Chamber swung in his direction. "I might add," he continued when he had their undivided attention, "that there was negligence on the Protector's part when he abducted the female and allowed a translator rod to fall into that Native's hands, which he used to injure a SESO crew. The crew is still recovering, however I see that the boy and the Native female who was caring for him at the time are sitting here in the Chamber and appear to be healthy."

He gave the closest approximation of a smirk an Other could manage and leaned back in his seat as his colleague whispered something to him.

Culley was livid. Shaking off Qaazi's attempt to retrain him, he jumped to his feet, pointed to Sally, and shouted at the insect-eyed humanoid. "Your captain, or whatever she is, almost killed that poor woman—and my son, too, for that matter. Look at her! She's barely able to hold her head up! You people ought to be ashamed of yourselves!"

Please, my love, Qaazi's mind cautioned as he returned to his chair, *do not upset them. It will only make matters worse. You will have a chance to speak soon enough.*

Culley's outburst caused a stir among the Council members, and once again the Chief Elder glanced to his right and left in an attempt to bring the meeting to order. After quiet had returned, he continued speaking: "Our SESO friends demand that we help them find their missing ship and Agent, which the bearded one relocated using one of their own devices. That we will do, although we do not feel that anyone deserves to be punished for what happened. There appears to have been provocation."

Then the Chief Elder turned once again to Qaazi. "I believe you plan to establish your experimental community in the country called Japan, am I not correct?"

Once again Qaazi rose to her feet. "Yes, Chief Elder," she responded evenly, "I had initially intended to establish the community you mention in the mountains of the main Japanese island. My kinsmen and I were impressed with the extent to which the local culture is compatible with our own."

She sighed aloud, human-style, and glanced lovingly at Culley. "But Doctor Wisdom has convinced me that the very homogeneity of Japan would make it difficult for us in the long run. It is also very crowded. In short, I now feel that it would be better for us to begin our experiment in a less crowded region of the planet, one that is perhaps more tolerant of small, unorthodox communities. I refer to the location in North America where Dr. Wisdom and I lived until I was abducted by Jaahaap, and where he and Dr.

Levine managed to rescue our son and Ms. Linker from the clutches"—Qaazi glared once again at the Reticulans, who remained impassive—"of SESO. The facility is no longer used by the Clan and the local technology is almost as advanced as that of the Japanese." As she spoke Qaazi broadcast a detailed mental image of the ranch and how she planned to remodel it—some of the ideas simply popped into her mind as she projected her thought-stream, but Culley quickly signaled his approval.

"All of us here," she went on, "including Professor Levine, Sally Linker, my half-sister Jaanii, and my cousin Waangaa, have committed themselves to the experiment." Qaazi turned around and indicated the small clutch of humans and Pleiadians seated immediately behind her, all of whom nodded and/or mentally signaled their agreement. "We promise you" she added after mentally thanking them for their support, "that we shall all continue to contribute to the Project and will collect DNA whenever any of the females conceives a child."

The Chief Elder stared at Qaazi for almost a minute before responding. "Would not the difference between you and your kin and the local population, even when you are disguised, pose a problem?"

"No, Chief Elder, it would not pose a problem," she replied, doing her best to maintain an even tone. "You must be aware that East Asians now live and travel all over the planet. We would not be conspicuous."

Qaazi's voice took on an edge Culley had never heard before, and the corners of her eyes shot upward. "There is so much we could learn from them, as well as teach them. Please, in the name of the Sacred *Gaandaa*, the prime symbol of rebirth and renewal, I beg you to affirm Jaahaap's protection and allow us to begin Phase Two!"

When she finished speaking, she remained on her feet, her body trembling and her fingers digging nervously into the arms of her chair. Her eyes flicked from one face to the other as she did her best to read the collective mind of the

Council. *They have all put up their screens, she whispered in Culley's head. Their mood is unclear.*

Hey, that's better than an outright rejection. You certainly gave 'em an earful! Let's hope they got the message. . . .

Then Jaahaap once again rose and faced the Council. "I thank the Chief Elder for his concern. In answer to his unverbalized question, yes, I endorse what Qaazi Qaan-gaa plans to do. That is why I have placed her and the others under my protection. You all know that she and I were once pledged. But I now formally release her to Doctor Wisdom, who will be the ceremonial father of all her children. In the name of the Winged One, I urge you to affirm my protection!" He bowed slightly in the direction of the Chief Elder, smiled a very human smile at Qaazi, and resumed his seat.

Well, he's certainly being damned decent about it, Culley's mind whispered.

Jaahaap apparently overheard this thought, for he turned his head toward Culley and grinned at him too. The grin seemed to say that he really didn't mind losing Qaazi to her beloved Native and that wished them well, though no words, verbal or mental, were uttered.

Once again, there was a long silence while the Council members conferred mentally among themselves. Then, with exaggerated slowness, Qaazgaa, the staunch, Niivaanaa-born conservative Elder whom Qaazi had warned him about on several occasions in the course of their odyssey, rose from his seat, glanced at the Chief Elder, and swept his huge eyes back and forth along the rows of desks. Culley would have sworn that the corners of Qaazgaa's tiny, slit-like mouth were turned down in what could best be described as a scowl, even though she'd assured him that only hybrids like her, Jaahaap, and Waangaa were fully capable of such a human gesture.

"Oh shit," he muttered, this time aloud, "here it comes. . . ."

CHAPTER SIXTEEN

After what seemed like an eternity, his four-fingered hands hanging limply at his side in what Qaazi later said was a characteristic, Niivaanaa-born gesture of contempt, Qaazgaa turned to face Qaazi and Culley. "I would much prefer to speak in the sophisticated cadences of our own language," he said calmly in mildly accented but hyper-correct English, "which I know our distinguished SESO colleagues understand extremely well. But I bow to the will of the Chief Elder and shall do my best to employ the crude Native tongue-there are so many of them!-in which he has agreed to conduct today's session."

Culley clenched his teeth. The *bastard does remind me of that asshole Fyfe. He's got the same condescending attitude, the same phony sincerity. I guess our cultures aren't really as far apart as I thought they were, at least when it comes to this sort of thing.*

I've been trying to convince you of that ever since Shinjuku, Qaazi's mind whispered in reply. *But soon you will understand why Qaazgaa is so dangerous. They pay close attention to him because he appears to be so reasonable—and so staunchly Pleiadian.*

"Yeah, I know what you mean," Culley muttered aloud. "That was the way Fyfe operated." He turned his attention back to the speaker.

". . . and as most of you know, I strongly oppose what Senior Native Affairs Specialist Qaazi Qaan-gaa plans to do," Qaazgaa intoned, his eyes still darting from one Elder to another. "It violates the most sacred and important of our rules, the Rule of Non-Interference, and ignores over ten Earth-millennia of experience managing the affairs of this planet and its inhabitants. More ominously, it violates the spirit, if not the letter of the Treaty.

"Qaazi Qaan-gaa's precipitous actions have already brought us to the brink of conflict with SESO, something that we have labored hard to avoid ever since the disastrous War which still sears the memories of several who sit in this chamber at the moment."

There was a cocking of heads, and some obvious telepathic interchanges among several Council members as Qaazgaa finished his sentence. He waited until the mental buzz died down before continuing.

"While I of course deplore what the Reticulans did to a member of the Clan, as well as to a Native bearing a Pleiadian implant"—the Pleiadian Elder stared with exaggerated balefulness at the SESO representatives—"I can understand their motives. If I were in their place, I too would resent what Qaazi Qaan-gaa and her co-conspirators have in mind. A Native-style family indeed!"

Qaazgaa emitted the closest approximation of a snort a Niivaanaa-born Pleiadian could emit, then paused for a second to let his words sink in. "It would be irresponsible in the extreme to expose one of our children, even a hybrid like Jaazaanii, to such a barbaric arrangement! Indeed, he has already been corrupted, as that ridiculous Native headpiece he persists in wearing in such a peculiar way clearly attests. I have researched its symbolism and find that it is associated with roving bands of young men that assault the innocent for no reason whatsoever." He paused again and stared intently at the boy, who averted his eyes but did not remove the cap. "And that vulgar clothing worn by the female Sally Linker, which, I have been informed, is also part of the Native wardrobe worn by our cousin, bespeaks a most unhealthy and uncivilized environment in which to raise a Pleiadian child."

This time, he fixed his huge eyes successively on Sally

and Qaazi, who, unlike her son, returned the Pleiadian Elder's stare, although as far as Culley could tell her mind remained a blank. "In truth, what our cousin proposes would be a giant step backwards," Qaazgaa continued, shifting his disapproving gaze to Qaazi. "It is redolent of what her grandfather tried to do in the land they call Mexico, or, more specifically, what that female technician, the one the Natives of the land called Babylonia eventually came to worship under a variety of names, attempted with her Native lover shortly before the War. Those adventures failed miserably, and this one will too, if it is allowed to go forward"

As he warmed to his subject, tiny beads of what looked like sweat appeared on Qaazgaa's ample forehead. He fixed his eyes on the humans sitting opposite him. "The Natives were not ready then, and they are not ready now," he went on, his voice oozing self-righteousness with every syllable. "They are still prone to do unspeakable violence to one other, as those conflicts in the regions called Bosnia, Kosovo, Rwanda, Israel, Ireland, and Afghanistan readily attest. Even in regions that are not at present engaged in full-scale genocidal warfare, ethnic, racial, and religious hatred are endemic, as was made abundantly clear when several adherents of the fanatical religion called Islam recently crashed commandeered aircraft into buildings in the cities called New York and Washington, thereby killing both themselves and thousands of others. Moreover, the constant degradation of the planet's environment, as well as widespread greed, rapaciousness, sexual perversion, and senseless violence of almost every sort, cannot be ignored. All such primitive traits must be eradicated before these creatures"—he stared in turn at Culley, Sidney, and Sally—"are ready to absorb our culture directly. We all know what happened to the Russian 'experiment' after our subject, the Native called Lenin, died. Several of us in this chamber witnessed it. Imagine what might happen if one of their leaders were able to equip an army with even crude approximations of our translators! There would be mass carnage, and we and SESO would be caught in the middle. The resulting tension could easily lead to renewed hostilities between our two races."

Qaazgaa hefted his wand ominously, then returned it to his belt. The SESO representatives seemed to be hanging on his every word. "Even if we could manage to keep our technology out of the Natives' hands, the impact of open contact would surely destroy their cultures. There would be mass hysteria, riots, and the breakdown of what little order these so-called civilizations currently possess. Indeed, by remaining aloof, we are doing them a favor!" The Niivaanaa-born Elder's tiny smudge of a mouth curled in what Culley would have sworn was a patronizing smile, even though he knew that the folks from the home planet were incapable of that universal human facial gesture.

"Yes," he concluded, "Phase Two will eventually come, and so will Phase Three, the final phase, but not until we have conditioned a vastly greater number of Natives to accept our way as the only true way. I therefore urge that Jaahaap Qaan-gaa's protection be overridden, that young Jaazaanii's transportation to Niivaanaa be implemented immediately so that he may experience a true Pleiadian environment, and that our cousin's reprehensible scheme not be allowed to proceed any further."

With that, Qaazgaa sat back and folded his long, spindly arms across his deep chest, his thin fingers tapping restlessly at each elbow. Culley could have sworn that Qaazgaa's forehead had turned red while he spoke of the possibility of death and destruction should their protection be affirmed. But there was really no discernible change in either his facial expression or, save for the beads of sweat, his skin tone; perhaps it was something he'd picked up telepathically. Or maybe he was still projecting his memories of Dean Fyfe onto their alien opponent. At any rate, the time had come for Culley to address the Council, and Qaazi did her best to encourage him: *It is now your turn, dear Culley; they have never before heard from a Native such as you. Do not speak in anger this time. Be eloquent, my love!*

Culley rose slowly to his feet, took a deep breath, and, as Qaazgaa had done, swept the room with his gaze. All eyes were on him now. Culley opened his mouth to speak, then, overcome by fatigue, hesitated for a moment and steadied himself by gripping the arms of his chair. "First, let me apologize for my earlier outburst. It was uncalled for and won't happen again." He stared evenly at the two SESO representatives, who remained impassive. "In any case, I'd be less than honest if I said I wasn't awed by what I've seen here and at your Antarctic Base. I'm sure I don't have to tell you that until recently most of us human beings, us Natives, have perceived you as supernatural beings and your technology as magic. Even now, as Qaazi well knows, I sometimes have trouble accepting that all this is real and that I'm not dreaming or having a religious experience."

He smiled briefly at Qaazi, projecting an image of her as the goddess Inanna on their private mental frequency, and then turned his attention back to the Council. "But intellectually, at least, I've come to understand that you're not gods and that what really separates us is a vast technology gap. I won't deny that I'd give anything to close that gap. Nor will I deny that portions of our planet would probably erupt in some fearsome nativistic movements, as we anthropologists call them, if and when Phase Two begins in earnest. I also can't guarantee that these experiments wouldn't be disrupted by terrorists. Lord knows, we still have more than our fair share of them, and many of them are indeed fanatical Muslims."

Culley paused for a couple of seconds to gather his thoughts. "Yes," he continued, "all of our major religions, including Islam, are largely based on woefully inaccurate and, for the most part, absurd attempts on the part of our remote ancestors to come to grips with the presence of the Clan and SESO. In fact, as I said a moment ago, I've had a problem coming to grips with it myself, and I'm the product of a modern intellectual tradition that prides itself on its rationality! But I can assure you that despite the inherent absurdity of their fundamental religious beliefs, the overwhelming majority of Muslims are decent people who deplore what happened on that day of infamy we've come to call '9/11' as much as you do. The same thing can be said about the majority of the people who live in the areas where the sorts of conflicts you mentioned have occurred or are still occurring, from Bosnia and Northern Ireland to Israel and the West Bank."

Pausing once again, he locked eyes with Qaazgaa. "As Qaazi indicated, there is so much you could teach us! How to cure AIDS. Or how to cure cancer, or how to ensure that every human being has enough to eat and a warm and safe place to sleep. Or how to tap new energy sources that won't pollute our environment. If you taught us how to do these things, the evils that you just enumerated would soon disappear. There'd be no more Kosovos, no more Rwandas, no more 9/11s."

Culley was about to add something about the morality of "raping" human females and then using their unborn hybrid offspring as DNA mines, and that it was as bad or worse than anything Qaazgaa had accused his people of doing. But Qaazi quickly intruded into his mind and warned him against it. *Now is not the time to bring this up, my love; remember, to most members of the Council this practice is not immoral. He will simply assert that the women aren't physically harmed, and that is, of course, true. To Qaazgaa and those who think like him, the degradation aspect is irrelevant. We will fight this battle when and if we convince them to affirm Jaahaap's protection. I also beg you not to mention what I told you about how they control the onset of our reproductive capabilities. That too is considered perfectly moral.*

He heaved a deep mental sigh, signaled agreement, and continued speaking-their entire mental exchange had taken but a fraction of a second-and there was no perceptible interruption in the flow of his words. "However, Qaazi once told us that although she knows vastly more about us, about our history and the evolution of our cultures, than we'll probably ever know, she's only just beginning to know us, that is, to empathize with what it really means to be a native of this planet. That's why, despite our present backwardness, I think that Qaazi's right when she says that we might have a few things to teach you, if you'll bother to listen to us. The human concept of family is one of them. In fact, Qaazi tells me that you yourselves once had a similar institution many thousands of years ago, Earth-years, that is. The way most of us humans see it, the family is a place where people nurture one another, where love can be freely expressed, not only between the sexes, but between father and son, or mother and daughter."

Culley placed one hand on Adam's shoulder and squeezed it tenderly. "I'm the father of a son by one of your people," he went on after a moment. "I gather that this, in itself, isn't all that unusual. But what is unusual is that the mother of that son—bless her!—wants to raise him with me at her side. I love her, and want very much to be at her side, as well as to be a true father to my son. So I urge you to approve Qaazi's request to let us be the nucleus of her experimental community. But if that's impossible, at least let the three of us live together as a family somewhere, even here! I'm sure you know what I'm trying to say; you've probably already scanned the thoughts behind my words, including the thought that my son's attachment to his new cap or the way he wears it doesn't mean he's become a member of a violent gang. Millions of decent young people wear such caps that way these days. It's simply a fad . . . just as the clothing currently worn by Ms. Linker and by Qaazi when she was abducted by Jaahaap"—he smiled broadly at the two women in his life—"is a contemporary female dress style and is in no way indicative of the behavior or character of those who wear it. In any case, I thank you for giving me the opportunity to speak. I await your decision."

This time there was complete silence, mental as well as auditory, as he slumped back into his chair, totally drained.

Sidney leaned forward and tapped him on the shoulder. "Way to go, buddy!" he whispered. "They seem to have heard you. Look at their faces."

"I'm not so sure," Culley replied as Qaazi's mental scan failed to detect any appreciable change in the prevailing mood.

"We appreciate your words, Doctor Wisdom," the Chief Elder said. "Does anyone else wish to make a statement to the Council?"

After glancing at Qaazi and seeing her almost imperceptible nod, Sidney rose and walked to the center of the room. "As you folks probably know by now," he said, facing the Chief Elder, "I'm a scientist. Not much of a one by your standards, but I do know enough to appreciate how much you have to teach us-not just about practical matters, but about how the universe really works, what time is, where energy comes from, and all that kind of basic stuff. There's nothing in this or any other world I wouldn't give to know what you guys know!"

Levine stared intently at the hologram suspended below the low ceiling, and then shifted his gaze to the Chief Elder. "That guy Qaazgaa over there says we're not ready for this knowledge, that we're still barbarians who do nasty stuff to each other. I can't argue that. Most of my European relatives died at a place called Auschwitz simply because they were Jews. But it was at that place that Qaazi first became to question the morality of one of your own rules, you know, the one that says 'thou shalt not interfere in Native affairs.' Well, she's now decided that time has come to discard that stupid rule, which probably sealed the fate of some of my Polish relatives, just as many of us are doing our best to see that what happened at places like Auschwitz never happens again. So we're really not all that far apart, after all, when it comes to fundamental morality!

"Nevertheless," he continued, his bearded chin thrust forward, his eyes blazing, and his voice tinged with a seriousness and passion that Culley never suspected was possible, "even if you decide that Qaazgaa's right and that we're still too uncivilized to be exposed to your marvelous science and technology, you've gotta let Qaazi and Culley settle down somewhere and raise their son! It's the only decent thing to do! I say this not as a scientist, but as a fellow sentient being. And yeah, I also think Adam's cap is totally harmless. Shee-it, I sometimes wear one that way myself!"

As the astronomer walked slowly back to his seat, Culley smiled and shook his head. The old Levine, the Levine he used to hate almost as much as he hated Fyfe, was long gone, and he had trouble recognizing this decent, caring man who had not only saved his son's life, but had just done his best to support their cause. After a long moment he said simply, "Thank you, Sid."

Qaazi smiled warmly at Culley's former enemy and gently patted his arm. "You certainly have become a good friend to us," she said softly. Then she looked at Sally, who had tears in her eyes. Her own eyes came as close to tears as it was possible for a Pleiadian's undisguised eyes to get.

Adam, who had sat quietly next to his father listening intently to all that was said, rose, removed the Raiders cap that had so annoyed Qaazgaa, and fixed his gaze on the Chief Elder. "I should like to support what my Father and Doctor Levine have just said," he asserted, his small voice sounding larger and firmer than ever before in the well-nigh perfect acoustics of the Chamber. "When Father and Mother took me from the crèche, I was not sure what to expect. Waangaa explained what was happening, and I saw the logic of it. However, after we settled into our life at the desert house, I quickly learned that my parents truly loved me, and that I loved them. It was a new emotion, but a most pleasant one. None of my previous companions has ever felt it, and that is sad. Please, Chief Elder, please let me live with my biological parents! I cannot and will not go back to life in the crèche. I would rather die!"

Sally hugged the boy, and tears streamed down his father's face. His mother sent him a loving and very private message, which made Adam turn red from embarrassment. But he also managed a wry smile.

Qaazgaa gave the Pleiadian equivalent of a shrug. "This is all very touching—I think that is the correct English word—but to let Jaazaanii live in such a fashion would violate ten-thousand Earth-years of Colonial policy and Clan tradition. As I said, the boy has already been heavily corrupted by his exposure to Native culture and desperately needs to be sent to the Home World. Only then will he become a true and productive member of the Clan. Once again, I urge you to override Jaahaap's protection!"

The Chief Elder held up his right hand and turned his head from side to side, absorbing the mental input of the Council. "I believe we have heard enough to make a decision," he intoned evenly, staring intently at the group seated across from him.

We have lost, Qaazi's mind whispered suddenly. *I'm picking up a preponderance of negative thoughts. They are all screened, of course, but the tone is unmistakable.*

Culley's face fell, and the other two noticed immediately.

"Well, we gave it a shot," Sidney muttered. "But what happens now? If you're right, do we all have to wear togas and that shit-eating grin? I'd rather go down fighting, if it comes to it."

"I agree with Sidney," Sally snapped. "What have we got to lose?"

Qaazi turned around and stared at each of them in turn. What had she done to these poor, helpless Natives? They had trusted her, believed in her, especially her beloved Culley. How had it all gone so wrong? She'd been absolutely certain that the Elders would listen to her!

It may not be quite as bad as you are thinking, my cousin, Waangaa's mind whispered in the special telepathic mode that they, as close lineage mates, were able to share. *As you explained to them, the Council will almost certainly let Sally and Sidney Levine return to their former lives after an extensive mind-wipe. Perhaps Culley Wisdom as well. I think even Qaazgaa might be persuaded to approve of this solution. If not, perhaps Jaahaap could intercede with the Chief Elder. But I agree that you and I will probably be sent to the Vegan colony rather than to a cattle research team . . .*

Qaazi felt drained of all feeling. Everything she had worked for had turned to dust, and her beloved Culley would soon be forced to forget that she ever existed.

If there had been an *aandii* on the wall of the Council Chamber, it would now be coal black. . . .

* * *

". . . and so that's where matters stand at the moment," Tom Johnson concluded. "Dr. Gibbs and I now strongly suspect that, until they flew to the vicinity of 'Oz,' Wisdom and the others were holed up somewhere in the central Mojave northwest of the Goldstone facility. At the moment, our people are operating on the assumption that the brilliant flash of light that lit up the sky from Las Vegas to L.A. yesterday evening is somehow connected with whatever they're up to. This is reinforced by the fact that there were several brief UFO sightings in the Barstow area both before and after the flash. But it's pretty rugged out there, and so far, I'm sorry to report, they've drawn a complete blank. Nobody's yet been able to pinpoint either the source of the flash or the exact trajectories of the UFOs. Is there anything you'd like to add, Dr. Gibbs?"

Wilma put on her thick glasses, looked around the room, and made eye contact with several members of the committee. "No," she said in that orotund voice that could intimidate even the most self-assured members of MJ-12, to say nothing of senators and presidents, "I think Tom's briefing has covered the main points pretty thoroughly, but I'll be happy to field some questions."

The table around which the twelve committee members

sat was made of solid oak and might have graced the board room of a Fortune 500 corporation. Along one windowless wall were ranged half a dozen aids, all of whom were hunched over small, portable terminals. Tom Johnson was the only non-member who occupied a place at the table—as always, at Wilma's right hand.

A three-star Air Force general, who was seated at the opposite end of the table, leaned forward and shot Wilma a quizzical look. "Do you think it's possible that Wisdom and the other subject—what was her name?"

"Linker. Sally Linker," she replied patiently.

"Ah, yes. Linker. She's a 'trance channel,' if I remember correctly."

"That is correct, General."

"Yes, well, as I was saying, do you think it's possible that Wisdom and Ms. Linker, as well as the Japanese woman, or whatever she is, will return to the Mojave in the near future?"

"It's hard to say, General, although Tom thinks they probably will, and, as you folks know, his instincts about things like this are generally correct." Wilma grinned at her assistant, who averted his eyes and fiddled with his glasses. "In any case," she continued, "we do, of course, know what both Wisdom and Linker look like. We also know that Linker drives a ten year-old Subaru wagon, California license number 1EFY256, and that the Japanese woman was driving a twelve year-old Ford Bronco, California license number 1SDZ525, that's registered to a person named 'Starbuck' whose home address proved to be a bare patch of ground. So far, we've refrained from asking the local law enforcement people to put out APBs on these vehicles; there'd be too many questions. But we are monitoring police reports, and our own people are keeping their eyes open. Groom Lake's on full alert, and the L.A. people are providing back-up. That's about the best we can do considering the security constraints."

She paused, waiting for further questions.

There was a general rustling and shifting of positions, coupled with several muted exchanges. Finally, the NSA representative raised her hand. "How about using a digital enhancer? I'm sure my people could come up with some sophisticated hardware that would allow us to—"

"No, Sarah," Wilma interrupted, her patience beginning to wear thin, "we've tried that. With all due respect, we probably have far more sophisticated equipment at our disposal here than you do. At present, there's simply no way we can enhance the images any further. As I keep saying, we're up against a technology here that makes ours look like it's still in the Old Stone Age."

Another pause, this time wholly silent.

The silence was finally broken by Lyle Steadman, a conservatively dressed CIA deputy director who reeked of Yale and the East Coast intelligence Establishment. "Have you tried making contact with them?" he asked, brushing back a stray strand of silver-grey hair that had fallen across his ample forehead. "Perhaps we could convince our diminutive friends to tell us what they're up to. After all, we've negotiated with them before."

Wilma sighed and glanced at Tom, who leaned forward and fixed his eyes on the speaker. "You must remember, Mr. Steadman," her assistant replied, "that they call us, not vice versa. The 'negotiations' you refer to were all on their terms. Dr. Gibbs and I are certain that they can tune in on us whenever they want to. Indeed, one of their monitors is probably picking up this conversation!"

He paused for a second and imitated the other man's gesture, only the strands that were pushed back were ten times thicker and blond. "Yes," Tom went on, "of course we've tried to contact them. But so far, at least, they've never answered our calls. When they want to communicate something, they let us know via the com-link, and if it's important enough, they transport Dr. Gibbs and her Russian counterpart to their headquarters and brief them. Questions are sometimes allowed, but rarely if ever answered candidly, or so I've been told."

Wilma chuckled softly. "Yeah, that's about the size of it, Tom. Now and then the Chief Elder answers a simple question, but usually she—that is, her hologram—responds with 'you will someday learn the answer to that,' or words to that effect. It's frustrating as hell, but there doesn't seem to be much we can do about it. Maybe someday, if they ever decide to launch 'Phase Two,' we'll be in a better—"

Steadman raised his hand again. "I think we've heard enough, Dr. Gibbs," he said evenly. "In light of these new developments, I think it's imperative that we brief the President. I call for a vote."

Wilma returned to her chair and stared at the ceiling for a long moment, then she swept her eyes across the twelve men and woman who were seated around the table. "How do we handle the Kennedy business?" she asked. "I mean, it's going be pretty hard to tell the Man that one of his predecessors may have been 'terminated' at the behest of this committee because he was about to reveal the truth to the American people. . . ."

"No one here today was a member of MJ-12 in 1963," the General retorted. "Besides, as I've often said, there's no reason to think that MJ-12 was involved. I'm sure our current commander-in-chief has enough sense to follow the rules and keep his mouth shut. I agree with Lyle. Let's bring him into the loop!"

There was a great deal of debate. Some members were for making an immediate phone call to the White House and telling all; others argued that the current policy should stand and that the President still didn't have a "need to know." Finally, a consensus was reached: The President would be briefed, but the committee's possible connection with the Kennedy assassination would remain secret. There was no reason to throw the Secret Service into a panic—or to set the stage for what might prove to be an embarrassing-and possibly catastrophic-investigation should "the Man" decide not to play ball.

Wilma still harbored some misgivings, not the least of them being how to tell her commander-in-chief that he was the first president since Kennedy to know the truth about UFOs without implying that that knowledge might have had something to do with his predecessor's demise. What if he asked her a direct question about it? They'd had several conversations about her work (her published work, that is) in the course of a reception after she returned from Stockholm, and she respected the man's mind; he was no dummy. She could keep secrets with the best of them, but was a terrible liar, especially when she was forced to lie to someone she admired.

In the end, Wilma agreed to go to Camp David, where the president was planning to spend the weekend. She would be accompanied by the general, Lyle Steadman, and, of course, Tom Johnson.

After a moment's hesitation, the formidable African-American physicist picked up the phone Tom placed in front of her and pressed a red button. "This is Dr. Wilma Gibbs. Please connect me with the White House. . . ."

CHAPTER SEVENTEEN

Culley stared dully at the shimmering hologram hovering above the Chief Elder's desk. The ethereal serpent-image writhed sinuously, its multicolored wings fluttering in the otherwise motionless and slightly ozone-scented air of the Council Chamber. There was no way any human being could resist the will of creatures capable of fashioning such an image, he mused, no way whatsoever. Sally and Sidney didn't yet fully understand the gravity of their situation. But Culley was now convinced that the three of them would be wearing white togas and vacant smiles before the "day" was out, despite Qaazi's attempts to cheer him up by sharing Waangaa's assessment of their likely fate. Indeed, the high probability that he would be forced to forget his beloved Qaazi, no matter what they did to him, was more than he could handle at the moment. And he hesitated even to contemplate what they might do to her and Adam. . . .

Then, out of the corner of a tear-filled eye, he saw a Council member whose rear-rank desk had been obscured by deep shadows rise slowly to his feet. When the Elder's classic hybrid Colonial features became fully visible, Qaazi suddenly stiffened. "That is Aavraa, my Ceremonial Father," she whispered hesitantly. "He was my mother's first 'husband.' I-I didn't realize he was here. I am certain he was not present when we arrived. Aavraa and I have never been close, but he has always been supportive. And he can be most eloquent. It's just possible that he has resisted Qaazgaa's poison and can persuade them to change their minds. . . . "

"Doctor Levine, you said earlier that your people consider you a scientist," Qaazi's Ceremonial Father intoned evenly, fixing his huge, unblinking eyes on the startled astronomer." As such, can you guarantee that if we teach you the rudiments of our science and technology that your fellow Natives will not upset the balance of nature on this planet, that you will not eventually render it uninhabitable through pollution, war, or over-population? You must remember that we have a far better grasp of your history than you do. I ask the same question of Doctor Wisdom, who would become my Clan-daughter's primary mate. Would not full-scale, open contact between us destroy your civilization and create chaos and disorder everywhere on this planet?"

Sidney gave Culley a quizzical look, then scratched his beard and adjusted his glasses while he searched for the right response. "No," he finally admitted," I can't guarantee that what we might learn from you in an open exchange of ideas wouldn't be used for selfish or evil ends. As you say, you guys know our history better than we do, so there's no way I can bullshit you here. Sure, wide-open contact would probably cause a helluva lot of disruption, at least at first. But that's Culley's field, not mine, so I'll let him take it from here."

He shot *Culley a glance that said: It's up to you now, 'ol buddy, hang in there!* as plainly as if he'd shouted it, and leaned back, letting the chair enfold him in its womb-like embrace.

Still shaken by the depth of the despair he'd glimpsed in Qaazi's psyche a few moments earlier and by the apparent hopelessness of their situation, Culley rose once more and stepped forward on unsteady legs. However, Aavraa had just given them a second chance, and he realized that Sidney's unspoken admonition, reinforced by Qaazi's whispered mental encouragement, was all that stood between them and the dreaded white togas.

"What Professor Levine says is unfortunately correct," Culley said after a moment's hesitation. "But if we start in a small way, with a loving, integrated family plus a few close friends and kin from both races, I think the disruption could be kept to a minimum. And if—"

Qaazgaa started to interrupt, but the Chief Elder silenced him with a baleful glance. Culley waited patiently until the mental buzz died down. "Yes," he continued, this time addressing himself directly to Aavraa, "if Jaahaap's protection is affirmed, I intend to become your Clan-daughter's first and only husband. I hope you have no objections, as we love each other deeply and in a way that's apparently rare in your culture. Anyway, among my people, it's customary for a prospective son-in-law to ask for a woman's hand in marriage. So I ask you for Qaazi's hand and your help in convincing the rest of the Council to let us get on with our lives." He returned to his chair and perched on its arm, staring intently at the Pleiadian who, he now began to hope, might someday become the alien equivalent of a father-in-law.

Aavraa returned Culley's stare for almost a full minute before responding. The silence in the Chamber was palpable. "I am not familiar with the details of your marriage customs, Doctor Wisdom," he finally intoned, "as I am not a specialist in your race. But I do understand the essence of what you ask. I hope that you and my Clan-daughter fully understand what is at stake here. Neither of your lives will ever be the same if you go forward with your plan."

The Elder's eyes contracted slightly, and Culley got the distinct impression that he'd made up his mind, an impression that was quickly confirmed by Qaazi. "However," Aavraa went on after a moment's hesitation, "Jaahaap Qaan-gaa has formally released her from her pledge, and if the Council votes to affirm his protection, I will ask the Winged One to-to 'bless' your union—yes, my clan-daughter's mind tells me that is the proper word in your language. You have also persuaded me that a Native-style family might well be a viable alternative to our traditional mating customs. I urge the Council to consider this possibility before they reach a final decision in this matter."

Aavraa returned to his seat and was once again swallowed up by the shadows. However, the psychic shadows that had all but devoured Qaazi's mind were fast disappearing, and she could barely contain her joy at this fortuitous turn of events.

The Chief Elder, who had remained standing while Sidney and Culley responded to Aavraa's questions, once again raised his hand. "It would appear that there is growing sentiment for reconsideration. Are there any more aspects of this matter that still need to be probed?" he asked in a flat voice that gave no overt indication of where he himself stood. There were none, although the pained expression on Qaazgaa's face seemed much more pronounced.

"We shall inform you shortly as to our decision," the Chief Elder announced impassively. "The Council session is now definitely at an end."

* * *

"For a while there, I really thought we were in deep shit," Sidney observed as they glided once again through the crystalline building. "But things seem to be looking up now. Ol' Aavraa really came on like gang-busters! He's one cool dude!"

Qaazi, greatly relived but still slightly shaken, nodded her agreement, as did Waangaa.

Jaahaap, who had been silent during the last exchanges, spoke up for the first time since they'd left the Council Chamber. "I did my best to probe the Chief Elder while you and Doctor Levine spoke. Qaazi and Waangaa did as well. We now think he was greatly moved by what you had to say in response to both Qaazgaa and Aavraa. And Aavraa's support will be very important. They cannot overlook the fact that he is her Ceremonial Father. Our chances now are far better than they were before he spoke. Qaazgaa, of course, will do his utmost to sabotage us."

"He reminds me of Fred Fyfe back at Graham," Sidney chimed in. The same kind of asshole! I hope he doesn't fuck us all up!"

Despite his fatigue and the effects of the emotional roller-coaster they were still riding, Culley laughed so uproariously that he almost lost his balance. "So you've noticed the resemblance too, eh?" he managed to gasp between spasms of laughter.

Sidney grinned wryly as Jaahaap led them through yet another crystalline panel. "Yeah, well, assholes are easy to spot, no matter where they come from. I used to be one myself, remember?"

"I remember. Boy, do I remember!"

"Speaking of assholes," the astronomer continued, doing his best to ignore Culley's riposte, "did you hear that Fyfe's now president of Graham? The Trustees gave it to him last year when that stuffy idiot who had the job when you were there had a massive heart attack. Old Fred finally got what he was after. They offered me the Deanship, but I wasn't about to wear a necktie every day, so they gave it to Roger Howell. You remember him, don't you? He's that incompetent guy that used to dress up in cowboy clothes. Ironic, isn't it?"

"Yes, indeed! Let's hear it for the 'Peter Principle,'" Culley muttered, shaking his head slowly.

Qaazi shot him a quizzical look. "I do not understand. Who is Peter and what is his principle?"

"If I remember correctly, he's the guy who said that incompetents always get promoted, which is why there are so many of them running things," Sally injected. "I'll bet it works here, too, as well as on your home world. That shithead Qaazgaa's living proof!"

Qaazi smiled at her and nodded agreement. She also heaved a huge sigh of relief; it was evident from Sally's strong psychic signature that she'd finally recovered fully from the effects of Djrnk's blast, which, Qaazi now realized, had come perilously close to being lethal.

They had just about reached what Waangaa said was an side exit from the wondrous building when Jaahaap suddenly stopped gliding, tilted his head to one side for a moment, and then turned around to face the others. "I have just received a message from the Chief Elder. The Council has decided that this matter is too important to be resolved here. Thus, no formal vote was taken. They are sending a full, holographic transcript of the proceedings to Niivaanaa for action by the Grand Council, who will deal with SESO directly. As a result, we are in what I believe you call 'limbo' at the moment."

The Pilot glanced at Culley, who nodded and mentally indicated that "limbo" was indeed the right word. "It will take the better part of an Earth-day to complete the transmission, and who can say how long it will take the Grand Council to make up its mind, or to complete negotiations with the SESO leadership?" Jaahaap continued. "They must be convinced to give up their objections to your plan, and to allow you to begin before they retrieve the ship and the Agent. I am afraid the only thing we can do now is wait for the response from the home world. The Chief Elder has promised to let me know as soon as it arrives."

"Hey, Culley, you were right!" Sidney said with a wry grin. "It was like a faculty meeting, wasn't it? The local honchos can't make a decision and are bucking it up to higher authority." He turned to face Jaahaap. "Do you know whether they attached any informal recommendation or statement?"

"Not officially," their protector replied as they removed their slippers and re-attached themselves to a glide strip. "However, I received the distinct impression that a slim majority of the Council are now willing to sustain my protection, and, if I am correct, that information will almost certainly be transmitted to Niivaanaa together with all of our statements and responses and the discussion that took place after we left."

"Then it looks like we're about to be in business, after all!" Sidney exclaimed.

"Well, maybe," Culley growled. "But I learned the hard

way a while back never to trust a committee. And that includes extraterrestrial committees!"

When they finally returned to Qaazi's quarters, via a shorter and much less spectacular stretch of the Central Plaza and several hitherto unfamiliar corridors, they discovered that the walls had been rearranged to form two sleeping cubicles. Each contained sections of the couches that had previously lined both sides of the larger room, as well as parts of the mood-reflecting light-painting.

Qaazi, Culley, and Adam took the largest cubicle, Sidney and Sally the other. Culley was not the only one who was ready to collapse from fatigue, and, except for Qaazi, who said she had business elsewhere in the complex and would return shortly, all were sound asleep within minutes.

It's sort of like laying out futon in the evening, Culley thought as he contemplated the new layout just before he dropped off. *Maybe she's right, after all, and we should set up shop in Japan—if we get to set up shop anywhere.*

A few feet away, Adam raised his small head and looked over at his father. "I would much prefer to return to the place in the desert. It was very enjoyable there."

That it was, Culley's sleep-shrouded mind mumbled. *That it was. . . .*

* * *

The next "morning"—Culley reckoned that it was around midnight, California time—the cubicles rearranged themselves back into a single room. There was no disruption of any kind; the walls simply slid noiselessly around them until the former pattern was in place. Culley was so tired that he slept through the whole thing and awoke to find himself lying next to Sidney.

After her "guests" had refreshed themselves in the cleansers, Qaazi suggested that they might be interested in seeing some sights they'd missed the previous evening. "Jaahaap will signal me immediately when the reply from Niivaanaa arrives," she assured them, "and it is a short trip to the Council Chamber from where I want to take you." Her mood, reflected in the bright colors and dancing spirals that animated the *aandii*, was upbeat, almost manic, a far cry from what it had been before Aavraa addressed the Council.

"Fine, let's do it," Culley replied between bites as he and the others finished a more substantial, but equally bland version of the "snack" she'd served them earlier. Sidney said something about missing his usual "power" breakfast, which caused general laughter and helped break the tension that was building as they waited for the "verdict."

They all commented on how refreshed they felt. Culley's watch no longer worked, but Qaazi told him he'd slept almost eight hours.

Yes, her mind told him privately, *I did help slightly. You were all tired, but your minds were keyed up. I made certain that a light "sleeping gas" was infused into the cubicles before I joined you. It helped me, too. Please do not tell the others, as it might upset them.* Shifting back to the verbal mode she added: "Last night, while you slept, I made the necessary arrangements. It appears that Jaahaap's protection gives us the run of the place, as Sidney might put it. When you've finished eating, please follow me."

However, just as they were lining up to follow her through the iris, Waangaa appeared and said he wanted to take Adam on a tour of the monitoring chambers. The boy's eyes widened. This was much more interesting than where his mother wanted to take the adults, and so they all arranged to meet later in the Monitoring Section.

The first stop on Qaazi's tour was what she called the "Museum of Time." It was housed in a series of artificial caves carved from the bedrock directly beneath the Central Plaza, and included a seemingly endless number of brightly illuminated, diorama-like "exhibits" that spanned over twelve thousand years of human history.

Every race and region of Earth was represented several times over, as was almost every culture that has exited since the first contingent of Pleiadians arrived at the end of the last Ice Age. However, it soon became apparent that the great majority of the exhibits, each of which occupied a fairly large niche, were devoted to the more complex human cultures and civilizations that have evolved in the last several millennia.

There were at least ten ancient Egyptian scenes. Some were of simple peasants frozen in the act of threshing grain or planting crops, while others depicted life as it must have been lived in the Pharaoh's palace. There were also scenes depicting the building of the Great Wall of China and the Pyramid of the Sun at Teotihuacán in southern Mexico. Another large group of scenes depicted daily life in both ancient Athens and ancient Rome; still others were devoted to medieval European castles and monasteries, the ancient Japanese court, and Ankor Wat, to say nothing of both American and Australian frontier towns.

Each exhibit, she told them, was carefully described on an instructional tape that could be accessed through the viewer's implant. Culley managed successfully to access the tape describing a scene in a Mongolian yurt circa the time of Genghis Khan, but all he got was an incomprehensible burst of Pleiadian.

"The people all look so life-like," Sally commented as they floated along a glide strip that paralleled the wall of one of the caves." Are they wax images, or something like that?"

Qaazi hesitated for a moment before replying. "No, Sally, they are not wax dummies. They are real human beings who have been placed in a form of suspended animation, as I think you term it."

"Are you telling us that all these people are really alive?" Sidney asked incredulously. "That's pretty hard to believe!"

"Yes," she replied flatly and with what passed for a frown among Pleiadians. "They are very much alive, and they could be revived with relatively little effort on our part. But to do so would deprive our Elders of one of their chief forms of entertainment: a trip to the Museum. Of course, it is all justified in the name of science. You see, you are not alone in these matters."

The chain of caverns was large enough to admit flyers, and as they floated from exhibit to exhibit several disks moved slowly past them.

"The flyers are carrying human subjects," their guide informed them. "A trip through this place is sometimes included in the conditioning process, especially if the subject has been selected for intense conditioning. There is an opening to one of the main docking bays at the far end over there." She gestured in the direction the taken by the flyer."

"Yeah," Culley observed. "I remember the woman from Massachusetts saying she saw something like this from the window of the disc that abducted her when she was a teenager, although when she recalled the experience many years later under hypnosis, she thought it was in a different place from the one where she watched the bird destroy itself. I can also see why she described it as an 'ice cave.' The crystals you've begun to attach to the walls and the ceiling might well give that impression."

Here and there they could see crystalline panels similar to the ones they'd seen in the Central Structure. Qaazi told them that eventually the "Museum" would be equipped with the same transport system that had been installed in the structure directly above them. The glide strips would be removed and viewers would be able to use glass slippers to float anywhere they wished.

As she described this project, which seemed to have a long way to go, she laughed sardonically, something Culley had never heard her do before. "Sometimes it takes us a very long time to complete a project, especially a project like this. You do not have a corner—yes?—on inefficiency!"

Sidney was awestruck by the scale of the Museum, as well as by its implications. "Shit," the astronomer said, his eyes riveted to a brightly lighted exhibit depicting daily life in what appeared to be a nineteenth century Jewish *shetel* in eastern Poland, "if I were an anthropologist, they'd have to pry me oughta here. My mother would have been in second heaven!"

Culley smiled. "Yes, I'm sure she would have. And someday I'd very much like to see more of it myself. But I'll bet it would take a month even to begin to get a handle on everything and everyone they've collected. Sort of like Disneyland . . ."

Qaazi winced as he said this. "At least your famous amusement park does not imprison people in the name of science."

"It could be worse," Sidney chimed in. "They could have killed and stuffed them. Maybe that's what the bug-people do with their human specimens."

"To the best of my knowledge, the Others do not have a place like this at their headquarters, which is perhaps a point in their favor," Qaazi responded dully, her eyes studiously avoiding the exhibits they were passing.

By this time, they had reached the last cavern and had begun to float upward toward the docking bay she'd mentioned.

As they left the Museum area her mood brightened somewhat. The bay was filled with flyers, as well as a fine gray mist that swirled in clouds around their feet and obscured distant objects. The environment in this part of the complex, she told them, was meant to resemble that of Aaraa, which, she reminded them, was the most important Pleiadian planet after Niivaanaa. The Aaraans, Qaazi explained, belonged to a separate section of the Clan that had its own symbols and rituals, although they also venerated the Winged Serpent. "Their planet is renowned for two things: a thick and almost perpetual layer of mist, far denser than the one that envelopes Niivaanaa, and excellent pilots. Indeed, the majority of our pilots, Jaahaap included, are descended from Aaraans who settled here in the early days of the Colony."

"Maybe their ancestors evolved better eyes as a result of having to peer through all that fog," Sidney observed, his tongue firmly in his cheek.

Qaazi laughed softly. "Perhaps you're right, Sidney. It is

as good a theory as any."

The misty docking bay, which seemed more like a storage area than an active port, was an interchange point, and they shifted to another glide strip that snaked between the parked flyers-some of them were hovering, others were resting on their landing pods-and toward another of those iris-gates that marked the boundary between zones.

"If I remember correctly, the Massachusetts lady visited this area too," Culley observed. "Were some of her abductors Aaraans, in addition to the pilot, of course?"

"I'm not sure," Qaazi responded dryly as she hovered above the strip, "You will have to ask Qaazgaa. He was in personal charge of that mission. Although now that you mention it I do recall that an Aaraan Native Affairs Specialist called Joohoop did like to bring his subjects in through here. As I recall, he was attached to Qaazgaa's own team for a while a few decades ago. Perhaps she did not misinterpret Jaahaap's name, after all."

She rubbed one of her eyes, and Culley noticed for the first time that she seemed tired. Not forlorn and hopeless, as she had the previous day in the Council Chamber, despite fact that their fate still technically hung in the balance. No, her eyes were faintly rimmed with red and their corners seemed, if anything, to sag slightly. She didn't seem sick; it was as if she simply hadn't gotten enough sleep.

You are correct, Qaazi whispered softly deep within his head. *I did not sleep very long last night, and according to our sleep-cycle pattern, I should have. As I've told you, we don't need as much rest as you do, but there are times when it is essential. Last night was one of them, unfortunately.*

Yeah, that's right. You were gone when I fell asleep. Where did you go? What time did you get back? He did his best to probe these matters, but her screens were firmly in place.

Please, dear Culley, be patient with me. No, I am not ill! I am totally healthy! I will share everything with you as soon as I have all the necessary data.

Okay, his mind responded. He knew Qaazi well enough by now to realize that further attempts to dig whatever it was out of her would be futile. She'd tell him about it sooner or later, and from the positive aura that surrounded her thoughts, "it" was almost certainly good news of some sort. So he turned his attention to what Sidney, unaware of this exchange, had been saying.

". . . there's something about all this I still don't completely understand," the astronomer mused. "Why didn't your ancestors simply settle here? When they first arrived there weren't that many of us, and we were pretty primitive. It would have been easy to eliminate us. Instead, you set up a long-term scientific research project, and later defended us from another bunch of ETs who wanted to do what I just said. Why? All this happened long before you realized you needed our DNA, didn't it?"

Qaazi nodded her head; most of the signs of fatigue he'd noticed earlier were gone. *What an amazing display of bio-feedback!* he mused. *The only thing she can't seem to do is control the corners of her eyes.*

She ignored Culley's unspoken thoughts and replied directly to Sidney's question: "You must realize that by the time we discovered you, we had long since colonized Aaraa and several other Pleiadian worlds. At that time, we had no need of your DNA, nor another home so far removed from our origins. But I guess the 'bottom line' here, as your people are so fond of saying lately, is that humans were on the threshold of a cultural evolution that would likely parallel our own. Such a race deserved to be studied and helped along now and then, rather than wiped out. That's why we opposed, and still oppose, the goals of the Others. Perhaps someday—"

Qaazi suddenly stopped moving and hung in mid-air for a few seconds without saying a word. Then the corners of her eyes began to dance upward. "Jaahaap tells me that word has come from Niivaanaa!" she exclaimed. We must hurry to the Council Chamber! Waangaa and Adam will meet us there."

* * *

As Qaazi and her human companions passed the image of the Great Bird their way the Central Structure, this time by yet another route, she found herself addressing a formulaic plea to the ancient totem in that secret place in her brain were even Culley couldn't penetrate. *Please, dear Winged-One-Who-Becomes-a-Serpent, whom we of the Clan have venerated since the beginning of time, please make them see the worth of what we propose, and how dearly I love this human and the child we have made together. I beg you!*

As soon as these thoughts had formed, she received the distinct impression that the Great Bird had heard her secret plea—it wasn't really a prayer in the Native sense—and had already done something about it. Indeed, she thought she heard the creature say that she had a great destiny to fulfill and that it would do its best to help her.

This is superstitious nonsense, she immediately told herself. *The Bird in all of its manifestations, including its Serpent incarnation, is but a sacred symbol that connects us with our remote past. Nothing more!*

But she couldn't shake the feeling that something was working on her behalf, and that she, Adam, and her beloved Culley would soon be allowed to begin their great experiment.

As the totem image disappeared behind her and the shimmering crystal panels of the Central Structure came into view, Qaazi did her best to convey her newfound optimism—even though there was no way she could share the very private mystical experience she'd just had, at least not now. *Dear Culley, her mind exclaimed, please do not worry so! We have won! Don't ask me how I know. I just do. Look! My eyes are level and I am no longer tired!*

He pulled up beside her and was relived to see that the corners of her eyes were firmly anchored down and that all signs of fatigue had disappeared.

It certainly seemed to be a good omen! But then, off to

his right, floating awkwardly in the opposite direction between two uniformed Pleiadians, he noticed a dark-haired, fully human young woman whose pale pink nightgown and fearful expression were not what one would expect to find on a Native Companion. She *had* to be an abductee, he surmised. Most likely she'd been sound asleep next to her husband or boyfriend when her alien abductors arrived. . . .

Culley tried to hail the woman, but she was oblivious. He wondered if they were about to take her fetus. Or whether she'd just been forced to fondle a tiny, big-eyed infant she didn't know she'd borne.

There is nothing we can do to help her, "Qaazi said quickly, confirming both of his suspicions," but if all goes as I now believe it will, these sorts of things will soon end. Do not be afraid! We are 'home free!'"

In spite of his lover's upbeat attitude and appearance, Culley's heart sank. There was no way they could beat this system . . . no way whatsoever. He glanced once again at the terrified young woman and her escorts, who were almost out of sight now, and then at his fellow humans. *That's the way we're all gonna leave here,* he fretted, doing his best to screen his thought-stream. Qaazi's grasping at straws. *They're gonna screw us over, just like Fyfe and his buddies screwed me over back at Graham.*

However, as soon as he and his companions passed through the Great Door and into the shimmering building, Culley felt the same calm and sense of well-being settle over him that he'd experienced the last time they visited the Central Structure. The anxiety was still there, but once again, out of nowhere, he heard that same small inner voice, the one he still couldn't quite identify: *Qaazi is not grasping at anything, it repeated several times. You really are home free! This is not Graham College!*

Culley was about to learn that both Qaazi and the voice were indeed correct. As it turned out, he and his human friends were not going to suffer the fate that had befallen that unfortunate young woman. This time, it seemed, the system—in this instance, Qaazi's Alien Raj—wasn't going to screw him over, after all!

CHAPTER EIGHTEEN

". . . thus, in the name of the Winged Serpent and his alter ego, the Great Bird, has the Grand Council spoken," the Chief Elder intoned in his stilted but well-nigh flawless English. "Supreme Elder Yaazdaagaa wishes me to convey her greetings. She, like the rest of us, both here and on Niivaanaa, will monitor your 'experiment' most carefully. Jaahaap Qaan-gaa's grant of protection is hereby affirmed in perpetuity."

Culley let out a tension-releasing whoop of joy and hugged Qaazi close while he and Sidney exchanged high-fives. Then he picked up his son, who'd been in the Chamber when they arrived, and planted a big kiss on his forehead.

For once, the boy didn't seem embarrassed by all the attention. "Now our new life really begins," he said as Culley gently lowered him to the floor and into the arms of his mother.

To be sure, they didn't get everything they'd hoped for. For one thing, the possibility of settling elsewhere, at least for the time being, was ruled out. Also, except for a few simple (by Pleiadian standards) medical supplies, they could have no Pleiadian technology whatsoever, and that included the presence of androids. The "psychic fence" that had protected the installation was to be removed permanently, and they would be on their own when it came to intruders. Whatever they might cobble together using Pleiadian knowledge and Native tools and resources was fine. But the Grand Council was reluctant to put any sophisticated hardware within reach of unconditioned Natives. It was simply too dangerous and might irrevocably upset the balance the Colony had spent so many millennia trying to maintain. The Others had insisted on this restriction during what seemed to have been some rather tense negotiations between Niivaanaa and SESO.

SESO also insisted that Djrnk serve as its liaison to the new community, and that Native Agent Hajime Nakamura be permanently attached to the group as her "observer" as soon as he was retrieved from wherever Sidney's blast had sent him.

Waangaa started to protest, but Qaazi gave him a quick mental kick in the shins: *Let us not look the proverbial gift horse in the mouth, as the quaint Native—*human!*—proverb has it. We will manage, and who knows how long it will take them to find the Man in Black? The important thing is that our project is launched!*

They were also enjoined from behaving in a way that would attract undue attention from their neighbors, which, of course, ruled out frequent visits by flyers. The Clan would provide enough perfectly counterfeited U.S. dollars to get them started, but eventually they were expected to become self-supporting.

Finally, the new community would be subject to the demands of the Project. This was no problem, Qaazi assured the Chief Elder, and she repeated her earlier promise that they would all donate the requisite human/Pleiadian DNA as a matter of course whenever a child was conceived. There would be no need for the infamous "holding tanks."

Culley started to raise the question of possible long-term genetic damage, but Qaazi detected this embryonic thought almost as soon as it emerged, and imposed a temporary block. *Bringing that matter to their attention now*, her mind whispered, *could well prove counter-productive. They have given us more than I dared hope for. Once we're settled, we'll do our best to convince them to begin a comprehensive testing program. So please, dear Culley, bear with me and abort that idea before it reaches your detectable thought-*

stream.

Okay, he responded, and immediately applied a thought-suppression technique she'd recently taught him. It seemed to work, as no member of the Council gave any indication, verbal or mental, of having picked up his thought.

You are an apt pupil! her mind exulted.

I have an apt teacher!

Meanwhile—the foregoing mental exchange took but a nanosecond—the Chief Elder went on to indicate that, after a great deal of discussion, Qaazi's half-sister Jaanii had been permitted to join them. He indicated that Medical Technicians were far more difficult to train than either Native Affairs Specialists or simple Technicians, like Waangaa, and that she would be difficult to replace. To Qaazi, this was welcome news indeed. Jaanii had been one her earliest co-conspirators, and it was only fair that she be included. Also, her half-sister's medical and genetic expertise would be invaluable, especially when the DNA testing program got underway.

And as it was now crystal clear that Sally fully intended to give Waangaa the "second chance" they'd discussed that evening in the safe-house kitchen, the fact that Jaanii found Sidney attractive, and vice versa, was a distinct plus. It would remove a possible source of conflict.

They also received word that Drusilla, the Native Companion who had shown Culley and the others how to use the cleansers, had requested permission to accompany them. Qaazi had no objections; indeed, she welcomed the challenge of reversing the centuries of conditioning that had almost, but not quite, reduced the blonde Companion to the status of a living robot.

As Qaazi and her party rose to leave the Council Chamber, the main iris opened to admit Djrnk, who seemed fully recovered from the effects of Sidney's zap, although it was impossible for a Pleiadian to mentally assess the true state of a Reticulan's health. The Chief Elder greeted the newcomer formally in the name of the Winged Serpent, and

Qaazi added her own polite greeting. She'd met Djrnk on several occasions over the years at joint conferences on Native affairs and still respected the SESO Commander's competence, despite her recent hostile actions and the ongoing competition between their two races for hegemony over the planet.

"I am pleased to see you again, Qaazi Qaan-gaa," the black-robed Other responded with equal politeness in accented but thoroughly understandable Pleiadian. "Please accept my apologies for abducting your son. It was inadvertent. I am glad that this unfortunate matter has been resolved and that we shall co-operate in bringing your idea to fruition." She stared at Sidney for a second, but gave no indication that she held a grudge against him. "Nakamura-san, our representative, will join you after you are settled. With the help of your Technicians, we have narrowed down the number of universes he may be in to a manageable number and expect to retrieve him in the near future."

Mentally, in the simple telepathic "pidgin" that Reticulans and Pleiadians used when they found it necessary to mind-speak, Djrnk added that she herself was sorry they would not have any advanced technology at their disposal, but that her superiors had insisted on it. She hoped that someday this restriction would be lifted, and that neither she nor her superiors had any objection to replacing Sidney Levine's SESO implant with a Pleiadian device. They did however reserve the right to claim a Pleiadian subject of equal or greater mental capacity at some later date.

Choosing her thoughts carefully, Qaazi thanked the SESO Commander for her apology and her sympathy, as well as her magnanimity as far as Dr. Levine was concerned. Although she questioned the Reticulan officer's sincerity as far as Adam was concerned, Djrnk's overall positive attitude was a good omen. It meant that SESO would probably not interfere adversely, or at least not too adversely. Indeed, maybe the Reticulans would finally see fit to stop spreading the monstrous lie among the Natives they abducted that the

Pleiadians were their biological creations!

Djrnk indicated that she had some business with the Chief Elder, and that they would be hearing from her after Nakamura-san had been retrieved.

Qaazi thanked her again, and joined the others as they filed out of the Chamber, her face wreathed in a smile as she contemplated the victory they'd won.

The Winged One had been right! She did have a destiny to fulfill, and so did Culley, Adam, and the others who had elected to join her. Together, they would lay the foundations for a new era in which overt and mutually beneficial cooperation between their two races would replace the covert exploitation and manipulation she'd so come to detest.

From now on, as Sidney Levine was so fond of saying, it was a whole new ball game!

* * *

Shortly after Qaazi and her companions left the Central Structure for what they hoped would be the last time, Jaahaap indicated that he'd been instructed to escort them to the "Infirmary." The Pilot informed them that Culley and his fellow humans needed to undergo some "treatments " before they departed.

"Professor Levine's SESO implant will be exchanged for one of ours," he explained while they attached themselves to yet another elevated glide strip and began to ascend.

The floor of the Plaza soon disappeared from sight, and the green mist they'd noticed the day before swirled beneath them. They were now so high that the scaly flying creatures seemed almost to be within arm's reach, although Qaazi reminded them that most were holograms and that the rest were as harmless as *raaghi*.

"We have been assured that his implant will be programmed only for communication and for interfacing with other aspects of our technology, should the ban someday be lifted," Jaahaap continued, as they wound their way between a series of tall pylons that loomed above the mist." The medical technicians will not, as Dr. Levine is now thinking, 'mess' with his mind. Qaazi, Waangaa, and I will observe the procedure and raise objections if we detect what Dr. Levine thinks of as 'funny business.' He will find it much easier to communicate when his new implant is in place."

"What happens to my old one?" Sidney asked with a straight face. "Do I get to keep it as a souvenir, or do you have to give it back to the bug people?"

Jaahaap took him seriously and started to explain in some detail why he couldn't keep the SESO device, and that any form of extraterrestrial technology was forbidden. The rest of the group, including Qaazi and Waangaa, did their best to keep from laughing.

Then Culley turned serious and asked why they were allowed to keep their implants at all, including the ones embedded in the three Pleiadian members of the group. "They're a pretty big part of your technology," he added, tapping his forehead at the spot behind which Qaazi once told him her own implant was located.

"That is correct," Jaahaap replied, nodding his head human-style, "but you will have no means at your disposal either to remove them or to modify their operation. However, I presume that if you are able to invent your own tools for extracting and reprogramming them, it would be allowed."

Sally, who had said little during the Council session but was now rapidly regaining her normal self-confidence, pivoted so as to face their protector. "Not to change the subject, but I've got a question for you. What are those 'treatments' you mentioned a while back? Culley and I already carry your implants. Are they gonna make some more adjustments before we leave?"

The Command Pilot brightened. "I am pleased to inform you that, after what seems to have been a great deal of discussion both here and on Niivaanaa, the Clan has decided that all of you should receive a series of anti-aging treatments. All of us receive them periodically."

"How often is that?" Sidney asked.

"Oh, I would say about one or twice in one of your centuries. The frequency depends on your specific genetic make-up."

"No shit?"

"I do not believe that the process involves fecal matter, although you might ask the Medical Techs. I am far from an expert in these matters."

Jaahaap wondered why Ms. Linker and Doctors Wisdom and Levine laughed uproariously. To make matters more puzzling, he noticed that Qaazi was also chuckling slightly. Mentally shaking his head, the Pleiadian suspected that he and others of his race who had never had a truly intimate relationship with a Native would never fully understand these remarkable Earth-creatures, despite the massive amounts of DNA they had come to share.

Then, as so often happened, Sidney shifted his mental gears and became serious. "No kidding?" he asked incredulously. "You're really able to stop the aging process? I thought Qaazi was just using a figure of speech when she mentioned the possibility to us yesterday."

"Yes, dear Sidney, it's true!" Qaazi exulted. She put her arm around Culley's waist so that they floated side by side. "Now we will all age together at the same rate! I had hoped from the outset that they would allow it, but I'm relieved to hear that it is now official. I can understand why there must have been some discussion, as life-extension has never before been granted to humans who are not Native Companions. We are already making history, my love!"

When they finally reached the Infirmary, Jaanii, who was waiting for them, took charge and led them one by one into the small cubicles where she and several other Medical Techs would perform these "operations."

Just before the small iris closed behind him, Culley suddenly remembered something important and started to pass it along to Qaazi's mind.

Not here, she replied quickly. *They may have instruments*

I know nothing about that can penetrate even the strongest mental barriers. I too have something important to share, at least I hope I have. But we will exchange these secrets later, in a more secure environment. Now I must observe the procedure they plan to use on Sidney. It is a most complicated one, and perhaps I can learn something from it.

Then she too disappeared through an iris, and Culley received a mental command to remove his clothes and float himself up to a table that seemed almost identical to the one they'd laid him on so many years ago.

For a couple of seconds, he felt the old fear rising in his gut—and just as quickly whatever was repressing it once again came to his rescue. A floating "eye" similar to the one he remembered so vividly once again examined every part of his naked body. When the "eye" completed its examination, Jaanii entered the cubicle, started intently at the device for a couple of seconds, and then inserted a small tube into Culley's abdomen. There was a momentary sensation of pain, followed by an indescribable feeling of lightness. It was as if he could float indefinitely with the aid of any device whatsoever.

After what seemed like several hours but was actually less than five minutes another Medical Tech, a male, who'd been monitoring a scope, removed the tube, grinned at him through bloodless, almost invisible lips, and mentally told him to get dressed. He wondered how many decades (or centuries) had been added to his life span and started to ask, but Jaanii had disappeared and the male Tech, a full-blooded Niivaanaan, seemed in no mood to communicate, so he masked his thoughts.

When Culley returned to the "waiting room," his mind was suddenly bombarded by a plethora of disparate thoughts and images, and he realized that, for the first time, Sidney was able to communicate telepathically.

Welcome to the club, Sidney! his beleaguered psyche exclaimed, *but please keep your thoughts down to a roar, at least until after you get the hang of that thing! Or until*

Qaazi shows me how to erect better barriers. I wonder where she is? I thought she was with you.

Sidney shook his head, mentally as well as physically, and nearly bowled Culley over. Then Jaahaap told them the time for departure was at hand.

After a brief stop to collect what few possessions they had brought with them, they proceeded to the docking bay where the Pilot's flyer was parked. Qaazi, with Adam in tow, soon joined them. She'd changed back into the jeans and newly-purchased tank-top she was wearing at the time Jaahaap abducted her, but was otherwise undisguised. As he watched her approach the group, Culley couldn't help thinking that the exotic combination of her undisguised, Pleiadian face and the sexy new outfit made her look even more desirable than ever-which caused Qaazi's mind to blush slightly when she tuned into his thought stream. *Adam does think that I now resemble Ms. Spears, her mind said softly, but with a strong undercurrent of pride. And Sally tells me that I look "totally awesome"!*

That you do, my love, his mind exulted. *That you definitely do!*

Their son had also not yet performed the biotension exercises that would transform his Pleiadian eyes, although Culley couldn't help noticing that he had shed his Pleiadian uniform and was wearing the baggy jeans, UCLA sweatshirt, leather jacket, and Air-Jordans he'd had on when they rescued him from the Reticulans. And, of course, the boy also wore his beloved Raiders cap, this time triumphantly, its visor, as always, shading the back of his tiny neck.

As Culley glanced affectionately at his son, he realized that Adam's unshielded thought-stream was dominated at the moment by his eagerness to surf the Web once again on his "primitive" laptop computer, this time actively as well as passively. *I'll bet that machine won't remain "primitive" for long after we get back!* his mind whispered. Adam simply grinned and sent his father a mental schematic that made no sense whatsoever. Nevertheless, Culley was willing to bet that it would improve the computer's performance a thousand-fold.

Qaazi moved up beside Sally, who was similarly clad, and took her human friend by the hand. Her face was wreathed with as big a smile as was possible for an undisguised Pleiadian face. "Dear Sally, I have something important to tell you! You are a mother! A few minutes ago I finally had a chance to check the Main Computer to see whether the child you and Waangaa conceived managed to survive, and found that she did! Indeed, the girl is here! In the Colony Headquarters crèche, only a few meters from where we are now! I have already requested that you be allowed to raise her. Her Clan name, by the way, is Qaanzaani, though you and Waangaa must choose a Native name too. I'm so happy for you!" She put her arms around the stunned young woman and hugged her close. Culley, who'd overheard their conversation, offered his congratulations.

"I really don't know what to say," Sally replied, her huge blue eyes misting, "except thank you, dear Qaazi! Thank you from the bottom of my heart! I really owe you one, big time!" Then her tears disappeared, and she beamed broadly at both of them." Hey, I've got a daughter! I can't wait to see her! Did they say when Qaanzaani—I hope I've got it right—will be allowed to join us?"

Qaazi smiled enigmatically. "Sooner than you are now thinking, I suspect!"

Thanks to this good news, all traces of Sally's injury, mental as well as physical, totally disappeared, and she practically danced the rest of the way to the Gate. The only thing that even slightly bothered her now was how to tell Sidney. But that was a minor problem. She was the mother of a healthy two year-old, who would soon be with her, and that was all that really mattered!

When the party finally reached the Security Gate, Jaanii and Drusilla were waiting for them. Qaazi's sister had exchanged her Pleiadian uniform for a pair of white coveralls that could easily have been worn by any Native laboratory technician. Moreover, she'd just undergone the medical procedure that gave her the capability of altering her features, and therefore looked far less alien than Qaazi did at the moment, despite the fact that Jaanii's first-hand experience with Natives (other than Native Companions) was limited to the abducted subjects on whom she had performed physical exams and fetal extractions.

Drusilla still wore her white robe, but Qaazi told her that the first thing she would do when they arrived was buy her some ordinary clothes. The blonde Native Companion seemed anxious, as she had never before been allowed to venture beyond the confines of the Headquarters complex. But her eyes sparkled at the thought of living for the first time as an ordinary human being.

Standing to one side was an impassive medical tech holding a small hybrid child by the hand. The child's huge, wrap-around eyes were sky blue rather than black and its tiny, heart shaped face was farmed by wispy, ash-blonde hair.

Sally sped to where they stood and gathered the startled little girl in her arms. "Folks, I want you to meet my daughter Qaanzaani! If Waangaa doesn't object, I want to call her Annie!"

Sidney had already been briefed on this turn of events by Qaazi and gave his former girlfriend a kiss on the cheek. "I couldn't be happier for you, Babe!" he said with a broad smile. "I know how much you wanted to have a kid, and now you've got one! She's a real cutie! *Mazeltov!*" Jaanii, who stood next to him, also offered her mental congratulations.

A few second later, Waangaa finally joined them; he'd been attending to some last-minute business elsewhere in the complex. Like Jaanii, he was wearing white coveralls, but was as yet undisguised. Sally handed Annie to him without a word and kissed his thin lips.

Embarrassed, but obviously elated, Waangaa picked up

the daughter that even he did not know existed until a few minutes ago and made eye contact. They engaged in a brief mental exchange, as the child could barely speak her native language and as yet knew no English.

Sidney was the first to extend his hand. He was followed quickly by Culley, who said, "Hey, Waangaa, welcome to the daddy club! We're gonna be a real community, now that there are two kids involved!"

The tech's undisguised features remained impassive, but the glow in his enormous Pleiadian eyes said it all.

Just before they passed in front of the scanner, Qaazi handed her wand to one of the security guards. One by one, they underwent a scan to see if the only items of Pleiadian technology on (or in) their persons were their implants and the small medical bag that hung from Jaanii's shoulder.

There were no hidden items, and Jaahaap was about to lead the way through the main iris when Aavraa, accompanied by Waangaa, caught up with them. While not actually puffing, it was clear that they had been moving as rapidly as it is possible to move along a Pleiadian glide strip.

"Thanks be to the Winged One! I am not too late!" Aavraa exclaimed as he slowed to a stop directly in front of Qaazi and Culley. "As I said in the Council Chamber, I bless your union, and, in the tradition of the Clan, wish to say the words expected from a Ceremonial Father. Since Doctor Wisdom's kin are not here, I must play both roles."

He raised both hands. "In the name of the Serpent-Who-Flies, and in the most ancient tradition of the Clan, I affirm Doctor Cullen J. Wisdom to be the Ceremonial Father of all offspring that Qaazi Qaan-gaa may bear."

He then said a few words in Pleiadian which Qaazi later said were among the most ancient in the language, words that descended from a time not only before her ancestors had begun to explore the Galaxy, but when they still thought their primordial world was flat. The best translation she could come up with was "Be fruitful and multiply," which

Culley suspected might not be fortuitous.

Once again, Sidney was the first to offer his congratulations. "Well, old buddy, it looks like you're now a married man again, at least in these folks' eyes. Best wishes to the both of you, and, of course, *mazeltov*! We gotta have a reception for you someday so I can say *lachiam*!"

Sally and Waangaa conveyed their congratulations both verbally and mentally. Adam threw his arms around his parents and hugged them close. "Now even the Winged One knows we are a family!" he exclaimed, his undisguised Pleiadian eyes glistening with excitement.

After returning his son's hug, Culley thanked Aavraa profusely. Two seconds later, oblivious of their surroundings, he and Qaazi shared a passionate kiss. *That's one of our cherished wedding customs, his mind whispered.*

It is a very pleasant custom, although that security guard over there will need her anti-aging treatment sooner than usual; we've shocked her out of at least a century's growth!

Jaahaap, who had watched the brief ceremony with mixed emotions, also extended his best wishes. Then, his innermost thoughts carefully masked, he led his protectees through the iris and into the corridor that led to the docking bay.

* * *

As the disk cleared the water and began its swift ascent to the edge of space, Culley smiled tenderly at his new "wife" and mentally asked her whether it was now safe to mention what he'd wanted to tell her at the infirmary.

Yes, Qaazi's mind responded, *although I already know what you're going to say: that we left some of my instruments-a communicator and a reprogrammer, as I recall-in a coin locker at Tokyo Station. The key is the uppermost drawer of the cabinet—I mean dresser-in our bedroom. I'm sure it is still there. After we're settled, you must return to Tokyo and retrieve them. The Monitors will not question such a trip. As far as they are concerned, your purpose will be to settle your affairs and bring back the personal possessions you left in Japan. Indeed, perhaps you will be able to recover the outer garment you left behind in the coffee shop where our current adventure together began-unless our new black-clad friend-to-be Nakamura-san is now in possession of it.*

They were now well beyond the range of the Colony Headquarters Monitors, and, as she was sure that Jaahaap would not betray them, she switched to the verbal mode: "I have taken the liberty of discussing this matter with Waangaa. He is convinced he can fabricate a crude but serviceable wand from the components of these instruments plus some of your own simple electronic devices, microchips and such. Once we have such an instrument, he can use it to fabricate larger and more sophisticated items. But we shall have to find a secret place for him to work—perhaps in one of those desert caves that you and Adam explored. Waangaa thinks it shouldn't be too difficult to shield such a place against detection." She went on to point out that they would also have immediate transportation. "Sally tells me that the keys to her Subaru, which you say survived the Others' attack, are in her purse, which should still be inside the house. Djrnk's appearance was apparently so sudden that she was unable to retrieve it before she was taken."

Then she grinned impishly. "Once place to which we shall surely drive it is the gambling city called Las Vegas. It's not all that far away, I believe. Indeed, as soon as we have a functioning wand, we will be able to amass as much money there as we need. We can use it to purchase the Native components we will need to further our technological development and to make our life as comfortable as possible." *And all the better to cope with my Alien Raj!* she added mentally.

Before Culley's mind could reply, Waangaa, who'd been inspecting the medical kit with an eye to cannibalizing some of its less crucial components, looked up, his newly transformed eyes wide with anticipation. "Yes," he said, doing his best to approximate an American accent, "one of those underground places you and Jaz-I mean Adam—I must remember to call your son and my daughter by their human names!—discovered will serve us well in this regard. Indeed, the elemental spirit that dwells in that place will be helpful, too. As my cousin told you, it is very much in harmony with us and our goals. And with the wealth you will acquire, I am sure that we will soon be able to-to beat the system. That is the correct idiom, is it not?"

Culley nodded and grinned broadly.

He started to explain to Waangaa in detail what he thought they might accomplish with a hidden wand at a Las Vegas roulette wheel when Qaazi's thought-stream once again interrupted, this time forcefully. *I have something very important to tell you, my husband, something that transcends all technology or any future efforts to augment our financial resources, including those that are technically illegal.* Her alien eyes sparkled and seemed even larger and more loving than usual. *The reason I stayed behind in the Infirmary, Qaazi's mind whispered in that special place that only the most intimate of telepathic modes could penetrate, and why I was so late in returning to the chamber and missed most of my sleep-cycle was to verify what I've suspected since I was unable to expel an ovum that last morning at the safe house. Our recent "bacon sandwiches" have born fruit!*

Culley started to chide her good-naturedly about mixing metaphors, but as the implications of what she'd just shared with him sank in his mind fell silent. There was no need for metaphors, mixed or unmixed, mental or verbal, only the most loving and tender images his psyche could muster.

Yes, dear Culley, her thought-stream exulted, *I am indeed pregnant again! This time it will be a daughter. With your permission, of course, we shall name her "Eve."*

EPILOGUE

"No, Mr. President," Wilma Gibbs insisted. "There's no doubt about it. Phase Two has definitely begun. Alexei and I heard it directly from the Supreme Elder's holographic lips. She told us the pilot project's been underway now for almost four months. That means it began just about the time we briefed you. You'll also be happy to hear that—"

Before Wilma could finish her sentence, there was a discrete knock. The President pushed a button, the door opened, and Carmen Belmonte, his personal secretary, appeared with the silver coffee service. He thanked the dark haired young woman and said he'd do the honors himself.

When they were alone again, the President poured his visitor a cup, then one for himself, and began rocking slowly back and forth in the antique Boston rocker. For a moment, cup in hand, he gazed absently through the large picture window behind his desk at the leaden February sky, half expecting to see one of their glowing disks land here at Camp David. Then he turned back to face Wilma.

"You were about to pass along some more news when Carmen came in," he said after a couple of sips.

"Yes. As I was saying, you'll be happy to hear that they've located the project in the Mojave Desert and not in rural Japan, where the Supreme Elder said they'd initially intended to put it. Except for a Native Companion of unknown ethnicity and a Japanese MIB—the Reticulans seem to have insisted on it—the human participants are all Americans. Alexei's miffed that no Russians are involved, though they took pains to assure him that it's only a matter of time before they establish a similar community somewhere in what used to be the Soviet Union, if not actually within the borders of the Russian Federation."

The President chuckled. "Adding insult to injury. I'll bet he was livid!"

Wilma grinned impishly and nodded her massive head. "You got that right, Sir! My Russian counterpart still hasn't totally adjusted to the current political reality."

The physicist's broad face seemed darker than ever in the fading afternoon light. But the effect served to highlight the whites of her eyes, which glistened with excitement about what she'd learned.

"Mr. President," she went on after a couple of sips of coffee, "I realize that you still haven't had time to fully digest what we shared with you the last time I was in this room, but the sooner you come to grips with this new development the better it'll be for all concerned."

"That's probably the understatement of the century," he replied softly.

* * *

As Wilma filled him in on the details, the President closed his eyes, steepled his fingers, and let his thoughts return to the day four months ago when he first heard about MJ-12. It was, as she'd just said, in this very room. He remembered staring open-mouthed as Wilma and her colleagues told him about the Pleiadians and how her group had come into being:

In July, 1947, two saucer-shaped alien space ships collided in mid-air near Roswell, New Mexico, strewing twisted debris and several small, humanoid bodies across several square miles of desert. Shortly thereafter, a handful of senior intelligence officers formed the nucleus of a super-secret UFO investigating committee initially called "The Majestic Twelve," from the fact that it reported directly to "Majestic," a Secret Service designation for President Harry Truman, and was composed of twelve distinguished people drawn from the ranks of the military as well as the intelligence and scientific establishments. However, thanks to the government's long-standing penchant for abbreviations, the name of the committee soon became simply "MJ-12."

In the months and years that followed, MJ-12 subjected the Roswell wreckage to exhaustive, albeit inconclusive analysis, performed autopsies on the alien corpses, and generally attempted to make sense out of what had happened that fateful night in the New Mexico desert. It also initiated the disinformation campaign that continues to ridicule ordinary citizens who claim to have seen UFOs, and, at the same time, did its best to establish communication with the aliens. This latter project was given the code name "Sigma."

At first, despite the best efforts of some of the brightest minds in the country, Sigma made no headway whatsoever. Whoever or whatever the "saucer people" were, they didn't seem interested in establishing a dialog or even recovering their dead.

Then, in the winter of 1954, at Edwards Air Force Base in the California desert, where a human being had first flown faster than sound, an event occurred that was so bizarre that even those who participated in it had trouble getting a handle on it, including President Dwight David Eisenhower. Some months earlier, a small, disk-shaped UFO bearing an insignia that looked like a flying snake had landed in a remote corner of Holloman Air Force Base in New Mexico. Both the craft and its two occupants were then trucked to a deserted hangar and sealed off from all outside contact.

MJ-12 was alerted immediately.

Within less than an hour, three members of the Committee, including the director of the Sigma Project, arrived at arrived Holloman and began the most exotic diplomatic negotiations the United States has ever engaged in. At first, it was not at all clear what the diminutive, huge-eyed humanoids wanted, even though both of them spoke fluent, almost unaccented American English, or why they had chosen this time and place to announce their presence. But as the dialog continued, it gradually became apparent that they wanted to make what amounted to a "deal."

Although they said little about themselves and where they came from, the visitors mentioned the Roswell incident and said that it had been caused by our "crude" radar beams, which for some reason seemed to interfere with their guidance systems. They offered us a more sophisticated radar technology, as well as several other high-tech items. In return, we were not to interfere in their ongoing "survey" of the planet, which, from time to time, included abducting people for what they said were "harmless physical examinations and experiments."

The MJ-12 people quickly realized that some fundamental decisions would have to be made at the highest political level, and so they decided to go directly to the President. A second meeting was arranged at Edwards several months later.

As luck would have it, Ike was scheduled to be in Palm Springs —less than two hours drive from Edwards—that winter on a golfing vacation. His disappearance for the better part of two days was later explained as a sudden bout of the flu coupled with a dental problem. Thus, Eisenhower became the first and so far only president to engage in face-to-face negotiations with creatures from another star-system.

Then came a real shocker. After Kennedy's assassination, the committee decided not to brief his successor. It seemed that JFK, who had learned the secret shortly before his inauguration but had not briefed his vice-president, was on the verge of going public when he was assassinated. Wilma assured her astonished host that he was only the second president since Kennedy—Nixon had managed to stumble on the truth late in his presidency—in whom the Joint Inter-Agency Committee on Anomalous Intelligence, as the Committee was now officially called, had seen fit to confide.

He'd started to ask some pointed questions about the Committee's role in the tragic events of November, 1963, but the pained expression on Wilma Gibbs' face warned him not to. Some questions were better left unasked, her eyes seemed to say. Nevertheless, her unspoken message was loud and clear: he was not to speak of these matters to his wife, the Vice-President, or anyone on his staff, let alone members of the media or the public at large. Unbidden, an image of Jack Kennedy's bloody head leapt into his mind; yes, perhaps it was better not to ask. He simply nodded, and the conversation continued as if nothing sensitive had been broached.

The President soon learned that the aliens had made similar overtures to the Soviets, and that Khrushchev was the first (and last) Soviet leader to know the full truth. However, despite the Cold War, which flared up and down with almost clock-like regularity, an unofficial communication link came to be established between MJ-12 and its Soviet counterpart, which was buried deep within the bureaucracy of the Academy of Sciences. Even during the height of the Cuban missile crisis in 1962, when the world teetered on the brink of a nuclear holocaust, the two super-secret agencies continued to compare notes.

Beginning in the early seventies, the Chairs of the American and Soviet committees were occasionally transported to "Dreamland," which soon became the principal code name for Colony Headquarters. (It was also sometimes referred to as "the Triangle" or "Oz Two.") In the course of these visits they managed to learn a few more things about their clandestine colonial masters: They were given some basic information about the Clan, about the "Native Companions," the Sacred Rule of Non-Interference, and the true nature of the Reticulans, the Men in Black, and the threat that SESO continued to pose, including its false claim to biological hegemony over the Colony. They were also briefed about the Project and why it was so crucial. Most important of all, they were told that the current "Phase One" in the aliens' contact scenario would eventually come to an end. Its successor, "Phase Two," would involve one or more "social experiments," in which groups of humans and aliens would live together in small communes, each learning from the other.

The final phase, which they referred to as "Phase Three," would evolve as these communities proliferated, and the two species began to meld. The end result would be free and open contact between their two species, coupled with what amounted to a junior partnership in the Pleiadians' ongoing effort to explore the Galaxy.

* * *

". . . so that's what's been happening, Mr. President. The Supreme Elder said they've arranged for everybody involved, including Wisdom and his alien girl friend, to be nudged along by some 'mystical' experiences."

"What sorts of experiences?" he asked, wrenching his full attention back to the current situation.

"She wasn't too explicit, but we got the impression that they included messages from talking coyotes and that sort of thing."

The President shook his head slowly. "It's hard for me to believe that the Pleiadian woman—what did you say her name was?"

"Qaazi Qaan-gaa."

"Yes, well, it's difficult for me to believe that this lady doesn't realize she's been set up. Are you absolutely certain about this?"

"That's what we've been told, Mr. President. The Edwards Agreement seems to be as big a secret in the 'Emerald City' as it is here. Even many of their senior people, like Qaazgaa, the one in charge of what they call 'Native Affairs' in this part of the world, are apparently out of the loop. How they manage to keep folks like him from picking it up from the heads of 'Natives' like us is anybody's guess. We suspect that they impose some sort of a block that prevents most of 'em from 'hearing' the thoughts we're thinking at the moment. I know all this sounds crazy, but we have every reason to believe it's true."

"Yes, indeed" he said softly, making a wry face, "it does

sound crazy. . . .”

The President stared at his hands for a moment, and then returned his attention to his visitor. “Okay, Wilma, let me see if I’ve got it all straight: Ms. Qaan-gaa will soon give birth to another child by the good Doctor Wisdom, who also has no inkling that he’s been set up. They‘re already the parents of a brilliant ten year-old boy whose IQ is way off both the aliens’ and our charts. Ms. Linker, the trance channel, is the mother of a hybrid, two-year-old daughter and is about to get pregnant for the second time by an alien named Waangaa, and her ex-boyfriend, an astronomer named Levine, has just impregnated Ms. Qaan-gaa’s half-sister. And there’s another human female, a seven-hundred years-old former Native Companion, who’s not yet pregnant by anybody. Is that the situation?”

The Chair of MJ-12 nodded, then took another long sip of coffee and smoothed a wrinkle or two in her skirt.

The President leaned back in his rocking chair and interlaced his fingers behind his head. He looked Wilma straight in those remarkable eyes, the most intelligent eyes he’d ever seen on any human being, for almost half a minute before saying anything.

“Recommendations?” he finally asked.

She tucked one thick leg underneath her in a characteristic movement he’d noticed when she visited the White House after receiving her Nobel Prize, and when they’d briefed him about MJ-12 and its work. “Well, Mr. President,” Wilma said after she was comfortable, “I suggest we simply leave ‘em alone, at least for the time being. Let the community develop on its own, giving it as much covert support as we can without upsetting the Pleiadians—especially the ones that have opposed even the idea of Phase Two, let alone the possibility that it could ever evolve into Phase Three. We also need to be careful not to upset the Reticulans; they’re the wild card in all this.”

“What you’re really saying, Wilma, is don’t rock the boat. Right?”

"Yes, Sir, that's exactly what I'm saying. I'm sure I don't have to tell you that we've already got people monitoring the situation there 'round the clock, both on the ground and from satellites. Indeed, we've been keepin' an eye on that place ever since Wisdom surfaced as a passenger in the Bronco and Ms. Linker's Subaru suddenly appeared in front of the house. That was way before we had any inkling that Phase Two was in the offing. But we're still bein' ultra discreet, and I suggest that we remain in this posture until we see where things are really heading. Rest assured, Mr. President, that I'll personally keep you on top of the situation. But for now, let's just let them have their babies and generally do their own thing."

"And you're *sure* the Reticulans are willing to play along with this experiment? No trouble on the horizon from that quarter?"

"None that I'm aware of. The Chief Elder told us that one of their MIBs will shortly join the community as a liaison. That seems to have been part of the bargain. We'll also probably get yet another round of crop circles, with no Pleiadian interference. Even Yaazdaagaa doesn't seem to know why they make those peculiar circles. But that's about all."

Once again, the President was silent for a few seconds. Then he rose, and she followed suit. "Thanks for the report, Wilma," he said, helping her on with her coat. He opened a small door that led directly to the parking area adjacent to the building and asked the Secret Service man who was posted outside the door to summon Wilma's driver. Before doing so, he scrutinized her with great care, just as his colleagues had when she arrived at the complex. Memories of 9/11 were still too fresh for them to take any chances with anyone who was in close physical proximity to the President, including Dr. Wilma Gibbs.

As they waited for the limo, their breaths hanging like pale smoke in the chill February air, the President noticed that several of the elm trees that bordered the driveway had begun to bud; it looked as if spring might come early this year—a good omen? . . .

"Yes," the stout Caltech physicist observed, following his gaze, "it does look like winter's on its way out, doesn't it? 'Course out there in the Mojave they don't have to worry about such things."

"I imagine that's about the only thing that Pleiadian lady and her people don't have to worry about at the moment," he chuckled as he helped her into the back seat.

"That's for sure! So please, Mr. President, let's leave 'em alone, at least for the time being. Okay?"

"Don't worry, Wilma, those people in the Mojave are the vanguard of the future. We'll do everything we can to help, but from a safe distance. You can count on it!"

As the sound of the limo's tires crunching against the frozen gravel died away, the President stood motionless, his hands thrust in his pockets against the cold and his eyes absently following the flight of a stray crow, while he did his best to digest the momentous news he'd just received. It was one more "brick" in what he'd come to regard as the massive pile of "bricks" that had fallen on him in the course of the last four months, altering his perspective on both the world and the universe beyond all recognition.

All of a sudden, the late afternoon stillness was pierced by the distant wail of a lone coyote; he'd grown up on a ranch in eastern Oregon, and the sound, although faint, was unmistakable. It seemed to echo (and, at the same time, amplify) what he'd just said to Wilma about "the vanguard of the future." He shivered slightly as he recalled what she'd said about "talking coyotes." Were they sending him messages, too?

But then he realized that there were no coyotes here in the Catoctins. Perhaps it was a stray wolf, if any were left hereabouts, or, more likely, his own vivid imagination. Nevertheless, whatever its source, the "message" certainly seemed appropriate.

The vanguard of the future . . .

As he walked briskly back to his study, intending to do some work before the evening's social obligations began, the coyote's "message" once again echoed in his head, and he knew, in a way he couldn't quite put his finger on, that the experiment would be successful. How he wished he could simply pick up the phone and congratulate them—just as he did when a team won the Super Bowl or the World Series!

Maybe someday—if and when Phase Three ever began. . .

* * *

Wilma had barely settled herself in the back seat of the limo when her cell-phone beeped. It was Tom Johnson, calling from the lab.

"How did it go?" he asked casually.

"Much better than I'd expected. I think he'll go along with our recommendations. But I know you too well, Tom. You didn't call just to ask how the meeting went. What's up?"

Her assistant hesitated for a moment. "Uh, yes, Dr. Gibbs, there is something else," he said finally. "We've just identified another subject."

"Must be somebody really important or you wouldn't buzz me here. Who is it?"

Another hesitation. "Are you certain your line's secure?"

"Yes, of course! I pushed the scrambler as soon as I heard your voice. Go ahead!"

"It's-it's the man you just left," Tom replied in a hoarse whisper.

She gave a short laugh and told him that she wasn't all that surprised. "That's why he didn't press me on the Kennedy business! Our little friends probably 'told' him not to. It all makes sense now. Good work, Tom! Bet he has no idea he's carrying an implant, which is probably just as well for all of us."

"I agree. Are you coming by the lab this evening, Dr. Gibbs?"

Wilma sighed. *There he goes again! Will that boy* ever

loosen up and call me by my first name? "No," she replied, "It's been a long day and I'm beat. Think I'll go straight home, take a long hot bath, and hit the sack." She started to say goodbye, then had a brilliant idea. It was off the wall, but it just might work.

"Listen, Tom," she asked, "you once told me you used to backpack in the Mojave. Is that correct? "

"Yes, it is. When I was at Caltech I used to go out there on weekends and hunt for rocks. Why?"

"Well, how would you like to do some more rock huntin'? Look, we really need to put somebody in there, and I can't think of anybody better qualified than you. Think you might be able to con your way in?"

There was a moment of silence. "It's possible," Tom finally replied, the excitement returning to his voice. "Yeah, they just might accept a guy like me, especially since there's an unattached female. . . . It's a long shot, Wilma, but I'll be happy to give it a try."

"Thanks, Tom. We'll talk more about it in the morning. 'Bye."

She smiled broadly. *Hallelujah! The boy's* finally *called me Wilma all on his own! That's a good sign. It means he's got the self-confidence to make 'em accept him. Now we'll really find out what's goin' on out there.*

As she stuffed the phone back into her bag, she noticed that they had crossed the Potomac and were heading toward her home in Leesburg. She closed her eyes and relaxed for the first time in what seemed like weeks. She'd never married, never had any children, but Tom—well, despite his skin color, he was about as close to a son as she was ever likely to get.

Although every test they could think of had turned out negative, Wilma sometimes couldn't help wondering whether both she and Tom also carried implants. *Maybe that's why I'm so certain now that Phase Two will be a success,* she mused as the sleep she'd postponed for so long finally began to catch up with her. *Then again, maybe my "son" and I have simply outsmarted 'em. . . .*

The thought stayed with her as she dreamt of a saucer-shaped nursery full of alien babies, all of whom looked suspiciously like Tom Johnson.

Author's Note

Although in fair measure inspired by the purported experience of Antonio Villas-Boas, an uneducated Brazilian farmer, who, in 1957, claimed to have been kidnapped by aliens, brought aboard a hovering UFO, and forced to have sex with an exotically beautiful member of the crew (see, for example, Michael Craft, Alien Impact, St. Martin's Paperbacks, 1996, pp. 25-26), *Phase Two* is a work of fiction. You won't find Graham College listed in any directory of American institutions of higher education. Nor do I know of any evidence whatsoever for the presence of alien facilities equivalent to Colony Headquarters and the Antarctic Crèche, or indeed, for the existence of the "home planet" Niivaanaa in the Pleione system. Likewise, with one possible exception, the characters who animate this novel-Qaazi and Culley, Adam, Sally and Waangaa, Dr. Wilma Gibbs, Tom Johnson, Jaahaap, Jaanii, Professor Sidney Levine, Drusilla, Djrnk, Dean Frederick A. Fyfe, and the rest-are all figments of my artistic imagination.

The possible exception is Qaazgaa, whose name, in a variety of transliterations ("Quazgaw," "Quazgaa," etc.), turns up in several unrelated UFO abduction cases that have come to light in the eastern half of the United States, from Iowa to Massachusetts. The diminutive, four-fingered "Gray" who bears this name (or title?) is invariably described as the leader of the alien team, or at least its spokesman, and often supervises the physical examination and whatever else happens to the abductee. The persona I have created for Qaazgaa is elaborated from these accounts (see, for example, Raymond E. Fowler, *The Andreasson Affair*, Bantam Books, Inc, 1979, p. 15 et passim; *The Andreasson Affair: Phase II*, Prentice-Hall, 1982, pp. 130, 257; *The Watchers: The Secret Design Behind UFO Abductions*, Bantam Books, 1990, p. 19 et passim; and the *National Enquirer UFO Report*, Pocket Books, 1985, p. 147).

However, if I have misrepresented him or his role in the "Alien Raj," I would certainly welcome his corrections!

About the Author

A native Californian, **C. SCOTT LITTLETON** received his B.A., M.A., and Ph.D. from UCLA, and taught anthropology at Occidental College in Los Angeles for many years. He is considered an expert in comparative mythology and folklore, as well as in traditional Japanese culture, having taught in Tokyo on several occasions. Littleton is the author of several scholarly books, including *The New Comparative Mythology* (3rd Edition, University of California Press, 1982), *From Scythia to Camelot: A Radical Reassessment of the Legends of King Arthur, the Knights of the Round Table, and the Holy Grail* (Garland Publishing Inc., 2000), and *Shinto* (Oxford University Press, 2002), and numerous articles in professional journals. He has also researched the mythological dimensions of the UFO phenomenon, and his article "Divine Rebels, Alien Dissidents: Does the Mythology Surrounding Lucifer, Prometheus, and the Ancient Mexican Deity Quétzalcoatl Reflect a Pro-Human Faction in the 'Alien Raj'?" recently appeared in *UFO Magazine* (April-May, 2002).

A dedicated runner, cyclist, and body-surfer, Littleton, who has two adult daughters, lives with his wife Mary Ann in Pasadena, CA.

Printed in the United States
82928LV00002B/172/A

9 781931 468091